S ELIS

By the Same Author

Medicus
Terra Incognita
Persona Non Grata
Caveat Emptor

Semper Fidelis

A Crime Novel of the Roman Empire

Ruth Downie

First published by Bloomsbury, 2013.

To Vicki and Mike Finnegan
(You'll know why.)

Hadrianus .... Britanniam petiit, in qua
multa correxit ...

Hadrian ... made for Britain, where he set
many things straight ...

Historia Augusta, *Life of Hadrian*

Semper Fidelis
A NOVEL

IN WHICH our hero, Gaius Petreius Ruso, will be …

accompanied by
  Tilla, his wife, a native Briton

avoided by
  Victor, a deserter

upset by
  Sulio, a recruit

set straight by
  Publius Valerius Accius, an ambitious tribune
  Geminus, a veteran centurion
  Dexter, another centurion

alarmed by
  Austalis, a youth with an injured arm
  Marcus, a British youth with splendid tattoos

The two shadows (names unknown) of Geminus
(See "Set straight by" above.)

investigated by

Septicius Clarus, prefect of the Praetorian Guard

ignored by

Suetonius Tranquillus, secretary to Hadrian and a well-known writer
Minna, Accius's house keeper
Lucios, son of Victor

quoted by

Pera, a former pupil

thanked (offstage) by

Corinna, girlfriend of Victor

undermined by

Metellus, head of security for the retiring governor of Britannia

misunderstood by

Valens, a former colleague

and in which he will seek to avoid

Hadrian, the emperor
Sabina, the empress
Virana, an unwise young woman, sister to Barita
(See below.)

Bella, a dog

while failing to meet

Dannicus, a recruit—because he is already deceased

Tadius, another recruit—see above

Barita, sister of Virana—because she refuses to leave home

Marcia, his own sister—because she lives in Gaul

Paulina, friend of the empress—because she lives in Deva

Lucina, Hedone, and Pamphile—because he is a busy man with no time to hang around chatting to girls in bars.

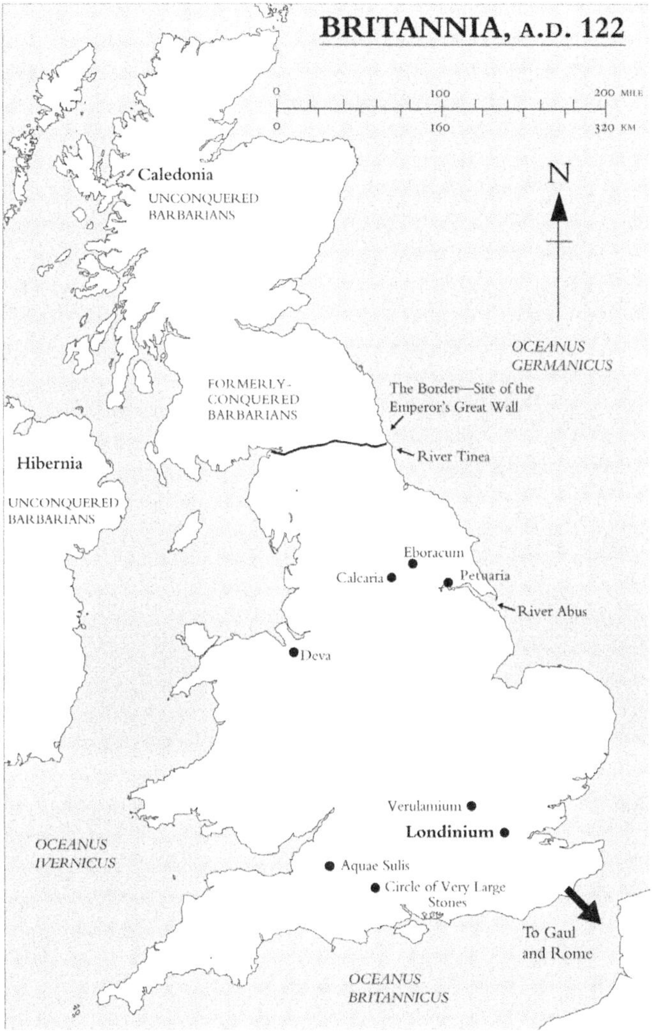

BRITANNIA, A.D. 122
0
100
200 MILE
0
160
320 KM
N
Caledonia
UNCONQUERED
BARBARIANS
OCEANUS
GERMANICUS
FORMERLY-
CONQUERED
BARBARIANS
The Border—Site of the
Emperor's Great Wall
River Tinea
Hibernia
UNCONQUERED
BARBARIANS
Eboracum
Calcaria
Petuaria
River Abus
Deva
Verulamium
Londinium
OCEANUS
IVERNICUS
Aquae Sulis
Circle of Very Large
Stones
To Gaul
and Rome
OCEANUS
BRITANNICUS

Semper Fidelis

1

Victor's left eye felt as though it was about to burst like a squashed plum. He ran his tongue along the inside of his gum, tasting blood in gaps that had not been there before. He made a tentative exploration of a couple of loose teeth, seeing how far they would move. It was a mistake. He gasped and fell back against the trunk of the willow as pain welled up and flooded the lower half of his face.

This will pass, he urged himself, all the while feeling that someone was screwing a hot poker into his jaw. *Count to ten. Breathe in... and... One. In... and... Two. Think of something else.*

But all that came was the memory of Tadius struggling to rise from the floor, and the voices roaring at him, *Get in there, or you'll be next.*

Tadius, lying very still.

Blood pooling in the dust.

As the pain ebbed he crept forward again, peering out between the willow fronds. The trumpets had sounded the hour for the midday meal and there was hardly anyone about. The girl was still alone on the sunny slab that overhung the water, her skirts hitched up and her bare feet dangling in the river. Beside her on the stone sat a wooden platter with bread and cheese and perhaps beer in the cup. She was busy looking at something in her hand. The willow hid her from the guards over on the fort gates. She had no idea that anyone was watching her.

The guards were standing in the shadow of the wall, leaning on their shields and gazing into the distance with the air of men expecting a quiet afternoon. Victor swallowed. There was a time—it seemed years ago now—when he had dreamed that being in the Legion would be a good life.

The girl sighed and flung down whatever she was holding. She pushed a wisp of blond hair out of her eyes and turned her attention to the platter. The sunlight flashed on a blade. His fingers slid toward his own knife, but she was only cutting the cheese. He let out his breath. He did not want to hurt her, but he had to keep her quiet. If she screamed, the guards would come, and he might not be fast enough to get away with the food.

He would stroll up and try to chat with her. If he said he was hungry, she might even offer to share.

He ran a fingertip over his injured eye. She might not. If the eye was as ugly as it felt, she might scream at the sight of him.

The guards were still looking vacant and bored. The girl tore off a big chunk of bread and put it into her mouth.

Victor stepped forward. "It is a good day to eat beside the river."

The girl jerked round. Her eyes widened in alarm, but instead of screaming she was convulsed by a choking fit. He reached for the platter, ready to grab the food and run before she could call for help, then saw one hand flapping helplessly toward him as she spluttered and tried to draw breath and thought, *What if she chokes to death?* He stepped behind her, hesitated for a moment, then smacked his hand against the middle of her back.

Moments later she took the beer from him and nodded her thanks.

When she could breathe again without coughing, he spoke slowly, trying not to let his swollen jaw mangle his words. "I didn't mean to startle you."

"If you don't want to startle people," she said with the accent of a tribeswoman from farther north, "Don't creep up on them. Especially when they are eating."

She was older than he had thought: perhaps in her mid-twenties, and attractive in a way that would have distracted him on better days. He took a deep breath. "I was hoping—"

Her gaze shifted past him. Too late, he heard movement.

As he hit the ground a boot clamped across the back of his neck, ramming his face into the grass. Pain flared from his jaw to his temple. Something hard slammed into the small of his back and a voice said in Latin, "We've been watching you, sonny."

"Please, sir, she was—"

"Shut up!" the voice said, reinforcing its meaning with another blow. "Who d'you think you are, striking an officer's wife?"

Oh, holy Bregans. She looked like a native. She spoke British. Where were the slaves? The jewelry? The fancy clothes?

"Sir, she was—"

"Shut up!"

There were two of them: one who gave the orders and one who looked as if he would obey them without question and without mercy. As they wrenched his arms back and lashed his wrists together, the woman began to say something. The soldier cut her short: "It's all right, miss, you're safe now."

"But—"

"We'll deal with him."

As if to show how, one of them rammed the pommel of a sword into his ribs. He had no idea why the woman cried out. She wasn't the one being hit. She wasn't the fool who had thrown away an escape for the sake of bread he couldn't even chew.

Half dragged, half stumbling, Victor was hustled up through the rough grass toward the fort gates. The officer's wife was hurrying to keep up, still talking.

"Don't you worry, miss," the senior one assured her. "He'll understand Latin when we've finished with him."

"I want to speak to him myself."

The men ignored her. A few paces farther on she appeared in front of them, holding her skirts clear of the grass with one hand and clutching a pair of battered boots in the other.

"So!" she said, looking from one to the other. "I am worth rescuing but not worth listening to?"

For a moment Victor thought they were going to barge her out of the way. Then the senior one seemed to think better of it and said gruffly, "The prisoner was watching you, miss. Hiding under the tree."

She said in British, "Were you watching me?"

He lifted his head to look into eyes that were not quite blue, and not quite green, either.

He staggered as a blow landed on his ear, muffling the roar of "Show some respect!"

Victor lowered his head. Trying to focus on the muddy toes poking out from under the woman's skirt, he heard himself mangle the words, "I'm very hungry, miss."

She said, "Have you no family?"

"Not here, miss." None who could feed him, anyway.

Pale curls tumbled forward as she bent to pull on her boots. "You should have gone to a farm."

He averted his gaze, afraid another clout would send him sprawling on the grass. He was not going to explain all the reasons why going to a farm was a bad idea. She seemed to think he was a civilian. If the men thought the same thing, there was a chance they might let him go with a beating.

She finished tying her boots and stood up to address the soldiers in Latin. "I thank you," she said. "Now, will you please fetch my husband? He will know what to do."

There was a moment of hesitation, then the senior one allowed himself a grunt of disapproval before ordering his comrade to take the message to the gate.

"And ask him to bring his case!" she called after him.

Victor closed his one good eye and prayed that the mighty Bregans would remember the pair of white doves he had promised to sacrifice if he got away safely. He was not to be taken into the fort yet: That was good. But now he had to explain to an officer why he had been hiding under a tree to watch a respectable married woman untie her boots, hitch up her skirts, and dangle her bare feet in the river. And as if that weren't enough, he had then stepped forward and hit her.

Of course, the man should never have allowed her to wander the countryside by herself in the first place, but in Victor's experience officers never took the blame for anything.

His new bruises had already begun to stiffen up by the time more men emerged from the fort. The two big lads in chain mail must be part of the German unit based here. The one in the middle was taller than some officers and scruffier than others, but he had the coloring of a man from a hot and dusty place where they talked too much and thought they were clever. Besides, there was no mistaking that walk. They all had it: the confident stride of a man who knew what to do.

Victor stifled the instinct to stand to attention while the men spoke in Latin about "this native" as if he were a stray dog.

The Germans saluted and marched back to the fort. The officer turned to his wife. "This had better be good," he said.

2

Ruso had already noted with relief that the young man's black eye and swollen jaw were too mature to have been administered by his wife. Or by the Germans, who had sloped off up the hill with obvious disappointment now that their sport had been taken away from them. "I've just left spiced chicken and a decent wine," he said. "Why aren't you over at the inn?"

Tilla frowned. "If I have to listen to the driver and that woman for much longer, I shall get off and walk. I went to eat in peace by the river and look at your sister's letter, and this man came to beg for food. Do you think his jaw is broken?"

Ruso, setting aside yet again the disagreeable prospect of a letter from his sister, cast an eye over the native's injuries. They looked like the result of a brawl. Perhaps somebody else had caught him pestering their wife.

The man had shortish ginger hair, appeared to be in his early twenties, and—apart from the bruises—seemed to be in excellent physical shape.

Still speaking Latin, Ruso asked, "Been in a fight, soldier?"

The native looked up. There was fear in his eyes.

"It is all right," Tilla assured him in British, but the words were still on her lips as the man sprang away and pelted down the slope toward the river.

"Stop!" cried Tilla.

Ruso seized her by the wrist before she could give chase.

"My husband is a doctor!" she cried. "He can help you! Come back!"

The man's tethered hands gave him a peculiar gait, as if he were trying to run through something sticky.

Ruso released his grip on her wrist.

"We will give you food!"

The man did not break his stride.

"What is the matter with him?"

Ruso folded his arms and watched as the man staggered across the river, lurching as the current pulled at him and then recovering to struggle up the slippery bank without the help of his hands. Finally he vanished into the woods on the far side.

"He's either stolen his civilian clothes," Ruso observed, "or his army boots. My money's on the clothes."

"Will you send the soldiers after him?"

He bent to pick up his case. "I've got enough patients without chasing after more."

"What will happen to him?"

"I'm guessing he's one of the British recruits they've started taking into the Legion. Not a very bright one. He's got rid of his belt, but unless he has the sense to change his boots and hide amongst the locals while his hair grows, he'll be caught."

"But he has the voice of a Southerner," she said. "He has no one around here."

"So?"

"The local tribe might sell him back to the army."

Ruso reflected that British tribes were always more complicated than you thought. "Well, it's not our problem."

Assuming that the spiced chicken would be cold and the wine would be finished by now, he accompanied his wife back to the river bank to compete with the local ducks for a share of her lunch.

"My brothers," said Tilla, raising her voice over the din of a squawking flotilla lunging for the bread as it hit the water, "would never have joined the Legion."

Since Tilla's brothers were not Roman citizens and had been killed by neighboring cattle raiders before they were twenty years old, this was not surprising. "And would they have said, *Our sister would never marry a soldier*?"

"You are not a proper soldier," she said, flinging the next handful toward a lone bird hesitating at the back. "You are a medicus."

Ruso glanced down at his army belt and reflected that this fine distinction might be a comfort to Tilla, but it was invisible to everybody else. He had renewed his vows to the emperor. He was an officer of the Twentieth once more, and it did not matter that he had only come back because he missed the salary and the camaraderie and because he never, ever wanted to work as an investigator again. As far as the rest of the world was concerned, he was just another soldier.

When all the food was gone, he escorted her back to the inn. "Just stay out of trouble this afternoon, will you?"

"If that driver is still in there telling stories about how stupid the natives are, I may punch him on the nose."

"Fair enough," he agreed. "If it needs straightening afterward, send him up to me."

On the way back past the gate guards he wondered if he should, after all, report the escaped Briton as a deserter. Then he remembered it was his own wife who had pried the man away from the guards, and decided someone else could do it.

3

Victor struggled on into the deep shade of the woods, his head pounding with every step. His throat was sore. His legs felt like lead. He was torn all over by brambles. He stumbled over a root and went headlong, crying out at the jolt of the landing but knowing he was lucky: The rotting leaves had broken his fall. He lay still, trying to listen over the rasp of his own breathing. Nobody seemed to be following him.

He began to squirm, curling up into a position in which he might be able to reach the clasp knife they had not taken because they had not searched him properly. What ever they had tied around his wrists was digging into his flesh. His fingers felt numb and clumsy. Slowly, patiently, he managed to tease the little knife out of its hiding place in the sodden sheepskin that lined his boot. Still listening for pursuers, he pried it open and tried to angle the blade against the binding without cutting himself. He could move it only a fraction of an inch at a time. He had no idea whether it was having any effect.

Suddenly the knife slipped out of his grasp. He yanked his wrists against the binding, but it felt tighter than ever. Groping for the knife amongst the leaves, he touched a smooth surface with the tip of one finger. He stretched out his hand. He had two fingers on the blade now, pressing down to get some purchase. It shifted, flipped away from beneath his fingers, and landed somewhere out of reach.

Victor lay back, exhausted. He was beginning to shiver. He thought: *I could die here.*

He dared not go back to Eboracum, but if he went home, what would he tell everyone? That he had run away in the fine army boots Corinna's family had given him for a leaving present? Even if his people took him back, what if Geminus and his men came looking for him? Whole families had been known to be condemned as traitors. There was always room on the ships for more slaves to feed to Rome.

He couldn't go to his own people. He wasn't going back to the army. He couldn't rely on hospitality from other tribes. There was only one place where he was wanted, and he definitely couldn't risk being found there.

He had made a mess of everything.

That was when Victor, champion wrestler of the Dumnonii tribe for two years in a row, only the second Roman citizen in his family, proud recruit to the Twentieth Legion, father of one, almost able to read and write, laid his head on the ground and wept like a girl.

4

The travelers from the Twentieth Legion reached a damp and blustery Eboracum early in the afternoon of the next day. The horses splashed across the ford while the pedestrians waited for the ferry. It was a slow and very visible approach, but no one came out from the fort to greet or even acknowledge them.

While the escort continued to thump on the south gates and bellow, "Open up for the tribune!" Ruso watched Tribune Accius himself glaring at the wood as if he expected to break through four inches of iron-studded oak with a hard stare. Or perhaps he was just mildly annoyed. It was difficult to tell with Accius. The sharply defined nose gave him an air of perpetual haughtiness, and the slight scowl about the dark eyes suggested a preoccupation with weighty matters that lesser men would not understand. Accius, as he had made quite clear, had no intention of spending his military service hunting and carousing like many of the young nuisances sent out from Rome. No: Accius was a nuisance of an altogether more dangerous sort. He was the sort who actually wanted to do something.

When there was still no response, the tribune twitched a rein and his horse obediently circled round, allowing him to frown at the ferrymen rowing the rest of his entourage across the river. Ruso followed his gaze and watched the first of the two baggage wagons venturing down into the choppy water.

"Something's not right," Accius declared, as if it were not obvious. "Stop knocking."

Ruso sniffed. The moist air was sharp with the smell of burning, but the casual whistling of a figure loading crates outside a warehouse downriver suggested that whatever was going on behind the ramparts of the vast and underoccupied legionary fortress was nothing unusual.

Accius said, "I sent Geminus a message. They should be expecting us."

Remembering that Geminus and Accius were related, Ruso did not venture to suggest that the aging centurion might have forgotten. Even if he had, the guards should have heard them by now.

He hoped the Sixth Legion had not arrived early. Accius had traveled from Deva to represent the Twentieth at the official handover, and his welcome would sound rather hollow if the new arrivals had already thrown down their bedrolls in the barrack rooms while their legate was happily sweating out the grime of the march in his private baths. He said, "Sir? The ferryman's trying to get your attention."

The standing figure in the ferry was pointing downstream past the warehouses, but his words were lost in a cacophony of yelling and waving passengers all trying to help him communicate. Behind them the mule team faltered, alarmed by all the shouting, and the driver struggled to keep the wagon moving across the ford. Finally someone gave the order for silence. A lone voice rang out, “East gate, sir!”

It was a poor start, and nothing on the short ride around the corner to the east gate suggested to Ruso that Eboracum was going to get any better. It pleased him enormously.

Ever since the emperor had declared the date of his visit, Britannia’s administrators had been working themselves into an increasing frenzy of counting and tidying and reordering. Everything that did not move was being painted—at least, on the side that faced the road—while inns were being improved and new buildings flung up in the hope that Hadrian might be enticed to stay in them. Friendly tribes in the South—and perhaps here too, if Tilla was right—were busy preparing a spontaneous explosion of joy to mark his arrival. He supposed the less friendly ones would be equally busy stashing away what ever weapons they still held after the recent troubles.

Meanwhile the Twentieth Legion had been swept up into an orgy of practicing, polishing, and sharpening, pausing to inspect, and then practicing, polishing, and sharpening some more.

Exasperated by all the fuss, Ruso had devised himself a tour to inspect the medical facilities of the most obscure outposts he could get away with. Eboracum, awaiting a new garrison and currently not home to anyone important, had seemed a good choice. He eyed the peeling paint and the sagging thatch of the civilian buildings with satisfaction. The few still in use stood out along the street like the remaining teeth in ageing gums. Ruso suppressed a smile. This was just the place for a man who wanted some peace and quiet to get on with his work.

Accius was not smiling. Glancing back down the potholed street, Ruso wondered if Centurion Geminus had said the wrong thing to somebody important. Nowhere looked inviting on a wet afternoon in Britannia, but Ruso had to admit that the faded glory of Eboracum was an especially forlorn place for a decorated war veteran to end his career.

The grand plaque honoring the late emperor Trajan looked out over a protective ditch choked with weeds, but as the ferryman had predicted, the heavy gates beneath it were open. The guards who stepped forward to greet them looked reassuringly smart and efficient. The tribune and his party were expected—yes, sir! There was accommodation prepared for him—yes, sir!

Evidently they had been taught to respond to questions in a manner that conveyed boundless enthusiasm. Only when asked where Geminus could be found did they falter. The blush and stammer that accompanied "He's dealing with an emergency sir!" suggested they were not sure there could be any crisis more pressing than the arrival of a legionary tribune.

"What sort of emergency?" demanded Accius, who evidently thought the same thing.

"He's up on the roof of the headquarters hall, sir."

"He's mending the roof?" Accius was incredulous.

"No, sir. He's trying to get somebody down."

5

Ruso looked up, tucking his flapping cloak under his thigh and raising a hand to shield his eyes from the spatters of rain. In the center of the fort, at least seventy feet above the ground, a lone figure had straddled the gable end of the massive headquarters hall like a mouse clinging to the neck of a giant stone horse. He was too far away for anyone to make out his features, let alone any expression that might hint at his state of mind. All that could be seen was a bright blond head above a brown tunic and one pale leg ending in a bare foot.

Below and to the man's right, about halfway up the building, several other figures were moving about on the wet tiles of the side roof. They were trying to maneuver a ladder so that the hand dangling a swaying rope from a high window could tie it in position. Ruso could hear them shouting to each other, but the breeze and the distance snatched their words away.

"There he is!" said Accius, looking at the rescuers. "That's Geminus."

The centurion must be the muscular, bald-headed figure directing the operation. Ruso shifted in his saddle. The roofs were not steep, but the wind was blowing in sharp gusts and the tiles were slick with rain. He had seen what happened when a body fell from a great height. He had no wish to see it again, nor to hear the voices of desperate comrades pleading with him to help, as if there were something that could be done.

He was startled by shouts from farther down the street. "Get on with it, then, sonny! We haven't got all day!"

"Are you jumping or not?"

"Silence!" bellowed a third voice. "You men, get back to work!"

Half a dozen legionaries in rough working clothes emerged from an alleyway and paused to gaze upward. One was clutching a trowel hastily scraped clean of plaster. Another was holding a brush against the side of a pot with bloodred paint dribbled down the sides. The painter jabbed a middle finger toward the figure on the roof and they all shambled away, failing to notice the visitors.

A thickset man with graying temples appeared from the same alley. He was stopped in his tracks by the sight of strangers on horseback. He saluted the tribune and introduced himself as Centurion Dexter.

Accius's scowl was directed at the man on the roof. "What's that idiot doing up there, Dexter?"

"Geminus will have him down in a minute, sir."

"No doubt," said Accius, sounding like a man who had just been proved right about something but was not pleased about it. He eased his horse forward to get a better view. "Or he'll kill himself in the attempt. I may order him to come down and send someone else."

"It's one of his recruits, sir. He insisted on going up there."

"He would."

The hand from the window swung the rope around and tied the ladder in position. Four men attempted to hold it steady while Geminus began to climb.

He was halfway up the ladder when it slipped and screeched down the tiles. Accius gasped. The lone centurion clung on, his tunic rippling in the wind. Above him the rope was hanging loose from the window, now with a detached rung swinging about at the end of it. The rung fell out of the rope, struck one of the men holding the ladder, and clattered down the roof, gathering speed before it launched off the edge.

Above them, the blond recruit was motionless, still straddling the ridge tiles at arm's length from the drop.

Geminus bent to say something to the men below him, who adjusted their positions one by one. There seemed to be a discussion going on. Finally the rope was retied to the side struts of the ladder, which was where it should have been in the first place. Accius muttered something under his breath as Geminus stretched up across the gap in the rungs, and kept moving.

This time the ladder held steady.

Ruso's attention was caught by the sound of running feet. Ten or twelve young men appeared around the corner with mattresses slung over their shoulders. The mattresses were silvered with drizzle and the straw had collected in the bottoms of the covers, so that they were swinging about and banging awkwardly into the men's thighs.

Directed by the centurion on the ground, they piled them up on the flagstones directly beneath the gable end. Ruso, afraid someone might now encourage the recruit to jump, nudged his horse forward and murmured, "Centurion, you do know he's too high for that to help?"

"Who are you?"

"Ruso, medical officer from Deva. I've seen this sort of thing before."

Dexter shrugged. "At least it'll be over."

"What's his name?"

"Sulio."

"Your comrade seems to think he can get him down."

Dexter snorted. "A real man would have killed himself in private, but the natives have to make a drama."

Ruso was aware of a mutter of prayer from one or two of the young men. All were gazing upward at Sulio, several clutching good-luck tokens strung alongside the lead identity tags around their necks.

"Move along there!" shouted Dexter, adding, "It's not a bloody show. Get back to training!" as they retreated.

Geminus was at the top of the ladder now, but he was still not high enough to step onto the roof. He put both hands on the tiles. Ruso could feel the thud of his own heart. Geminus looked very small against the dull gray sky. One leg rose tentatively, then he grabbed the ladder again.

Ruso instinctively groped behind him to check that his medical case was still strapped behind the saddle. As if it would do any good.

Geminus repositioned himself, raised one knee, and finally eased himself up over the edge and onto the roof. Ruso wiped the rain off his face and spotted a medical team assembling a couple of stretchers against the wall of the hall, out of the recruit's line of vision. They had brought a box of dressings but also—more realistically—a bucket of sawdust, a broom, and a shovel.

Geminus was now picking his way diagonally across the roof toward the gable end. The blond head turned toward him. Geminus came to a halt while they were still ten feet apart. Nothing seemed to be happening. Perhaps they were talking.

Down in the street, the arrival of breathless runners signaled the delivery of more mattresses. Dexter busied himself directing their arrangement as if they would make a difference.

Above them, the conversation—if that was what it was—seemed to be over. The recruit was hitching himself backward along the ridge toward safety. Ruso let out a long breath, and then Geminus moved forward.

Seeing him coming, Sulio stopped. Then he edged back toward the drop. Geminus, concentrating on his own progress, did not seem to have noticed that his man was moving in the wrong direction.

"Wait!" Ruso yelled, aware that he might be making things worse by interfering. He cupped his hands around his mouth. "Stay still!"

Dexter, seeing what was happening, shouted at his men to stand clear.

"Centurion Geminus!" Accius's clipped voice rang out across the street. "This is Tribune Publius Valerius Accius. Halt!"

Geminus looked down, and paused. Just out of his reach, Sulio clambered awkwardly to his feet. He swayed above the drop, then steadied himself. His wet tunic flapped against his thighs.

"Sit down!" Everyone was yelling now. Cries of "Don't do it!" and "Stay there!" and "Don't be a fool, son!" filled the street, but Sulio did not seem to hear them. He looked back over his shoulder again at Geminus, who raised both arms as if he were trying to hold him steady by embracing the air between them.

Sulio turned away. He stretched his hands toward the dull sky. He looked as though he was praying.

"Sit down!"

"No!"

The street was silent for one long and terrible moment. Then Sulio hit the ground.

6

Wherever two main roads met there were soldiers, and wherever there were soldiers there were women, and wherever there were soldiers and women there would sooner or later be small boys, and one of the great delights of small boys was to watch the roads for the arrival of weary civilians and then descend upon them like a cloud of midges.

On the way into the fort, Minna had slapped at the grasping hands and shouted insults in Latin. The small boys called her names in British that she did not understand, which was just as well. When Tilla emerged from the gates a short while later, still struggling with damp bags and boxes of medicines but no longer with a wagon to put them in, she was glad she had not joined in the trading of rude words. It made it less likely that the scrawny, barefoot helper she now chose to escort her to the official inn would run away with her luggage. In case he was thinking of it, she looked him up and down and said in British, "Don't I know your mother?"

Perhaps encouraged by this connection, or perhaps in the hope of a larger tip, he gave her a commentary on the sights of Eboracum as they passed. Tilla, however, was not interested in knowing where Demetrius, the famous grammarian, used to teach, or how to find the temple of Mithras or the bar where the deaf wheelwright had murdered his wife's mother. What she wanted to do was get out of the wind and rain. What she wanted to know was whether the official mansio was better than the ghastly centurion's quarters she had just been offered inside the fortress.

She shuddered at the memory of a kitchen spattered with mouse droppings, a dining room with a gray fan of damp spreading out from one corner, and a lone and worm-eaten cupboard with the door hanging off. She supposed that once it was clear the previous legion was not coming back, the few troops left to garrison Eboracum had looted the unused buildings and then abandoned them. The cupboard was probably too damp to burn.

"This is it!" announced the boy.

Tilla gazed at a wooden building on a prime corner site. It was obviously a bar, well used and properly maintained. It was also very obviously a whorehouse. Watching them from the shelter of the doorway with his one good eye was a man shaped like a bear.

"Ah," said Tilla.

The boy swung one of her bags toward a freshly painted slogan on the wall outside. "Look!"

"Yes," said Tilla, squinting past the hair blowing into her eyes. "Are you sure this is the—"

"I can tell you what it says!" announced the boy. "It says, 'Lucina, Pamphile, and Hedone welcome our heroes from the Sixth Legion.' Lucina is Mam's special work name."

" 'We speak Latin,' " added Tilla.

The boy looked at her in amazement. "You can read?"

"A little," confessed Tilla, who was still not sure it was a good idea.

The boy called across to the doorman, "Is Mam around?"

"Working."

The boy shrugged and apologized to Tilla, who said, "We mustn't disturb her."

He took up the bag again. "I'll take you to the mansio now."

Evidently nothing worth telling her about had happened on the next street, possibly because hardly anyone was living there. A shop was offering bread along with a pile of unidentifiable meat, a box of cabbages, and five cheeses arranged in a pyramid on a tray, but at the moment she had no use for any of them. Nor for the shoemaker on the corner, who broke off from his work to offer instant repairs and grease to keep the rain out. A third shop seemed to be offering the sorts of things soldiers collected in barracks and then found they could not carry with them when they left: an old carved chair, a birdcage repaired with twine ...

The official inn was just beyond the east road, and it was a surprise. Its walls were bright with fresh white limewash. Its doors were in place. Its windows had glass, its roof looked intact, and there was no sign of women or cabbages for sale inside. Two slaves in matching cream-and-brown tunics rushed forward to take her luggage. Relieved, she paid the boy more than she should have, and they were both happy.

The slaves took her to a downstairs room that looked out over the dripping courtyard garden. It was not cheap, but it smelled clean and it had all the things she needed: two narrow beds, two lamps, one table with a jug and bowl, and a wicker chair with a faded scarlet cushion. Better still, there was no sign of anything with more legs than herself living there already.

The slaves bowed and retreated. She opened the boxes of medicines to check that none of the bottles was broken and that the linen bags were dry after their journey, then slid them away under the beds. There was nothing to replace or refill: They had barely been used on the trip so far. She pulled her sister-in-law's letter out of its safe place, tucked away in her tunic, and left it in the middle of the table.

She had no idea what the letter was about. Marcia's writing was like nothing she had ever seen before. She had given up trying to make out anything beyond *Dearest Gaius*. Gaius was what the family called him. *Dearest* was what they added when they wanted something. No wonder he was putting off looking at it. That was one of the bad things about being able to read: people could nag you from a great distance.

She washed her face and pulled a comb through her hair before twisting and pinning it tight at the nape of her neck. The pleasure of a proper wash and dry clothes would have to wait: she must face the weather again to catch the shops and the shoemaker before they closed, and perhaps have a quiet word with the bar staff before Lucina and her friends were busy selling their wares in a language that all men understood everywhere.

She hurried around the covered walkway that enclosed the courtyard garden, patting the purse slung from her belt. She was reassured by the chink of several large but not very valuable coins. They would be enough for bread and boot grease and whatever else she would need to buy to get into conversation. With luck, the tradespeople would spread the news that a very experienced and skilled army doctor was staying at the mansio for a few days, along with his wife who was a midwife. Both would be available for consultation when his military duties allowed, and their fees were very reasonable. In amongst the curious, the desperate, and the ones who had fallen out with the local healers, there might be people they could actually help, and who would be willing to pay.

Two matching slaves emerged from one of the doors ahead of her. They paused to let her pass and bowed at exactly the same time. She was wondering whether they held bowing rehearsals in spare moments, when she heard a voice inside the entrance hall that was familiar but not welcome.

"And a private kitchen!" it was saying. "A proper kitchen, that is, not just a brazier in a corridor somewhere. The cook needs space to prepare the tribune's food. He is very particular about his diet."

It seemed Accius's staff had not been impressed with the housing inside the fort, either.

Tilla glanced round the courtyard. There must be a way out that did not pass through the entrance hall. One of those doors must lead to the street, but which? Now that she needed them, the bowing slaves had disappeared. She wondered whether to go back to the room, then realized how ridiculous it was for an officer's wife to be hiding from someone else's slave. Pulling her hood up over her head as if it were blustery indoors as well as out, she stepped into the entrance hall. The tribune's house keeper was still in full flow.

"Ah! There you are, madam!"

Tilla clenched her teeth. She had spent most of the journey listening to Minna and the driver competing to see who could find the most to complain about. She had silently added *Must understand about speaking only when spoken to* to the list of qualities their future slave must have when they finally got around to buying her. Or him. The disagreement was one of the reasons they were still paying the neighbors back at Deva for the services of a borrowed kitchen slave. The other was that most of her husband's earnings went back to his family in Gaul.

"Here I am," she agreed politely. Minna might be a slave, but her master was a powerful man—as she never tired of pointing out.

"I was just explaining, madam," Minna continued, "that house over in the fort is a disgrace. I've never seen anything so filthy in my life."

Tilla bit back *Then you are a very lucky woman.*

"I see you weren't prepared to put up with it, either, madam."

"I am staying here," said Tilla, not wanting to give her the satisfaction of agreeing.

"You see?" Minna demanded of the manager, as if the state of the military accommodation were his fault. "It's not even good enough for the natives!"

As Minna carried on ("My master is a tribune, not just some passing centurion!"), Tilla felt the blood rising in her cheeks. *Not even good enough for the natives?* One of the local staff—who were probably listening somewhere out of sight—ought to hide a frog in the wretched woman's bed. Better still, a cowpat. Perhaps she would do it herself.

Instead of telling Minna to go away and use the servants' entrance, the manager was promising her that the very best suite was being prepared at this moment.

"Well, I hope they're doing it properly. I know what you people are like."

Tilla paused in the doorway to give the manager a sympathetic glance, but his face was still a mask of politeness. She said, "I shall be out for a little while, and I may have some visitors later."

The manager bowed. "Yes, madam."

"I will come back for dinner."

"We shall look forward to it, madam."

She made her way down the steps outside, leaving Minna complaining that it wasn't as if the soldiers hadn't known her master was coming. Perhaps she thought the poor man might feel sufficiently outraged to go up to the fort and berate the Twentieth Legion for negligence.

7

Doctor Ruso, sir?" The voice echoed around the empty benches in the entrance hall of Eboracum's hospital.

Ruso would have been hard-pressed to recall many faces from the ever-changing trail of young hopefuls who had followed him around the wards back at Deva, supposedly watching and learning. But standing before him was an older, thinner version of a short curly-headed youth whom he remembered only too well.

"It's Pera, sir. I was—"

"You were at Deva," said Ruso, grateful for the reminder of the name.

"We got your letter, sir," said Pera. "Welcome to Eboracum."

"Thank you," said Ruso, trying to remember anything Pera might have done to distinguish himself apart from that unfortunate prank in the mortuary. The awkwardness of the pause that followed suggested Pera might be trying too.

"So, who's in charge here?"

"I am, sir." He sounded as if he was expecting this mistake to be rectified at any moment.

"Really?" said Ruso, recalling the disciplinary hearing where Pera had explained how, instead of leaping out from beneath a shroud to terrify his fellow students, he had made the catastrophic blunder of doing it in front of half a dozen relatives grieving for the man on the next table. "Excellent," he said, realizing Pera had heard *Really?* as an expression of disbelief. "Well done."

Pera looked relieved. "Thank you, sir."

"Perhaps you could explain the setup here. I'd imagine the camp prefect's rather busy welcoming the tribune."

It was one of those conversations that reminded Ruso of all the things he liked about military medics. Pera, his confidence restored, did not waste time with rambling discourses on why all his rivals were fools, or praising his own secret medical recipes, or blaming the patients for his failures. Within minutes Ruso had a clear picture of the varied needs of two centuries of experienced but aging legionaries, a small auxiliary unit, and forty-eight recruits in basic training who were barely out of their teens. "Sorry. Forty-seven now, sir."

What Pera did not say did not need saying. There was no need to elaborate on the usual struggle to impose ventilation, cleanliness, and sobriety upon men who would happily spend their off-duty hours drinking the local beer and their nights huddled in a warm fug of unwashed bodies. Nor did he need to explain that Eboracum, like much of Britannia since the uprisings in the North, was chronically undermanned. Pera's small team was rattling around in a hospital built for a garrison ten times the current size. It was just as well the rebellious tribes had retreated to lick their wounds and bury their dead. Hadrian, who seemed like a sensible man, was seizing the chance to bring reinforcements and a fresh legion.

Pera was ushering Ruso through the side door and into the corridor when an orderly came to ask for guidance about a diet and a bandager wished to report that he thought a sprained wrist might be fractured.

Pera settled the diet question and promised to have a look at the wrist shortly. Turning to Ruso, he said, "What would you like to inspect first, sir?"

"Let's start with the wrist."

Pera looked pleased. Clearly the last thing he needed was to waste time escorting visitors around. By the time he pushed open the door of one of the treatment rooms to reveal a woebegone young man clutching his right arm, three more men had come to ask him for help or instruction, two of them wanting orders about what should be cleared out and what should be packed for the impending move to Deva.

"Why don't I see to this chap?" Ruso suggested, making a mental note to talk to Pera about training and delegation.

"He'll be honored, sir."

"Then we'll both be out of your way."

When Pera grinned, he looked almost as young as the recruits.

Sulio had confounded Dexter's attempts to clear the area by leaping beyond the straw mattresses, and several men had fallen awkwardly in the rush to get clear of the plummeting body. As Ruso splinted and strapped up the wrist and congratulated the orderly on spotting the symptoms that might indicate a cracked bone, he went through the usual speech about the bandaging being loose enough for swelling. "Come straight back if your fingers start to tingle or go numb. We'll splint it properly in a couple of days, then you'll have it held in position for about six weeks."

"Will I be discharged, sir?"

Ruso looked up from the wrist, surprised. "Gods above, no. It'll probably be fine in a couple of months. I'll give you a chit to show your centurion at Deva, so he won't undo all my good work with sword drill." He turned to the orderly. "Could you organize that straightaway, do you think?"

The orderly turned to leave. One of the men who had been on the roof limped out ahead of him on a bandaged foot.

When they had gone Ruso said, "You can do any training that doesn't involve the arm. Keep the wrist in a sling during the day for at least a week, and don't use it until we say you can."

The youth said, "Thank you sir," with all the gratitude of a man who had just been handed a bagful of snakes.

Ruso said, "How's the pain?"

"Not too bad, sir." The youth seemed almost disappointed.

"You'll be excused from carrying your kit back to Deva."

Most men would have been pleased to hear that, but this one seemed not to care. Ruso was tempted to point out that, compared to the dead man, he had little to complain about. Instead he said, "I'm sorry about your comrade. Did you know him well?"

"It's all right, sir," said the youth, staring at the floor. "You don't need to pretend. We know nobody wants us at Deva."

Ruso frowned. "What's given you that idea?"

"We're an unlucky unit, sir." The youth's weary gaze met his own. "They say we're—"

Before he could finish, a voice from the doorway called, "You there! Get a grip!" The youth gulped and fell silent.

Pera appeared, clutching a bottle of green fluid. He crouched down beside the youth and hissed in his ear, "Sulio chose to take his own life. The others were accidents. Any more talk like that and you'll be on a charge. Understood?"

"Yes, sir."

"*Is that understood?*"

The youth straightened his back, squared his shoulders, and stared into the middle distance. “Yes, sir!”

Ruso wondered who “the others” had been, and reflected that the prankster from the mortuary was much changed.

8

The occupied rooms of Eboracum's hospital were at the front by the entrance hall, while the kitchens were in one far corner and baths in the other. Kitchen staff and bathers were thus obliged to traverse long corridors lined with gloomy wards whose shuttered windows would have offered a fine view of native weeds strangling the herbs in the courtyard. Ruso waited until they were alone in such a corridor before he asked Pera to explain *The others were accidents.*

"This way, sir." Pera looked both ways before ushering Ruso through the nearest door and closing it behind him. "Is that why you've come to inspect us, sir? Because of the accidents?"

"No, this is just routine." It was true. A routine invented only last week was still a routine if one had plans to stick to it. "But since I'm here, can I help?"

Instead of answering, Pera opened the door and stepped back into the light of the corridor. "Sorry, sir. Wrong room."

Ruso stayed where he was. "Tell me about the accidents."

At the sound of distant voices, Pera flattened one arm against the door as if to hold it wide for his old tutor's exit. "We're not using this ward anymore, sir. I forgot."

"The accidents, Pera?"

Pera glanced back along the corridor, but no help came. Still Ruso did not move. Eventually Pera's arm dropped. With the door safely closed again behind him, he went across to peer through the cracks in the shutters before saying, "We've been ordered not to talk about it, sir."

"Not in front of the men," Ruso agreed. "That's understandable. But if any of this has involved the medical service, I need to know."

Pera massaged the back of his neck with one hand, as if it would ease his obvious reluctance to speak. Finally he said, "It's all nonsense, sir."

"Nonsense or no," said Ruso, "the lad's right: If word reaches Deva that they're an unlucky batch of recruits, they won't get much of a welcome. What happened?"

"You'd have to ask Centurion Geminus, sir."

Ruso sighed. "Pera, if you invite someone into a private room and close the door, he expects something interesting to happen."

"But I can't tell you anything, sir."

"So it seems. Although anyone who's watching will think you have."

There was a silence, and Ruso guessed Pera had not thought of that. "Never mind," he said cheerfully. "I'll go and ask the patients."

"No!" Pera sidestepped to block his exit. "Sir, there was a recruit who drowned when he was crossing the river."

"When was this?"

"About six weeks ago. And then two days ago a man had an accident during training. You know how superstitious the Britons are, sir. Once they get the idea of a curse—or anything, really—into their heads, it's hard to knock it out again."

"Yes."

"Ah." Pera must have picked up something from his tone. "Sir, I didn't mean to insult your—"

"I know," said Ruso, who was frequently baffled by Tilla's intransigence himself.

"The ones whose fathers were in the Legion have more of an idea, sir," continued Pera hastily. "But some of them are full-blooded natives. They're only citizens because their fathers are officials. It's not like the old days."

"True," observed Ruso, wondering whether Pera really imagined he was ancient enough to remember the days when most recruits were sent out from Italy. He was right, though: it was not like the old days. Nobody had explicitly stated that standards were to be relaxed, but Ruso was not the only doctor to end up arguing with the recruitment officer when a medical board rejected more men than was convenient.

That, however, was a battle for another day. In the meantime two fatal accidents in six weeks was unusual, but he was not an investigator now. He was not going to start imagining curses and conspiracies around every corner. He had seen the difficulties of crossing the river for himself, and deaths in training were not unknown. Men had nasty encounters with the moving parts of heavy weaponry. They wandered across a firing range, or got too close to a sharp edge, or were trampled by horses. Sometimes a man simply succumbed to a physical weakness that had revealed itself under the pressure of the demands upon him. Once the facts were clear, even the Britons might begin to grasp the concept of coincidence. "What happened to the lad in training?"

"He was dead before they got him here, sir."

"Is there something wrong with your neck?"

Pera retrieved the hand. "Sorry, sir. I was told he fell and hit his head."

"But presumably the lad this afternoon went up on the roof of his own accord. Do we know why?"

Pera's hands were clamped behind his back. He glanced down as if he could not remember where he had put them. "I think Centurion Geminus might be the best person to ask, sir."

"I see," said Ruso, curious to know what Pera was hiding and wondering whether he was more wary of the curse than his official position would allow. So far he had revealed nothing that Ruso could not have found out by asking around the barracks.

"Well, we can't do anything for dead men," he said, hoping he would get more sense out of Geminus later. "Let's go and see what we can do for the rest."

None of the half dozen men occupying hospital beds was suffering from anything that was of great interest to anyone except himself. All appeared well kept, adequately fed, and appropriately treated. The couple of recruits amongst them appeared subdued to the point of sullenness, but Ruso supposed that, after losing two comrades in two days, it was only to be expected.

There was one remaining patient: a youth with haunted eyes and a heavily bandaged upper right arm. His name was Austalis and he was being kept in isolation between two other vacant rooms, presumably in an attempt to provide peace and quiet. His response to "How are you today, Austalis?" was a worryingly weak "Very good, sir."

"I hear you had a knife injury. Mind if I take a look?"

The patient appeared indifferent. Ruso lifted the edge of the bandaging with a finger and did not like what he saw. "That looks painful."

"A bit, sir."

Ruso glanced at Pera. "What are you giving him for pain?"

Pera looked at the two junior medics who had crowded into the room behind them. One of them said, "He hasn't complained before, sir."

"Did anybody ask him?"

Nobody answered.

"What's in the compress?"

"Elm leaves and vinegar, sir."

Ruso nodded. "We'll give you some poppy tears for the pain in a minute," he promised, surprised that Pera had not seen to it before. There was no stool, so he sat on the edge of the bed, feeling a pulse that was thin and too fast.

"Are you normally in good health?"

"Yes, sir."

"How's your appetite?"

The youth's hollow eyes turned to the bowl of something brown that sat untouched beside the water jug on the bedside table.

Pera said, "We weren't sure whether to feed him, sir, but he didn't want it."

Ruso lifted the spoon a fraction. A skin like a leather tent rose up with it. He handed the cold bowl to one of the juniors. "Get rid of it."

Outside the room he said, "I'll clean the wound up in the morning. Meanwhile, move him where you can keep a close eye on him. Give him half a lozenge of poppy, make sure he takes plenty of water, and call me immediately if there's any change."

"I would have moved him, sir, but he's supposed to be kept away from the other men."

"Why's that?"

"Centurion's orders, sir. The injury was self-inflicted."

"The centurion doesn't know how ill he is," said Ruso, not wanting to pick a fight with Geminus over a man who had probably sliced up his sword arm to get out of training. "Move him carefully, straightaway, and if there's any problem I'll take responsibility."

For a moment Pera looked like a man who did not know which way to run. "This is the hospital, Pera," he said, trying to keep the impatience out of his voice. "I'm the medical officer."

Pera looked relieved to be given no choice. He gave instructions to prepare a room opposite the staff office.

Two accidental deaths in six weeks, not to mention one suicide and one potentially fatal self-inflicted injury. The recruits of Eboracum did indeed seem to be under some sort of malign influence. Geminus was trying to impose discipline. Pera was trying to patch them up. Maybe it was his own role to introduce some logical thinking around here.

Meanwhile, he realized there was one place he had not been shown. "Where's your mortuary?"

An expression that might have been embarrassment passed over Pera's face. "I didn't want to disturb them while they're preparing the body, sir."

"You did tell your staff there would be an inspection?"

"Oh, yes, sir."

"Then just point me in the right direction. I won't disturb them any more than necessary."

9

The mortuary floor was being washed by a lone orderly who leapt to attention, displaying large yellow teeth protruding from a face the color of chalk. Beyond him, Ruso was surprised to see not one but two parallel tables with white-shrouded figures laid out beneath the flickering lights on the lamp stands.

He bowed to the shrine in the corner and introduced himself to the orderly, adding, "I believe Doctor Pera told you I'd be here?"

The youth nodded and formed the words "Yes, sir" round the teeth.

"And no doubt he told you to answer my questions honestly?"

The nod was less enthusiastic, the "Yes, sir" a little more hesitant. Wondering exactly what Pera had said to his staff, Ruso glanced at the shrouds and had a momentary and inappropriate vision of one of them sitting up and shouting, "Help me! Where am I?"

"So here you have—"

"Sulio came in this afternoon, sir." The youth pointed to the nearest corpse, which was the smaller of the two. "Both going for cremation this evening."

Ruso made his way between the bodies. The incense in the burners was fighting a good battle against the smell of death, and what he had momentarily taken for stains in the light from the high windows were pale pink rose petals scattered across the crisp linen of the shrouds.

He had only to lift the cloth over Sulio's head to satisfy himself that the body had been treated with respect. It was both reassuring and alarming how the features relaxed in death: apart from a cleaned graze on his cheek, the blond recruit looked as though he were enjoying an untroubled sleep. He also looked about fifteen years old. Ruso lowered the cloth and sprinkled a few of the displaced petals over the shroud. What ever the hospital staff thought about the manner of Sulio's death, they were being very careful not to enrage his spirit.

"And the other one is ... ?"

"Tadius, sir."

"The training accident?"

"Yes, sir."

As Ruso reached for the cloth the orderly said, "Sir, I was ordered not to—"

"I'll take responsibility ..." The word trailed into silence as he stared down at the dead face. According to Pera, this man had fallen and hit his head during training. He also appeared to have given himself several bruises and broken his nose. Ruso reached forward. The lower jaw grated unnaturally when he tried to move it.

The mortuary attendant had retreated toward the door.

Ruso said, "What can you tell me about this man?"

"I—I'm not usually here, sir."

Ruso noted with interest that he seemed far more nervous of the accidental death than of the suicide. "I gather the cause of death was a blow to the head."

"Please, sir, I don't know. I don't know anything at all."

Ruso crouched beside the body. Whoever had washed it had missed a trickle of blood from the opening of the left ear. That could be the result of a head injury he could not see without rolling the body over. "Perhaps," he said, getting to his feet, "you could ask Doctor Pera to step in here when he has a moment?"

The youth nearly tripped over his own bucket in his eagerness to escape.

Pera found a moment almost immediately, but had the demeanor of a man who wanted to get a tricky job over and done with. Ruso apologized for interrupting him. "Just a few questions about this chap."

"That's Tadius, sir."

"The one you were told fell and hit his head."

"Yes, sir." There was no hesitation this time. "The occipital bone's fractured: you can't see it from there."

"I just wondered," said Ruso, who had already discovered the fracture for himself, "what you make of the broken nose and jaw, the broken fingers on the right hand, extensive bruising to the face and torso, and the circular abrasions around one ankle."

"I'd imagine he got into a fight, sir."

"Doesn't anyone supervise them?"

"You'd have to ask their centurion, sir."

"You didn't query it at the time?"

Pera cleared his throat. "He might have fallen off the stretcher, sir."

"Fallen off the stretcher?" It was such a farcical excuse that Ruso could not resist seeing how far his former pupil would take it. "This was after he'd received the blow to the head?"

"Yes, sir."

"Was this in the hospital or outside?"

Pera seemed to be having trouble with his neck again. "On the steps outside, sir."

"I see." If the injuries had been more plausible, he might have believed it. Accurately noting a cause of death was one thing; admitting to dropping a patient was quite another: It was the sort of embarrassing mishap that nobody wanted on record, except perhaps the outraged patient himself. "So if you question the fight injuries, this fall will come to light?"

"Perhaps, sir."

Ruso nodded. "I suppose if he was dead when he came in, a few more bruises wouldn't have made much difference."

"Exactly, sir. He—" Pera stopped just on the edge of the trap. "Well, he wasn't quite dead sir, but as good as. He was clearly slipping away."

"I see."

"There was just time for the bruising to develop before he died," Pera explained, digging himself deeper into the hole.

"I see," said Ruso, baffled as to why the man would lie over a small mishap when it was clear that Tadius had been in much bigger trouble than anything that could be inflicted by incompetent stretcher bearers.

"Sir, there was nothing more we could have done for him."

Ruso smoothed the young man's hair, then lifted the cloth and laid it over the body, adding another scatter of rose petals.

"Are we in trouble, sir?"

"I don't know," said Ruso. "But somebody should be."

10

Ruso left Pera to worry, and seated himself on a wobbly stool in the office. He was aware of his every move being scrutinized by a hefty clerk who, despite being told to stand easy, still looked as though he were being squeezed into a small space on one of his own shelves.

Medical records, as Ruso had insisted to Pera and dozens like him over the years, were crucial. They told the next medic what you'd seen and done. They told *you* what you'd seen and done, after a string of night duties when it was hard to remember your own name, let alone anything about the patient. If you took the time to review them, they helped you to decide which treatments were useful and which weren't, or which patients were genuinely ill and which were constant complainers. The trouble was, when you were the doctor, there was always something more urgent to do. And when you were supervising other doctors, the prospect of sitting down to read their notes made you aware of a pressing need to go and do… well, almost anything.

Like asking what that wooden box with "Sulio" chalked on the side was doing here.

"It's his effects, sir. We're waiting for someone to collect them."

Ruso eyed the bloodstained writing tablet sticking out from a fold of cloth. "Did he write a last note?"

The man leaned forward and pulled it out. "Tucked into his belt, sir."

Ruso had begun to read by the time the clerk added, "It's a letter from his mother, sir."

He had already skimmed far enough to know that the mother was praying for her son's success and enclosing some lambskin to line his boots. He slapped it shut and handed it back. "If I'd known that, I wouldn't have asked."

He tried not to imagine the woman's pleasure at receiving a reply. Eager for news, she would take it to someone who could read—perhaps the scribe to whom she had dictated this—and he would read out Geminus's words informing her that her faraway son had been dead for several days.

"A waste of a life," he said, feeling as though he should make some comment.

"Yes, sir."

Still, Sulio's mother was not his problem. The medical service was. The clerk was watching him: he must make a good show of inspecting the records.

"Right," he said, wishing as he always did at this stage that his own clerk—who genuinely loved this sort of thing—were still in the army, instead of hanging around down in Verulamium while a local woman decided whether or not she wanted to marry him. "Show me what you've got here, will you?"

Moments later a set of extralong wooden tablets listing admissions was laid out before him on the desk. Running a finger down the entries, he noted the acceptance of a body into the mortuary some weeks ago: *Dannicus. Dead on arrival. Drowned.* After that he could trace the seasonal transition from cold-weather coughs and catarrh to stomach problems and runny eyes and fevers. Something else was apparent too.

"What can you tell me about the training regime here?"

This was clearly not a question the clerk was expecting. "You'd have to ask Centurion Geminus about that, sir."

"I will. But first I'm asking you."

"Well, it's just... basic training, really. Drill and military pace, learning the commands, physical training... jumping and vaulting, that sort of thing."

"I see."

"Use and maintenance of weapons," added the clerk, evidently keen to show that he had not forgotten.

"So—"

"Throwing missiles, sir. And swimming in the river."

"So would you say it's significantly different from your own training?"

"Running, sir. That's another one. Plenty of running. Long-distance marches with full kit twice a week."

"So nothing unusual?"

"I don't think so, sir."

"There seem to be a lot of training injuries."

"It's the recruits, sir," said the clerk cryptically.

"The recruits?"

"They keep having accidents, sir."

It might not be as ridiculous as it sounded. Hadrian's promise of reinforcements had aroused fears amongst senior officers in Britannia that they would be fobbed off with all the idlers and trouble-makers that none of the other legions wanted. The consequent pressure for hasty recruitment was bound to result in some bad choices. This bunch might be clumsy rather than cursed. Still, that did not explain either of the bodies in the mortuary.

He found the second death two sheets further on. The entry was dated the day before yesterday. The word *Deceased* was written next to Tadius's name. Squeezed above it in a different hand, a word that could plausibly have read *Postmortem* was followed by a squiggle that must be a signature.

When he asked to see the postmortem report on Tadius, the clerk looked blank. "There isn't one, sir. Dead on arrival."

Ruso pointed to the register. "Whose signature is that?"

The clerk peered at it. "It's hard to say, sir."

"Where would I find the records for Tadius?"

Moments later the clerk was apologizing as he fumbled with the twine holding the postmortem report together. "I can't understand how it got there without me seeing it, sir. They usually just leave everything in a heap on the desk for me to put away."

On separating the pair of wax-coated leaves, Ruso was gratified to see a full set of neatly written notes covering both sides, dated the same day as the admission. His insistence on the value of record keeping had not been wasted. The hurried scrawl by the admission notice had belonged to Pera.

There was, of course, no mention of the nonsense about falling off the stretcher. It was a thorough report detailing the injuries he had seen just now: injuries sustained by a man who had died from a blow to the head following the sort of fight that should never have been permitted to take place on a training ground.

Pera had recorded the evidence, yet for some reason he had taken the matter no further himself and seemed desperate to keep Ruso out of it too.

Ruso closed the report, handed it back to the clerk for filing, and sighed. Eboracum should have been such a simple trip. If only Pera had come up with a good reason for silence, he would have been happy to collude with it, on the grounds that what ever they did, the man would still be dead. But Pera had not.

Meanwhile, the recruits seemed to believe that they were cursed. And the glum recruit with the broken wrist had been right: If the story reached Deva, he and his comrades would not get a warm welcome.

Ruso left the office deep in thought. He was not an investigator now. He could leave the business of Tadius's death alone and decide it was someone else's problem. But it involved the medical service, which was his responsibility, and what was the point of inspecting if he was not going to act on what he found?

Nodding to the statue of Aesculapius in the hospital entrance hall, he could not help wondering if the gods had noted his decision to avoid all the fuss and bother of Hadrian's visit and decided to have some fun with him.

11

As Ruso hurried down the hospital steps, the wind snatched at his cloak and spattered cold rain down his legs. He paused to get directions to the mansio from a gate guard who looked as though he had just swum to his post, then sped past the luxuriant weeds waving in the fort ditch and tried to dodge the worst of the puddles as he sprinted down the street.

One of the potted trees beside the mansio entrance had fallen over. He paused to set it upright before entering. He was stamping his clammy boots on the mat when he heard the thud of the wretched thing blowing over again.

The manager confirmed that, yes indeed, the Medicus's wife was here, and rang a bell to summon a servant. While he was waiting to be taken to the room, Ruso was treated to the sight of another visitor tottering up the steps toward the entrance hall.

The girl was clothed in a style that was appealing rather than appropriate. Below the look-at-us-boys cleavage, the flimsy pink dress that appeared to have been shrunk onto her was grubby and mud spattered.

This was as much as Ruso saw before the door slave stepped into his line of vision. "Guests only."

She craned to see past. "Is he the Medicus? It's urgent."

"This is an inn," the slave pointed out, "not a doctor's house."

"Well, that's not very nice! I just picked your tree up for you!"

Ruso moved away from the doors and stood examining his damp boots and his conscience. It had been a long day. Now he needed to tell Tilla that he had been invited to dine with the tribune this evening, while she had not. Experience had taught him that women did not like this sort of news, even if they had never wanted to go in the first place. He was also fairly confident that the last thing Tilla would want to hear next was that his best kit needed to be polished before tomorrow morning and that he didn't have time to do it himself, because he could neither arrive at dinner smelling of horse nor keep the tribune waiting, so he needed to rush off to the bath house straightaway.

Meanwhile, the young woman outside was urgently seeking a doctor.

"It's all right," he said, noting the unkempt hair and the wide eyes peering over the door slave's outstretched arm. The body was mature but the face above it was that of a child. "You can let her in."

The slave withdrew the arm and the unescorted girl stumbled past him, too busy taking in her surroundings to look where she was going. Noting the expression on the manager's face, Ruso drew her away from the desk and into a corner beside a shrine garlanded with wilting flowers. "I'm the Medicus," he explained. "But I can't—"

"I'm Virana."

"I can't see you this evening, Virana."

The girl was looking him up and down with undisguised admiration. "You are an officer!"

"Someone has to be."

She shook her head. A loop of brown hair escaped from whatever was supposed to be holding it in place. "I am not here to see you. They said if I want to see your wife, I must come to the mansio."

"Ah," said Ruso. He turned to the manager, who was eyeing the girl as if he were planning to have her swept into the drain as soon as Ruso had gone. "Did my wife tell you that she might have visitors?"

"She did mention something, sir."

"Well, this is one of them," said Ruso, wishing Tilla had explained more clearly who those visitors might be. "Can she wait here while I fetch her?"

It was not really a question, and the manager knew it.

Virana was clearly delighted to be given more time to examine her surroundings. As Ruso left the hall in the company of one of the mansio slaves, he heard the manager snap, "Don't touch those flowers!"

The walkway provided some shelter as the slave led him out around the courtyard and tapped on the fourth door. Beyond it he found a simple room, and in that room was just the sort of domestic scene a man wanted to come home to after a long day. A beautiful blond woman was presiding over a small table laden with a selection of salads and meats, a flagon of wine, a jug of water, and two cups.

"I did not know when you would be back, so I thought cold food would be easiest."

"Ah."

Tilla reached for his hand. "You look tired, husband. Is it true that a man jumped off a roof and killed himself?"

That was how it was in places like this: A man inside a fortress had only to sneeze and moments later half a dozen people on the far side of the wall were wishing him good health. He said, "It hasn't been a good day."

"It is over now. Sit and eat."

"There's someone waiting—"

"Let them wait." She pulled the chair out for him, then handed him a cup. "Why did he do it?"

He took a sip of the wine and hoped they would not have the nerve to charge much for it. "I don't know."

"They said he was from the Atrebates."

"Was he?" Nobody had mentioned Sulio's tribal origins. Probably because only other Britons would be interested. "Tilla, I can't stay. I'm sorry. I have to go and talk army business over dinner."

"But I thought—"

"And there's a patient waiting for you in the entrance hall."

She sighed, looking at the food. "I suppose if I put a cloth over the top, it will do for breakfast. So you are going back to the fort?"

"I'll be here, planning the move back to Deva with the tribune and the local centurions."

"I do not like that tribune."

"I didn't know you'd spoken to him."

"When you are not there, he looks at me."

"Really?" He would keep an eye on Accius from now on.

"Not in that way," she added quickly. "At least, I think not. More as if I am something strange and interesting."

"What a perceptive man."

"And, unlike you, he has never been rude to me."

Ruso grinned, just to show he was not in the least bit perturbed by Accius being younger than he was, almost handsome, powerful, rich, and unable to keep his eyes off other people's wives.

Tilla had moved on to a new subject. "I suppose Minna will be there, too, bossing the slaves around." She wrinkled her nose in distaste. "Finish the wine at least. It will help you put up with all the boring soldiers."

"I'll be as boring as I can. Then perhaps we'll finish early."

She leaned across the table and kissed him. "I am sure you will be very good at it."

It was not until he was sitting on a towel in the hot room of the mansio bath house, feeling the sweat begin to sting his eyes and trickle down the small of his back, that he realized he had forgotten to ask her to clean up his kit.

Later, perhaps while they were both polishing in a scene of domestic harmony he could not quite picture, he would see if she could shed any light on this business with the recruits. Despite a brief fling with the followers of Christos in Gaul, Tilla retained a firm belief in the power of cursing and blessing. She might have some insight into what the Britons thought was going on here. And then he could work out how to deal with it.

Ruso did not know a great deal about curses, but he did have a wide experience of army recruits. The impression he had formed at medical examination boards was that most of them were very young and poorly educated. Many were away from home for the first time, and even the best were trying not to show how nervous they were. His limited contact with them farther down the road suggested that Geminus's men would now be exhausted by the rigors of training, feeling trapped inside the fort, struggling with a level of discipline they had not known at home, and no doubt wondering if they had made a terrible mistake. Isolated from their own tribes, fed on rumor and grieving for lost comrades, he could see how these young men had worked themselves up into a panic.

Accius, evidently well briefed, had done his best to settle them down before they went back to barracks for their evening meal. As befitted a young man with an expensive education, he knew how to give a speech. Better still, he knew when to stop. In a very short space of time he had said all the things they needed to hear. He had looked out over the men of the Twentieth assembled beneath the roof from which the recruit had jumped. He introduced himself with the clarity and authority of a man twice his age. He offered them his sincere condolences on the death of Sulio, whose mind had gone. He honored the bold rescue attempt of Centurion Geminus and the men who had supported him. He commended their example to the recruits, reminding them that soon they would be back at the Legion's main base in Deva, where the discipline, bravery, and loyalty they had begun to develop here would bring them the advancement they deserved. They would be a credit to their centurion and their families back at home.

Finally, he announced a dawn parade at which he would personally preside over the sacrifice of a prize ram to Jupiter. Prayers would be said for the safety of the emperor and the spirits of the departed, and every man would be there in full dress uniform to witness it.

Accius was undeniably impressive, and it had seemed to Ruso that the young men whom Geminus marched out of the hall were less wild-eyed than before. Perhaps it was the presence of an officer of

Accius's standing. Perhaps it was the prospect of a long evening shining up such parade kit as recruits in basic training might manage to muster. Most likely it was the neat way the tribune had managed to respond to their fears without openly acknowledging them. He must have known what had been going on, and the people who had briefed him must be the centurions with whom Ruso was about to spend the evening. Perhaps he would find out what really had happened to young Tadius—and why Pera wanted it kept quiet.

Ruso wiped the sweat from his eyes and breathed in gently so as not to scald the lining of his nose. Deciding he had suffered enough, he got up from the bench and clacked across the hot floor on wooden sandals. A quick scrape of the dirt, a cold plunge, a rubdown, and he would be ready for a dinner which might turn out to be much more interesting than he had led Tilla to believe.

12

The black beads were cheap and the pink dress had been made for someone much slimmer. The first owner had probably abandoned it when efforts to scrub out a spatter of grease spots across the middle of the skirt had left them marooned in a faded patch.

Before Tilla could speak, the girl said in British, "Are you the doctor's woman?"

"I am the midwife," said Tilla in the same tongue. The girl was too young to be the boy's mother, so she was not Lucina come to ask why some stranger had been claiming to know her. It must be Pamphile, or Hedone, or some other working girl who was supposed to be looking forward to the arrival of the Sixth Legion. Which was more likely to mean her owner was looking forward to a rise in his profits.

"I am Virana." The girl glanced over her shoulder at the manager. "Grumpy over there doesn't like me. But you did say to come here, didn't you?"

Tilla gestured toward the courtyard door. "Come with me. We will speak in private."

"You are not Parisi," the girl guessed, following her along the walkway. "From your accent—Brigante?"

"Near enough," agreed Tilla, because no matter how many times she explained about the Corionotatae, people only remembered the names of tribes they had heard of before.

"You are Brigante, and you have married an officer!" It seemed the girl had never heard of such a thing. "How did you do it?"

"That is a long story." Tilla ushered her into the room and gestured toward the chair with the red cushion.

The girl seated herself and gazed around her, lifting the corner of the cloth to see what was laid out on the table. "Is this your dinner?" She tipped the flagon toward her and sniffed the contents. "I don't like wine," she said. "Beer is much nicer."

"Yes," said Tilla, putting the flagon back and replacing the cloth. She had left Marcia's letter on the table, hoping her husband might read her some news of his family in Gaul. Now she moved that out of the girl's reach too, hoping this was indeed a patient, and not just a local nuisance whom the mansio manager had failed to keep out. "You look in good health, Virana."

"Oh, I am! Is that your husband's armor?" The girl reached out and ran a fingertip along the curve of the metal plates.

"Yes." Who else's did she imagine it might be? "How can I help you?"

Virana, having finished her inspection of the room, leaned across the table to where Tilla had seated herself on the bed, and beamed. "I think I am with child!"

"That is good news," said Tilla, not entirely sure that it was. "I have herbs that will help the baby grow and keep you strong. I can give you something to take when the time comes, and an egg charm to hold in your hand when you give birth, but you will have to find your own midwife. We are only here for a few days."

"And then you are going back to Deva with the soldiers," said Virana, her eyes bright. "Tell me, is it true there are stalls selling silk and ivory and spices and eastern perfumes? And I can wear my shoes outside, because there is no mud in the streets, and nobody needs buckets, because the water flows to every house?"

"No."

"Well, never mind." Virana reached back to retrieve a bone pin and shook her hair loose. "I'm sure it will be better than here. I know the Sixth Legion are coming, but they'll send all the best ones up north to build the Great Wall, won't they? We'll just be stuck with the old fat ones again. So I thought you would know what to do."

"What to do about what?"

"I don't mind if he doesn't marry me. I know it's not allowed unless he's an officer."

"It is not recognized," corrected Tilla. "But if you have chosen a soldier and he has chosen you, that is none of the army's business."

"That's what I think too."

"When your man is moved, you will have to follow. It will not be easy, but plenty of women do it."

Virana pouted. "But that's the trouble. Nobody wants me to follow. They all say the baby is somebody else's."

Tilla suppressed a sigh. Was there no end to the supply of stupid girls living near army bases?

"Please don't shout at me. Everyone else does."

"I am not going to shout at you. I am going to work out some dates. It is hard to be certain about these things, but at least we might know where to start."

The girl shook her head and her hair came loose again. "I don't know anything about dates. One day is much like another here. We don't have all those big festivals and games like you have in Deva."

"You must have a market day."

Virana brightened at this, but it seemed one market day was also much like another, and the boredom of life around Eboracum was only made bearable by friendly encounters with young recruits on their weekly afternoon out from the local fort. "I was going to wait and see who it looked like," she said, "but now they're going back to Deva there isn't time."

"I will examine you now," Tilla told her. "But these things are very uncertain, and if you cannot remember when things happened, I am not sure how else I can help."

The girl lay down on one of the beds as instructed, then sat up suddenly. "You aren't going to take it away, are you?"

"No."

"Because if you take it away, I'll have to stay here, won't I?"

The examination revealed nothing new. The girl was indeed pregnant and all appeared to be well. Tilla felt a wave of jealousy. Why this stupid girl? Why almost every other woman in the world and not her? She swallowed, hearing the echo of her mother's words after she had voiced some forgotten complaint: *Nobody likes a person who feels sorry for herself.*

You don't understand, Mam.

No. And nobody else will, either. It's no good moping, girl. There's work to be done!

Virana was still prattling. "What I was thinking," she said, "was that if you tell your husband that you know who the father is, then he could order him—"

"My husband is not allowed to do that sort of thing."

"But how else will I get out of this place?" Virana sat up and gave the pink dress a violent tug to straighten it. A bulge of pale flesh appeared through a hole in the side seam. "They won't even let me in to talk to anybody."

"They are not going to help you," Tilla agreed.

"Those horrible centurions don't care about anybody."

"It is not their job to care about you."

The girl swung her feet to the floor. "They don't even care about their own soldiers!"

Tilla said, "My man does his best."

The girl put a hand to her mouth. "I am sorry. I meant no insult."

"You can speak the truth, Virana. I am not in the Twentieth Legion just because he is."

Virana glanced at the window, then said softly, "You should tell him to be careful in there."

"Why?"

The girl leaned closer and mouthed, "People keep on dying. They say there is a curse."

"I heard about the man on the roof."

"Not just Sulio." Virana glanced at the window again, and fell silent.

Tilla checked that no one was listening at the door. Then she closed the shutters, plunging them into near darkness. "What do you mean, 'People keep on dying'? What sort of people?"

"I don't want to get into trouble."

"There will be no trouble if you tell me the truth."

The girl sniffed. "First Dannicus. Then Tadius. Then Victor ran away, and now Sulio lies dead too."

Tilla paused. "This Victor—does he have ginger hair?"

In the gloom she could just make out Virana's nod.

She said, "I think I have seen him," but Virana was not listening.

"Fortune has turned her back on them!"

"But you still want to go to Deva with them?"

"They say the tribune will offer a ram to Jupiter in the morning. Perhaps things will be better after that. But tonight—"

"I will tell my husband to be careful," Tilla agreed. "These deaths—what causes them?"

"Dannicus drowned in the river." Virana shuffled on the bed. "So you cannot help me?"

"I cannot see inside the womb, sister. Think who you lay with at about lambing time and try to work it out."

Virana began counting on her fingers and murmuring names. There seemed to be a lot of them. Tilla opened the shutters again.

"They were all nice to me." Virana stopped counting. "I wouldn't do it with the rude ones."

"Of course not."

"They bought me beads."

"So I see."

"I felt sorry for them."

Tilla, trying to remember if she had ever felt sorry for a soldier in her life, said, "Why was that?"

"Mam said to stay away from them, but what does she know? I shall have plenty of time to grind flour and milk cows when I'm old like her."

"There is no need to feel sorry for soldiers, Virana. Especially when they ask you to comfort them."

The pout reappeared. “They won’t have me back at home now. My aunt says I’ll turn the milk sour.”

“I am sad to hear it.”

“It wouldn’t be Tadius, would it? I only did it once with him because of my sister.”

“Once is often enough,” said Tilla, pushing aside the thought, *but not for me.*

“Well, I’m sure it isn’t. Anyway, I need somebody alive. Marcus is nice…” The girl looked up. “You won’t tell my sister about me and Tadius, will you?”

“I do not know your sister.”

“She thinks she was the only girl he ever looked at. Now she is lying at home, sulking.”

Tilla dismissed the question of what the parents had done to deserve two such daughters, and tried to steer Virana back toward the danger the Medicus might be in. “Could the father be either of the other men who died?”

“Oh, Sulio and Dannicus weren’t interested in girls. You know. Like they say about the emperor.”

Tilla was not going to discuss the emperor’s bedroom habits with a girl who could not control her tongue or, it seemed, much else. “So the boy who jumped off the roof was the lover of the one who drowned?”

Virana nodded. “After Dann was drowned, Sulio was so frightened he couldn’t eat. He wanted to run away. I told him not to be silly.” She sniffed. “I should have said, *Yes, go,* shouldn’t I? If he had run away, he would still be alive.”

"Why was he frightened? Was he to blame for the drowning?"

"Tadius and Victor were really cross with him."

"He was frightened of the other recruits?"

But Virana had moved on. "Now Tadius is dead and Victor knew it would be him next and Corinna would be left on her own." She sniffed. "Like I will be if I'm not careful."

While the girl paused to wipe her nose on the back of her hand, Tilla tried to make sense of what she had said. "Three soldiers are dead, but from different causes, and one has run away."

Virana nodded vigorously, shaking the remaining strands of hair loose. "Corinna really is Victor's wife. But that's none of the army's business, is it?"

Talking with this girl was like trying to catch fleas: you never knew which way she was going to jump. "That depends on who you ask."

Virana thought about that for a moment. "It's not so bad for me, really, is it? I mean, I've got plenty to choose from. Corinna never lay with anybody else, so she can't get them to help now that Victor's gone."

It seemed the local girls had rushed to make the new recruits very welcome indeed. A harder woman would have told them that if they must take on a soldier, go for an older man who was about to settle down with his retirement fund. The young ones had no money, little free time, and no choice over where they were posted—but of course they had clear eyes and smooth skin and full heads of hair, and they thought they were immortal. Until, it seemed, they came to Eboracum.

She decided to approach from a different angle. "Who spoke this curse, Virana?"

The girl glanced at the open window again. "I do not think one ram to Jupiter will make much difference."

"What should I tell my husband to look out for?"

Virana got to her feet and adjusted the pink dress again. "I have to go now. I don't have to pay, do I? You didn't help me."

"I need something," Tilla insisted. "I have done everything I can for you, and I cannot have word go round that I see patients for free."

Virana pulled at a strand of her hair. "I have no money."

"You hoped I would help you because I am generous?"

"I hoped if I warned you about the curse ..."

"What you have told me is gossip. I need to know exactly what my husband has to fear in the fort. Who spoke the curse, and why?"

The girl twisted the hair around her forefinger until the fingertip went white. "It will probably be all right," she said at length. "It is only the recruits that bad things happen to. An officer from Deva will be safe."

"I hope so, Virana. Because if you have lied to me, I will find you, and you will be sorry."

13

The empress Sabina had long ago formed her own theory about the nonsense in travel books. No traveler, having gone to the expense and trouble of venturing where most civilized people were too sensible to go, was going to come home and admit that it had been a waste of time. Instead, he had to pronounce his destination to be full of strange wonders, like the elk with no knees that could be caught by sabotaging the tree against which it leaned when it slept (Julius Caesar) or the men from India who could wrap themselves in their own ears (reported by the elder Pliny, who seemed to have written down everything he was ever told), or the blue-skinned Britons (Julius Caesar again).

Strangely, no traveler ever brought one of these creatures home for inspection. Doubtless they were impossible to capture, or died on the journey, or the blue came off in the wash.

Travel, in Sabina's experience—and the gods knew she had suffered enough of it in the last twenty years—was less a matter of wonder than of discomfort and disappointment. Londinium was no exception. It had been as empty of blue-skinned natives and promiscuous Druid women as she had feared. Instead, the outgoing governor had led them on a tour of the local forum, followed by an interminable display of marching, fighting, and killing in the amphitheater. In the evenings she and the emperor had been trapped for hours in the palace dining room with provincial administrators and hairy native chieftains. As if the emperor could not see fora or amphitheaters, or eat oysters, or meet barbarians who spoke Latin everywhere he went! The irony, which of course the native chieftains would never be subtle enough to grasp, was that while they were eager to be Romans, their esteemed Roman leader liked to pose as an intellectual Greek.

But since Julia had fallen pregnant—no doubt on purpose in order to avoid this trip—there was no friend with whom she could share the joke. The slaves were all chosen by Hadrian, and presumably primed to report her every complaint, yawn, and mutinous scowl.

The governor's wife, poor woman, was as tedious as Sabina feared she herself might become if she were obliged to spend much longer marooned in the provinces. She was desperate for the latest gossip from Rome—as if Sabina had been there recently, instead of dutifully shivering through a Germanic winter that froze your teeth if you opened your mouth, and turned the slaves' feet and noses blue with cold.

Perhaps things would be better when they finally arrived in Deva. Paulina had sounded positively thrilled to know that her distant and now very famous cousin was coming to visit. She had promised to keep Sabina entertained while the emperor and her husband did all those important things that emperors and legates had to do. Meanwhile, Sabina had asked the governor's wife in vain for the locations of singing stones, statues that spoke, stuffed monsters, giants' bones, or relics of Helen of Troy. She supposed pyramids were unlikely in Britannia, as were temples filled with treasures, or elephants trained to write, or fountains that miraculously spouted wine—although admittedly she had never been able to pin down the last two herself. But it seemed even the distant hills of the North and West boasted no steaming sulfurous craters or fissures belching poison gases. There was not even an oracle.

"There is the circle of very large stones, madam."

"Do they do anything?"

"Not that I know of. But you might like the temple of Sulis Minerva at Aquae Sulis."

"What does that do?"

"It is an old and very holy place where a constant supply of hot water springs out of the ground."

"How very convenient," she conceded. "If one were short of slaves."

"The people throw in offerings to the goddess and curses on their enemies."

"Well, I suppose it will have to do. Is it nearby?"

Sadly, it was not.

The only way to get to Paulina at Deva was to travel north with the emperor. Even that was a better prospect than staying in Londinium, discussing cushion covers with the governor's wife. Besides, there was always a faint chance that the stories of a northern land of perpetual daylight might be true. Even if they were not, Tranquillus and Clarus would be amusing and intelligent company on the journey. Although they did not dare say so, she was sure they, too, wished they were back at home: Tranquillus working on his writing, and Clarus, who always looked as though his uniform belonged to somebody else, with his nose buried in a scroll.

Hadrian could find someone else to bore with his lectures about drawings and measurements. His latest project might be the biggest and best wall in the empire, but it was still just a wall. Of course, she was the only one who had ever dared to tell him so.

An auspicious day had been chosen for the start of the voyage, and the omens had been good. Even so, things had gone wrong almost straight away. The dress she wanted to wear turned out to be in one of several trunks loaded onto the wrong ship. Clarus had been assigned to another vessel with most of his men, while the quiet and nondescript man who had been hanging around in the governor's palace—and was undoubtedly some sort of spy—turned up on deck and then vanished, giving her the uneasy feeling that he had hidden somewhere to watch everybody. Or perhaps just her.

Tranquillus had shrunk yet again from letting her read his *History of Famous Prostitutes* and still refused to tell her stories from it lest the emperor should disapprove. Then after two days, the wind had risen. The mounting seas had hidden Clarus's ship along with the vessel carrying her luggage and the motley collection of ambassadors seeking an audience with the emperor. She had felt increasingly ill. Tranquillus had retired to his cabin "to work on his latest biography." Her maid reported that the only sign of productivity was the occasional emergence of a slave clutching a covered bucket.

She no longer cared. It was impossible to be amused or intrigued when the wallowing and heaving of the gray waters outside seemed to be competing with what was going on in one's stomach. It was a great pity that the author who had declared the sea around the north of Britannia to be "sluggish and scarcely troubled by winds" was already dead. She would have taken great pleasure in arranging to have him tied in a sack and thrown into it.

The emperor, of course—that was how she thought of him these days: *the emperor*, not *my husband*—the emperor was still striding about the deck, giving orders to the captain and encouragement to the crew before expecting his weary companions to join him for stimulating conversation over platters that slid about on the table. Hadrian had scant sympathy for those who succumbed to seasickness: evidently it was one of the many forms of weakness to which one should not yield.

There was a soft tap at the door.

"Come!"

A blast of damp air blew a slave into the little cabin. The slave was clutching a tray in one hand and had a cup clamped onto it with the other. She fell backward, slamming the door with her bottom.

Faintly recollecting that she had asked for some water, Sabina said, "Just leave it on the floor."

The slave, appointed by the emperor and so doubtless a spy, did as she was told and withdrew. A moment later the ship gave a violent lurch to starboard. Somewhere outside, a woman screamed. The cup fell over, sending trickles of water exploring first one way and then another across the boards. Every timber around her seemed to be creaking as if it was straining to part from its neighbor.

Men were shouting. Footsteps hurried past the cabin. The bedchamber slave crouched to wipe up the water just as the ship hit another wave. The girl fell sideways, grabbing at the end of Sabina's small sleeping platform to steady herself. Seawater slid in under the door and sloshed across the planking. Normally silent unless told to speak, the girl began to gabble prayers to her gods.

More shouting. More lurching.

The empress Sabina lay on her side, closed her eyes and prayed for sleep. Or death. Either would do, so long as she stopped feeling like this, but neither was happening. The pitching and rolling of the ship grew worse. She clung to the edge of the sleeping platform to steady herself. Finally the prayers ended in a shriek as the world rolled sideways. Sabina lost her grip and landed on top of the struggling slave.

The women slid in a heap of limbs into the corner. Water was streaming in from all directions now. They clung to each other, the slave sobbing and wailing and Sabina trying to call out prayers to Neptune over the crashing of waves and the straining of timbers.

They both screamed as the door burst open and a bedraggled figure staggered in, clutching a knife. It bent to slash the ropes that held the trunk containing her jewelry in place beneath the sleeping platform and dragged it toward the door.

Remembering her duty, the slave made a lunge for it. "Thief! Stop!"

"Captain's orders!" he yelled.

Sabina pulled her back, put her mouth against the girl's wet hair, and shouted, "They are throwing everything over to make the ship lighter. Be glad you are not going with it. If this does not work, we will all drown."

14

Accius reclined on one of the rather worn couches that graced his private dining suite in the mansio, and Ruso congratulated himself on his mature lack of jealousy as he noted that this room alone was three times the size of the space he was sharing with his wife. The housekeeper who had irritated Tilla bustled around straightening covers while Ruso and the remaining guests spread themselves across the other couches.

While the mansio slaves in their matching cream-and-brown tunics trotted in to serve drinks, a confusing set of introductions was performed. There were four centurions, plus a man from the auxiliaries who explained that he was in charge of road patrols and proceeded to say nothing else all evening. Perhaps he was overawed. The others all had at least three jobs each. The granite-faced Geminus appeared to be in control of the recruits and of everyone else. Dexter had something to do with the maintenance crews. The plump one was in charge of stores and supplies, and smelled as though he had been checking out the wine stocks before he arrived. The one with thinning hair and a careworn expression was tasked with fobbing off the complaints of the locals, or as it was officially known, "Civilian liaison." All gave the impression that they would be happy to shed a few titles in exchange for being posted somewhere else.

"So," said Accius, helping himself from a bowl of hard-boiled eggs that had been cut into halves and dolloped with some sort of green sauce, "no problems getting things lit in the rain?"

Geminus said, "All done, sir. Quick, quiet, respectable."

"Good. I didn't want funerals hanging over the proceedings tomorrow. How are the men?"

"Our lads are all right, sir," put in Dexter, apparently speaking for the plump one and the careworn one as well. "It's the recruits."

"Hearing about the sacrifice to Jupiter seems to have settled them down a bit, sir," said Geminus. "And they took heart from what you told them about Deva. We shouldn't have too much trouble on the march."

The recruits Ruso had met seemed glum rather than rebellious. It had not occurred to him that there might be any trouble on the long march west to legionary headquarters, but as he listened to the practical arrangements for packing and transport being discussed around him, it became evident that the recruits were being treated with a certain wariness.

"As soon as we get them back to base," said Accius, dabbling his hands in the finger bowl held out to him by one of the slaves, "they'll be split up between the centuries." He smiled. "And while the rest of us continue to endure the ghastly conditions on this island, Geminus, you'll be sitting in the sunshine on your little farm in Campania."

Geminus inclined his head and said, "I shall, sir," without a trace of humor.

Ruso reflected that Hadrian, who insisted on mixing with the ranks and sharing a military diet, was probably the only man in the army who did not grumble about his working conditions. No doubt the incoming troops would have plenty to say about the state in which the Twentieth had left the fortress at Eboracum. Meanwhile the Twentieth would have the satisfaction of knowing that the headquarters and their one occupied corner showed they were civilized men, even though they had long ago stripped the remaining buildings of anything that might contribute to the domestic bliss of their successors. Anyone who imagined that the legions were happily united in the service of the emperor was woefully naïve.

Reaching for a spoonful of the fish with leeks that had been a favorite recipe of his first wife, it occurred to Ruso that Claudia would not have been impressed with his conduct so far this evening. *You must make an effort, Gaius! Do try and join the conversation. People will think you don't approve of them!* He doubted they cared whether he approved of them or not, but it was clear he was not going to find out anything interesting unless he asked.

"I was wondering, sir," he put in when they seemed to have run out of things to say about the crop yields of the farm Geminus had bought in Campania, "why the recruits were sent here instead of being trained at Deva."

"Because somebody has to garrison Eboracum while everyone's up on the border building the emperor's wall," explained the tribune, as if it were obvious.

"And they look like soldiers to the natives," added Geminus.

"Ah," said Ruso, suspecting he now appeared dim rather than sociable, and not sure what to say next.

"It was thought," continued Accius, helpfully filling the silence, "that if we trained them over here, they wouldn't pick up bad habits from the older men back at Deva."

"But it turned out they'd got plenty of their own," observed Geminus.

"You've all done everything that could possibly be asked of you," Accius assured the centurions. "I saw that for myself this afternoon."

Geminus said, "I should have got rid of that lad before, sir. But sometimes a recruit like that comes good."

Dexter wiped his bowl with a chunk of bread. "You can't do anything with a man whose mind has gone." He crammed the bread into his mouth as if there were nothing more to be said on the subject.

Ruso felt there was a great deal more to be said, but not here. Instead he reached for the water jug. "So how did they get the idea they were cursed?"

No one replied. He glanced up. The others were looking at him as if he were an earwig that had just crawled out of their lettuce. He had a feeling this was not the sort of reaction Claudia would have intended.

"The curse of the Britons," said Geminus finally, "is that they don't do what they're told. A couple of them found out the hard way that they should have paid more attention in swimming practice."

"Geminus dived in and rescued one of them himself," said Accius, as if he were afraid his relative might be too modest to mention it.

"Lost the other one downstream." Geminus shook his head, acknowledging defeat. "Then this week we lost one in a training accident, and they've put the two together and made up some tale that means none of it's their own fault." He clapped his glass down on a side table as if signaling the end of this depressing subject and turned to Accius. "I noticed the mention of discipline in your speech, sir. Very appropriate."

"Ah, yes." Accius reached for his own wine. "Of course, you know why we have altars to Disciplina."

"To encourage the men, sir?" ventured the plump one.

"The same reason we have coins celebrating Concordia," said Accius, taking a sip and looking around the room. "Because we like to pretend we've got it."

"We do, sir," agreed Geminus. The plump centurion gave a grunt that might or might not have been assent, the thin one looked round for a cue, and the silent one busied himself with his dinner.

Ruso wondered how much wine Accius had drunk. The wording stamped on coins was chosen at the very top, and—given the bad relations between the Senate and Hadrian—it was hardly tactful for the son of a senator to be heard criticizing imperial policy in a building where any member of the staff could be a spy. The spies, on the other hand, would not be anywhere near as interested as Ruso was in the loss of a few unimportant Britons—something Accius should have been concerned about but apparently wasn't.

"I was wondering, sir," he said, "if the second recruit who died had been in some sort of a fight."

Geminus frowned. "Where did you get that from?"

Too late, Ruso realized that a fight might suggest Geminus had failed to keep control, whereas an accident could be blamed on the gods. "The body," he said, unable to think of a suitable lie and wishing the tribune had found some women to invite. Women were good at filling embarrassing silences. Except for Tilla, who was good at creating them.

This time it was Accius who restarted the conversation. "Did Geminus ever tell you," he said to the centurions, "how he and I first met?"

The fat and the thin centurions greeted this opening with the eagerness of men stranded on a lonely road spying an approaching carriage. The silent one did not appear to notice.

"We're related, you know," Accius explained. "On my mother's side."

Ruso, who knew this much already, surmised that Geminus was a useful sort of relative: distant enough not to be a social embarrassment but close enough to be claimed as family when he had marched home from the Dacian campaign, his chest sparkling with decorations for bravery. Apparently the eight-year-old Accius had been escorted onto the streets of Rome to watch him in the victory parade. Later, he had followed Geminus around the house asking every question he could think of about life in the army.

Geminus's hard features softened slightly as his protégé reminded him of the marching lessons around the fishpond in the garden, and how Accius had taken to demanding the day's watchword before allowing anyone to enter his presence.

"Do you remember that wooden sword you gave me?"

"Very well, sir."

"Did Mother ever tell you Father confiscated it? I knocked over one of the statues in the garden while I was practising the thrust and twist. I wrote to the praetorian barracks to ask you for another one, but I think the slave must have been told to lose the letter."

"I never got it, sir."

"And finally, after all these years, I heard we were serving in the same province and I had the chance to thank you."

The bald head dipped in acknowledgment. "You've made me very proud, sir."

"And to apologize to you for being an insufferable brat."

There was a brief silence while everyone waited to see if Accius would smile. Then they all laughed. Even Geminus. The subject of dead recruits was forgotten.

15

By the time Ruso headed back around the courtyard toward his own room, the blustery rain had put out all but one of the torches, which was why he failed to see the puddle before he trod in it.

To his surprise he found his wife still awake and sitting at the table. Whatever was left of the food had been pushed to one side beneath a cloth. The flames of a triple-wicked lamp were dancing in the sudden draft from the door as she rolled up a scroll that had been laid out in front of them. He recognized the collection of poetry a friend had lent her for reading practice.

"If one of our poets had spoken this rubbish," she said, tying it closed, "nobody would pass it on, and it would be forgotten, and good riddance. But this man wrote everything down, and now it floats about like somebody else's hair in the bath. Who cares if his lady's pet sparrow is dead?"

He sat on the bed and bent to tackle his wet boots. "The only other scroll Valens could lend me wasn't fit for a decent man to read with his wife. It's a foul night out there. How was your patient?"

"Pregnant, and very silly. Is it true three recruits have died?"

"And one's deserted."

"He is the one we met on the way here. His name is Victor. I hope he is somewhere safe in this storm."

"I'm surprised more haven't run off. They seem to be an unhappy bunch." He tossed the boots into a corner.

Tilla retrieved them and put them on the windowsill to dry in the draft. "The girl said Fortuna has turned her back on Eboracum, and you should be careful. She thinks it is only the recruits who are cursed, but I have prayed to Christos for you—"

"I wish you wouldn't keep doing that."

"—and I will find a place to leave a gift for the goddess, just in case."

"Did she say how the second man died?"

Tilla frowned, as if she was trying to remember exactly what she had been told. "The recruits were frightened of each other after the one who jumped off the roof lost his boyfriend in the river."

"His boyfriend?" That might explain the suicide. "Why were they frightened of each other?"

"She said, after the drowning, two of them were angry with Sulio."

"Was it his fault?"

"I do not think so. By the end I was as confused as she was. But one of the angry ones is dead—"

"Tadius?"

"Tadius, yes—"

"Does she know how he died?"

"She was more interested in telling me how he bedded her and her sister. The other angry one is Victor, and he deserted because he thought he would die next."

Victor, like Tadius, had been beaten up.

"Why?"

"I do not know. I do know he has a wife called Corinna."

Ruso scratched one ear. Civilian gossip might move fast, but it degenerated into nonsense the farther it traveled. If Sulio had killed himself out of grief for a lost lover, he had waited a long time to do it. In the meantime Victor had run away and Tadius was dead. "I'll see if I can make some sense of it tomorrow," he promised her.

"Be careful."

"I'm always careful."

"Is it true the tribune will try to lift the curse with a sacrifice in the morning?"

"Oh, hell." Reminded, he reached down and lifted the shoulder plates of his armor. The attached segments rose one by one into a shape that could enclose a man's chest. "He's offering a ram," he said, scowling at the orange specks of rust. "Best not to ask why. Have we got any rags and some oil?"

She delved into one of the boxes and pulled out a frayed linen bandage. "There is no sand."

"We'll just have to rub harder."

Moments later he was wishing there had been an artist present to record the ensuing scene of domestic bliss, marred only a very little by Tilla saying, "If my ancestors are looking, I hope they know that I am only helping you because you are just a medicus and not a proper soldier."

He let it pass. "By the way, I think I've found out what our noble tribune is really doing here, so far away from all the action."

She paused with a length of oily bandage in one hand. "Husband, are you jealous?"

"Of course not," he said, demonstrating his indifference by the casual tone of his denial. "But Accius made a tactless remark, and when it was obvious people had noticed, he was very careful to explain that he isn't deliberately avoiding the emperor."

"The tribune told you he is not avoiding the emperor?"

"Not directly. But he says he volunteered to come here because he wants to see Geminus before he retires. The old man's hanging up his vine stick after he's marched his men back to Deva."

She frowned. "But if Geminus is marching his men back to Deva, why come all this way to see him? Would they not meet there anyway?"

"Exactly!" Even Tilla could see how obvious the tribune's lie was, but she did not seem as impressed as he had hoped. "Accius is the son of a senator," he explained, realizing he should have explained the background. "Most of the Senate didn't want Hadrian in charge. They don't trust him."

"And because the father is not a friend to the emperor, you think the son would travel all this way to avoid him?"

"Four of Hadrian's opponents in the Senate were conveniently murdered when he came to power. I have a feeling Accius may be distantly related to one of them. Even if he isn't, people find it very hard to forgive that sort of thing. Of course Hadrian had nothing to do with their deaths—"

"Why not?"

He blinked. Even now, there were times when his wife took him completely by surprise.

"Well, because... because you can't do that sort of thing these days." The gods alone knew what went on amongst the Corionotatae when a new leader took over. He said, "Everyone knows he wasn't involved, because he said so," but this well-worn joke made no impression upon his wife. She had already moved on to the next question.

"And did you tell him that is also why you are here inspecting the medical service?"

"That's not the same thing at all," he said. "I just didn't want all the—"

"Polishing?" she said.

"Fuss." Outside, he could hear something loose banging about in the wind. "Is there anything left in that jug?" He lifted the cloth. The movement revealed the dark rectangle of his sister's letter.

"Ah!" Tilla reached out and thrust it toward him before he could cover it up again. "You can read while I finish this. Quick, while there is still oil in the lamp."

"I'll read it tomorrow in daylight."

She shrugged. "Perhaps I shall take it and ask that handsome Tribune Accius to read to me."

"It's no good," he told her. "I'm not jealous."

She took the bandage from his hand and replaced it with the letter. Then she slid the lamp nearer. The flames wavered in the draft from the window.

"All right," he conceded, not sorry to abandon the cleaning. "Let's get it over with."

Most of his relatives never wrote unless they wanted something, but, as the head of the family, it was his duty to find out what it was before he refused it. He turned the thin wooden leaves to face the light and leaned forward to make out the crowded lines his sister had inked onto them several weeks ago in the sunny south of Gaul.

No wonder Tilla had struggled with it. Marcia's spelling was always creative, but she could write perfectly legibly when she wished. This, however, seemed to have been composed with her eyes shut. If their father had lived to see the outcome of her expensive education, he would have demanded his money back.

He ran a forefinger along the uneven line of script.

"'Dearest Gaius,'" he read, with difficulty. "'Greetings from your loving sister. I hope you and Tilla are well and so are we although to listen to some people around here you would never believe it. Little Lucius fell off a fence yesterday and knocked his front teeth out. His mother made a great fuss. Your brother complains all the time, and now he is shouting at me because the man who says he will take this letter wants to get home before dark but it isn't my fault that nobody told me he was coming and I am writing as fast as I can. Our mother and Diphilus are planning an extension on the west wing and he and your brother argue a lot.' "

He paused. "The tribune will be sorry he's missing this."

"The tribune would read faster than you."

" 'Good news,' " he continued. " 'Unless you have the same news for us we have beaten you to it.' "

The swish of linen on iron fell silent. "She is pregnant."

"It might not be that."

It was.

He put a hand on her knee. "I'm sorry."

"You must wish them well from us both."

He carried on reading, not because he was interested in what his sister had to say, but because he had long ago run out of reassuring things to say about their own failure to conceive.

" 'Tertius is very pleased with me, as he should be, and is making sure I take plenty of rest every day. I expect Mother has written to tell you we will not have enough to live on when we are a family.' "

"Has she?"

"No, but it's good to be forewarned."

" 'As you know, poor Tertius has never really got the advancement he deserves. Well, really there is no future in making clay pots for the next-door neighbor, is there? Of course he was grateful for the job when he was injured and I'm sure they are very good pots but now he is as fit as you are and probably fitter because you are so old.' "

He paused again, waiting in vain for his wife to disagree.

" 'He is also brave and honest,' " he continued, " 'and quite clever in his own way.' "

He said, "Not clever enough to keep away from Marcia."

Tilla had gone back to polishing. He scanned the rest of the letter in silence. *So as you are the head of the family and Tertius has nobody else it must be up to you to help, Gaius. We all know you are hopeless at putting yourself forward but please think of other people and make an effort.*

Gods above. His sister was starting to sound like Claudia before the divorce. Unfortunately, he supposed she was right: He ought to try and do something for Tertius.

Having settled that, Marcia was displaying an unusual interest in current affairs.

Did you know that Hadrian is on his way to Britannia?

The reason became clear in the next line.

I hear he has thousands of people on his staff. I'm sure he could find something for Tertius if you ask him nicely enough.

Ruso shook his head in disbelief. He supposed it was his own fault. He had once held several short and dust-covered conversations with Senator Publius Aelius Hadrianus about treating the injured in the aftermath of a terrible earthquake that had flattened most of Antioch and nearly killed the reigning emperor Trajan. Some years later, when Hadrian had risen to even greater fame, Ruso had been foolish enough to mention these fleeting encounters to his family. Instead of being mildly interested, his stepmother had been convinced that persistent demands of *And what else did he say?* would help Ruso remember a series of cozy chats that ended with Hadrian saying, *If there's ever anything I can do for you, my friend*... and Ruso thanking him and promising to be in touch *as soon as my stepmother's told me what I want.*

He continued to read. *Please don't let us down, Gaius. I know we are a long way away and you probably don't think about us much now you have managed to get back into the army, but we are your family, and we will never get another chance as good as this.*

He sighed. Marcia was in for a disappointment. With luck, by the time he had made his way back to Deva via every possible outpost and watchtower, the imperial tour would have passed by.

He felt Tilla's hand close over his own. "We will have a good life," she said softly.

For a moment he had no idea what she was talking about. Then he realized she had thought he was sighing over their lack of offspring. "Of course we will," he promised.

16

Ruso woke in darkness and stumbled across the room to find a bleary-eyed matching slave waiting outside the door with a lamp. Tilla muttered something about getting up to help and promptly went back to sleep. He shrugged his way unaided into his heavy armor, which still smelled of olive oil, eased the hooks into place, and fumbled with the slippery leather thongs in the poor light. When they got back to Deva, he really must find the money for a slave boy.

The storm had cleared overnight. Munching on a wine cake he had grabbed from the table on the way out, he made his way to where Accius's flunkies were tacking up the horses by torchlight. After a brief acknowledgment when the tribune strode out of his suite to join them, the men from the Twentieth rode across to the fortress in silence.

Ruso, who was on foot, left the others to dismount in the courtyard of the headquarters building and walked around the outside. The street was empty now. In the dull predawn light he stood on the spot where the blond figure of Sulio had fallen. The flagstones had been washed clean, the gravel raked. He bent to pick up something beside his foot. It was a strand of straw that might have come from one of the mattresses.

Above him, the gable end rose black against the clearing sky. What had passed between Geminus and Sulio in those last moments? How had Geminus tried to entice him down, and why had Sulio refused to listen? Did the deserter, Victor, have anything to do with it? Did Tadius? There was definitely something odd about the death of Tadius. Or was Sulio overwhelmed with grief about his drowned lover? He didn't know. Somewhere in the southern tribe of the Atrebates was a mother who would never know, either.

He tossed the straw aside and headed into the headquarters hall for morning briefing. The dead had never been his patients. This morning he needed to concentrate on the living recruit who had taken a slice off one arm.

The briefing was a formality, since most of those present had already met and discussed the same issues over dinner last night. The sun was just gilding the tops of the surrounding roofs by the time the men were marched into the courtyard, ready to watch the sacrifice. Ruso slipped in next to Pera. The plump centurion poked the line straight with his stick and then moved on. After he was gone, Pera murmured, "Sir, I'm assigned to sanitary inspection this morning. Can you do the ward round?"

As the senior medic Ruso would have expected to be consulted about where Pera was assigned, but this was not the time to say so. Barely moving his lips, and with his eyes focused on a dent in the helmet of the man in front of him, Ruso said, "Of course." Then he added, "I read your postmortem report."

When there was no reply, he glanced at Pera, who was standing like a statue. He showed no sign of having heard. "Why can you write the truth but you can't speak it?"

Still no reply. More men took their places ahead of them. One recruit was hauled out of line for some misdemeanor. As he was being marched out of the courtyard by a pair of Geminus's junior officers, Ruso heard Pera murmur, "Geminus's two shadows."

The miscreant had barely disappeared when the tinny sound of a rattle being shaken around the courtyard served as a warning that the procession was on its way. There was no chance of further conversation now, with the centurions glaring along the ranks like schoolmasters watching for bad behavior.

Ruso had to admit that Accius looked imposing in his toga. The aristocratic voice rang out clearly, reading the traditional words with confidence. There was no stumbling and no interruptions—not only auspicious but a relief, since it meant they would not have to go back to the beginning and start again. The ram appeared content to be led up to the altar: another good sign. The blade flashed in the early morning sun. The animal barely struggled. The blood spurted.

It was all very professionally done. Even to a man whose religion consisted mostly of half-formed and unanswered questions, it was strangely reassuring.

Ruso hoped the men would be impressed. What ever words might be necessary to pacify the spirits of the dead would have been said over their pyres last night, and with this performance the pollution of the deaths and the nonsense about the curse should be over. The men now marching out of the headquarters courtyard in their best kit would soon head west across the hills to Deva, where they would be split up and assigned to their centuries. Older, wiser, and better disciplined, they would each make a fresh start in the Legion.

On his right a quiet voice said, "That question you asked me earlier, sir ..."

"Don't tell me to go to Geminus."

"It's best not to ask that sort of thing at all, sir. You really don't want to know the answer."

17

Two days' march south of Eboracum, another dawn sacrifice was offered with more than the usual gratitude. This one was to Neptune and Oceanus. Sabina watched the smoke rise into the clear sky, fingered the cluster of emeralds in her one remaining pair of earrings, and tried to be grateful that the rest of her luggage had been saved instead of furious that most of her jewelry was at the bottom of the ocean. She was not sure where this outpost was, but of one thing she was certain: she would never set foot on a ship again until it was time to leave this ghastly island behind.

She left the emperor striding about the place, deep in conversation with Clarus and the local centurion. The centurion was probably still reeling from the shock of sighting a battered imperial flotilla in the estuary. Hadrian would be doing the rounds of the survivors, pausing to chat to exhausted sailors, inquiring about injuries to the horses, and sympathizing with the comrades of the men washed overboard. Meanwhile she was taken to the local inn, where she was to lie on a couch in some other woman's clothes while her staff went in search of her missing luggage. She glanced across at the emperor's secretary, busy scribbling despatches explaining the change of imperial plans.

"Tranquillus?"

"Madam?"

Watching poor Tranquillus trying to conceal his excitement at being noticed was an entertainment in itself.

"I hope you are taking notes on all this so that you can tell the world what we have had to suffer."

"Indeed, madam."

"Because you will hardly get a whole book out of Interesting Things to See in Britannia. A few statues of dead emperors, stones arranged in a circle, and burial mounds of people no one has ever heard of."

"Indeed, madam."

"I have been wondering if Clarus and I could persuade you to include the present emperor in your list of biographies."

Tranquillus swallowed. "I am delighted to say that the present emperor is still with us, madam. It would be premature to attempt to summarize his already great achievements when there will doubtless be so many more to record."

"Ah, yes," agreed Sabina. "Of course." There were times when she wondered whether she should be kinder to Tranquillus. Then he came up with an answer like that and she wondered whether he, too, was enjoying the game.

Tranquillus was not fool enough even to consider writing about Hadrian, but as the limping chambermaid from last night took her arm to escort her around a pothole, she wondered if he was thinking of the scandalous material he could include if he did. Nothing as scurrilous as the depravities that he had related from the old days, of course, but Hadrian would not want the world to read about that sordid squabble with Trajan over the pretty boy. Nor about the dubious manner in which he had become emperor. She did not believe for a moment that Trajan had named Hadrian on his deathbed. The old man's widow, the only witness, was one of Hadrian's collection of devoted middle-aged women. All of them thought they understood him better than she did. But what normal man preferred the company of his mother-in-law to that of his wife?

Neither she nor Tranquillus, of course, would ever mention these things. The quiet man who had appeared on the ship had vanished, but the slaves were always there, and always listening. She knew that because once she had invented an overpriced diamond and spoken of having it imported from India, and sure enough the emperor had later accused her of wasting money. He had not been in the least perturbed when she complained about him spying on her. "Of course," he said, as if it were as natural as breathing. "Do you have something to hide?"

"How could I?"

"Precisely." He had turned away to discuss the defense of Lower Pannonia, and that was the end of the interview.

Now, of course, he really would have to buy her some jewelry.

The sound of hammering and sawing rose from the wharf: They were starting the repairs on the ships already. She turned to Tranquillus. "I begin to understand why you refused your first posting here."

Tranquillus turned pink again and mumbled something about not refusing exactly; it was simply that at the time he had been inconveniently unable—

"Do you know whether one can travel by road to the place where the hot springs rise?"

"It is even farther from here than from Londinium, madam." Tranquillus's apologetic tone suggested this was his own fault.

"What about the land of endless day?"

"Many miles to the north of us, madam."

She sighed. "Well, if you can think of anything at all that might relieve the ghastliness of this place, please do suggest it."

18

She had dreamed the dream again.

Tilla lay in the warmth of the blankets, gazing past the empty bed beside her to the bright streaks of light around the shutters. The storm seemed to have blown itself out during the night. Sparrows and pigeons and a blackbird were celebrating the morning in the courtyard, hardly disturbed by the slap of sandaled feet passing along the walkway.

The house in the dream was always endless. Last night there had been a broad fan of gray damp spreading from one corner, but the rest was always the same: empty rooms and steps and corridors that she wandered through with no clear idea of where she had come from or how she would ever get out.

She had dreamed about it so often that when a traveling interpreter came to Deva, she had paid good money to find out what it meant.

"Ah, yes!" The interpreter had looked into her eyes while clasping his hands together as if he could squeeze the meaning out from between his palms. "And are the rooms collapsing?"

"I don't think so."

"Any smoldering or ash?"

"No."

"I am happy for you, mistress. If a room burns brightly without falling down, then you will come into riches."

When she failed to look pleased, he said, "You are quite sure there is no ash? Because damage warns that something bad is on the way. A burning bedroom signifies ill fortune for a wife. Damage to the men's rooms means ill fortune for a man."

"I see."

"The meaning is quite clear, even if only one wall is collapsed. The wall with the door in it represents—"

"What if the rooms are not on fire at all?"

"Not on fire?"

"No."

The man laid his hands flat on the table. "Then it is very hard to say."

She was glad she had not told her husband where she was going.

She could see now that the meaning was obvious. It did not matter that she had risen from slave to housekeeper, from housekeeper to wife. It did not matter how many babies she helped other women to bring into the world. Marcia's letter had been a sharp reminder that her days were destined to be spent moving between empty rooms, with no family of her own to fill them.

She closed her eyes, listening to the voice of her mother.

It's no good moping, girl. There's work to be done.

But Mam, the slaves do all the work in a mansio, and I cannot make women have babies to deliver. Besides, do you not see how it breaks my heart to hold them when I have none of my own?

Have you forgotten? Nobody likes a person who feels sorry for herself.

I try not to, Mam. And when we get back to Deva, I shall have plenty to do.

Lighting fires and fetching water? Cooking?

Not every day. Some days we rent next door's kitchen girl.

What other wife of a Roman officer ever does those things? You shame us by marrying him and then you shame him by acting like a slave!

He is not ashamed of me!

No? What do his friends think? Why were you not invited to dinner with the tribune?

Nobody's wife was invited, Mam. And I had a patient to see.

You spent the evening with a silly girl who said you were no help, and reading about dead sparrows. I don't know what to make of you. One minute you are cleaning his armor like a slave, the next you are trying to read as if you were some rich foreigner.

You were the one who told me to get on and do things and stop moping, Mam! Now I am doing things and still you are not satisfied!

She could hear again the sniff of disdain that meant her mother might be losing the argument, but she was still right. *You are trying to be many people at once, daughter. But you know from the dream that you are not going to be a mother, and you are a terrible cook. Why do you not ask your husband to buy some help?*

We cannot agree on what sort of slave to buy.

Nonsense. That is an excuse.

Mam, I am not going to be one of those wives who hang around the bath house all morning eating cakes and complaining about everything.

Then find yourself something better to do!

Tilla, who in low moments long ago had considered trying to join her lost family in the next world, decided she was glad she had stayed in this one.

The blackbird was still singing outside. Over in the fort, the sacrifice to Jupiter would be complete. It was a good morning to make a new start. Then perhaps the dream would go away.

19

Ruso yawned and made his way across to the hospital to shed his gear and see what fate had decreed for Austalis, owner of the wounded arm. As he approached, the acrid smell of burning filled his nostrils. A couple of bonfires were alight in the middle of one of the unused streets. The Twentieth were clearing out their rubbish and preparing to leave.

The room opposite the office had a different and worrying stink, and Ruso was annoyed to see that nobody had opened the shutters. He was not fooled by *We didn't want to wake him, sir.* When had hospital staff ever shied away from waking their patients?

The light revealed a figure whose sunken eyes were too bright. Sweat-darkened hair lay flat against his scalp, and the sheets were damp with perspiration. When Ruso spoke, he tried to reply but seemed unable to form the sounds into words. His pulse was still fast and faint. Ruso turned to the man who was hovering at the door.

"I left orders for someone to call me if there was any change."

The only response was a meaningless "Yes, sir!"

As Ruso suspected, nobody had checked the catheter. Another food bowl, this time of thin gruel, had gone almost cold beside the bed. Apparently Austalis had been fed a couple of spoonfuls earlier and had vomited. So much for not wanting to wake him.

Ruso gave a few terse orders and the dressings tray finally appeared in the hands of the chalk-faced youth, who seemed to be the one given the jobs nobody else wanted and now looked as though he might faint at any moment. He was followed by a porter, who delivered a jug of clean water and a smaller jug of vinegar inside an empty bucket and then hurried out as if he was afraid he might be asked to assist. Ruso called him back and ordered him to summon all the staff to the office at the start of the next watch.

The chalk-faced youth seemed to have some idea of what to do, but Ruso was forced to stamp on his toe as the bandages were unwrapped. It was not until the wound had been cleaned out and redressed with a poultice of ground pine needles and they were splashing water over their hands down in the latrines that he could explain.

"Looking at a wound and saying "Ugh" is hardly going to boost the patient's confidence, is it?"

"Sorry, sir," said the youth. "I didn't think he could hear me."

"That belief has been the downfall of many great men."

"Yes, sir."

Ruso found the driest corner of a towel that someone should have changed this morning. "Apart from that, you did well."

"Thank you, sir." A little color appeared in the youth's cheeks as he ventured, "I haven't done anything like that before, sir."

"You'll get used to it," Ruso promised him, wondering if that sounded more like a threat.

"He will be all right, won't he, sir?"

Ruso handed the towel over. "If we keep on with the treatment, there's a slim chance he might get better by himself and still have two arms."

"What if he doesn't, sir?"

"Taking the arm off might save the rest of him. But the longer we wait and the weaker he gets, the worse his chances are."

The color in the cheeks drained away again. "I can't believe any man would do that to himself, sir."

Ruso said, "I doubt he intended it to end up this bad. Any idea what drove him to it?"

The youth looked around him, but the wooden rows of latrine seats provided no inspiration. He said, "You could try asking Centurion Geminus, sir."

Geminus, the man who seemed to know the answer to every question. The man with two shadows.

By the time the trumpet sounded the next watch, Ruso had been relieved to find that Austalis was the only neglected patient. He had discharged a couple of men who looked sorry to be leaving; admitted another who arrived doubled over with stomach cramps; and been almost certain that the recruit who claimed to have walked into a door was the man who had been marched away by Geminus's shadows. He checked on the wrist and the injured foot from yesterday, and looked in on Austalis again. When all the staff on duty had crowded into the office, he chose the most sensible-looking orderly to be responsible for Austalis. "I want him kept clean and comfortable, and I want to be told straightaway if anything changes. And I want it made known that he's allowed a visitor. Just one friend, and very briefly. I don't want him worn out."

The orderly raised a hand. "Sir, he's supposed to be in isolation."

"I take it his centurion wants to put the others off trying the same trick?"

If any men in the room had dared to guess at the centurion's intentions, they were not fool enough to admit it.

"I'll square it with Geminus," he assured them. "And given the condition of the patient, I think we can count on his visitor to spread the word about the stupidity of self-inflicted injuries."

20

The mansio slave's directions were good. It was barely two hundred paces upstream along the muddy path from the wharf to where the old willow bent to dip its leaves into the glittering silver of the river. She raised one arm, counted to three, and flung the coin. The small splash was washed away in the flow. While the gift was sinking, she said a prayer to the river and to the goddess to look kindly on her husband and keep him safe. Then she asked for a blessing on her new start, and for courage, because the decision that had seemed so clear this morning had faded in the sunlight.

Who has ever heard of a woman being a medicus?

What will your husband say?

You can hardly read Latin, and nearly all the recipes for medicines are written in Greek. You cannot even understand Greek, let alone read it…

Who will do all the work you do now?

Do you really want another woman in the house?

What if you get the wrong sort of slave—one who needs constant watching, or one like Minna? That would be even worse. What if…

Something white caught her eye. Two swans, a cob and a pen, were gliding downstream. She watched as they drifted past the fort walls, smoothly changed direction to pass behind the approaching ferry, and disappeared beyond the warehouses. It was a sign. She let out a long breath and whispered a prayer of thanks, remembering the wounded Brigante warriors she had tended with stolen bandages and medicines during the troubles. None of them had complained about her being a woman.

All will be well. All will be—

"There you are! They told me you were here! What are you doing? Can I help?"

She turned, startled and not pleased. The pink dress was no cleaner than yesterday. "Good morning, Virana."

"Are you looking for plants for healing?"

"Not this morning."

Virana parted the fronds of the willow as if she hoped there might be something interesting beyond them, then let them fall. "This is where Sulio came to pray for the soul of Dannicus."

"Is this where he drowned?"

"No, farther down by the ford. Sulio tried to save him but he couldn't, and then the Centurion had to get Sulio out too."

"It must have been frightening."

"I suppose so. I was at home with my family." She hauled the beads out of her cleavage and hung them down the front of the pink dress. "They were all being horrible to me, as usual. Did you hear the trumpets this morning? They don't usually sound like that. Was it because of the sacrifice?"

"Sulio must have been a brave man."

"Oh, he didn't jump in. He was there anyway."

When Tilla looked puzzled, she said, "He hurt his knee while he was on one of those long marches they do, and Dann stopped to help him, and then they had to get back across the river. Well, that's what they're saying."

Tilla frowned. "Why did they not use the ferry?"

The girl began to fiddle with the beads again. "I wasn't there myself."

"You can tell me the rest of the story while we walk back to town."

The string had twisted and hooked over one bead, making a loop. Virana frowned as she tried to straighten it. "If I tell you, will you tell your husband?"

"My husband is a medicus. He understands about secrets."

The bead was finally disentangled. "I only know what I heard."

"That will be fine."

"You must swear on the bones of your ancestors that you won't say who told you."

"I swear."

The path was only wide enough for one. Tilla's skirts brushed through the overhanging grass while Virana's voice sounded in her ears.

"The river is always cold," the girl said, "and it rises with the tide. It's worse after a new moon. And it had rained a lot, so the water was almost at the top of the landing stage."

Tilla could not remember much about the landing stage; she would have to go down and take a look. "So it was dangerous to cross?"

"Even the ferrymen don't like it when it's like that. Anyway, they were late back and the centurions were waiting for them and somebody heard Geminus shout across to them that he wasn't going to send the ferry because it was their own fault. And he told them to swim."

"Did he not see it was dangerous?"

"Dann was never any good at swimming."

What had her husband said? *I'm surprised more haven't deserted.* She was beginning to see why.

She did not need to ask why the recruits had obediently entered deep fast-flowing water. She had spent long enough in and around army camps to know that they would not dare to refuse an order, in case something worse happened to them.

Virana said, "They got sticks to keep themselves steady and they tried to cross hand in hand, but the current was pushing them, and then Dann lost his footing and they both went under. Then Geminus dived in on the end of a rope and they got Sulio out."

"But not Dannicus?"

She shook her head. "The ferrymen found him washed up on the north bank the next day. He was a long way downstream."

There was only one question left now. "Did the centurions know that Dannicus couldn't swim?"

"Well, I knew," said Virana. "And my friend knew. And I heard the other boys teasing him about it. So I should think everybody did, wouldn't you?"

21

Ruso was searching the office in vain for the post-mortem report he had read only yesterday when he was startled by a rap on the door. He shoved the box onto the nearest shelf and turned just as a young man burst in wearing a sweat-stained tunic, exuberant tattoos, and an anxious expression.

"Can I help you?"

In Ruso's experience, recruits were perpetually hungry, but this one seemed to have given up the battle with the chunk of tough barley bread clutched in his hand. He also seemed to have forgotten how to speak.

"The clerk's gone to find some lunch," continued Ruso, who had chosen this moment to visit the office for that very reason. "I'm the doctor."

The man glanced down at the bread, then tried to hide it behind his back before more or less standing to attention.

"Are you looking for somebody else?"

"No, sir."

"So," said Ruso, wondering if his visitor was also on a mission to sneak into the records while the clerk was absent, "why are you here?"

"I was told to come and see Austalis, sir."

"Ah," said Ruso, helping himself to a seat. "Stand easy, er..."

"Marcus, sir."

A man called Marcus who spoke Latin with that accent had probably been given one of the few Roman names his parents knew. Ruso guessed he was a full-blooded native son of some sort of local chief. "You'll find him in the room opposite. Don't stay too long: He's very weak."

"I have seen him already, sir. He looks terrible."

Ruso said, "We're doing everything we can."

"I think he will die."

"Not necessarily."

Marcus ran a hand back through his hair, inadvertently giving Ruso a better view of the blue horse rearing up his right arm. "He was fine just a few days ago."

"I've been wondering why a man who was fine would deliberately take a slice off his own arm."

The young man hesitated.

"There are safer ways to remove tattoos."

His visitor's face brightened: Ruso had guessed well. "Are there, sir?"

"Nothing's completely safe, but I'd suggest burning them off slowly with a caustic potion."

"Can you do these?"

"Turn around and let me see."

A serpent slithered down the other arm toward the left wrist.

"If you had a slave brand," he said, "I could understand it. But as tattoos go, those are rather good. Marcus, haven't I seen you somewhere before?" Or his arms, at least.

"You were one of the doctors who said I could join the army, sir."

"I imagine that seems a long time ago."

"A whole life, sir. What is in the potion? Can you do it before we go to Deva?"

Ruso angled himself on the stool so that it was resting on the back two legs, and dismissed a distant echo of his first wife's warnings about ruining the furniture. "First," he said, dodging the first question lest the patient should decide to slap lime all over himself, "tell me why you would want to bother."

Moments later he was recalling a conversation with a young lawyer in Antioch who had insisted that he was not ashamed of his own people. "I simply want to go to the baths and not be *noticed,* Doctor. It's bad for business. Other men get *Oh, look, there's the lawyer.* Or: *There's the man who won the Stephanus case.* Or: *There's a man who looks reliable.* I strip off and I get *Oh, look, there's a Jew.*"

Ruso had explained the difficulties of the surgery, the inevitable pain, the possible consequences of serious inflammation at the operation site, and the fact that nothing would fully restore what had been lost. The lawyer, who seemed to think he was bargaining, begged him to reconsider and offered more money. That evening Ruso's ex-wife, who had recommended him through an acquaintance, demanded to know why he had embarrassed her by refusing the case.

"Because it's unnecessary, nasty, and dangerous."

"But it must work or people wouldn't do it."

"True."

"And if you get a good reputation for doing this epispasm thing, he'll send all his friends, and—"

"I don't want any sort of reputation for surgery people don't need."

"But he thinks he needs it! Now he'll have to go to somebody who's not as good as you. And when his thing drops off, it'll be your fault."

Sometimes Ruso thought it was a wonder he and Claudia had stayed married for as long as they did. They had still been arguing when the earthquake struck. The lawyer was only one of a great number of people he had never seen again.

Now he was facing a man with a similar problem. The trouble with tattoos, apparently, was that when legionaries of any rank saw them they thought, *Oh, look, there's a Briton,* and lowered their expectations accordingly.

"It's bad enough to be in an unlucky unit, sir, but if the rest of the Legion think we are no good because we are barbarians..."

"Do they?"

Marcus twisted the rough bread between his hands. A shower of crumbs fell to the floor. "I am a Roman citizen, sir," he insisted. "Just like the rest. My father has a copy of the citizenship order. Signed by the emperor Trajan himself."

Ruso said, "To be chosen by the emperor is a great honor." It was true, although Tilla would have said that any Briton chosen by the emperor had obviously done something to be ashamed of. "Are you the first legionary in the family?"

Marcus nodded. "Everyone's very proud of me at home, sir." He looked up. "How can I tell them what it's really like?"

"It'll be better when you get to Deva and you're assigned to your century," Ruso promised him. "It's not all like basic training."

"Austalis will never go to Deva now, sir, will he?"

"I don't know." Austalis would be lucky if he survived at all.

"It's not right, sir. Me and Austalis grew up together. We had our first tattoos on the same day. We enlisted together. And now... now..." Marcus, unable to find the words, gestured helplessly with the bread. Then he raised the arm with the horse tattoo. A roar of fury and despair covered the sound of hard bread crashing against shelves. The British curse on the name "Geminus!" was clear enough, and so was the threat to kill him.

In the silence that followed, a stack of record tablets teetered, then clattered to the floor.

Marcus slumped back against the wall. As they both surveyed the chaos he had caused, someone knocked hard enough to rattle the door latch. "Are you all right in there, sir?"

"Fine, thank you!" Ruso called, glad the bread had not been aimed at him. "Just give me a few minutes."

The Briton put his hands over his head. He slid down the wall until he was cowering on the floor like an animal expecting to be beaten.

Ruso shifted his weight forward. The front leg of the stool landed on the floorboards with a gentle thud. He said, "While we pick all this up, Marcus, I want you to tell me exactly what happened to Austalis."

Once he had accepted that he was not about to be clapped in irons and flogged, Marcus made distracted attempts to tidy up, consisting mostly of stacking tablets vertically and then failing to catch them as they slid sideways along the shelf and fell over. Ruso, crouched on the floor, took his time retrieving the strays from under the desk, because the lad had started to talk.

Austalis, it seemed, had committed some minor offense. Geminus had discovered it and delivered one of those devastating streams of abuse that centurions were fond of serving up to recruits at high volume in front of anyone who happened to be around at the time. Geminus had scorned Austalis's intelligence, his personal hygiene, his prospects, and his parentage before singling out the tattoo of a stag on his arm as symbolic of his inferior status.

"It was a beautiful tattoo, sir. Even better than mine. And Austalis, he decides this is enough. He says, 'What is wrong with it?' and the bastard with the two shadows hits him round the head with his stick, and shouts, 'You might as well write up your arm, *Look at me, I'm a barbarian and I'm stupid.*' "

It was not hard to picture the scene. "So then what happened?"

"Austalis shouts back. Geminus calls it insubordination. They make him stand outside HQ for hours holding a clod of turf, sir."

Ruso had seen this many times. It did not sound like much, but the heavy turf would have to be held at arm's length, and before long the muscles would be screaming for relief.

"After they let him go, I think he went to find the beer supply—" Marcus stopped.

"This is why you aren't supposed to have one," Ruso pointed out, guessing they had stashed it somewhere in the unused buildings, and wondering how Geminus and his shadows had managed to miss it.

Marcus rammed the last of the records into a space on the shelf. "When we found him, he was drunk and bleeding, with the stag cut out of his arm."

Ruso handed up the last of the record tablets. Somebody had to tell the truth around here. "Geminus probably didn't mean it," he said. "Centurions sometimes insult their men to test their self-control."

Marcus stared at him. "Is that true?"

"I've seen it." And so had plenty of other men, and somebody should have had the grace to warn these lads.

The lad stiffened. "You must think the Britons very funny, sir."

"If I thought the natives were a joke," said Ruso, "I wouldn't have married a Brigante."

Marcus seemed to be pondering this as the trumpet sounded the next watch. "I must go," he said. "If I come back tonight, can you start the potion?"

"Let me talk to your centurion first."

"But, sir—"

"Leave it with me," said Ruso, who had no idea what he was going to say to Geminus the war hero, but knew that what ever it was, it needed saying.

22

The clerk returned not long after Marcus left. He was reeking of bonfire and surprisingly sanguine about the disorder on the shelves. It did not matter, since he was currently engaged in a sorting-out anyway.

Ruso sniffed. "What have you been burning?"

"Old rubbish we don't need to take to Deva, sir."

"Medical records?" Ruso was on his feet. "Show me."

The charred edge of the tablet that Ruso rescued with the end of a hoe almost certainly said *Tad*—but he was too late: the words inside had run away with the wax. He slid the hoe beneath it and tossed it back onto the foully smoking heap just as a voice said, "How was ward round, sir?"

Pera's hair was even wilder than usual. His tunic had damp patches and there were smudges of black muck on his elbows that he had failed to quite wash off. Ruso said, "That idiot clerk's just burned your postmortem report."

Pera squinted at the untended bonfire, where it seemed only the hospital records were burning with any vigor. Thick smoke was pouring from the old bedstraw and worn-out rags that made up the rest of the pile. "I told the clerk to get rid of any useless junk, sir."

"Not things you only did the other day."

Pera was rubbing the back of his neck again. "I'll have a word with him, sir."

Ruso propped the hoe back against the wall, next to a bucket of water. "The ward round was fine apart from Austalis," he said, glancing around to make sure that no one was close enough to listen before he went on to explain gravity of the situation. "I wasn't impressed with the staff. They seem to be trying to avoid him."

"I'll have a word with them too, sir."

Ruso eyed his disheveled state. "Who put you on sanitary inspection?"

"Geminus, sir."

"Don't you have engineers for that sort of thing?"

"I was with an engineer, sir. The sewer outlet's out of bounds otherwise."

Ruso wondered what possible reason Geminus could have had to send a medic crawling around the drains. Pera should not have needed to do any more than ask the engineers whether what went in at one end of the sewer was coming out at the other. It was hard not to suspect that he was being punished for something, and—given the timing—it was probably something that Ruso had ordered him to do.

He was wondering how to tackle the subject when the heavy figure of the clerk appeared, lugging the remains of a broken chair and a sack of something that proved to be old wood shavings mixed with floor dirt, some of them rich red-brown with the dried blood they had been scattered to absorb. They crackled and spat as he poured them over the flames.

"Go to the baths before ward round," Ruso told Pera. "You'll frighten the patients."

"Clean men are healthy men, sir."

Ruso grinned, recognizing his own words. "Name the deadliest enemy of an army."

"The deadliest enemy of an army is disease, sir."

When the clerk was safely out of earshot, Ruso said, "He didn't seem to know that any report on Tadius existed before yesterday."

"He didn't see it, sir. He wasn't on duty, so I put it away myself."

"And then I brought it to his attention."

Pera said nothing.

"It was a good report."

"You always taught us to record everything, sir."

"And the purpose of that was … ?"

"In case we could learn something from it later."

"It seems you were listening after all."

"Thank you, sir. But we can't learn anything from it now, can we?"

Ruso glanced at him. "If you're going to fake a tone of regret, Pera, you'll have to try harder than that."

"I'm very sorry, sir."

"That's better. I'm sure between us we could remember most of it."

"I can't be of much help, I'm afraid, sir. And it's not going to bring him back, is it?"

"That's generally true of postmortem reports," Ruso observed. "Was the clerk ordered to burn it?"

"Sir, please don't ask. Nothing good will come of it."

"Why not? Give me a good reason and I'll leave it alone."

"I—I can't, sir."

"I've wasted enough time on this. Perhaps I'll get more sense out of Geminus."

"Yes, sir. I expect so."

"That's the wrong answer, Pera."

"Yes. I know it is, sir."

A gust of wind sent thick smoke billowing down the street toward the hospital. They stepped apart to avoid choking. Ruso leaned on the wall beside the hoe, waiting for the air to clear.

"Let me tell you a better story," he said through the smoke. "Tadius died as a result of a severe beating. There was a cover-up, which you cooperated with, because you were ordered to, but privately you were so outraged by what had happened that you recorded the truth. Then you hid it in the files, perhaps hoping to bring it out at Deva once you were safely clear of Eboracum."

The breeze dropped almost as suddenly as it had risen. The buildings across the street began to reappear. Pera remained silent.

"Well?" Ruso squinted through the smoke.

The shape standing against the far wall was too big to be Pera. On either side of it stood two junior officers.

"Do us all a favor, Doctor," said Geminus. "Leave the lad alone. He's only doing what he's told."

Ruso felt his heartbeat quicken. He wanted to ask, *How long have you been standing there?* What he said was "Why did you send him off to inspect the sewers?"

"And the drains, and the water supply," said Geminus affably. "Can't have the Sixth thinking we're dirty."

A section of the fire collapsed, sending out a fresh gust of smoke. Geminus stepped round it. His henchmen moved to reposition themselves on either side of him. "I hear you've been inviting young Austalis's pals in to visit him."

Ruso had hoped to be better prepared for this discussion. "Just one," he said. "It'll do him good to have a visitor."

Geminus shook his head sadly, as if such ignorance was a disappointment to him. He gestured for Ruso to follow him. "You and I need to have a word," he said. "In private."

23

When a centurion lived with female relatives, entering the house on the end of his barrack block was like visiting a family home where a couple of rooms were set aside for the work of keeping eighty legionaries in order. Geminus was a single man. The corridor was empty apart from scuff marks on the limewash. The office into which Ruso followed him bore no personal touches beyond the smell of dog and Geminus's parade uniform with its white-crested helmet looming over them from a stand.

Geminus made a sign to a junior seated behind a plain desk, who hastily set down his abacus. His boots made a hollow sound across the floorboards as he went to join the two shadows outside.

Ruso heard the latch fall into place behind him and stifled the foolish thought that nobody could rescue him, because nobody knew where he was.

Geminus did not waste time with niceties like sitting down. From the middle of the room he said, "If you don't like my orders, come and see me. Don't cause trouble behind my back."

"What's the problem?"

"I've enough to do here without being undermined by some smart-arse fresh out from Deva. You need to listen to your men. Austalis was on his own because if I give the recruits half a chance to get together and stir each other up, we'll have a whole lot more trouble. And before you ask, I do know why he took a slice off his arm."

Ruso swallowed. Austalis might have been cheered by the visit, but Geminus had a point: Marcus had certainly been stirred up. Still, there was a principle at stake. "Where I come from," he said, "the medics decide what goes on in the hospital." If they were lucky.

Geminus appeared ummoved.

"I had a morning's work lined up for Pera, and instead he went off looking at drains."

"I was trying to keep him away from you." The gray eyes traveled slowly over Ruso, who was reminded of times when he had been summoned to his father's study. Geminus gave a "Hm," as if he had just reached a decision. He reached for a stool and nodded toward another. "I was hoping to keep you out of all this, but now that you've insisted on poking your nose in, you'll have to know too."

Ruso sat. He felt as though he had shrunk since he entered the room.

Geminus let out a long breath and began. "You want to know what happened to Tadius."

"What people are saying doesn't make sense."

"What's it to do with you?"

"I'm concerned about what's happening to the men."

"And you think the rest of us aren't."

Ruso shifted position on the stool. "You didn't seem keen to defend them at dinner last night."

Geminus grunted. "You saw what they did to Tadius."

Ruso stared at him. "Tadius was killed by the other recruits?"

"Who did you think it was? Me?"

The question hung between them, unanswered.

"There was some native festival a few nights back. I forget what; you'll have to ask your wife."

Ruso did not ask how Geminus knew about his wife.

"A bunch of my lads take it into their heads to play this tribal hunting game. They name one man as the stag and then they chase him all over the fort. Things get out of hand. I get there with Dexter and a couple of my men and find the stag dying from a beating in a back street and the rest running away in the dark."

He paused, perhaps to let Ruso imagine the scene.

"There could have been fifteen or twenty of them; we could only pick out two. One was a lad called Victor. We think he hid out somewhere and then went over the wall."

"Ginger hair?"

"Silly bugger should have worn a hood if he wanted to get up to mischief."

"I ran into him just outside Calcaria," admitted Ruso. "He escaped into the woods."

"Did you report it?"

Ruso said truthfully, "I didn't realize he was one of yours."

"The other one was Sulio."

So that was why Dexter had not cared whether he jumped.

"And now you're wondering why I haven't chained the rest of them up and flogged the truth out of them."

"Why haven't you?"

"And then what?"

Ruso scratched one ear thoughtfully.

"I can't kick that many men out of the Legion without authority from higher up."

"Can't they be tried at Deva?"

"We've got to get them there first. Five days' march at least. Do your arithmetic, Doctor. Forty-seven Brits, fit young lads who've just had a bloody good training in the use of weapons. Then count the men we can rely on if they turn ugly and divide it by four, because the auxiliaries are staying here and a lot of the maintenance crews are going north in a day or two to help with the wall. Between you and me, they're a bunch of lazy lard-arses anyway. Whatever happens, there'll be plenty of stitching practice for your boys afterward."

It occurred to Ruso that, being Britons, the recruits were unlikely to agree amongst themselves for long enough to organize a full-scale mutiny. But they could certainly cause trouble if they turned violent, and the opposite problem—a mass desertion—would be seriously embarrassing.

"Nobody's going to send us any help," continued Geminus. "We need to keep them calm and get them to Deva." Geminus was a tough man, but he was no fool. He was not going to sacrifice himself for a legion that he would be leaving behind in a matter of weeks. "Once they get there they'll have a shock coming, but they're not bright enough to guess and nobody's going to tell them, are they?"

"I see."

"See lots of things now, don't you?"

"Did the hospital clerk alert you to the postmortem report?"

"Young curly was trying to be too clever," said Geminus. "You medics need to know when to stop. Leave it to us."

Ruso was rapidly reassessing his understanding of what was going on here. If what Geminus said was true, then he had contradicted and undermined a centurion who was already in a difficult position. "Is there anything I can do to help?"

"Yes. Stay out of it, and keep your mouth shut."

24

Virana said, "it was here."

Tilla stood on the edge of the landing stage and watched the river drifting past the heavy oak posts below her. At the moment it would be a tricky jump down into the little flat-bottomed boat moored up with its ropes at full stretch. The ferryman assured her that in a few hours the boat would have risen and it would be an easy step.

Leaving Virana to chatter to the ferryman—both seemed flattered by the attention—Tilla tried to picture the scene when the centurion had ordered two of his men to swim across. She had been nervous when the wagon driver's mules had stopped on the ford in mid-river. The two recruits would have been contending with much deeper water and no animals or vehicle to hold them steady. What had the centurion been thinking? That a man thrown into fast-flowing water would suddenly discover that he could swim? It might work with dogs, although even that was doubtful. It had not worked for Dannicus.

She was pondering the stupidity of the order when shrill screaming cut across her thoughts. It was not a scream of anger or excitement. It was the relentless, terrified, out-of-control shrieking of a child in serious trouble.

Tilla hitched up her skirts and ran toward the sound, with Virana following her up the street toward the east gate, shouting, "Wait for me!"

People were already clustering around the shop. A sheep's carcass swung wildly beneath the awning as a mostly female crowd elbowed past the cheeses and cabbages. From somewhere inside, the child's cries rose above a woman's wailing and shouts of "Put him in the river!" and "Fetch a healer!"

"The washing cauldron," a woman was announcing as Tilla pushed her way toward the front. The listeners gasped in sympathy. "Boiling linen all over himself, poor little beggar. Scalded like a pig."

Tilla stopped. She was not a medicus. She was just someone who delivered babies as best she could for women who knew they were in danger anyway. She had thought that nothing could be worse than the sight of those warriors hacked apart by the army. She had been wrong. *Boiling linen all over himself. Scalded like a pig.*

She was not a medicus, and she did not want to be one.

"The doctor's woman is here!" cried Virana.

Other voices took up the cry. "The doctor's woman!"

"Let her through!"

Hands reached out to seize her. She was hustled forward.

She opened her mouth to explain that she was not what they needed, but nobody was listening.

This is like helping to bring out a baby. Stay calm. Keep your mind on what needs to be done. Do not be put off by the screaming. And never, ever show that you are afraid too.

"Corinna, the doctor's woman is here!"

Tilla paused in the doorway, glimpsing a small struggling form between the cluster of women gathered around it. She took a deep breath. She was not what they needed, but for the moment she was all they had.

"Everyone out!" she yelled over the din.

Nobody moved.

She seized two of the women who had been pushing her forward. "You, clear the room except for the child's mother. You, send to the fort for Medical Officer Gaius Petreius Ruso and tell him his wife needs help with a scalded child."

"I'll go," insisted a third woman. "She's too fat to run."

"What?" demanded the plump one. "I'm not—"

"Water," Tilla told her. "We need lots of cold water—quickly. And then the whites of eggs." And then a miracle.

She began to shake only when it was all over and she was sitting on the faded red cushion back in their quiet room in the mansio.

"You did well," he said.

She watched the surface of the water tremble as she lifted the cup. "I wanted to run away."

"So would anyone."

She let him think he had said something comforting. She did not tell him about her wavering resolve to become a medicus. He would have stayed no matter what he felt like doing. She had only stayed because she'd had no choice: Virana had announced her. She said, "If he really had been scalded all over, what would I have done?"

"Exactly the same as you did."

"He would be dying now."

He said, "Yes."

"That neighbor needs a good slap for telling lies."

Her husband did not seem to share her outrage. "People panic."

In a better light Tilla had been able to see the angry red scald down one side of the struggling child's leg, and secretly rejoiced at the healthy skin everywhere else.

She knew her husband had worried about putting too much poppy inside such a small body, and then about not giving enough to dull the pain. Whatever he did, the child would not feel as lucky as he undoubtedly was. The mother, who lived next door, had been baking and did not want him near the oven, so she had left him playing in the yard. He had crawled under the gate into the back of the shop and tried to stir the washing cauldron.

She put the cup down. "I do not like this place."

"I don't think anybody likes this place." He pulled off the tunic that was splattered with water and the egg white they had smoothed over the angry red skin.

"Your Jupiter has not defeated the curse."

"There is no curse, Tilla. Just a mother who didn't know her child could get under a gate."

"Corinna has many things on her mind," Tilla explained. "She is the wife of Victor, who deserted."

"That explains it, then. She's distracted."

"Did you know people are saying your centurion drowned one of his men?"

When she had finished telling him, he carried on buckling his belt in silence. Then he said, "Your secret informer—it wasn't the scalded-like-a-pig woman, was it?"

"No!"

"But this person didn't see it happen."

"Lots of people saw it. My informer says they are too scared to talk."

Instead of answering, he pulled the tunic straight, then bowed his head and ran both hands through his hair several times as if that would improve it.

She said, "Why would somebody make up things like that?"

"Why," he said, "would a centurion deliberately drown his own man in front of witnesses?"

"You don't believe me?"

"I didn't say that. But they might not have understood what they saw. And it's none of our business. I'm not an investigator now."

"Be careful of that man."

He picked up his case. "I need to get back. I've got a critical patient to keep an eye on."

"I will pray for him."

"Tell the gods his name is Austalis." He leaned forward and kissed the top of her head. "You did well with the boy."

"What will you do about the centurion?"

"I'll think about it." He paused in the doorway. "What festival did you miss while we were on the road here?"

She frowned. "Festival?"

"Some native tradition, or a god of some sort? Might have something to do with hunting?"

"I have not heard of it."

"Ah. Just for men, perhaps."

She wanted to say, *And you think that means a woman would not know of it?* but he was gone.

25

Austalis's face was the color of porridge, and a sheen of sweat lay on his skin.

Resting his fingers on a cold wrist with a pulse that was too weak and too fast, Ruso told him that Tilla was praying to the local gods on his behalf. The lad's cadaverous attempt at a smile of thanks was interrupted by a hiccup. Ruso exchanged a glance with Pera, who had just entered the room. Hiccuping might sound trivial, but for a man in Austalis's condition it was a bad sign.

Ruso observed him for a few minutes, checked the dressings, and promised to return in a couple of hours, not adding that there would still be enough light to perform the amputation. He had no idea whether anything would have changed in two hours. He was just putting off the decision, and he knew it. Geminus had shaken his confidence. How could he have been so wrong? Why had he listened to the recruits but not to the medics? Why had he believed every word he had been told?

Because he liked the recruits, and he didn't like Geminus. Because Geminus and Dexter's blame-the-natives attitude had annoyed him from the moment he'd arrived here. Because they would have said the same things about Tilla, and even if they were partly right, he would still have wanted to punch them.

"Sir?"

Ruso realized Pera had been talking to him since they set off down the corridor.

"Say that again. I wasn't listening."

"A word in private, sir?"

"Is it urgent? I've had enough words in private for one day."

Pera conceded that it wasn't, but his expression said something different.

Ruso owed the lad an apology anyway. "Come on," he said, taking him by the arm and skirting past a squeaking trolley loaded with linen baskets into one of the unused rooms. He closed the door. The squeak faded into the distance. He said, "I'm listening now."

"Sir, I apologize for that excuse about the man falling off the stretcher."

"It wasn't very convincing."

"I'm usually much better at lying, sir."

"Perhaps you'd like to tell me the truth now?"

"I'd rather try for a more convincing lie, sir."

"I've had a conversation with Geminus," Ruso said. "He's explained some things I didn't understand about the situation here."

"Yes, sir."

You should have listened to your staff. "So is there anything else you think I ought to know? Anything you haven't just invented, that is."

"If the centurion has explained everything, sir, then I have nothing to add."

"Good," said Ruso, noting the odd formality of the response. "That's all right, then."

"Yes, sir. Thank you, sir."

"That's all you want to say to me?"

For a moment he thought Pera was going to offer something new, but all that came out was another bland "Yes, sir."

Ruso opened the door again. "You can go."

Alone in the empty room, Ruso leaned back against the wall. Conscious of the distant bellowing of orders and the steady tramp of boots, he found himself wondering how many of the healthy recruits being drilled up and down the parade ground had been involved in the killing of Tadius. He closed his eyes, imagining the broken body lying in the street and the guilty men fleeing away into the night. Someone—the centurions, perhaps—had gathered Tadius up and carried him to the hospital, where Pera had recorded the details of the injuries straight away in the postmortem report.

Ruso frowned. He was not an investigator now. He never wanted to be one again. He just needed to satisfy himself about one thing, then he would be able to concentrate on Austalis.

Pera was halfway across the entrance hall when Ruso grabbed him by the shoulder. "Tadius," murmured Ruso, in a voice so low even the statue of Aesculapius, benignly gazing out to welcome his new patients, would have struggled to hear. "What time was he brought in?"

Pera thought about it. "It was after the evening meal, sir, but it wasn't dark. About the tenth hour? The days are very long at the moment."

Ruso nodded. "It was still light enough for you to do a detailed postmortem report the same day."

"Yes, sir."

"Which ankle was the shackle mark on?"

"I can't remember, sir."

"But you can confirm that there was one."

Pera's hand rose to rub the back of his neck. "It's hard to remember anything, really, sir."

Ruso sighed. "Never mind."

"Will you be joining me on ward round, sir?"

"No," said Ruso, heading for the street. "But get a trumpet call out for me if there's any change with Austalis. I need to go somewhere else."

26

As he walked toward the east gate, Ruso could make out the shouts of men in training. The watch captain was talking to a couple of his men beneath the stone arch of the gate. Ruso lingered in a doorway, pondering what Geminus had told him about the guilty recruits running away in the dark. It must have been a simple slip of the tongue. After all, how visible would Victor's ginger hair have been if there was no light?

As soon as the watch captain strode off toward the north gate, Ruso stepped out from the doorway. The guards on the east gate did not dare to ask why a doctor wanted to see the cells where the unruly were usually dumped overnight to consider the folly of their ways. He found, as he had expected, chains attached to iron rings in the wall. But they were too high: The prisoners here must be cuffed by the wrists.

The guards directed him to the north gate in his medically inexplicable hunt for custody cells, but since he had just seen the watch captain heading in that direction, Ruso decided to take his time. Without much hope, but not knowing what else he could do, he made his way along the walkway of a deserted barrack block, shouldering open damp doors as he went.

Normally the first room behind each door would be used to cook and store equipment for the eight men who slept in the room behind it. Now in the gloom he found untidy splatters of pigeon droppings, broken furniture, abandoned rags, an occasional worn-out shoe, and one wriggling nest of kittens. A small dead animal lying on a windowsill turned out to be a lady's hairpiece, the presence of which would be forever unexplained.

By the time he reached the third block, he had to acknowledge that the search was hopeless. Even assuming that what he was looking for existed, and that he would recognize it when he saw it, the fortress was the size of a town. Laid out between the main roads were dozens of buildings with hundreds of rooms. Even if he ignored all the doors blocked with weeds, and anything that was locked, that would still leave more places than he would ever have time to check.

He crunched over broken glass in the doorway of a storeroom, wrinkling his nose at the stench. Crisp brown leaves had blown in across the floor, and the dung suggested the most recent occupants had been goats. He turned on his heel and walked out, heading for the north gate. A couple of soldiers clutching brooms appeared from between two buildings and passed him with the purposeful gait of men who might be on their way to doing something, or might just be wanting to look as though they were.

The north cells turned out to have the same security arrangements as the east. This was a waste of time. Trudging down a street between two rows of store houses, all of which proved to be locked, he tried to assess the situation logically. The first two deaths were not connected. The drowning had been bad luck, or maybe bad judgment on the part of the centurion. The training accident was a murder.

Army basic training was not a pretty sight, with free men apparently being treated like slaves and pushed beyond what they believed to be their limits in body and mind. All of them loathed the men who were making them suffer, and many would grumble freely to anyone who would listen. Normally, as the grueling weeks wore on, most of them found strength and resilience they did not know they possessed, and by the end they were proud of having survived the trial. But according to Geminus, these recruits had turned on each other like animals. They were lucky not to have been caged and whipped. He had no doubt that the punishment waiting for them back at Deva would be imaginative, memorable, and very nasty indeed.

The men with the brooms appeared in front of him again, then vanished around a corner.

Maybe he should go back and confirm the time of the death with Geminus, just to allay any lingering doubt. Maybe he should ask him about that shackle mark. There was probably a simple explanation.

He was trying the door of an abandoned centurion's house when the trudge of boots and jingle of strap ends woke him from his thoughts. He turned to see two men in patched work tunics. The one with the shovel said, "Looking for something, sir?"

"Just checking."

It sounded ridiculous and it was, but he was an officer and they weren't, so they would not say so to his face. He wondered how long they had been watching him, and what they could possibly imagine he was doing trying to break into empty buildings. Fortunately, compelled by the need to look busy in his presence, they would not be able to hang around and find out. As soon as they were gone, he turned and headed in the opposite direction.

It was only then that he noticed a gap between the barrack blocks that he had already passed once without thinking. It was not the gap itself that was remarkable: The buildings were the standard ten-doors-per-century blocks with the centurion's house on the end and a narrow break before the pattern was repeated. What struck him was that the gap was unusually well-trodden for a passageway leading from one empty street to another. At first he thought it was a goat track, but as he moved closer he could see that the edge of the puddle filling most of its width bulged into the ovals of boot prints.

He was about to leap across the puddle when he heard someone whistling. A lone and overweight soldier rounded the corner and began to shovel the accumulation of dead leaves and dirt from a doorway where it must have lain moldering since last winter. "Are you lost, sir?"

Ruso indicated the passageway. "What's down there?"

The man paused from his work to peer between the two buildings before declaring, "Nothing, sir."

"There's a lot of boot marks."

"That'll be our lads, sir," the man explained. "That's how we get round the back to paint the walls and fix the windows and what have you."

"Ah," said Ruso. He wondered what strange diligence might lead the maintenance gangs to converge on the backs of these buildings when the fronts were so neglected. Before he could speak again, the man gave a yell of alarm. There was a thudding of hooves and a black and white billy goat leapt over a broken door and cantered away down the street, leaving a distinctive waft in the air behind it.

Ruso said, "Doesn't anybody round them up?"

"Only for dinner, sir. Goats keep the weeds down."

He resumed his walk back to the hospital. The man followed him. He turned right. The man was behind him. He turned right for a second time. The man with the shovel had gone. In his place were the two with the brooms.

Ruso stepped off the track and into a doorway. The men trudged past with barely a glance. He waited until they were twenty paces in front, then set off after them. Sure enough, one of them turned to see where he was. He lifted one hand in a cheery wave. The man pretended not to notice and kept walking.

There was nobody behind him now. The men in front turned off down an alleyway. He sidestepped into the muddy passage. Beyond the barracks, the timbered walls rising on either side of him were no longer accommodation but some sort of large warehouses. Each had a couple of shuttered windows just above head height: too small for thieves to slip through.

Emerging onto the street at the far end, he followed the muddy trail round to the right and found himself in front of a nondescript wooden building about thirty paces long. At first sight the double doors were padlocked like all the others, but then he saw that although the lock had been slid across, it was not secured into the body. He glanced round to check that nobody was watching, slid the lock open, and stepped into a silent darkness.

With the door closed behind him he could see nothing. Then he could make out bright lines around the shutters. He picked his way across what felt like a bare earth floor to reach up and let in the light from the passageway. He turned and waited for his sight to adjust to the gloom.

Gradually, the object he had been searching for took shape in the middle of the floor.

He had seen this sort of thing before. A shackle and chain attached to a heavy stone block. It was where the captured animal or the condemned prisoner was attached, so that it could not escape from its tormentors while the crowd in the amphitheater cheered them on.

Ruso perched on the edge of the block and fastened the cold shackle around his ankle. He stood. Two experimental paces away from the stone, the chain jolted him back. He tried to move as a man would who was trying to defend himself. The chain wrong-footed him. It wrapped around his free ankle so he had to hop to release himself. Then he tripped over the block and sat heavily on the floor. That was when he noticed darker patches on the mud around him. He ran a forefinger over one of them and sniffed it.

Blood.

Blood, and a shaft of light spreading across the floor, and the broad silhouette of a legionary in the doorway. Centurion Dexter's voice said, "Best to stay out of here, Doctor. The roofs are none too good in some of these buildings. That's why we keep them locked."

Ruso said, "The place looks used."

Dexter made his way across the room and slammed the first set of shutters closed. "Crafty buggers had a stash of beer hidden in here."

"Is this where Austalis was found?"

"I hear he's dying."

"Not if I can help it."

The second set of shutters slammed. "When I joined up, we got paid to keep the Brits out. Now we invite 'em in and give 'em weapons."

As he followed Dexter toward the door, Ruso said, "What's the block and chain for?"

Dexter halted in the doorway and turned to gaze across the room as if he had not noticed the stone cube he had just walked around.

Ruso pointed to it.

Dexter shrugged. "Something left by the last lot, I suppose."

The statement was plausible. The pretended ignorance was not. Ruso was beginning to think that something even worse than Geminus had described had happened to young Tadius. This did not look like a hunting game that had gone wrong. The blood could have belonged to a drunken Austalis, but the presence of the shackle made it look very much as though Tadius's comrades had taken him here, chained him to a stone, and beaten him to death.

27

Corinna's son was lying motionless on the little bed in the alcove, his eyes closed and one plump arm flung above his head. Tilla bent over him, relieved when the faint rise and fall of the covers told her he was breathing. His skin was pink: His hand was warm. The poppy had done its work safely.

"I always check too." Reassured, Corinna teased out more wool from the combed fleece by her stool and twirled the dangling spindle. "As soon as they are born, you worry about them."

Tilla noticed again the soft burr of the South West in her voice. This girl was a long way from home. She left the curtain drawn back so they could see the little bed from where they sat talking in low voices by the hearth. It seemed the family lived in this one narrow rented room, with a loft above, a small plot behind where Corinna had planted a few vegetables, and an empty shop counter at the front under which they kept a stock of firewood that had almost run out. It was clean and homely and probably as good as anything they had grown up with. The child was bonny and

Corinna seemed a gentle sort of girl. Wondering what could make a man leave all this behind, Tilla gave her the bag of dried honeysuckle leaves to help against weariness before passing on the news that she thought she had seen Victor at Calcaria two days before.

The girl's eyes widened. "You know about him?"

"Virana told me."

Corinna gave the wool a sharp tug. "I've had no message. There is nothing I can tell you."

"The army are not chasing him, and if they were, I would keep silent unless you asked me to speak. Someone tried to help him, but he ran away."

The girl laid the spindle in her lap. "How was he?"

"Bruised, but well able to run."

"Hm." Corinna did not seem to be sure whether she was pleased about that or not.

Tilla said, "It is not easy to be married to a man who is supposed to be married to the Legion."

Corinna glanced over at her son again. "I thought at first that I could manage."

"You are a strong woman. And your son will heal."

"I want to go home."

Tilla sat back in the battered chair. "Tell me about your home."

"It is very beautiful," Corinna said. "The army hardly bother us. The seas are wild around the rocks but there is good fishing. The land is rich for cows and good for crops if you lime it, but things do not change very fast. And Victor is a man who always thinks there is something better somewhere else."

She picked up a rag from the wool basket and wiped the grease off her hands. "I tried to tell him it was a good life, but he wouldn't listen. He is a fighter: a champion wrestler. In the old days he would have been a warrior, but of course at home he was not allowed to train for battle or carry weapons. He used to talk all the time about the legions—how he wished he had joined when he had the chance."

"This was after you were married?"

"I doubt he meant it as an insult, but he kept saying I was the only thing that stopped him from joining. I knew the army would treat us as divorced, but he spoke of it so often that I was afraid he would run off and join anyway."

"So it was better to agree than to lose him."

"That is what I thought back then." Corinna shrugged. "My mother said he was a fool, and so was I, but my father had a pair of soldier's boots made for him as a gift. We traveled for weeks to get to this place of terrible winters. Then he was only allowed out for one afternoon every week, and when we saw him, all he wanted to do was quarrel or sleep."

"I have met other women who say the same."

"Perhaps it is different if your husband is an officer. The Legion was not the life he was expecting. The training is hard, even for a strong man. There were a lot of arguments."

Tilla said, "Did he tell you he was leaving?"

The thin fingers rubbed a fold of her skirt. "He said we would slow him down. The soldiers came here to look for him, but I do not think they were sorry to see him go."

"Was there something that happened that made him leave, Corinna?"

The girl eyed her steadily. "It was not for any reason they will tell you. That is all I can say."

"Who hurt him?"

"Tadius."

Tilla frowned. "I have been told wrongly. I thought Tadius was his friend."

"He was. A good friend."

"Then why—"

"There are things you don't know."

"Tell me."

The pale lips twitched into a smile that did not reach the eyes. "If you don't know, you are safe. You don't have to decide what to do. You can keep quiet and not call yourself a coward, because you know nothing. And if you are a friend to my family, you will forget I have ever spoken to you of this."

Tilla puzzled. "But if there is something wrong—"

"Don't complain. Tadius complained. Victor wanted to."

"About what?"

"About lots of things," said Corinna. "But look what happened. The Legion always wins in the end."

28

"No, no, no, no, no!"

The orderly seized Austalis by his good arm and wrestled him back down onto the bed.

"No, no!"

Ruso raised his hands to show they were empty, but Austalis was too frightened to care. The orderly kept him pinned down while Ruso retreated and leaned against the wall.

"No."

"I'm not doing anything," Ruso assured him, which at that moment was true.

The "No!" was more of a whimper now: Austalis had reached the end of his strength.

Ruso stood motionless, as he would have with a frightened animal. Eventually he said, "Would you like some water?"

"No."

"You're very ill, Austalis."

"No."

"The surgery would help."

The voice was very weak now. "Don't… cut."

Ruso nodded to the orderly, who stood up, hitched his torn tunic back over his shoulder, and retreated to a corner. To Austalis he said, "You're in a bit of a mess there. Shall I put your bed straight?"

There was no sign of Austalis caring one way or the other. Ruso straightened the bedding and poured a few drops of water between the cracked lips.

"Let me tell you about Clementinus," said Ruso. "Clementinus used to be a vet in the Twentieth. Now he earns a good living as a dog breeder and he's fathered two children. Or there's Amandus the brewer. He's got a wife and a son. Both men lost an arm at about your age, and I did the surgery."

A whisper of "No."

"We can give you something to dull the pain and I'll be as quick as I can."

"No."

"If it's the arm or you, I know which I'd choose."

The silence was encouraging.

"It's the best choice. We'll get rid of the diseased—"

The door burst open and Geminus strode into the room. He loomed over the end of the bed, eyed the startled patient, and announced, "That arm's coming off, then."

"Out!" Ruso had him halfway to the door before he recovered his balance.

Geminus twisted free and blocked the exit. "He's my man."

"He's my patient."

Ruso was taller. Geminus was solid muscle. There was no sign of his shadows, but they were probably out in the corridor somewhere. Ruso said, "Not here."

"You didn't listen."

"Not here!"

Ruso was conscious of a faint voice behind him. The words were in British. "Not my arm—no."

"Don't worry," Ruso assured him in the same tongue, keeping his eyes fixed on Geminus. "Nothing will happen here unless I say so."

"Outside," growled Geminus, stepping back to let him pass.

Ruso murmured, "Stay here and keep him calm," to the wide-eyed orderly, and gestured to Geminus to go first. He was not giving that man a chance to get near his patient again.

"You were told to mind your own business."

Ruso envied Aesculapius, whose tranquil gaze across the entrance hall was undisturbed by the centurion's tone. He had brought Geminus here because if there was going to be a fight, he wanted witnesses. He also wanted help, but he doubted he would get any. Still, at least there was no sign of the two shadows. He said, "If you want to talk to my patient, you talk to me first."

"I should have known you'd be trouble."

"Did you have me followed?"

Geminus glanced around to make sure no one but the god was listening. "My men have better things to do than get you out of places you shouldn't get into."

"You told me Tadius died at night."

"I told you everything you need to know." Geminus moved closer. He smelled of the sweat of the training ground. Ruso stood very still.

"When I heard you were coming," Geminus said, "I asked some questions. And I got some very interesting answers. Why was it you left the Legion last time?"

Ruso knew now where this was heading, and he did not want to go there. "I was injured. By the time I'd recovered, my contract was over."

"Nothing to do with your woman, then?"

Ruso took a slow breath. "That's old news."

"But I'll bet it hasn't reached the tribune, has it?"

"I've no idea."

Geminus's smile was even more fearsome than his scowl. "We're all on the same side here, Doctor," he said. "You leave me to get on with my business, and I'll leave you to get on with yours."

29

After last night's costly mistake, Tilla did not order the evening meal until her husband turned up. At the same moment a local man and his nephew arrived to show him a limp and complain of a bellyache. Then the stew came, and he ate in silence, listening to his own thoughts. It did not seem the best time to ask for a slave so she could learn to be a medicus, so she said, "How is your difficult patient?"

"Mm?"

"Your patient. Austalis. How is he?"

"Desperate to keep the arm. I'm leaving him for one more night."

"Perhaps he will improve."

"And perhaps I'll have killed him."

So that was what was troubling him. "I went to see Corinna's boy again," she said. "He was asleep."

"Mm."

"She told me something I did not understand."

He tore a chunk off the bread and dropped it into the liquid.

"Shall I tell you what it was?"

"Uh—what? Yes."

"She said Tadius and Victor were good friends, but then they had a fight."

He scooped the bread out on his spoon. "Friends fall out."

"She says there are things we don't know."

"Maybe we don't need to know them."

"Did you think about that centurion?"

He looked at her. "That centurion knows why we had to go to Gaul."

She put her spoon down. "But how—"

"Apparently he's been asking around. It's not exactly a secret, is it? Metellus circulates his security lists. That's the point of them."

Her throat was suddenly dry. "I thought that was all forgotten."

"So did I."

"I always knew that centurion was—"

"I know what he is!"

The force of his reply startled her.

"Sorry," he said. "Don't worry. You're none of his business, and Metellus will be busy up on the border, arresting anyone who isn't a loyal subject of Hadrian."

As she said, "I hope so. That man is a snake," there was a rap on the door and a slave announced more visitors for the Medicus. Tilla sighed and put the bread platter over his bowl in the faint hope that the stew might not be stone cold when he finished.

The back sufferer turned out to have tried every remedy that was suggested and refused to believe that gentle exercise would help. The child who could not speak was deaf. She had devised her own gestures to communicate with her family, and seemed to have accepted the situation far more readily than they had.

Tilla had just lifted the bread platter from his bowl when they both looked up, uncertain. He called, "Come in!" and the movement of the latch confirmed that there was indeed somebody there.

A bent and wrinkled slave shuffled in. Tilla recognized the figure she had seen hoeing the weeds out of the rose beds, but when she greeted him with "You are the gardener!" he shrank away and begged them not to tell anyone he was there. The reason became apparent as he explained his symptoms: stiffness in the hips, painful knees, difficulty in movement, hot and swollen joints in the hands… None of these was desirable in a gardener. He was terrified of being sold and replaced with someone younger and fitter.

Tilla, seated on the bed and halfheartedly scanning the poetry scroll in the poor light, reflected that any decent owner would buy a boy who could learn from the older slave and take over the heavy work. But while the old man had worked in the mansio gardens for as long as he could remember, managers came and went. And new men liked to make sweeping changes.

She glanced up and saw that her husband was scratching one ear in the way he did when he was thinking. The treatment she had seen him recommend for this sort of thing would be of no use to a slave who was more likely to sleep in a damp bed than be able to lie in a hot bath. And if he managed to scrape together regular warm fomentations of bark and barley meal, where would he find the privacy to apply them?

Finally she heard "Tilla, can you get me the bottle of mandrake in wine, and a spoon?" and, to the patient, "Do you grow dill? And rue?"

"Dill, yes. Rue smells. I could find a patch outside."

While Tilla rummaged inside the case, her husband explained how to boil the herbs together to make a medicine that was good for easing joint pain.

When she handed the bottle across, he checked the thin wooden label tied around the neck as usual and frowned. "Mandrake," he repeated, handing it back.

She took it, glanced at the two bubbles near the base of the thick green glass, and offered it back to him. "Mandrake," she confirmed.

Silently he pointed to the label.

"Mandrake," she insisted.

He gave her a look of mild alarm that said, *You don't read the labels?* and reached for the case himself, picking out one of the three remaining bottles he usually carried with him.

"That is iris, for purging!" she whispered, placing her hand over his. The patient, who was sitting on the end of the bed nearest the window, was beginning to look worried.

She placed both bottles on the table, pulled out a stopper, and sniffed before passing the bottle to him. He lifted it to his nose, paused, and turned to the patient. "Sorry about that. Have you finished work for the night?"

The man nodded.

"One and a half spoons in a cup, please, Tilla." To the patient he said, "I don't recommend you take a lot of this, but for once it should give you a decent night's sleep."

Tilla handed over the cup with a warm smile that defied any questions about whether this traveling medicus and his woman really knew what they were doing.

After the slave had drunk the medicine and gone, Tilla watched her husband line up all four bottles on the table and scowl at them. "You must be more careful, Tilla."

"Me? I am the one who got it right!"

"Just as well." Leaving the bottles on the table, he snapped the case shut and tightened the strap so that the buckle slid into the groove it had made in the leather.

The stew bowl was barely warm, although he had not had time to find that out when there was yet another rap at the door.

Tilla called, "The Medicus is eating! Come back tomorrow!"

"The tribune wants him."

Tilla would have told the tribune to wait, but her husband was already on his feet. That was the sort of thing they were trained to do in the army: obey without question or delay. When they were ordered to swim across a swollen river, they did it. Or died trying.

"Can you sort those bottles out while I'm gone?"

"I did not tie the wrong labels on."

"But it's obvious you don't read them." He scooped a last mouthful of stew.

"Why bother when it is quicker not to?" She reached for the bottle of purgative and examined the knot in the twine. "This is someone else's work, husband. I always leave a loop and an end so it undoes easily."

He was not listening. "If there's a message about Austalis, tell them where I am and tell them they absolutely must interrupt."

And then he was gone.

30

Accius had disrupted the end of Ruso's meal, but he was not allowing anything to distract him from his own. While the tribune picked at a bowl of olives and perused a scroll on the table in front of him, Ruso stood as silent and unnoticed as the slave in the corner, and wondered why Tilla was always determined to argue instead of apologizing. He had enough troubles without standing here feeling annoyed with her. He was probably about to be reprimanded for his public quarrel with Geminus.

Had he been too harsh on Geminus? The man was undoubtedly a bully who frightened his men into taking dangerous, sometimes fatal risks. On the other hand, he had dived into the river to save Sulio and then later climbed onto a roof to try to talk him out of suicide. He was a centurion with years of experience. He had been specifically chosen for the job of instilling into raw recruits the discipline that would send them out to fight.

What did Ruso know about training recruits?

Nothing. He could not even persuade one to sacrifice an arm to save his own life.

Accius was still eating. Ruso shifted his weight onto the other foot. Beside him, the slave watched for a signal from his master with the air of a man used to making himself invisible.

Whatever had happened to Tadius—and Ruso was convinced that he still wasn't being told the whole story—he had to admit that it was up to Geminus to deal with it. Looking at the situation from the other side, he could see how annoying it must be to have an unknown doctor arrive and start interfering. Almost as annoying, in fact, as it was for that doctor to have a centurion dictate what should happen to his patients.

On the other hand (did that make three hands? He had lost count), if the man had nothing to hide, why start making threats about reporting Tilla's past to the tribune?

Accius spat out the last olive stone, looked up, and said, "Ah, there you are!" as if his visitor had just walked in through the wall.

"Sir."

"How are your medics doing?" Before Ruso could answer he said, "I went to the hospital but you weren't there."

"They've mostly done a good job in difficult circumstances, sir."

"Good. Are all your patients fit to move?"

"One's doubtful, sir."

"Then we may have to leave him with the Sixth and have him sent back later."

When Ruso looked blank, Accius said, "That's what I called you over to tell you. Apparently the Sixth are only a couple of days' march away."

"I see, sir." Ruso felt the muscles in his shoulders relax. He was not here to be reprimanded. Nobody had reported his disagreement with Geminus. Why would they? He was getting as nervous as the recruits.

Accius was talking about the arrangements for the takeover. "So our recruits will have their final trials the day after tomorrow, and then we'll be ready to march them to Deva as soon as the Sixth take over."

"I'll tell my men, sir."

"Good." Accius paused. "How did you think the ceremony went this morning?"

Ruso said, "Very well sir."

"Yes." Accius appeared pleased, as if some other answer had been possible. "I thought so too. I think we've cleaned off the slate so we can start again."

Ruso took a deep breath. "Sir, there's something I need to mention to you." He glanced at the slave. "It's confidential."

"Is this really necessary?"

"Yes, sir. I think it is."

Accius glanced at the slave. "More wine, and then clear out till I call you."

"It's something I should have mentioned before, sir," Ruso confessed. When the slave had refilled the wine—with none offered to the visitor—and cleared away the olive stones, Ruso began to attempt a version of events that laid out the facts while skirting round the truth in the middle of them. "It's all been dealt with, sir, but I think you ought to know that some time ago my wife received some coins that turned out to be from a stolen pay wagon."

"And did she report this?"

"She didn't realize, sir." At least, not until he had pointed it out to her. "We were about to leave for Gaul and she spent some of the money. When we returned, I found the governor's security adviser had put her name on one of his wanted lists."

"Would that be Metellus?"

"Yes, sir."

"I hear he's a useful chap."

"He's very thorough, sir." Ruso could have added *sly* and *vindictive* and *My wife calls him a snake,* but did not.

Accius said, "Do they know about this at Deva?"

"I'm not sure, sir."

"You didn't think to mention it when the Legion offered you a new contract?"

"No, sir."

"So why is it so important to tell me now?"

Ruso cleared his throat. He could hardly say that Geminus was attempting to blackmail him. "It was starting to worry me, sir."

"Gods above, man! I don't have time to sit here while you tell me what's worrying you!"

"No, sir."

"Make sure you report it when we get back to Deva."

Ruso hoped his relief did not show. "Thank you, sir."

"Frankly, I'm surprised to find an officer married to a local. Not that she's not attractive. Some of them do have a kind of…" He paused, searching for a word. "…rustic charm. But surely marriage was hardly necessary?"

"It wasn't necessary, sir, no."

Accius looked at him for a moment. "I see. Yes. Very forward-thinking of you. Mingling with the natives. Setting an example. Bringing up standards."

"I do my best, sir." Usually without success.

"Just be careful they don't use you."

Ruso lifted his chin. "Use me, sir?"

"Begging for sympathy. Expecting special treatment. That sort of thing. If they think you might be on their side."

Ruso cleared his throat. "I think we're all on the emperor's side here, sir." Accius was the son of a politician. He would be used to hearing pompous platitudes.

"Yes, of course. But given your wife's unfortunate history, you need to make it clear where your loyalties lie."

"You needn't have any concerns about my wife, sir." Suddenly he saw his opening. Geminus was not his personal problem. He would do the correct thing and refer any decisions up the chain of command.

At the same time he would establish Tilla's loyalty. "In fact, that's the other reason I wanted to talk to you. Only today she reported a worrying rumor she'd heard in the street. She thought we should know."

"Really?"

No, not really, but it was close enough. "The locals are saying that the lad who drowned was well-known as a poor swimmer, and the river was exceptionally high, but Geminus refused to allow the ferry across to pick them up."

"I hope you explained that Geminus entered the water himself to try and pull the men out?"

"It's why they got in to start with that's the issue, sir."

Accius did not look pleased to be brought back to the point. "The recruits are here to be challenged and stretched, Ruso. Not to enjoy themselves. No doubt that looks a little harsh to the locals."

"Yes, sir." He had begun now, so he might as well finish. "There's something that concerns me about the second death as well, sir. The training accident."

"Geminus has briefed me on that one." The fierce eyes met his own. "I believe he's spoken to you as well."

"Yes, sir. But if something's affecting the welfare of the men, it's my duty to try and deal with it."

"The live men," Accius agreed. "I don't expect you to resurrect the dead ones."

"I believe the victim was shackled to a weight before he was killed, sir. It wasn't just a piece of horse-play that went too far."

Accius shook his head. "It's not pretty, I know. We have an intake of recruits who can't be trusted. To be frank, I think they dressed up a murder as an accident and invented a native rite to explain it. Keep this to yourself, but at one point Geminus was seriously concerned about mutiny. Personally I'd discharge the lot of them, but it's politically sensitive. Some of their fathers are the heads of tribes who are supposed to be our allies. I'm telling you this because we'll have to keep a close eye on them all the way to Deva."

"Yes, sir." Accius, he decided, would go far—if only he could resist the urge to outshine the men above him.

"Anything else bothering you?" Accius's tone suggested that if there was, he did not want to hear it. Ruso told him anyway.

"Sir, we're accusing the deserter of murder, but the locals are saying he was a good friend of the victim."

Accius scowled. "What did I just warn you about? That pretty wife has you dancing on a string. Civilians don't know the facts, so they speculate. No doubt some of them are saying Geminus forced that man off the roof."

"Not to my knowledge, sir. I appreciate that he's a relative of yours, but—"

"Are you saying I can't form a fair judgment?"

"No, sir. I'm saying Geminus's men are unusually frightened of him."

Accius reached for the water and topped up his wine. "Doctor, do you really imagine that nobody has looked into all this other than you?"

"No, sir."

Accius took a long drink and placed the glass exactly back over the damp ring on the table before speaking. "I've spoken to Geminus at length about the suicide," he said. "He tried to persuade the man to come down, but Sulio had convinced himself that he was personally under a curse. His last words were a confession about his involvement in the death of Tadius."

Ruso said nothing.

"Recruits complain, Ruso. You should know that."

Ruso had heard far more complaints than would ever reach the noble ears of the tribune, but it would not be tactful to say so.

"Especially Britons," Accius continued. "They're not used to discipline. Even the ones whose fathers are soldiers have grown up running wild with their native cousins. The gods alone know what they get up to at those shrines in the woods that they aren't supposed to have. Add that to the usual behavior of recruits—spending all their wages on extra food and drink and impressing the local girls, so they have to send requests home begging for things like socks that they haven't bothered to buy for themselves ... If we didn't stop their wages for the basics, half of them would have no boots."

"Yes, sir."

"Frankly, anything your wife has heard is likely to be a long way from the truth. Get her to give you the names of the rumormongers and I'll have them brought in and spoken to."

Ruso's stomach clenched. This was not at all what he had expected or intended. He said, "I'm not sure she knows, sir. She may have just overheard something in the street."

"Well, tell her to find out. If she was close enough to listen, she must have a description."

"Sir, I saw evidence of the shackling."

"Then for all our sakes, keep it to yourself. We don't want the recruits any more stirred up before the march. As for the rest... well, it never does any harm to know what's being said around the enemy campfires."

"I'll let you know if she hears anything else, sir."

"Oh, there's no need for that. We need to deal with the gossipmongers now, before any of this nonsense gets passed on to the Sixth. I'm sure you can explain to her why she needs to be more helpful this time than she was over the pay wagon."

Ruso swallowed. "The Britons have loyalties just like we do, sir."

"She's your wife, Ruso. Her loyalty is to you."

"Yes, sir."

"And you, of course, are loyal to the Twentieth. Which, as you helpfully reminded me earlier, serves the emperor."

31

"I can't stop to argue." He swung his cloak around his shoulders. "I'm going back for a last check on that arm. And then there's something we need to talk about."

It was not something good: Tilla could tell from his voice. "There is no need to argue," she told him, following him out onto the walkway, "because I am right. The other knot was the same. Be cross with someone at the hospital, not me."

He called from the walkway, "Nobody over there has any right to go into my case!"

"Well, someone has, and they are not very good at it!" Too late, she added, "What is the thing we need to talk about?"

But all he said was "Don't speak to anyone till I get back."

Tilla closed the door and surveyed the room. Two bowls, one half full of cold stew. A scroll of stupid poems. And nobody to talk to.

It's no good moping, girl. There's work to be done.

She lit the spare lamp. Then she set out to reassure herself that nobody had meddled with the rest of the medicine bottles, the little linen bags, and the limewood boxes in the case, and to make sure that the salves were still in their right containers. It was one of those times when a person could see the use of being able to read.

The medicines were neatly stacked in their compartments and the extra lamp had fizzled out by the time she heard footsteps on the walkway. She snatched up the scroll, but the footsteps went past. She put the scroll down again. If her husband had to do an emergency amputation, he could be gone all night. She might as well go to bed.

She was on the way back from the latrine when a voice said, "Stop there, miss!" In the torchlight, one large figure separated itself from another. Before she could dodge, the second man had placed himself behind her. She told herself not to be afraid. This was the mansio: There were plenty of people around. Anyway, he had called her "miss." But then, a man could hide bad intentions behind good manners.

She said loudly, "Who are you?"

"The tribune wants you."

"What for?"

"Follow me."

If they tried to take her out of the building, she would scream. Faintly consoled by the thought that she had a plan, she set off behind them.

The torchlight glinted on the scabbard of his sword. He was, at least, some sort of soldier.

"The Medicus's wife, sir."

Accius was scowling at a map on the desk in front of him while a secretary hovered at his elbow. Tilla was not greatly reassured to see Minna perched on a stool in the corner, where it was much too dark to see the sock she was supposed to be darning.

Finally Accius rolled up the map and sent the secretary away with instructions about messages to the forts on the route. Then he dismissed the guards. Tilla heard the door clamp shut behind them. She fought an urge to haul it open and run.

"Tilla," he said, looking her up and down as if he were trying to decide whether he would allow her to keep the name or give her another one.

The black smudge of soot across his forehead made his dark features even crosser than usual. A man this rich would not light his own fires, so she supposed he must have been to a temple.

"Real name," he continued, "Darlughdacha. From a small tribe amongst the Brigantes known as the Corionotatae."

Tilla stared at him. How did he know all of that? He had even pronounced it correctly.

"My attention has been drawn to the security records at Headquarters. Your people were involved in the recent troubles on the border. Restoring order cost us a lot of men."

"Some of my people are—" No, that was wrong. Latin was always harder when she was nervous. "Some of my people were involved, sir. Many just wanted to bring up their families and tend their sheep." Why was he talking about this now? Why was he talking to her at all? Was that what her husband did not have time to say: that he had told Accius all about her? It was all very well saying "Don't speak to anyone till I get back," but what should she do now?

"Your concern for the Legion's reputation is noted."

What concern?

"I hear you've been collecting information from the locals for us."

She was aware of Minna in the corner listening to every word. Did he know about Virana? Or maybe even that she had befriended Corinna, wife of a deserter? How could she know what to say without knowing what he had heard?

"I have spoken to your husband," he told her. "Since you are not…" He paused, searching for a word. "Since you do not have the usual background for an officer's wife, I have decided to make some things clear to you personally."

By the time she realized she was supposed to thank him, it was too late. "As the wife of an officer of the Twentieth Legion," he continued, "your duty is to support your husband in the home. You need not trouble yourself with military affairs. In any way."

Tilla opened her mouth, but before anything could come out, he said, "Civilians have no idea of the facts. They have no appreciation of all that your husband's legion does for them. Any hint of encouragement from someone connected with the Legion merely fuels unfounded rumors that we then have to go to the trouble of correcting."

He paused to let her regret any encouragement she might have offered.

"You will confine your discussions with the natives to the necessary business of running your household."

Minna's needle had stopped moving.

"Your husband will be giving me a list of the names of the people who are behind this latest gossip, so we can visit them and correct the false statements they have been making."

Tilla knew about visits from the army. They were not easily forgotten, even after the damage had been repaired and the bruises had healed.

Minna had put the sock down and was watching to see her response. Tilla suddenly remembered how stupid most Roman officers thought the natives were. She let her mouth fall open and gazed at Accius with an expression of wide-eyed, tongue-tied awe.

Was that a faint relaxation of the scowl? He said, "Meanwhile, madam, the Legion appreciates your wish to be helpful. If we ever need your assistance, I will let you know."

Finally Tilla managed to speak. "Sir, what must I do next time people try to tell me things?"

The scowl returned. "Tell them that complaints should go through the proper channels."

Tilla bowed her head demurely. "Thank you, sir," she said. "I will ask my husband to explain to me what the proper channels are."

32

Ruso took another swig of the wine with rose petals steeped in it before he set off, but by the time the torchlit entrance to the mansio came into view, his headache was showing no sign of clearing. Still, Austalis seemed to be stable, and with luck Tilla had heeded his message and gone to bed. the last thing he wanted tonight was an argument. That could wait until morning, when he would have to admit that his attempt to call Geminus's bluff had achieved exactly the opposite effect to the one he had intended.

If only he had kept his mouth shut.

That pretty wife has you dancing on a string. Perhaps Accius had a point. Other officers' wives stayed back at base, tending their homes and children and meeting up at the bath house to gossip. Other officers' wives did not follow them around the countryside raising awkward questions to which they would never understand the only answers their husbands had to give. In fact, now that he thought about it, Tilla's presence and her insistence on voicing the demands of the women outside the camps made his job infinitely more difficult. It was time they bought a slave. Next time he was away, the slave could look after him and the wife could stay at home.

He strode on, not looking at the light but at the surface of the street. He did not want to round off a difficult evening by stepping in a pile of dung.

There had been an accumulation of small exasperations back at the hospital: first the cook's failure yet again to remember his instructions for Austalis's diet; and then someone had packed the pharmacy scales ready to travel, and when they were needed, nobody could remember which box they were in. The search was complicated by a period of semidarkness when it was discovered that nobody had filled any of the lamps, owing to the nonarrival of the oil that Stores insisted they had sent, but the hospital staff were adamant they had not received. An emergency request to Stores to allocate some more had resulted in the messenger being told to piss off, which was more or less what Ruso had been told himself—only more politely—when he went across to insist on some action. He had been on the verge of losing his temper when the first amphora was traced to the headquarters building, lying in a side room with the words *Hospital, Urgent* clearly chalked on the side.

A less rational man would begin to think the gods didn't like him. A rational man would conclude that someone at the hospital—and he certainly didn't trust that clerk—was deliberately making his life difficult.

He was so preoccupied that the rapid thud of hooves and the yell of "Look out!" took him completely by surprise. He felt a rush of air as the horse swerved to avoid him, no doubt as alarmed as he was by the sudden appearance of a pedestrian in the middle of the road in the dark. The rider yelled something at him and hurtled on toward the east gate. Ruso stepped aside in case there were more horses, but the cavalryman seemed to be a lone late arrival.

He took a last deep breath of cool night air before making his way up the mansio steps. If Tilla was awake, he would begin with the good news. "I've cleared up this Metellus business with Accius," he would say. "We can stop worrying. He's not bothered."

Seconds later, he found that rehearsing his lines had been a waste of time. He had started the scene in entirely the wrong place. Not only had Tilla received no message to say he would be late, but the first words after an accusatory "I was worried!" were "What have you been saying about me to the tribune?"

The headache gained him no sympathy at all. He helped himself to a cup of water—clearly none was going to be offered—before sitting on the edge of one of the beds and trying to explain. "I thought he would listen," he said. "I even thought he might look into it. I never thought it would come to this."

"But I told you it was a secret! How can I give him a name when I swore on the bones of my ancestors that I would not?"

He heard himself offer the lame "It seemed like a good idea at the time."

"And it is not me who mixes up your medicines."

"Forget the bloody medicines!" Had she sat here all evening making a list of things to argue about?

"But the first thing you will be thinking is *It is Tilla again.*"

"I think it was someone at the hospital."

"Yes. But first you will be thinking it is me."

She was getting her tenses mixed up, something she rarely did now unless she was very agitated.

"I am a nuisance to you."

"Oh, gods above." He lay back on the bed and pressed his hands to his temples. "Not tonight, Tilla."

"No," she agreed. "Not tonight. But this is worse than the pay wagon. This time I swore an oath to say nothing."

He was not fool enough to think he could change her mind. "You realize if we don't come up with something for him, there will be consequences for both of us?"

"That is his choice, not ours."

"But we're the ones who will suffer for it."

"Something in this place stinks," she said, lifting her chin as if the smell were under her nose at that moment. "I should have tell him he must deal with what is wrong, instead of trying to silence a person who tells the truth."

"I'm glad you didn't."

"Perhaps we should say that to him."

"Perhaps you should try presenting your witness so he can hear the accusations for himself."

She shook her head. "The tribune would not believe a word this person said."

"Marvelous." He raised himself up on his elbows and took another swig of water. "The only way out of this is to convince Accius that the rumors about Geminus are true. And the only way to do that is to present a witness we can't produce." He glanced at her. "There must be other witnesses. It's not just this one person, is it?"

"I could ask, but I do not know anyone who will talk."

"Better and better."

Tilla was silent for a moment. Finally she said, "We could go back to Gaul."

That pretty wife has you dancing on a string. He was only here in Britannia because of Tilla. "Last time we went, I was on sick leave at the end of a contract," he pointed out. "This time it would be desertion." He pulled off his boots. "What I want," he said, "the only thing I've ever wanted, is a job where all I have to deal with is what's in front of me." He slung his belt over the bedpost. "Is that too much to ask?"

She said, "What is in front of you?

He hauled the covers over himself and closed his eyes. "A good night's sleep, I hope."

"And tomorrow?"

"Amputation of the right arm at the shoulder."

"In front of me is a girl many weeks' walk from home, abandoned with an injured child. And a centurion with something to hide."

He sighed. "Stay out of it, Tilla. There are any number of veterans who will swear to you that the training isn't as tough now as it was in their day. Geminus is a bully, but no doubt he sees himself as trying to restore standards." He opened his eyes. "Did you do any reading this evening?"

"He should have sent the ferry."

For a moment he thought this was her last word on the subject. Then he heard "Do you think he was angry because two men were fond of each other?"

"They shouldn't have made it obvious," he said. "Somebody should have warned them: Never do anything to make yourself a target in basic training."

"But when the emperor himself runs after boys ..." She paused. Some sort of commotion was going on outside. There were doors banging. Raised voices. Footsteps and the jingle of military belts approached the window. Ruso lifted his head to listen, but the soldiers carried on past.

"The emperor can do what he likes," he said, relieved that whatever the fuss, it did not require a medic. "He's not answerable to Geminus."

"Geminus likes to frighten people."

"Recruits have to be toughened up. And taught to obey orders. They don't drill them for fun. Discipline saves men's lives, Tilla. If I didn't believe that, I'd have no business being in the Legion."

One of the soldiers was coming back. She had just said, "It is not saving very many lives here, is it?" when someone thumped on the door and shouted, "Message for the medical officer!"

Ruso sighed, rolled off the bed, and padded barefoot to the door. His eyes widened as the captain of Accius's guard whispered the message in his ear. He said, "Is this some sort of joke?"

"I hope not, sir."

Reflecting that this was not going to help his headache, he buckled his belt and retrieved his boots from under the bed. "Don't wait up," he told Tilla. If the guard had not been standing three feet away, he would have told her the news. Instead, all he could say was "Something's happening. You'll find out in the morning."

33

Tilla took a moment to recognize the hideous screeches that had woken her as the sounds of heavy furniture being dragged across the floor of the room next door. Outside she heard urgent voices, the slap of mats being beaten, and the frantic swish of scrubbing brushes. Distant and discordant clanging told her that more than one blacksmith was up and working. She rolled over and opened her eyes. The rumpled bed beside hers was empty. Why was everyone making so much noise? How late had she slept?

That was when she remembered the second knock on the door, just after the Medicus had hurried away without telling her where he was going. That time it was Minna, bundled up in a shawl, pushing her way in without invitation and hissing in a stage whisper, "Have you heard? The emperor is coming!"

"I know," Tilla had said, bemused and not a little annoyed at the late invasion. "Everybody knows."

"No, he has landed somewhere called Petuaria. His ships were damaged in the storm and he's coming here tomorrow!"

Tilla's first thought had been that she did not much care where the emperor went. Her second was that this would give the snooty tribune something bigger to worry about than tracking down local people who said things he did not want to hear.

Minna had probably thought the smile meant she was excited about the visit.

Tilla splashed last night's cold water from the bowl over her face, imagining the panic in the fort after the news arrived. Few of them would know any more about Hadrian and Sabina than she did herself, but they would know how vital it was to please them.

Tilla had always felt sorry for Vibia Sabina, who appeared from her statues and coins to be both beautiful and vacant. Sabina too was childless, and after more than twenty years of marriage. There were people who wondered why the emperor had not divorced her and found someone fertile. Tilla was glad he had not.

Hadrian himself always appeared on his coins and statues with a heavy jaw and a curly beard, an odd little crease in each earlobe, and beady eyes that were too close together. He was supposed to be a clever man and a fierce improver of poor standards. It pleased her to imagine those eyes taking in the shameful state of the officers' empty houses at Eboracum.

The breakfast tray and the fresh water finally arrived with two girls who were so busy whispering and giggling that they forgot to bow altogether. From somewhere beyond the rose beds she could hear Minna's voice raised in complaint. Moments later the manager, flustered and apologetic, arrived to explain that he had been given orders to prepare for ten very senior officials and their staff, and would she and the Medicus mind moving to another room? Behind him, she could see more staff scurrying about with piles of bedding. "It's quite comfortable," he assured her. "Compact. Very convenient to the dining room."

She felt too sorry for him to ask if the tribune would be moving too.

The room was, as she had expected, only big enough for one bed and a chest, and potentially very noisy, but it was clean. She was checking that the staff had brought all the luggage when a shadow fell across the courtyard window and a voice she had not expected said in British, "There you are! I couldn't find you!"

"Virana! What are you doing here?"

"It's all right, nobody is looking. I got in through the side door. I have decided what to do. Let me in so I can tell you."

They sat side by side on the bed, since there was nowhere else, while Virana revealed that she had not one plan but two. The first was for Tilla's husband to give her the password so she could get into the fort and make a last-minute appeal to whichever of her former lovers she could find, since they might not be allowed out again before they marched away. When Tilla explained that this was impossible, she said, "I thought you would say that. But it doesn't matter, because the emperor is coming!"

"I know."

"So I got this." She delved into her cleavage and pulled out a rolled and squashed scrap of parchment. "Look!"

Tilla unrolled it and made out the words *Your Majesty*. She stopped. "What is this?"

Virana beamed. "The scribe down the road wrote it for me. He was very nice. I'm going to—"

"He should not have taken your money," Tilla told her.

"Oh, he didn't want money!"

"He knows as well as I do that you are not a citizen of Rome," said Tilla, guessing what he had taken instead. "The emperor is the most powerful man in the world. If the officers here will not listen to you, why would he?"

Virana looked crestfallen. "But he's the emperor! He goes around the world giving out justice!"

"Not to you and me."

"But somebody has to take me to Deva. I can't stay here!" Virana threw the parchment aside and clasped her hands together. "Let me come with you. Please. I could help you. You need a servant."

It was true, and it irritated Tilla that even this silly girl could see it. "Go home," she said. "You should not be wandering unescorted around here."

Virana pouted. "*You* wander unescorted!"

"That is different."

"The Sixth Legion will be here soon, did you know? And the new governor will come with the emperor and there will be the cavalry escort and the Praetorian Guard with the scorpions on their shields ... Is it true they are all six feet tall and very rich?"

"The Praetorian Guard would swallow you whole and not even notice," said Tilla, who had never met them except by reputation. "Go home."

Virana's lower lip began to tremble. "Please don't send me away! Nobody wants me!"

Tilla sighed. "Very well. You can stay with me just for this morning."

Virana clutched at her arm. "Yes! Oh, thank you, thank you! Where shall we go? Can we go inside the fort?"

Tilla detached her grip. "No. You can wait while I visit Corinna, then you can take me to talk to your family."

"My family?" The girl grabbed at her again, then remembered and let go. "My family will not listen to anyone. Not even you. Anyway, I can't miss the emperor! And Vibia Sabina. Did you know the empress was younger than me when she got married?"

"The emperor will not be here until this evening. Perhaps your family will bring you back to watch."

"No they won't. They're horrible. Anyway, I can't walk that far. I feel sick."

"Some exercise will do you good."

"My brothers are nasty and violent. And they don't like strangers."

"I am Brigante, and the wife of a Roman officer," said Tilla, squaring her shoulders. "Your family will not frighten me, and unless they are very stupid they will not hurt me, either." At least, she hoped not. Anyway, she could not spend all day sitting in this room with nothing to do or wandering about the streets. None of Virana's family was in the army, so she could truthfully say she was obeying the tribune's orders not to get involved in the Legion's affairs. She got to her feet. "Are you coming, or will I have to find the way by myself?"

Virana was chewing her lower lip. "They will tell you lies about me."

"Then it will be best if you are there to tell the truth," said Tilla, bending to tighten the laces on her boots and reaching for her bag.

34

The lazy lard-arses of the maintenance crews were lazy no longer. It was a bright morning, and everywhere Ruso went, men in brown working tunics were hammering wooden shingles onto roofs, sweeping up old leaves, filling potholes, clearing dumped rubbish, scything grass, slapping on paint, greasing hinges, and opening windows to air long-neglected buildings. The granaries had been opened to release extra wheat, and pink-eyed slaves who had been up all night grinding flour were now shambling back and forth to the ovens with trays of loaves.

An arrhythmic clanging had been echoing across the fort since first light as the sweating blacksmiths labored to keep pace with the demand for tools and repairs. Evidently they were not succeeding: Ruso had been called upon earlier to patch up two men injured in a fight over a rusty spade, and a third who had been knocked out by the ill-fitting head of an axe. A long queue outside Stores was jeering as the clerk who had refused to give Ruso more lamp oil last night was being told by a man twice his size exactly where he could shove his official permit.

Ruso had snatched barely three hours in bed after Accius's emergency planning meeting last night. The hospital's role—to open up the empty wards to accommodate the Praetorians—was decided early on, but clearly there was no hope of being sent away to get some sleep. As the discussions wore on, he found himself reflecting that at least they had some warning. He could only imagine the consternation of the man in charge at the humble ferry port of Petuaria when Hadrian's ships had been sighted in the river Abus instead of the Tinea. There had been a collective sigh of relief at the meeting when Accius announced that the tides were not high enough for Hadrian's rowers to bring him upriver as far as Eboracum. At least, if he were traveling by road, it would be possible to monitor his progress.

Ruso had just left Accius's second briefing meeting of the morning, where a dusty cavalryman had confirmed that the imperial invasion—which was how Ruso thought of it—was still six or seven hours away. He strode back toward the hospital, anxious to see Austalis, who to his immense relief seemed to be showing signs of responding to treatment. He had set aside his plans to amputate, pleased that his visit here might at least have achieved one useful outcome. As for the Geminus business... it was unfortunate, but with the tramp of the emperor's escort growing closer every second, it was hard to see who would care about the loss of a few recruits.

As he rounded the corner, he was startled by a rumbling growl. Furious, deep-throated barking. Something huge and brown with teeth hurtling toward him. He flung himself sideways, hauled open a door—thank the gods, it wasn't locked—slammed it shut and threw himself against it, feeling the jolt as the massive creature collided with the other side.

Back to the door, gasping for breath, he marveled at the closeness of his escape—until the room went dark and the snarling dog crashed in through the open window. Wrenching himself away from something tearing at his tunic, he was out of the door and scrambling up the nearest pillar with the dog snapping at his feet. Finally he collapsed, breathless, on the shingles of the walkway roof. Below him he could hear the dog scrabbling against the pillar, still barking and snarling as if he'd just attacked it, instead of the other way around. He ran a hand over the back of his left thigh, feeling torn flesh and the warm stickiness of blood.

Somebody was yelling over the din. He lifted his head to shout, "Careful, it's vicious!" just as the barking stopped.

"Here, girl," said the gravelly voice of Centurion Geminus. He sounded almost affectionate. Then he called, "Sorry about that, Doc. Did she get you?"

Cautiously, barely able to believe what had just happened, Ruso peered over the rough edge of the roof. Geminus was standing next to a creature that was part large hunting dog and very definitely part wolf. Man and animal were joined by a slack rope that looped around the dog's neck.

"Is that yours?" demanded Ruso, eyeing it with suspicion. "She tried to have my leg off. She shouldn't be out."

"Oh, she wouldn't have had your leg off," said Geminus cheerfully. "Not Bella." He patted the dog. "Would you, girl?" Then he said, without a hint of irony, "If she was serious, she'd have had your throat out."

Ruso maneuvered onto his back and lifted his leg to examine the bite. It was messy but, as far as he could make out, not deep. The hem of his tunic was shredded and soaked with blood. He was aware that he was shaky and not thinking straight, his body still fearful even though his mind knew the danger was over. Geminus was saying something, but it was a moment before he could unscramble the words.

"It's all right, Doctor, you can come down. She won't touch you."

Insisting on escorting him back to the hospital, Geminus apologized again for his dog, but in a tone implying that Ruso should have known better than to be walking around while the dog was loose. Then he moved on to discuss the plan to invite Hadrian to watch the recruits' final tests tomorrow morning.

Ruso, forcing his jittery mind to concentrate, gave him the latest news on Austalis.

"Pity about that one," Geminus said.

Ruso had just remembered that he had promised to talk to Geminus about tattoo removal when the centurion said, "No hard feelings over your complaint, by the way."

"Complaint?"

Geminus chuckled. "You thought he wouldn't tell me?"

When Ruso did not reply he said, "We're all grown men here, Doc. Good men have to stick together, not tittle-tattle like children." He gestured around him. "After all, you can't trust this bunch."

Ruso could not think of a reply. His leg hurt, and the revelation reverberating around his mind was leaving no space for anything else. He had dared to complain to Accius. Instead of keeping it quiet, Accius had told Geminus about their conversation. Now Geminus's dog had attacked him.

Geminus was still talking. "Only fair to give a man a chance to tell his side of the story, eh? You were honest with him, he was honest with me, I'm being honest with you. You only had to ask about the river. I'd have told you. Both those lads had swimming lessons. I taught them myself. They knew what to do. They'd have been all right if young Dannicus hadn't panicked. As for what went on with Tadius: You're right. Shameful." He broke off to shout, "Oi!

Sharpen your blade, son!" To a youth who was ineffectively swinging a scythe at a patch of nettles.

They were outside the hospital entrance now. Geminus clapped a hand on Ruso's shoulder. "Sorry about the leg," he said. "But you look to be walking all right. Tell Stores I said not to bill you for another tunic. And let me know how young Austalis does, will you?"

Ruso stood in the hospital doorway, feeling the blood pooling inside his boot. He watched man and dog walk away. Geminus had not explained what the animal was doing loose in the street at the very moment Ruso had been approaching. *If she was serious, she'd have had your throat out.* She had seemed serious. If he hadn't moved fast enough, would Geminus have stopped her? When nobody in authority cared about the fatal bullying of a few humble recruits, how closely would anyone have questioned the loss of one medic? His death would be just another accident for the unlucky garrison of Eboracum.

This time he had escaped with a warning. Next time there might not be a roof within reach.

35

As she left Corinna's house, Tilla realized that reaching Virana's family was not going to be as easy as she had thought. News of the emperor's arrival had galloped ahead of him. The streets of Eboracum were already thick with people and vehicles. Drivers were yelling at each other, trying to keep their animals under control and ignoring the attempts of the legionaries stationed on each corner to direct the traffic. The air was thick with curses and children crying and the calls of bewildered sheep and cattle being driven in for slaughter. She had hoped they might be able to pick up a lift out of town with a passing carter, but as they dodged their way through the crowds and a flurry of plucked chicken feathers, it was clear that the world was converging on Eboracum. Farther out, innocent of the chaos ahead, still more muddy farm vehicles were lumbering toward town, stacked with produce to sell. Everybody seemed to have brought something: a loaded mule or a handcart or a side of bacon or a couple of hens in a basket or just handfuls of freshly picked flowers. One old woman was trying to sell lucky pebbles from the shore where the emperor had landed, while her husband had carved wooden souvenirs depicting the great man as a lumpy figure with bulgy eyes. All were hoping for a good price and a view of the famous couple. Tilla almost had to drag Virana away from a group of entertainers whose cart had a juggler balanced on top of the luggage, entertaining any other travelers willing to throw him a couple of coins.

The road grew emptier and Virana's spirits visibly sank as they turned north. Finally they were on a track that was mostly churned mud with patches of grass sprouting in the middle. After a few minutes Tilla saw smoke, and beneath it the thatched cones of three or four buildings. "Is that it?"

"I feel really, really sick." Virana's head hung down. She had let her hair fall forward over her face. "I think I'm going to faint."

Tilla tucked one hand firmly under the girl's arm and urged her forward. "Not far now."

Beyond the gate, a pair of geese announced their arrival to two young men who were loading a mule cart. Farther back toward the houses, a barefoot girl of about ten was milking a goat. It was a scene that reminded Tilla of her own home in the good days. Before the raiders came.

The girl moved the bucket out of kicking distance and abandoned the goat, running toward one of the buildings. "Mam!"

A woman emerged, pushing graying hair out of her eyes with exactly the same gesture as Virana. She stared at the two figures by the gate. "Where have you been, then?"

"As if we can't guess," put in the smaller of the young men, sounding more disdainful than fierce.

The girl chased the geese away and dragged the gate far enough open for them to squeeze through. "You're in trouble!" she announced gleefully. "Barita's still sulking and I'm not big enough to do things. Who's that?"

Virana glanced at Tilla and mumbled something. The bigger brother looked Tilla up and down and gave a noisy sniff through a flattened nose before observing, "She can bring you here anytime."

Tilla introduced herself as a friend from Eboracum.

The smaller brother swung a basket of cabbages up into the cart and said, "At least this friend's not in uniform."

"Remember your manners, you!" snapped the mother. She turned to Tilla. "You'll have to excuse them: They take after their father—not that he cares. I do my best, but they take no notice. None of them. *Will* you get off that gate? How many times?" The small girl grinned and slithered to the ground. The woman turned to Virana. "You, get in the house and put some proper clothes on. What do you think you look like, running around like that?"

Virana cast Tilla a look that said, *I told you so!* although she had not.

Tilla said, "Perhaps—"

"She looks like what she is," observed the smaller brother. "A cheap little bitch who opens her legs for the soldiers."

"Shut up!" Virana shrieked at him. "Just shut up!" Then with a sob she buried her face in her hands and rushed toward the house, the pink skirt trailing in the mud.

Her mother rounded on him with "Now see what you've done!" as if it were all his fault. To Tilla she said, "Nothing but trouble since the day she was born, that one."

Tilla said, "I think she has a kind heart."

"Hah! That's what they used to say about me. Too kind, I was!"

"What about you, then?" The smaller brother, who really was very rude, had turned to Tilla. "You another friend of the soldier boys?"

"Take no notice of him, miss," put in Flat-nose. "All mouth and no manners, him."

"I came to bring your sister home," said Tilla, deciding the rude one was not worth the bother of slapping. "She was not sure she would be welcome."

"She don't have to be bloody welcome," observed the rude one. "She lives here. What's it to do with you?"

"I am a friend of your sister," said Tilla. "And since you ask about soldiers, my husband is a senior medical officer with the Twentieth Legion."

In the silence that followed, she was conscious of them all staring at her.

"Well done," muttered Flat-nose to his brother.

The small girl said, "Are we in trouble, miss?"

"Not you," Tilla assured her. She turned to the brothers. "Perhaps, when you have finished loading all those things you are hoping to sell to the soldiers you despise so much, you will escort me into town?"

"They'll escort you into town and like it, miss!" said the mother before they could answer. "And they'll keep their big mouths shut for a change. Miss, you come into the house for a sit-down and a drink while you're waiting. You two, get that load on. You should have been off at dawn. At this rate, the emperor will be gone before you get there."

Tilla's eyes adjusted to the gloom inside the house while she breathed in the familiar smells of wood smoke and cabbage water and dog. Virana approached and offered a cup of fresh goat's milk. She had changed into a dull brown tunic tied loosely around the middle with braid. Her eyes were swollen and her hair was even more disheveled than usual. Tilla said, "Virana, your mother needs you. And it is safer for you to be here." Safer, at least, than ending up in a whore house in Deva. But she could hardly say that in front of the mother, and without it she was not sure her claim sounded very convincing.

Virana sniffed and went back to sit next to her little sister on the log by the hearth. Her mother thanked Tilla for bringing her home, adding with a sidelong glance, "The longer she hangs around the fortress, the more shame she heaps upon us. At least her sister got herself properly betrothed to a decent—"

"She wasn't betrothed!" interrupted Virana. "Only officers can get married, Mam. Everybody knows that."

The mother sighed. "Well, he can't marry her now, that's certain." She raised her voice and called into the shadows behind her. "Barita, come and say hello to the officer's wife!"

A muffled voice from the darkness said, "Leave me alone!"

"If your father were here, my girl, he'd have you out of that bed in no time!"

No reply.

The mother shook her head but made no attempt to roust her daughter. "I've told her she can't keep this up. There's plenty of lads round here would take her on. She's not disgraced herself like this one."

Suddenly there was movement. A wild-haired, blinking figure in creased clothes shambled into the light. She moved toward her mother. "You don't know what you're talking about!" she hissed. She turned to address her sisters and Tilla. "You will never understand! None of you!" With that, she shuffled back toward the darkness.

Tilla said, "I am sorry for your loss."

The girl spun round. "You? What do you care?"

"Oh, Barita!" sighed her mother. "There are plenty of other lads!"

"You are right," agreed Tilla, wishing she had kept quiet. "It is none of my business."

"It was never anyone's business," retorted Barita. "You're just like the rest of them. Wash your hands and walk away!"

Virana folded her arms. "Anyone would think she is the only one with troubles."

"Oh, will you two stop!" cried the mother. "Barita, put on your good tunic and comb your hair."

Tilla drained the milk and said she would go and see whether the cart was ready. She was halfway across the yard when Barita's voice called after her: "They place bets! Geminus and his men were betting on whether Dann and Sulio would get across the river!"

"Enough!" Tilla spun round, raising one hand for silence. "Say nothing more."

"Walk away, officer's wife! Pretend you haven't heard. Just like everyone else."

Even with her hands over her ears, Tilla still heard, "Tadius and Victor tried to get it stopped. None of the others had the courage to help. Not one!"

Tilla could feel her own heart beating. Flat-nose and the rude one had paused to watch her from the far side of the cart. The girl was standing with her hands on her hips, waiting for a response. Tilla walked over toward her. "You have not spoken about this," she said. "I have not heard it, and neither have your mother and your brothers and sisters."

"So, Brigante woman," said the rude one, "you are just as bad as they are."

"And you are a fool!" snapped Tilla. She turned back to Barita. "I am already in trouble because I repeated what a person told me, hoping as you do that something would be done. They have done nothing to help, and now they are trying to make me say who told them."

"Tell them it was me! Tell them Barita of the Parisi told you. Tell everyone what I said. If I die, I will be in the next world with Tadius."

"They will not just come for you, girl! Have you not seen what they do to troublemakers? They will come for your family as well. When they have finished with you they will feast on your animals and sell you as slaves. Do you want that to happen?"

"But your husband—"

She seized the girl's thin shoulders. "Understand this. I have already explained it to your sister. My husband is a good man, but he is only a doctor. He cannot tell the other officers what to do."

The girl's red-rimmed eyes glared into hers for a moment, then she lowered her head. "It was my fault," she whispered. "All my fault. He talked of nothing but the drowning and how wicked it was. I grew weary of listening. I told him he must either stop complaining or do something about it. So he did something." She looked up. "If you want to keep your man, tell him to stay silent."

Tilla gathered the stale-smelling girl into her arms. "Your revenge is to live," she murmured. "They will go back to Deva in two days. Say nothing to anyone else, and you will be safe."

"They tried to send a message to the legate in Deva, but they were betrayed." Barita drew back. "I have no weapons to avenge my man, but I tell you this: There really is a curse upon that place, and upon Centurion Geminus. I know this is true because I am the one who put it there."

36

Tilla had left the room in the mansio with its shutters closed. It seemed very gloomy after the sunlit courtyard. That was why she took a moment to notice the figure in the bed. She stepped back, wondering if the slave had let her into the wrong room, but no: There was her bag, and the medicine boxes on the floor. She was not the one in the wrong room.

She opened her mouth to call the slave back, then stopped. There was something odd about the sleeper. Keeping away from the bed and ready to spring toward the open door, she reached out and fumbled with the window latch. Eventually one shutter swung open.

That was when she screamed.

A couple of flies rose from the pillow and circled around the room.

The slaves all arrived at once and crowded into the doorway, craning around each other to gawp at the bloodstained snout of a dead pig poking out from under the sheet. The pig was lying on the pillow where Tilla had woken this morning next to her husband.

Somebody said, "Who put that there?"

Tilla swallowed and forced herself to step forward. Gripping the bedding between finger and thumb, she whipped the blankets back. The "body" was nothing but a couple of cushions.

Standing above the bed, she could see that the spatter of blood up the snout was an arrangement of letters. They were clumsily done—it must be hard to write on a pig's snout with blood—but she managed to spell out enough to know what it said. One word.

TRAITOR.

She turned to face the slaves. "Did anyone see who put this here?"

But of course nobody had. The manager appeared, stared at the head in horror, and then hurried to promise investigations, punishments, and disposal of the offending object. He assigned Tilla a new room on the opposite side of the courtyard, escorting her there personally while the slaves followed with her baggage and the boxes of medicines. He promised to send warmed wine to soothe her nerves, and a message to alert her husband.

In the end, he seemed so worried about her that Tilla found she was trying to comfort him instead of the other way round. It was only a pig. Just someone's idea of a silly joke. She was not hurt. She just wanted a clean bed, and this one would be fine, thank you. No, there was no need to leave one of the girls with her.

But when she was alone, someone rapped on the door of the new room and she found herself on her feet, knife in hand, before she had time to reason with her fear. It was a struggle to form the words "Who is it?" and only when it really was the slave with the warmed wine did she feel safe enough to put the knife away.

37

The problem with the dog bite—apart from the damage, the shock, and the pain—was that it was behind him. From the front, Ruso looked perfectly capable of paying attention to someone else's problems. Greeted by "Sir, the window in the blanket store's been leaking and the bedding is all musty," he was tempted to reply, *I don't care! I've just been chased and bitten by a bloody great wolf dog!*

Instead he said, "Oh?"

"Should we launder it, sir? Do you think the emperor will mind a few wet blankets?"

"The Praetorians will," he pointed out. "They're sleeping in them."

"We'll just air them, then, sir, shall we?"

"Good idea."

He was relieved to find the treatment room empty. It was only a bite from a dog that wasn't mad. There was no point in wasting other people's time, and besides, he was no longer sure he trusted anyone else.

With the worst of the blood wiped off, he lay on his back on the table, raised his left leg in the air, and contorted himself to an angle at which he could examine the jagged tooth marks. It was perversely disappointing not to have something more dramatic to prove how nearly he had ended up as dog food. He reached for the cloth, took a deep breath, and swore as the vinegar penetrated the torn skin.

He was concentrating on the agony of prodding one of the deeper recesses when he heard a discreet cough, glanced through the crook of his left knee, and saw three men standing in the doorway, watching him.

"I see I'm interrupting," said Accius.

Ruso rolled over and sat up, wincing as the wound came into contact with the wooden bench. "I was bitten by a dog, sir."

"I'm here to inspect and encourage," Accius informed him. He might have added, *Not to hear more of your complaining.* "Any problems?"

"None that I'm aware of, sir."

"Good." Accius squinted at a couple of writing tablets held out to him by a secretary. "Looks like the heralds have whipped up a good crowd," he said, handing the first one back. "Tell them to send plenty of patrols out to keep order. And make sure the crowds know to cheer and wave, not just stare like simpletons."

The news on the second tablet seemed to surprise him. "Already? This is turning into a circus. Tell them to wait outside. They'll have to give them to his secretary at Headquarters tomorrow."

He turned back to Ruso. "Embassies and petitions. Swarming round like ants after honey. Anyway, it's just as well I had the men smarten up their kit yesterday, don't you think?"

"Yes, sir."

"I think we'll put on a good show. Which reminds me: your wife."

Ruso felt himself tense.

"She seems like a practical sort. Ask her to report to the legate's house, will you? Some steward chap of Hadrian's has turned up to oversee things, and he's making a fuss. I've sent my own staff in to help, so she won't be on her own."

Housework. All he wanted was housework. Nothing to do with informants and names and consequences. Ruso should have been insulted to hear his wife and Accius's slaves mentioned in the same breath, but instead he was relieved. Hoping she was somewhere a message could reach her, he said, "I'll see what she can do, sir."

"She doesn't know any decent entertainers around here, I suppose?"

"I don't think so, sir."

"No, of course not. Respectable married woman. Well, we shall have to do without. Somebody found a juggler, but he wasn't up to much. Did Geminus have a word, by the way?"

"After his dog bit me, sir."

"Good. I had a chat with him on the way to worship last night. He took it like the man I always knew he was. Shame you weren't there. He could have put your mind at rest personally."

"Yes, sir."

"You're not a follower of Mithras, are you, Ruso?"

"No, sir."

"You should consider it. Not only an inspiration, but you make good contacts. Friends wherever you go."

Ruso, whose former clerk was miles away in Verulamium and whose old friend Valens was somewhere sucking up to people more important than himself, felt suddenly like the only man left out of the club.

"Geminus has his rough edges, but he's a fine centurion. Staunch. A lot of men owe their lives to him. I couldn't allow the end of his career to be blighted by unfounded rumors."

"Yes, sir."

"So, onward! Tell your men to keep up the good work."

Accius was enjoying himself. Hadrian might not be his family's choice for emperor but this was his chance to shine, and he knew it. "Not long to go now. Eboracum's luck has turned."

"I hope so, sir. Is there anything else I can do to help?"

"There is," said Accius. "When Hadrian gets here, stay out of his way."

38

Motionless, silent, gazing at the crested helmet of the man in front of him, Ruso marveled at the way a couple of trumpet blasts had conjured these splendid ranks of legionaries out of the chaos of half an hour ago. The first call had been the signal for every man to abandon what ever unfinished task lay in front of him, run to his quarters, and scramble into full parade uniform. The second was the signal to assemble. They were now standing like parallel rows of statues lining the road from the marketplace to the east gate, waiting in the low evening sun for the most powerful man in the world to pass between them. All around, an excited rabble of civilians chatted and laughed and argued in the sunshine, waiting for the free show. Youths dangled their legs from the eaves of buildings. Children had been hoisted up on parents' shoulders. A white-haired woman was clinging to a donkey.

Ruso shifted his grip on his shield and watched a fly land on the helmet and begin to crawl up the crest. His bandaged leg was aching and his mind kept going back to two conversations. The first was with Marcus.

He had spotted the tattooed recruit moving toward the barrack blocks with the cautious gait of a man in pain. He offered what was intended to be a friendly greeting. Marcus jumped as if he had felt the cold touch of a ghost, then turned and gave an awkward salute.

His upper lip was swollen to twice its normal size. There was dark blood congealed around his nostrils and a jagged wound at the edge of his hairline.

"What happened to you?"

"Nothing, sir." The swollen lip distorted the edges of his words.

Ruso wondered what else was concealed beneath the tunic. "A training injury, perhaps?"

"Yes, sir." The Briton glanced around awkwardly, as if he were trapped with a bore at a party and was longing to get away.

"I haven't forgotten our conversation. I'll talk to your centurion—"

"No, sir, don't—"

"I'm speaking!" Ruso was not used to being interrupted by his juniors. "I'll talk to your centurion when things aren't so busy."

Marcus's eyes widened with desperation. "Please, sir. I've changed my mind. I want to keep them, sir."

"Keep the tattoos?"

"Yes, sir." A slave emerged from one of the barrack rooms. "I have no complaints, sir," Marcus announced in a voice loud enough to be overheard.

And that was all Ruso could get out of him.

The second conversation was with Tilla. His message to report to the emperor's steward had allowed her into the fort, where she had arrived at the hospital with some medicines he didn't need in order to tell him things he didn't like the sound of.

First, someone had been in their room in the mansio and left a gruesome souvenir of the visit, and she was clearly not as calm about it as she was trying to pretend.

"I'm going to have this out with Geminus," he fumed. "It'll be him, or one of his shadows. And I'll see the manager. I can't believe a thing like that can happen and nobody sees anything. It's outrageous!"

"The manager is asking his staff," she said, "but there are always people coming and going there. Lots of them are carrying things. Nobody would notice one more sack."

"Surely the room was locked?"

"Lots of people can pick locks."

"I don't want you going back there without me."

"Then where am I to go when I have finished cleaning and sweeping up for your emperor? It will be all right. We have another new room, and the staff are watching. Now, stop making a fuss, because there is something else I must tell you."

He did not like the second piece of news, either. Had he not been so busy nor she so pale, he would have quarreled with her, demanding to know why she had allowed herself to listen to more scandalous gossip about Geminus.

"Somebody will have to do something," she said. "They cannot ignore something like this."

"I can't do anything now, Tilla. This is not the time."

So she had looked him in the eye and said, "Then when is?"

Ruso opened his mouth very slightly and directed a stream of air at the fly. It flew off on his second attempt.

Geminus was strutting up and down the silent ranks, prodding the occasional offender back into line with his stick. Ruso found himself eyeing the end of the stick for traces of Marcus's blood. He was certain that the clerk had overheard the conversation in the office and reported every word.

And now there was Tilla's news. *They have been placing bets on the recruits…*

It made sense. It made sense of the dangerous order to cross the river. It made sense of the training injuries, incurred when the British recruits were urged to compete with each other. It made sense of Austalis and Marcus's desperation not to be marked out as Britons when they reached Deva, lest they be exposed to more men like Geminus. Geminus, or perhaps his shadows, had beaten Marcus into silence. Now he had taken steps to frighten Tilla. If it was true that Tadius and Victor had been caught trying to report their centurion's twisted abuse of power to

Deva, then perhaps they had been not only threatened but silenced.

On the other hand, it was hard to be rational about a man after being attacked by his dog.

He tensed the muscles in the injured leg. A fresh stab of pain cut through the ache. There were times when it did not matter whether you were rational, as long as you were right.

There had been no physical coercion of Sulio, but there had been no need. Recalling his early conversation with Geminus, Ruso doubted that the centurion had really persuaded the lad to stay in the army. If the conversation had taken place at all, it was far more likely that Geminus—knowing what Sulio might reveal once he was freed—had refused him permission to leave. Trapped inside the fortress, perhaps fearing that he too would shortly meet with some kind of "accident," Sulio had attempted the only escape that seemed open to him, and Geminus had followed him onto the roof to make sure he succeeded.

Ruso focused his gaze on the blank faces of the men lining the far side of the street. How many of them could testify to Geminus's bullying? There must be witnesses standing all around him now, too frightened to speak. If only Pera had kept his nerve and clung to the courage that had caused him to slip an accurate postmortem report into the records without anyone else seeing it. He must have watched with horror as Ruso blundered in and drew it to the clerk's attention. Now the report was destroyed, and Pera had fallen silent. Just like all the others who had failed to support Tadius and Victor. Perhaps it was too far-fetched to imagine that all those minor annoyances at the hospital had been arranged by Geminus. But someone had put that thing in the mansio bed. And then there was the dog. The dog had been a deliberate attack.

If only he had known all of this when he first approached Accius. The tribune would have been compelled to do more than have an informal chat with an old friend.

He caught a snatch of conversation behind him. A woman was saying in British, "... to see how she gets it to stay up in coils like that."

"It isn't hers," said a second woman. "It lifts off at night."

"Really? She must have to pin it very tight to her real hair."

"Well, I don't suppose she moves much," replied the first woman. As their voices faded Ruso heard, "They don't even wipe their own backsides, these people. They have slaves to—oh! Is something happening?"

There was indeed a stir in the crowd. While the legionaries stared stoically ahead, the civilians were craning for a view of what was approaching down the east road. The chatter died away. The bark of an order was followed by the tramp of heavy boots approaching from the fortress gate as the guard of honor, with Accius at its head, marched out to meet the imperial party.

The trumpets wailed above the sound of cheering and applause. Forbidden to turn and see what was approaching, the legionaries had to wait until the procession passed in front of their eyes, but all around them Accius's instructions seemed to have had the desired effect. The locals cheered and whooped and waved at the horse guards as if Hadrian's cavalry were riding in to liberate them from the blighted presence of the Twentieth Legion. Behind them came the Praetorian Guards, identifiable to anyone who did not know them by the scorpions on their shields, and to anyone who did by their air of owning the place already. Ruso could see their officers scanning the crowd for trouble, as if they did not trust the local garrison to keep order. It was strangely satisfying to think that these highly paid arrivals from Rome would be obliged to march across Britannia in the rain just like everyone else.

The noise of the excited crowd rose even higher. Across the street, a couple of youths on a roof clambered to their feet, raised their hands in the air, and began to wave their arms from side to side on their precarious perch as if they were swaying in the wind. Ruso caught sight of the thin civilian liaison centurion trying to order them to sit down. It was hopeless. Others followed suit, and soon the buildings opposite were crowded with arms swaying back and forth in time with the chant of some sort of cheerfully chaotic native greeting.

Geminus raised his stick twice in the air. The ranks of the Twentieth erupted into a roar of "Caesar! Cae-sar!"

And there he was. A lone figure with a glittering breastplate over a surprisingly plain tunic, seated on a white stallion, one hand raised in greeting. The face a little heavier than Ruso remembered from Antioch, surveying the crowd with an air of approval. The lanky rider behind him must be the prefect of the Praetorians. Then more guards, and shrieks of excitement from the crowd as six bearers in scarlet tunics appeared, carrying an open litter.

Children were held up to fling handfuls of white petals into the air. They caught in the breeze and floated down like snowflakes. The empress Sabina looked out from beneath her elaborate hairstyle with no obvious emotion. Ruso tried to suppress the question of whether there really were slaves whose job it was to wipe the imperial backsides, and wondered whether the empress's pallor was white lead makeup or the aftereffects of a rough sea trip and the knowledge that if she wanted to escape this island of dancing and screaming barbarians, she would have to repeat it.

Moments later, on the far side of more ranks of marching Praetorians, Ruso glimpsed a blond woman smiling and waving at him. No doubt she was just caught up in the excitement of the crowd, but he felt oddly moved. It was not often that Tilla appeared to be proud of him.

Then he remembered what they had been talking about earlier, and he knew it wouldn't last.

39

The dog, Ruso reminded himself, would not be loose in the streets without Geminus. Geminus was definitely busy because he—and conspicuously not Ruso—had been invited to dine with Accius and Hadrian and Hadrian's friends and officials this evening. Still, as he set off on the few minutes' walk from the hospital to the mansio, Ruso found himself alert to the sounds and shadows in the dusk around him. As he rounded the corner he was not sorry to see the lanterns outside the mansio entrance flare into life, and to notice the door slave making his way back inside carrying a taper.

Reassured by the nearness of safety, Ruso clumped up the steps and sat on the bench next to the unstable tree, whose pot now seemed to have been roped to a post. In a minute he would go and find Tilla, but for now he leaned against the wall, stretched out his aching leg, and surveyed the street along which the emperor had passed earlier this evening. Noise and light were spilling out from the bars. Groups of native men stood outside drinking, talking, and laughing. A couple had their arms around skimpily clad girls. The respectable women would all have gone home, or to wherever respectable women went at night when it was too far to get back to their own hearths.

Ruso filled his lungs with cool evening air that smelled of beer and roast meat and spice and roses. A man needed to sit quietly and think after such an eventful day.

They have been placing bets on the recruits.

This is not the time.

Then when is?

Hadrian had been impressive. He had barely paused to recover from the march before going across to the headquarters courtyard and greeting the assembled men of the Twentieth, calling them "fellow soldiers," which pleased them, and adding, "Now that I've experienced the climate of Britannia for myself, I'm even more proud of you." There was a gust of laughter. Ruso could see from their faces that the older men liked him. The recruits, who might be excused for not trusting anyone in authority, seemed to like him too.

He thanked them for their preparations for what he called "this unexpected honor." He was, he said, "aware of the disruption an imperial visit can cause, even the most welcome one."

Watching him, Ruso was impressed. This man had risen from being the son of a provincial senator to become a general, a scholar, and now emperor.

There was no sign of the country accent that had made him the butt of jokes when he first entered the Senate. He appeared relaxed, well-groomed, and confident despite just having completed a long march after the terrors of a near shipwreck. It was clear that Hadrian was a very determined man.

As expected, he informed the recruits that tomorrow he would be pleased to observe their final trials before their full admission to the Twentieth Legion. He would also oversee the discharge of veterans. The veterans cheered. Ruso had glanced across to where Geminus was standing as straight as a board beneath the magnificent white crest on his parade helmet. The silver disks that testified to past bravery were polished and gleaming on his chest. If he was concerned about how his men would perform, it did not show. As for the recruits themselves, Ruso was not sure it was possible for them to be any more terrified than they already were.

He stood up slowly from the bench, feeling the stitches pull in the back of his leg. The manager of the mansio leapt up when he saw who it was, assuring him his wife was safe and well and that the staff were keeping an eye on the room.

He found Tilla practicing her reading while she waited for him. Evidently they were now to sleep in a large cupboard and to be entertained by the merry whistling of the cook in the kitchen next door.

She was wrinkling her nose before he was fully in the room. “Fish sauce?”

"Good for dog bites. You won't notice after a bit." He had expected her to launch straight into the subject of Geminus, but instead she busied herself rolling up the poetry scroll. He said, "Have I missed any patients?"

"A boy who jumped off a wall and sprained his ankle, and one old lady who fainted and fell off a donkey. I have bandaged them both. Everyone else is too excited to be ill, or too drunk to notice. How is it in the fort?"

He hung his cloak on the back of the door and joined her on the bed. "The Horse Guards and the Twentieth are eyeing each other with mutual suspicion," he said, "and the hospital's full of Praetorians who haven't spoken to anyone so far except to complain."

"But they are all on the same side."

"Only if there's an enemy."

There was a shout from the kitchen and the clang of a metal pan hitting the floor. He said, "We need to talk. I don't doubt what you say about Geminus. But if Accius finds out you've been listening to more rumors after he told you to stay out of it—"

"I tried not to listen, but she was determined to tell." She paused, running one finger slowly down his forearm. "Husband, if I tell you who said it, will you swear not to tell Accius?"

"I suppose so."

"That is not swearing!"

"Tilla, you know I won't tell." That was not swearing, either, but she let it pass.

She leaned back against the side wall and tucked her bare feet between his legs while she explained about the farm she had gone to visit. "Virana is a very silly girl," she said, "but now I have met her family I am not surprised."

He shook his head. "What is it about soldiers that sends girls silly?"

"You should be glad of it," she said, wriggling her toes.

"Ow."

"Sorry." She moved her foot away from the bandage. "So the tribune did nothing about this Geminus?"

"Oh, he did something. He conveyed my 'complaint' word for word to him. Geminus assures me he has no hard feelings over it."

"And now his dog has bitten you."

"Evidently the dog doesn't feel the same way."

"You could have been killed!"

He slid a friendly hand up her thigh, reminding her of what she might have lost. She did not seem to notice.

"This proves Barita was telling the truth!" she said. "Now he is trying to frighten me with a pig head and silence you too."

"One of the recruits who complained has been beaten up."

"Has he lost his mind? He cannot go round threatening and killing everybody!"

"He doesn't have to. He just has to make them think it's not worth making a fuss."

"We must stop this man!"

He slid the hand higher. "Accius won't do anything. If he believes anything's wrong—which I doubt—he's waiting for it all to blow over."

"You will have to talk to someone more important."

"There's no one here—" He caught her expression. "Oh, no. No. That would be ridiculous."

"You have met him before. You could remind him. I will pray that he will listen."

"You're starting to sound like my stepmother. Besides, I've been told to stay away from him. I'll talk to the camp prefect about it when we get back to Deva. Until then I'll just have to be careful. I don't imagine any more of the recruits will step out of line."

She grasped his hand. "Not now. I am trying to think. And I am thinking you should be very careful. I saw that pig's head. I think Geminus is mad enough to try to stop you from getting back to Deva."

"Unless he thinks he can make me keep my mouth shut."

She brought his hand up to her lips and kissed it. "You are a good man in a bad place."

"And if I'm not prepared to risk my neck to make that place better," he said, "will I still be a good man?"

"I do not know," she said. "But you will still be alive."

40

The dawn briefing was a crowded affair, but Ruso was greeted by nobody except the plump centurion, who looked too hungover to know who he was grunting at. He was not sorry to make his way back to the hospital, where he intended to remain while men with fiercer ambition tried to impress each other.

Austalis's smile of greeting was encouraging in more ways than he could know. Ruso supervised the changing of his dressings and, since the kitchen orderly had been commandeered by Hadrian's cook, went to fetch the breakfast nobody had remembered to bring. This took longer than expected, as he was called upon to intervene in a squabble over what the Praetorians called "requisitioning" of saucepans and the kitchen slave called theft. Thus he emerged completely unaware of the panic that had gripped the other end of the corridor.

The kitchen slave had ladled a generous helping of honeyed milk into Austalis's cup. Ruso was concentrating on not spilling it across the tray when the sound of footsteps and voices caused him to glance up to avoid a collision. Half a dozen men were bearing down on him. At their head was the tall figure of Hadrian. The short, flush-faced man next to him was Pera.

Recalling the tribune's order to stay out of Hadrian's way, Ruso stepped aside to allow them to pass just as the emperor reached the end of a sentence.

"That's him, sir!" declared Pera, with obvious relief.

Hadrian stopped. So did everyone else. Ruso, back to the wall and still clutching the tray, felt a sudden sympathy with patients who found themselves surrounded by a gang of apprentices and an instructor ready to show them how to conduct an intimate examination. He could not salute without dropping the tray, and without the salute his "Hail Caesar!" sounded rather odd.

Hadrian put his well-groomed head on one side and peered at Ruso. "Don't I know you?"

He really must insist that Tilla stopped praying for things. "Ruso, Your Majesty. We met after the earthquake in, um…" Gods above, what was the place called? His memory had deserted him.

"I thought so," said the emperor, seeming not to notice his confusion. "I never forget a face. I don't know why I bother having a man to tell me who people are: Half the time I know more than he does. Ruso. You were one of the rescuers in Antioch. A terrible business."

"Yes, sir."

"So you're in charge here now?"

He said, "I'm only here for a few days, sir. Pera's usually the man to talk to."

Pera, who must have thought he had escaped, did not look grateful to be placed back in the target area.

Hadrian glanced from one to the other of them with an air of amusement.

"Ah, Pera. Back to you. So what can you tell me about the Britons?"

Pera's hand rose to his neck. "Th-they've calmed down a lot since last year, Your Majesty."

"So I hear," agreed Hadrian, apparently satisfied. "But I'll be leaving the Sixth over here in case there's any more trouble."

Pera swallowed, as if he was not sure whether he should thank the emperor or not. Hadrian, evidently used to smoothing over conversations with the tongue-tied, turned to Ruso. "So, Doctor Who Isn't in Charge, how are you finding things in Eboracum?"

Ruso glanced round at the faces: one or two sympathetic, most bored, Pera rigid. They were waiting for him to answer this bland question with something suitably reassuring.

This is not the time. The emperor had affairs of state waiting for him, and a crowd of ambassadors following him around like a long unwieldy tail. He didn't want a litany of complaints any more than Ruso wanted a list of symptoms after casually asking an acquaintance about his welfare.

But Geminus's regime in Eboracum had left recruits dead and injured, families bereaved, a woman and child abandoned…

He was conscious of Hadrian assessing him, the famously piercing eyes seeing an officer who was too nervous to go far.

He took a deep breath. "It's a lot better than Antioch, sir."

Hadrian chuckled. "Indeed. Now, while the pair of you decide who's in charge, I shall visit some of your patients."

Later, Ruso could remember very little about Hadrian's tour of the hospital. Austalis, whose injury was not explained, was declared to be "a brave lad." There were occasional silences that Pera stepped in to fill. Meanwhile Tilla's question was echoing around his mind. If this was not the time, then when was?

As the senior doctor, he was surely not just here to patch up the sick and wounded as they were presented to him, any more than a commander's only role in battle was to stand in the front line and stab the enemy one by one. It was his duty to organize the defences, to devise strategies that might prevent them from harm in the first place. It was his duty to challenge something that was making the men here very sick indeed.

Yet, when a man with the power to change things had asked him how things were in Eboracum, he had pushed aside his duty and said the sort of thing his superiors wanted to hear. Thinking of Marcus's battered face as he remembered the glib *It's a lot better than Antioch, sir* made him feel hot with shame.

Hadrian was leaving the bedside of the last overawed patient. "Well, your men seem to be doing a good job in here."

Pera said, "Thank you, sir."

Everyone else began to shuffle out behind him. It was over. Hadrian was happy. Everyone was satisfied. The reputation of the Twentieth was intact, and Ruso had missed his chance.

As the last flunky filed out, Ruso dodged past him into the corridor. "Your Majesty! Sir!"

Everyone turned. The hangers-on looked shocked. Hadrian looked impatient, then glanced at his friends. "Did I forget something?"

"Sir, you asked a question and I didn't answer it properly."

Beyond Hadrian he could see Pera in the corridor, eyes wide in horror. He should have rehearsed this, he realized now. Hadrian was used to receiving ambassadors who had been polishing their speeches for months. But it was too late. This was his moment, and instead of feeling bold he was shaking as if he had just offered himself up to an underfed tiger.

One of the flunkies stepped forward and murmured, "Sir, the recruits will be waiting to start their trials."

"In a moment," Hadrian snapped. Ruso quailed at the annoyance in the voice.

"My lord," he said, switching to Greek. At least the patients wouldn't understand. "My lord, I think I should tell the truth."

Hadrian's expression was stern. "I think that would be a good idea."

"My lord..." He stopped, conscious that everyone was waiting to hear what he had to say. If only he could speak privately with the great man...but Hadrian, by dint of his very greatness, was perpetually surrounded by other people.

Hadrian indicated his rotund secretary and the lanky Praetorian prefect. "These are my friends. You can speak openly."

That was when Ruso noticed the nondescript man loitering at the back of the group. Metellus, security adviser to the outgoing governor. Metellus, who had put Tilla's name on one of his infamous lists. Metellus, whom Ruso had last seen flailing about in the muddy waters of the river Tamesis—after Ruso himself had pushed him in there.

"Well?" said Hadrian.

Ruso cleared his throat. "My lord, there are good men here in Eboracum. But there are also men who order their juniors to face dangers just for the plea sure of betting on the outcome. Three Britons who joined your legion to serve you are dead because of it."

He stopped speaking. Somewhere, someone slammed a door. The crash echoed down the corridor. Everyone except Metellus was watching Hadrian to see how he would respond. Metellus was watching Ruso.

This was not the time. He saw that now. He had allowed Tilla to push him into a terrible, catastrophic mistake.

The great man lifted his head. "I see." Behind him, faces appeared, peering round the end of the corridor. Even if they didn't understand, someone would be bound to translate for them as soon as the emperor was gone.

"Have you informed your superiors?"

It was a question he should have foreseen.

Tell the truth again. Just leave parts out. "Tribune Accius is aware that something's wrong, my lord, but I've only just found out the details for him."

"Well, I'm sure he will deal with it appropriately."

And with that, the moment was over. Hadrian and his entourage swept out of the hospital entrance and away down the street.

Pera must have slunk away. Ruso was alone in the entrance hall. He leaned against the wall, feeling nauseous.

At a time like this, a man should be comforted by philosophy. Virtue, said the Stoics, was the only possession worth having. But he was no longer sure that he knew what virtue was, and the faint whisper that Tilla would be proud of him was not going to be enough to sustain him through the storm that was to come.

41

"I am only saying what you are both thinking," declared Sabina, pushing away the bowl of dates whose shape and color had reminded her that this place might have cockroaches. "Germania was bad enough. Did you see all those ghastly people?"

"I am sure the emperor knows best, madam," Tranquillus assured her.

"And I'm sure this couch is damp." She gestured to the steward. "Have them find me something else to sit on."

The steward nodded to one of the slaves, who flitted out through a side door.

"Britannia is a very prestigious posting, madam," said Clarus.

Sabina frowned at the flaking paint of what was supposed to be the best room, and ordered more coals for the brazier. "If Britannia were so marvelous," she continued, "Tranquillus would have come here when he first had the chance, instead of finding ways of wriggling out of it. Wouldn't you, Tranquillus? You could have had a glittering military career."

Tranquillus modestly inclined his head. "I am honored to be the emperor's secretary, madam."

"Oh, be honest, both of you. You would both rather be at home with your noses stuck in scrolls than trailing around all over the empire. And after all this bother, not a blue face to be seen anywhere! Do you think the painted ones have run away?"

"I believe they are on the far side of the emperor's Great Wall, Madam."

"Along with the land of eternal day, I suppose."

Clarus examined a date before biting off one end. "Very possibly, madam."

"They murdered Lollia's husband, you know. And both of poor Favonia's sons."

Tranquillus said, "I am sure the emperor will not put you in danger, madam."

She sighed. "No. I'm not even allowed to risk listening to your book about prostitutes."

"Madam, if the emperor thinks it suitable—"

"We both know that if the emperor thinks it will entertain me, it will not be suitable."

Clarus glanced at his friend, but Tranquillus had developed a sudden interest in rubbing an ink stain off his forefinger. Clarus helped himself to another date while he was still chewing the first one.

"Surely there must be something both respectable and interesting to do here while one's husband talks about walls?" demanded Sabina. "What about the famous native warrior women? Could you find one of those for me to look at?"

"I believe they're all dead, madam." Was that a touch of condescension in Clarus's voice?

"Oh, dear. I shall have to spend the afternoon writing to tell Julia that you're both terribly boring and she isn't missing anything."

Tranquillus looked worried. "Madam, if there is anything we can do..."

"You can introduce me to someone who isn't a homesick officer's wife, a screaming barbarian, or some dreadful woman married to a tribal chief with hairs in his nose."

Somewhere in the distance, a military trumpet sounded. The silence inside the room was finally broken by the faint sound of someone clearing their throat. She turned. "You have something to say?"

The steward took a step forward and bowed.

"Speak."

"Madam, there is a native midwife who is married to one of our officers. She came to help prepare the house for you."

"Really? Is she a better midwife than she is a cleaner?"

The steward did not know. She glanced at Clarus and Tranquillus, who were clearly hoping the steward's intervention would divert some of her irritation from them. "Shall we have her fetched?"

Tranquillus looked appalled. "A *midwife*, madam?"

Clarus said, "A *house cleaner*?"

Sabina smiled. "And an officer's wife. I think I should like to meet her."

"She'll have to be checked first," insisted Clarus. "I'll need a name."

Sabina sighed. "Clarus, you have a very large sword. We are surrounded by the servants and you can call your guards. If none of those can deal with her, Tranquillus will stab her with his stylus. I think I shall be safe from one woman, don't you?"

42

The legate' s house still smelled of fresh paint, and the slave girl who had told Tilla to wait in the yellow entrance hall had a smear of the same color on the shoulder of her tunic.

Tilla, left alone to wonder why the empress wanted to see her, glanced out at the courtyard garden. It had been a mass of brambles before yesterday's desperate slash-and-burn preparations. Plants in pots had been commandeered from somewhere, and slaves were scurrying back and forth between the rooms she had helped to sweep and air yesterday afternoon. Through an open door she could see the wall hanging Minna had ordered put up to hide a damp patch. She wondered what it would be like to live surrounded by servants, with everything you wanted supplied for you, and with hundreds—maybe thousands—of armed men outside who would do what ever your husband told them. It might be very lonely.

An approaching male voice said, "They have searched her for weapons, I take it?"

Oh, yes, thought Tilla. *Very thoroughly, and not with respect.*

The slave with the paint on her tunic reappeared. "The empress will see you now."

Moments later Tilla was announced as "The British woman, madam."

She stepped into the big room with the cracked windowpanes and found herself under scrutiny. There were four women, three of whose plain slave tunics were finer than anything she had ever owned, and two ill-matched men in middle age: a lanky bald one looking uncomfortable in Praetorian uniform and a short one with a pot belly and inky fingers.

Sabina herself was seated in a basket chair and draped in pale gold silk. While two of the slaves adjusted the curls on her complicated hairstyle, she surveyed Tilla as if she were examining a piece of fruit for blemishes. The beautifully made-up eyes were puffy, and Tilla suspected she had not slept well.

The slave girl who had brought her in stepped forward and murmured in Tilla's ear, "Do not stare at the empress!"

"Her hair is rather scruffy," observed the empress. "And she isn't blue at all. Ah, well. Do we have anyone who can translate?"

"I speak Latin, mistress," said Tilla, addressing the thin fingers resting in the imperial lap. She was not sure what to call this woman. She did not want to get her husband into trouble. On the other hand, if empresses were fussy about who looked at them and what they were called, then they should arrange for someone to say so earlier.

"How convenient," said Sabina, not sounding in the least embarrassed about her rudeness. "Not quite the barbarian I was hoping for, but never mind. Cheer up, young woman. I have not brought you here to terrify you."

Someone must have told the empress about her. Perhaps she was here to be thanked for all her hard work.

Sabina said, "I hear one of our officers has married you."

"I have married him also, mistress," said Tilla. "My people choose our own men."

"So I hear. Well, I am glad not all the Britons are hostile to us, although you are rather forward. Tell me something. I have also heard that your men share their wives."

Tilla hesitated. Wretched Julius Caesar again. "I cannot speak for all the tribes, mistress. But I can tell you that no woman of my people would lie with a man she does not like."

"You are very frank for a young woman with no position."

Tilla was tired of looking anywhere but at the woman's face. "I am trying to answer honestly," she said, meeting the empress's scrutiny. "You are a guest in these islands, and it would be inhospitable to lie to you."

The men looked from her to Sabina. The empress's brittle laughter seemed to come as a relief to everyone. "A guest in our own province! How quaint! Tell me, why are none of you blue?"

What was it that made Romans so interested in this sort of thing?

"Warriors paint themselves, mistress. Perhaps everyone did it in Caesar's day, but I have never heard of it." Just to be helpful, she added, "I have never heard of men hunting each other for sport, either."

"Really?" The girl doing the hair above the left ear let go just in time as Sabina turned to the men. "You see? Even the barbarians have stricter standards than we do."

"I suppose there's no money for games here," put in the lanky man. "It does look horribly poor."

"Well, so far this is rather disappointing. Is it at least true that you are a midwife and your husband is a medicus with the Twentieth Legion?"

Relieved to be asked something sensible at last, Tilla said, "I deliver babies, mistress, and I help my husband with the civilian patients and medicines." And perhaps, she saw suddenly, she could help someone else. "My husband is a good man," she said. "He is trying to stop a centurion who is gambling away the lives of his recruits while the tribune stands by and does nothing."

Sabina's face tightened. "The army is not our concern. The emperor does not need advice and he would not like anyone to interfere in his business."

The empress was not as empty-headed as she pretended to be. "I try not to interfere, mistress. I just try to find something useful to do, as the gods have not yet granted us children."

"I shall pray for you."

Tilla bowed her head. "And I for you, mistress. There is always hope. Not long ago I delivered a first child for a woman who had been married for seventeen winters."

"I see," said Sabina, not warmly. "Well, this has been very interesting." Again the hairdresser slaves lifted their hands just in time as Sabina turned to consult the men. "Do we have any more questions for her, gentlemen?"

They did not.

"You may leave us now. Oh, and, girl … ?"

"Mistress?"

Was that a faint smile creasing the makeup on the imperial cheeks? "Do not pray too hard."

As she backed out of the room, Tilla heard the empress laughing. She hoped it was nothing to do with her.

43

It was mid-afternoon before the summons came from the tribune. Ruso finished splinting the broken wrist he had treated on his arrival, then handed over his responsibilities to Pera, who was the only person with any authority who seemed prepared to speak to him. Neither of them had said a word to the other about Ruso's conversation with the emperor, but just as he was leaving, Pera murmured, "Good luck, sir."

"I don't think I've been much help here, Pera."

"Only the gods can work miracles, sir. We mortals just have to do our best."

Ruso shook his head. "I must have been a pompous ass as a tutor."

"Not as much of an ass as I was, sir."

They clasped hands, then Ruso turned on his heel and followed the messenger down the corridor. He gave Aesculapius a farewell nod before he stepped out into the street.

"You should have—come—to me—first!" hissed Accius, leaving gaps between the words for emphasis, as if he would have liked to shout but did not want to be overheard by any of the men passing back and forth across the headquarters hall outside.

"You deliberately undermined me! I had to sit next to him for hours, looking like a complete idiot while he oversaw the exercises. As if I don't know what's going on in my own unit!"

"Sir, I told him—"

"I ordered you to stay away from him. You disobeyed me."

Common sense and experience were telling Ruso not to argue, but he was not in the mood to listen to either of them. "Sir, the emperor asked me—"

"Of course he did: That's what emperors do! The answer was *Yes, everything is fine,* because it is! Our men were having a simple run of bad luck. Everything was getting back to normal until you and that native woman started stirring up malicious gossip."

"Sir, I was going to—"

"You ran after him to tell him! And you did it because you thought I wouldn't listen!"

There was no point in denying it. "Yes, sir. I did it because—" The back of Accius's hand hit his face with a force that stunned him.

"Don't speak! Guards!" The men Accius had stationed outside the door stepped in. "If this man speaks again, run him through."

Over the ringing in one ear Ruso heard, "You are demoted to the ranks, confined to the fortress, and forbidden to speak until further notice. You can reflect on your disloyalty while you scrub out the sewers. As for that woman: Have her sent back to wherever you got her from. You're divorced."

Ruso opened his mouth to protest, heard the swish of swords being drawn, and thought better of it.

Accius shook his head sadly. "You're a fool, Ruso. You could have used your time with Hadrian to get yourself noticed. Instead you've ruined yourself and embarrassed everybody else." He gestured toward the guards. "Take him to the sewers."

Ruso tied his neckerchief over his nose and mouth. He turned aside, took a deep breath, hooked his fingers through the iron rings, and heaved. The trapdoor lifted. He did not need to inhale the stench: He could taste it.

The guards, one of whom Ruso vaguely recognized as a former patient from Deva, stepped back.

"The tribune didn't order you to stay," said Ruso. The pair looked at each other, evidently wondering whether to run him through for speaking, then shrugged and walked away.

44

"Well," said Sabina when the woman had gone, "what did you make of her? Shall I take her with me?"

"Take her with you?" At the sight of Tranquillus's mouth forming an "O" of horror in his little round face, Sabina felt a shiver of delight. This afternoon had been the best entertainment she had had since coming to Britannia. "Oh, Tranquillus! You look almost as amusing as she did when I said, 'Do not pray too hard.' "

"Madam, the woman is a native!"

"That is what makes her interesting. Clarus, what do you think?"

"And very impertinent!" put in Tranquillus before he had a chance to answer.

Sabina sighed. "Yes, I suppose so. Sooner or later I should be obliged to have her beaten, which would be a pity. Do our centurions really gamble away their men, Clarus?"

"It's not customary, madam. I think that woman must be the wife of the rather wild-eyed doctor who ran after the emperor this morning."

"Really?" Sabina sat forward, felt herself jerked backward, and aimed a slap at the slave who had failed to let go of her hair in time. "A doctor ran after the emperor? How wild was he? Did he have to be restrained?"

Tranquillus said, "He was not quite that wild, madam."

"A pity. Still, at last, something interesting! I love a good scandal."

"But, madam—"

"Don't pretend you don't, Tranquillus. We all know what you wrote about Tiberius. So what will happen to the gambling centurion?"

But disappointingly it seemed nothing would happen to the centurion. The case had been referred back to the tribune. "The same tribune that the woman said does nothing?"

"Perhaps because the centurion is innocent," said Clarus, setting aside the usual disdain of the Praetorians for everyone else in order to defend a fellow officer.

Tranquillus said, "One cannot believe everything the Britons say, madam."

Sabina sniffed. "She seemed alarmingly honest to me. And not unintelligent."

"She may believe what she says," put in Clarus. "Apparently the natives here imagine all sorts of nonsense."

"I see," Sabina said. "Perhaps I shall bring her back and ask if she believes in men who wrap themselves in their ears."

The chief hairdresser was hovering in front of her, clutching a mirror. Sabina snatched it from her, because no matter how many directions one gave, a mirror in someone else's hands was never at quite the right angle. She moved it about, examining the result of their efforts, and saw the relief on their faces when she said, "I expect that will do. It is rather hard to tell. Why is it that no one has made a mirror in which a person can see all of herself at once?"

It was one of those perfectly sensible questions that left everyone in the room looking worried, as if she were about to order instant execution if they failed to produce what ever it was she wanted. The next question was just as good: "And why," she said, "do our officers leave it to some mad-eyed doctor and a barbarian woman to discipline one of our centurions?"

45

Tilla held her head high as she stepped into the entrance hall of the mansio. She was not going to allow a group of spoiled rich people to upset her. The manager, looking concerned, hurried to greet her. The last time he had seen her, she was being marched off to the fort by four Praetorian Guards. "It is all right," she assured him, not sure she wanted to tell anyone about her meeting with the empress. "It was nothing bad."

But he was not interested in where she had been. He was interested in where she was going, which was anywhere but in his building. He was very sorry, but there was no room any more.

"But I have nowhere to go! Everywhere in Eboracum is full."

"I'm sorry, madam. You can't stay here. We've had orders."

"But why? Is the tribune's household still here?"

"I can't discuss other guests, madam."

She was about to answer, when she heard shouting outside. "They're here! The Sixth are here!"

The manager straightened up, craning past her to look out through the open doors. She could hear the steady tread of boots now. This was not good. In moments the street would be filled with a blue and silver river of men in armor, sweeping away everything in its path. She would have to find a way out through a side door and hope that there would still be somewhere in the fortress for an officer and his wife to spend the night.

"I need to find my husband."

"There is also the matter of payment—"

"Send the bill to my husband at the hospital."

"Madam, our usual policy—"

She straightened her shoulders and looked him in the eye. "Do you want me to leave, or not?"

Corinna was kind, and surprised, and reassuring. No, they had no right to throw her out like that. "You are safe here," Corinna assured her, handing her a piece of bread and giving another to her son, distracting him from tugging threads out of the bandage on his leg. "The door is strong, and there is no one here but us."

As if to reinforce what she said, the sound of raised voices came from the street. Corinna looked up from stirring something that smelled good, and sighed. "It was noisy last night too. All these new people arriving. You must stay here until your husband comes to take you to the fort."

Tilla ripped a chunk off the bread. "I sent a message. I hope someone will give it to him."

She had managed to snatch a word with the lame gardener, who had been sympathetic but able neither to help nor to explain. He did whisper, though, that he thought the order to throw her out had come from the tribune. He did not know why, and Tilla could only guess. Was it something to do with what her husband had said about Geminus? Surely they were not being thrown out because she had stared at the empress?

She glanced up, startled by a sound that seemed to come from the top of the ladder leading to the boarded loft under the thatch. "What is that?"

Corinna took a sip from the spoon and said calmly, "Just the rats. A nuisance, but last night they put off two ambassadors from Baetica who banged on the door demanding beds. If we stay here, I must find a cat."

Tilla shuddered and hoped the message would get through quickly. She had thought about asking if she could spend the night here, but how could anyone sleep with rats running about the house? Was nowhere safe? She needed to be settled somewhere else before dark. She needed the Medicus.

Someone banged on the door, but it was only a mansio porter bringing her luggage, just as the embarrassed manager had promised. She checked the contents, only too aware of how easy it would be for a slave to hide something and sell it quietly later on. When she had finished, she sank down onto the stool by the hearth.

Corinna said, "Is it all there?"

She nodded.

Corinna wrapped a cloth around her hands and poured broth from the pan into the two bowls she had set on the table. "Eat," she said, wiping the drips from the metal rim of the pan. "We will think of something more cheerful. Tell me about the empress."

"You know about that?"

"This is a small place. People talk."

"She wanted to meet a Briton," said Tilla. "I think I was a disappointment to her."

"So is it true what they say about them? That he prefers boys and they hate each other?"

Tilla looked up from her bowl. "They hate each other?"

Corinna dipped a piece of bread into the broth, shook off the drips, and tested the temperature before handing it to her son. "I hear he was always more friendly with his mother-in-law than his wife."

Tilla's spoon came to a halt as she heard an echo of her own voice. *I can tell you that no woman of my people would lie with a man she does not like.* She hoped the empress had not thought it was a deliberate insult. "Perhaps that is why she has no children," she said. "I thought she might have sent for me because she wanted medicine, but she did not ask."

"They say she makes sure she will never give him children. I heard that she says any child of his would harm the human race."

Tilla stared at her in mounting alarm. "Are you sure?"

"Who knows?" Corinna shrugged. "That is what I heard."

"Perhaps you heard wrongly," said Tilla, feeling her intestines writhe as she recalled the sound of laughter following her around the courtyard. So that was why the empress had said, *Do not pray too hard.*

She had spoken with the best of intentions. She had tried to be kind. She hoped the empress realized that. Still, no matter what the empress realized, the words were out now. *There is always hope.* And then she had made it worse by gabbling about the patient who had been married for seventeen winters.

Tilla pushed a chunk of bread under the surface of the broth with her spoon. She was no longer hungry. She had made a fool of herself. It should not be any worse because it was in front of the wife of the most powerful man in the world, but it was.

"So what did she say to you?"

Tilla watched the brown liquid soak up into another piece of bread. It was bad enough to be laughed at without having to relive the embarrassment every time someone asked. "I can't tell you," she said, shoving the second piece of bread down below the surface. "It was a secret."

46

Nobody seemed to know how the fighting started, but for once it was impossible to blame the recruits. Despite putting on a remarkably good show for the emperor, they had been ordered to celebrate within the walls of the fort. Outside, there was talk of a local trader quarreling with men from the Twentieth about settling their bills before heading west; but the putative trader seemed to have fled, and if the departing legionaries were involved, they were not going to admit it. There was talk of a fight erupting between the Sixth and some of the maintenance crews, who did not take kindly to being called old men who could piss off now that the professionals were here. That version had the Praetorians trying to restore order. Other accounts had the Praetorians involved from the start, with comrades on all sides weighing in to defend each other and nobody attempting to halt the spread of the mayhem until a gang of centurions and their staff charged out of the east gate, beating their sticks on their shields. By this time teeth and noses were broken, furniture had been dragged into the street as weaponry, and someone's roof was on fire.

In the confusion, it was a while before anyone noticed the soldier from the Sixth who was leaning quietly against the wall of the temple of Mithras, clutching both hands to his head and staring in puzzlement at the dark liquid dripping into his lap.

Meanwhile Ruso, denied access to the bath house, had resorted to washing by stripping off beside the nearest water trough and tipping several buckets of water over his head. He had then dunked his stinking tunic and loincloth into another bucket and given them several rinses before hanging them outside the crumbling barrack room where he would spend the night alone, since no one wanted to share with him. Those were the only clothes he had with him, and he supposed they would still be wet in the morning, but a man had to keep up some sort of standards.

He untied his boots, which he had slung around his neck after a bath house slave had taken pity on him and slipped him a pair of wooden sandals. In a reversal of the usual practice, he now put the boots on to go indoors.

He had been allowed the concession of a straw mattress, although not a clean one, and a thin gray blanket into which he now rolled his aching and chilled body. Stretching out on the mattress, he reminded himself that virtue was sufficient for happiness.

The man who thought that one up evidently had no need of clothes. Or a fire. Or dignity. Or dinner. Or a wife, who might or might not get the message that he had paid one of the bath house slaves to give to a friend who might or might not be going to the mansio.

He hoped Accius would leave Tilla alone. He hoped Pera would make sure the staff didn't neglect Austalis. He hoped the emperor would get to hear about the plight of his old comrade from Antioch and order his immediate reinstatement. He hoped he wasn't becoming as deluded as his stepmother. After that, he could think of nothing else to hope for, so he closed his eyes and attempted to enter the last refuge of the desperate: sleep.

He had almost made it when someone crashed open the door and started shouting about needing a doctor.

"I'm not on duty."

"You are now," said Dexter. "Get out of bed. Jupiter's arse, something stinks in here. One whiff of you'll kill the poor bastard anyway."

"On my way," said Ruso, flinging the blanket round his naked shoulders.

"Like that?"

"Or not at all."

It was Pera who had insisted on having Ruso summoned to help with the injured. A spare tunic was swiftly produced, after which cuts were bathed and stitched, noses straightened, and one or two hopelessly loose teeth removed before the owners sobered up enough to care. In the midst of all this, a semiconscious and dramatically bloody man arrived on a stretcher, and Ruso spent some time cleaning him up, searching for the source of the bleeding before he could staunch it.

Eventually the waiting area was cleared and the man with the bleeding head admitted for observation. Tomorrow the centurions would have to sort out the recriminations. Tonight, since Dexter must be busy elsewhere and had left no instructions, Ruso and Pera left the orderlies to clear up the treatment room and headed off down a poorly lit corridor to take advantage of what ever warmth was left in the hospital baths.

On the way, Pera murmured, "I'm very sorry to hear about your situation, sir."

"You don't have to call me sir now."

"I know, sir."

They had just stolen one of the few lamps from the corridor to light the changing room, when Ruso said, "The password hasn't changed since this morning, has it?"

Pera paused with his tunic halfway over his head. "Sir, you can't—"

"Yes or no?"

"Not as far as I know, sir. But—"

"Then I'll thank you for the respite, wish you good night, and go back to barracks."

Before Pera could extract himself from his clothing, Ruso had snatched up the cloak he had just spotted abandoned in an alcove and was back in the corridor with it bundled under his arm. He hid it behind his back to stroll past a couple of off-duty Praetorians. True to form, they ignored him.

The office door was ajar. He heard the murmur of conversation from the late-duty staff, but nobody seemed to notice his passing. He waited until he was out in the dark of the street and well away from the hospital before flinging the Praetorian cloak around his shoulders, tugging the hood over his head, and fumbling with the arrangement of loops and toggles that seemed to fasten it together at the front. The last thing he wanted was for anyone to spot that they'd taken away his army belt.

The guards on the east gate looked at him strangely, but decided to err on the side of caution and added a "sir" to the very reasonable question of "At this hour?"

Ruso said, "When the emperor says *now,* he means *now.*"

They stepped aside to let him pass.

Whatever had gone on out here an hour ago, the streets were quiet now. The slave on duty at the mansio took one look at the cloak and let him in, but the door to the courtyard rooms was locked and he insisted he could not open it without authorization. Ruso stood in the entrance hall, still concealed beneath the hood, hearing a distant clatter from the kitchen. The convivial murmur of a dinner party swelled suddenly, then faded with the click of a door latch. A pair of matching slaves scuttled across the entrance hall, not pausing to bow. Moments later the manager appeared with the rumpled look of a man who had finally managed to snatch some sleep and had now been woken by someone he neither expected nor wanted to see.

"My wife," said Ruso without preamble. "Is she here?"

The manager was eyeing the stolen cloak with an air of confusion when someone else hurried in from the street and clacked across the tiles in studded boots. Ruso shrank deeper into the hood as Dexter demanded to know if Centurion Geminus was on the premises. The manager consulted with the door slave and confirmed that he was not. "Then I need to talk to the tribune," declared Dexter, ignoring the lone Praetorian hunched over the counter with his back to him.

To Ruso's relief, Dexter was sent into the courtyard to await the tribune's response. When he had gone, the manager reached underneath the counter. Etched across a wax tablet in a large and unevenly formed hand that Ruso recognized as Tilla's was *Come for me at the house of Krina.*

Mercifully the clouds had cleared. The moon was silvering one side of the street and plunging the rest into deep shadow. Ruso walked quickly, pushing aside thoughts of dogs and Geminus and what any stray Praetorians might do to a legionary deemed to be impersonating one of their own.

Tilla answered his knock so quickly, she must have been waiting behind the door. "At last!" she whispered, giving him an unexpectedly warm embrace and murmuring in his ear, "There are rats!"

He closed the door behind him. "Rats?"

She sniffed. "What have you been doing? Are you all right? Were you in the fighting?"

He shook his head. "I can't stay. What have they told you?"

"We must go to the fort. If you take that box, I can carry the bags, and on the way you must tell me everything you know about the empress Sabina." She stopped, and pulled his hand toward the light from the fire. "Is that blood?"

"Work." He wiped his hands on the borrowed tunic, but the ingrained red needed to be scrubbed. "Tilla, I'm in trouble."

When he had finished telling her, she was silent for a moment. Then she took his hand. "This is my fault. I prayed that you would talk to him."

"I chose to do it."

She said, "Are we divorced? Will you ask me to go back to my people?"

"Of course not. Lay low until the Twentieth march out tomorrow, and I'll send a message here for you. This will probably all blow over."

" 'Probably'?"

"I don't know," he confessed. "I've never betrayed a legion, harassed an emperor, and humiliated a tribune before."

"You are not the one who has done wrong here."

"I deliberately disobeyed an order."

She began to rifle through one of the bags.

"I've made a bit of a mess of this," he said, feeling the stitches pull in his leg as he crouched beside her.

"It does not matter," she insisted, placing a hand on his knee. "You have done a brave thing." She turned back to the bag.

"What are you looking for?"

"I am taking out the things we do not need," she said, tugging at some sort of female undergarment. "If we do not carry too much and we start now, we can be ten miles away by morning."

"What? Tilla, I'm not—"

"Shhh!" She put her fingers on his lips. "Corinna and the boy are sleeping in the loft."

"I'm not going to run!" he whispered.

"Then what are you going to do? The Legion will not want you!"

He shrugged. "I swore to serve."

"But—"

"Besides, where could we go where we wouldn't be noticed, you and I?"

Her silence was his answer. She said dully, "They execute men who disobey orders."

"Oh, it won't come to that," he assured her, pushing aside the moments in the dark depths of the sewer this afternoon when he had felt almost paralyzed with terror. If disease really was caused by foul air, then spending time down here could kill him as surely as having his head severed—only more slowly. "I'll send a message as soon as I can. Have you got enough money?"

She cast an eye over his beltless tunic. "Have you any to give me?"

"No."

"Then I have enough."

He took both her hands in his bloodstained grasp and kissed her on the lips. "Be safe, Darlughdacha of the Corionotatae."

She stroked his hair. "May the gods smile upon you, Gaius Petreius the Medicus."

"Look after my kit, will you?" She nodded. Halfway out of the door, he paused. "Why did you want to know about Sabina?"

"Is it true she and her husband hate each other?"

"I believe so."

"Why did you never tell me this?"

He shook his head, baffled. "You never asked. Does it matter?"

"No," she said. "Not now."

47

The men of the Twentieth had been ordered to have everything packed and ready so they could march out at sunrise, but when dawn came, there was no call to assemble. The old hands began to gather round the water fountains, rinsing and filling their leather bottles for the journey. With no orders to follow, the men stood chatting in the cool air, checking the comfort of their boots, rearranging their packs, and occasionally glancing up into a cloudless sky, hoping to get going before the sun was too high. Loaded mules flicked their tails and looked bored.

When the trumpet finally sounded, it was not to assemble the men but to summon the Legion's officers. Ruso, who would normally have been amongst them, was left to wait in ignorance along with everyone else. Some of the recruits began to look anxious. Grumblers demanded to know the point of getting up in the middle of the night only to stand around and wait. Meanwhile, several of the more experienced men propped themselves against the barrack walls in the early sunshine, closed their eyes, and appeared to fall asleep.

One of Geminus's shadows finally appeared with instructions to return to barracks, where they were to sweep the floors and scrub the walls. There were groans of disbelief, and several voices demanded to know the reason for the holdup.

"None of your business," said the shadow.

"He doesn't know," interpreted one of the complainers.

"Yes I do," retorted the shadow.

"How long's it going to be, then, sir?"

"Just go and clean up. I'll be round to inspect in an hour. Not you, Ruso. You're on latrines."

Catching the spirit of the moment, Ruso asked, "Why me?"

"Because you ask bloody stupid questions. And if anyone's seen Centurion Geminus since last night, speak up."

That got their attention. "Geminus is missing?" demanded one man, evidently sharper than another who asked, "Where is he?"

"Has any man here seen the centurion since last night?"

While Ruso's mind scurried round a series of possibilities, nobody replied.

"Then go and get scrubbing," said the shadow.

"Sir, are we leaving today, or not?"

"You'll be told later."

To be an officer on latrine duty added humiliation to the routine discomforts of tedium, loneliness, and bad smells, but Ruso had one great advantage over the men consigned to sprucing up their barrack rooms: A man who kept his head down and appeared to be concentrating on scrubbing the flagstones could overhear a regular stream of outside gossip from the occupants of the wooden seating that ran along both sides of the room.

"He'll turn up. He's just gone off somewhere to see someone."

"One of his many friends, eh?" The confidence of the sarcasm told Ruso the voices did not belong to recruits. "And then what: He got lost?"

"Perhaps he's been struck down for not believing in the curse."

"Perhaps he's on a secret mission."

"Perhaps he's saying good-bye to his fancy woman."

"Lucina is as fancy as he gets."

"Lucina? That's it, then. He'll be waiting in the queue."

"Have the Twentieth found their centurion yet?"

"Don't think so. They're even more hopeless than they look."

"They're searching all the empty buildings now."

"They ought to set his dog to find him."

"A dog needs to follow a trail, dim-brain. His stink'll be all over the place."

"Like yours."

"Ha ha." A pair of broad feet stepped past Ruso, and a sponge on the end of a stick was lowered into the channel that ran along the middle of the floor. Ruso shuffled out of splashing distance as the sponge was pumped up and down several times to rinse it. A voice said, "Perhaps he's deserted."

"Never. Not this close to his retirement money."

The man smacked the sponge on the edge of the paving to shake out the worst of the water, then thrust it back amongst the others in the bowl of weak vinegar solution. "I heard he didn't want to retire anyway," he said, "but it sounds like he'll have to now."

"Aulus says the medic's a crank. The tribune's backing Geminus."

Ruso, who had no idea who Aulus was, resisted the urge to look up and see who was talking.

"He might be a crank, but he's forced the tribune into a corner."

"I wouldn't like to be him right now."

"The tribune?"

"The medic."

Ruso remembered he was supposed to be working. The men's departure was drowned out by the swish of bristles on stone.

He's forced the tribune into a corner. Rumors of his conversation with Hadrian must have spread through the fort. Geminus would have heard of the allegations of betting that had been made against him. Now he had disappeared.

Ruso dropped the scrubbing brush back in the bucket and sat back on one heel with his injured leg stretched out in front of him. Geminus the war hero was not a man to run away—but if not, where was he?

I wouldn't like to be him right now.

Ruso was not enjoying being him, either, but at least his misdemeanors had brought about some good. Geminus had bullied his last recruit. He would retire with a tarnished reputation. His handsome discharge bonus might be in doubt too.

Ruso emptied the bucket into the drain and rinsed the brush. He was not fool enough to expect a release, nor a reinstatement. Accius could still make plenty of trouble for him, both within the Legion and beyond. But he had known that when he took the risk of speaking to the emperor. He would just have to console himself with the thought that, somehow, justice had been done.

He was about to put the bucket back in the corner when he was startled by the sound of shouting and running feet. Still clutching the bucket, he opened the door and slipped outside to watch.

Pera and three men he recognized as hospital orderlies were hurrying toward the east gate with a stretcher. Two members of the Sixth were running in the opposite direction, one of them shouting, "Where's the emperor?"

A passing Praetorian asked who wanted to know.

"Primus, optio in the century of Proculus. Important visitor for the emperor."

A skeptical voice from back in the latrines said, "Another one come to lick the emperor's arse."

The Praetorian directed the man toward the legate's house, adding in a superior drawl, "Try not to make too much fuss. They aren't always as important as they think they are."

Ruso glanced around. Nobody was paying him any attention. He weighed the bucket in his hand for a moment, then set it down, swiftly washed his hands, and sprinted down the street after Pera.

Pera's men were hampered by the stretcher and a box of supplies, and Ruso caught up with them just before they reached the gate. "Want some help?"

Pera looked alarmed but then grasped the situation and gestured to one of the orderlies to hand over the box. Ruso hoisted it onto his shoulder. The men of the Sixth, who had taken over guard duties—Accius must have made his handover speech—were standing strictly to attention at the gates. They paid no heed to the unknown medical team and their shabbily clad slave.

Pera murmured, "You've heard, then, sir?"

As they emerged from the archway of the gate house he saw a carriage approaching, pulled by a team of four matching bays. There were dark patches of sweat on the horses and the red paint was dull with dust. The man had been right: This was somebody important. "Who is it?"

"He's dead, sir."

Ruso said, "Who's dead?" but his voice was lost beneath the rush of the carriage and its guards sweeping past them into the fort.

Pera led his men for about thirty paces along the outside of the perimeter ditch to where a burly squad from the Sixth Legion stood, apparently guarding the weeds that the maintenance crews had failed to clear in time for the emperor's arrival.

Pera beckoned Ruso to follow. Then he stepped forward and peered into the ditch. "It's true, then," he said.

Below them, protruding from a battered patch of nettles, was a muscular and blood-smeared arm. Centurion Geminus had been found.

48

"What do we do?"

Ruso stood beside Pera at the bottom of the ditch, running one hand through his hair. He could not believe what he was seeing. Geminus's throat had been cut open and his head pulled back with an efficiency that suggested the practiced butchering of an animal. A bloodstained dagger lay beside him.

He crouched beside the body, feeling the tingle of nettles against his skin. The dagger slid neatly into the empty sheath at the centurion's side.

Pera said, "He couldn't have done that to himself, could he, sir?"

"No."

"What do we do?"

Ruso closed his eyes for a moment and tried to detach his mind from the shock. " 'Time of death, cause of death, any other matters of note,' " he recited. "You can do the rest of the details up at the mortuary. Did you bring anything to write with?"

"Sorry, sir."

Pera extended a hand, put it on the centurion's arm, and then quickly withdrew it. "He's cold, sir."

"Sometime last night. Cause of death, severing of right and left carotid arteries. Anything else of note…" He stood, slapping at the nettle stings. "Did you slide down here or jump?"

"Jump, sir."

"So did I." Ruso peered at the side of the ditch, where he could now make out smears of blood. Several clumps of grass were hanging by pale roots. "Looks as though they did it up there," he said, "and then tipped him in."

"'They'?"

Ruso said, "You think one man could take Geminus?"

There were two thuds as a couple of the orderlies landed in the ditch behind them. They complained vigorously about the nettles as they lifted the body onto the stretcher and maneuvered it up to their comrade waiting at ground level. The men from the Sixth finally produced a ladder from the gate house and Ruso was halfway up it when he heard a growing sound of tramping boots and jingling belt straps. It was followed by a cry of "Make way for His Honour the Praetorian Prefect and Tribune Accius!"

Pera emerged from the ditch and crouched to wipe his hands on the grass before saluting. Ruso recognized the lanky man who had been riding behind Hadrian in the procession: Praetorian Prefect Clarus, the only man authorized to carry a sword in the private company of the emperor. Accius was beside him, looking like a man who had not slept well, and behind them Dexter was craning to see what was on the stretcher. Prefect Clarus approached and gestured for the orderly to draw back the top of the sheet. Both he and Accius blanched and turned away from the sight. Dexter stared down at the mutilated body of his comrade, betraying no emotion. The man replaced the sheet.

Clarus said, "Is that him?"

Accius swallowed. "Yes, sir."

"Who found him?"

"The perimeter patrol, sir," said one of the Sixth.

Accius shook his head. "Terrible. Terrible. He was just about to retire. What a tragedy." Suddenly he noticed Ruso. "You!" His voice was hoarse. "Get away from him!"

"Sir, if I can help—"

"Arrest this man!"

"But, sir—"

"Have him chained up in the guard house."

"Sir, I didn't—"

The blow to his head sent him staggering sideways.

"Speak when you're spoken to!" snarled Dexter. "And show some respect to the centurion. Like a flock of vultures, you lot."

Dazed, he was aware of Accius somewhere in the distance saying, "He can speak at his trial. Until then, get him out of my sight or I'll have him killed on the spot."

49

Ruso's head was throbbing. He supposed he should be glad that they had left him the dignity of a loincloth, but the stone walls of the cell were cold and unyielding against his naked back, and the iron bands he had seen two days ago were now cutting into his own wrists. He could not even scratch at the crawling itches of the nettle stings because the chains were too short, clamped to the wall in such a way that it was impossible either to stand up properly or to lower his hands from shoulder height when he sat.

What a fool he had been. What a pompous ass. *I swore to serve* indeed! At every crossroads, he had taken the wrong turn.

Pera's careful report about Tadius had been destroyed because he had blundered in, trying to help.

Hadrian's annoyed expression as he had called "Your Majesty!" should have warned him to shut up, but instead he had plowed on.

He closed his eyes and pictured Tilla pulling clothes out of their luggage. *If we do not carry too much and we start now, we can be ten miles away by morning.*

If only he could have that moment over again. He would say, *Give me both bags and you take the box.*

She had said, *May the gods smile upon you, Gaius Petreius the Medicus.*

What ever the gods were up to, smiling was not a part of it.

He was drifting into a fitful sleep when a key rattled in the lock and the door crashed open.

"On your feet!" bawled a guard. "Septicius Clarus, prefect of the Praetorian Guard, and Tribune Accius to see the prisoner!"

Ruso struggled to his feet and stood with his back straight and his knees bent. It was marginally more respectful than leaning against the wall with his legs stretched out, but much less comfortable.

Clarus stepped into the cell. When Accius joined him, there was barely room to shut the door. Ruso, forcibly shortened and with his thighs already aching from the effort of his unnatural posture, looked up at them and waited while Clarus angled a wax tablet to catch the light from the small, high window. Accius glowered at a space somewhere above Ruso's head. Normally a disciplinary investigation would be conducted by a tribune, but there were all sorts of reasons why Accius was the wrong man to investigate this, and Ruso guessed he had been forbidden to speak.

"Gaius Petreius Ruso," Clarus declared, looking up from his notes and addressing him as if he were making a speech in the Forum. "As you are known to the emperor, I will be making the inquiries relating to the accusation of murder that has been made against you."

"I didn't do it, sir."

"I am instructed to inform you that if you confess, things will be easier for your wife."

"I have no wife, sir. I'm divorced."

Clarus looked down his nose at him for a moment, then continued. "Last night you were confined to quarters."

"I was called to a medical emergency, sir."

"Yes." Clarus ran one finger over the notes until he reached the point he wanted. "And when the emergency was dealt with, you went out through the east gate disguised as one of my men."

This was not going well.

"You were seen at the mansio asking for your wife."

Ruso swallowed.

"There was blood on your hands."

"The blood was from a patient, sir."

Clarus let that rest. "There are some doubts about the loyalty of your wife, are there not?"

"I have no doubts, sir."

"You wouldn't deny that you asked to see her?"

"I needed to inform her that our marriage was no longer legal, sir. Because I'd been demoted."

"But you still think of her as your wife."

The burning in Ruso's thighs was becoming unbearable. "I didn't kill Geminus, sir."

"Several people have told me that you had a grudge against him."

"Not him personally, sir. The things he did. He caused the deaths of three of his recruits and then made threats against me when I tried to look into it. I wasn't the only person who—" He stopped just in time and finished with "who had trouble with him" instead of *who wanted him dead.*

"The tribune here was already dealing with the business of the recruits."

"Yes, sir." He could stand it no longer. He wriggled round until he could lean against the wall with his aching legs stretched out in front of him.

Accius burst out, "Stand up straight!"

Clarus shot him a warning glance while Ruso shuffled back to his original position. He turned to the prefect. "Sir, I'm not going to escape. Could I have the chains removed?"

"Other men, perhaps," said the prefect. "A man with your history, no."

"My history, sir?"

"Your record of violence against fellow officers."

Ruso frowned. "What?"

Clarus sighed. "You see, Ruso, we know a great deal about you."

Ruso closed his eyes, realizing at last what—or rather, who—was behind Clarus's interest in him. "I once pushed Metellus into a river, sir. I did it because he deserved it."

"And did Geminus deserve what you did to him too?"

"What happened to Centurion Geminus wasn't justice, sir. And the person who did it is still free." He took a chance. "I've worked as an investigator in the past, sir. I could help you track down the guilty men."

Clarus snapped his writing tablet shut. "Do the honorable thing and confess, Ruso. You don't want to meet the questioners, and we don't want to have to use them on a man of your former standing. It's undignified." He turned and thumped the door with his fist. "Guards! We've finished with this man."

50

Where are your toes?" asked Tilla. "Can you show me where your toes are?"

Lucios, seated on a rug on the mud floor, grasped the end of one chubby foot and looked up for approval.

"Oh, clever boy!"

It was hard to reconcile the grinning toddler with the red-faced, screaming creature she had seen thrashing about in his mother's arms three days ago.

"Now where is your hair? Where's Lucios's hair? Shall I show you?"

The wispy blond hair was duly located and admired. "How about your ears? Oh, look! There they are! Two ears!"

Tilla hoped his mother would be back soon. The child was barely old enough for stories, she was running out of games and she would be glad to get away from this place. Corinna had clearly not been pleased to come down and find her still here this morning, and was even less pleased when Tilla explained that her husband had told her to wait here for a message.

So Tilla had promised to find lodging elsewhere, and although they both knew that rooms were as rare as fish feathers in Eboracum at the moment, Corinna had thanked her and offered to pass on the message when it came. Meanwhile, perhaps Tilla would wait behind and watch Lucios while she went out to buy bread?

Tilla had duly noted that she was not to let the boy eat mud, or pull off his bandage, or go near the hearth or out of the gate (which was now barred) or up the ladder (a board was tied across the rungs to keep him off); and at the least sign of fidgeting or hiding in a corner, she was to insist that he sit on the pot.

Corinna had been gone a long time. There must be queues at the bakery, and no doubt much gossip to be exchanged after the rioting last night. Perhaps Corinna was glad of the break: Caring for a small child all day and night must be tedious. Was that how it would be if they ever had children of their own? And where would "home" be if Accius had her husband thrown out of the Legion?

She wished the message would come.

"I think," she said, "it must be time for your milk."

Lucios, easily contented, bounced with delight. While he slurped at the pointed spout—he insisted on holding the cup himself—she busied herself checking the repacked luggage. Essentials were in one bag and things that could be abandoned in the other, just in case she had to move quickly. The medicines would have to stay here until she could collect them. Corinna, whose son had benefited from them, would not begrudge her that.

She divided her small stock of coins into three. Some went back into the purse that she would tie to her belt. She glanced up to make sure Lucios was still safely occupied, then slipped others into a little linen medicine bag slung on twine around her neck, hidden inside her tunic. Then she unrolled a bandage, knotted the last remaining coins inside it, and hitched up her skirts to tie it around her waist. It was difficult to form a knot by feel, especially with the skirt fabric getting in the way, and it took several attempts, but finally she was satisfied that if she found herself traveling alone, she had done all she could to fool anyone who wanted to rob—

Lucios was not on the rug. Her heart beat faster. He was not in the room! Holy mothers, where—"Lucios?" she called, trying to sound calm. "Lucios!" She stopped. "How did you get up there?"

The toddler was balanced on the top rung of the ladder, just out of her reach. He was holding on—loosely—with one hand. The thumb of his free hand was stuffed into his mouth.

"Stay still!" she urged, untying the wretched board that was stopping her from reaching him. He must have bypassed it by climbing up the cupboard shelves. "Hold tight and don't move, I'm coming!"

By the time she reached the top of the ladder, he was waddling away across the gloomy loft, giggling as if this were a fine new game. "I can see you!" she declared, hoping her voice would frighten the rats into hiding. "Here I come!"

There was no point in being cross. It was her own fault for not watching. She hoped she could get him safely down again before Corinna came home.

The boy threw himself onto a striped bedcover laid out on the floor. She moved toward him, ready to make a grab if he tried to run but keeping a wary eye on the dark expanses under the eaves lest something should scurry out. A misshapen pile hidden by an old gray blanket looked particularly suspicious, but that thing poking out from it was not moving. It was only an old sandal…

She stopped. There was nothing unusual about an old sandal in a loft, but this one had toes inside it.

Lucios had tired of the game. He held his hands out toward her. She scooped him up, then retreated carefully down the ladder, holding tight as he wriggled under her arm. As soon as they reached the ground, she carried him out onto the sunny cobbles beside the vegetable patch and placed herself in a position where she could watch the back door of the house. She sat with him between her knees and sang him a please-go-to-sleep song—not too loud, in case she missed the sound of a messenger from the fort knocking at the front.

She had heard nothing from either the door or the loft when Corinna returned. Lucios was finally asleep on a blanket in the shade, thumb in mouth and looking like a cupid in one of those dreadful paintings that decorated the stepmother-in-law's dining room in faraway Gaul.

"I am sorry I am so late," whispered Corinna, gathering up her sleeping son. "The army are out on the streets arresting people. I had to hide until they were gone."

Tilla stabbed a finger toward the thatch and whispered back, "There is someone up there!"

Corinna glanced at her, then carried the boy into the house and lowered him onto the little bed in the alcove. He wriggled and opened his eyes, then found his thumb and drifted back to sleep. She beckoned Tilla across to the dead hearth. "Please tell no one. He has nowhere else to go."

Tilla said, "It is not my business to tell. So there are no rats?"

Corinna managed a weak smile. "Just the one big one with ginger hair."

"I will leave now," said Tilla, wondering what he had overheard. "I will find somewhere else to stay."

Corinna shook her head. "You should not go yet," she said, reaching for the wicker chair. "Something very bad has happened." Sitting on the wooden bench by the ashes of the hearth, Tilla learned that the Twentieth were still here, and did not look likely to leave today.

"Geminus is dead?" Tilla was stunned. This was not how it was supposed to end.

According to Corinna, the army were stopping people to question them about last night. Anyone who did not answer in the way the soldiers wanted was being arrested and taken away.

"What about my husband? Is there any news?"

"I heard..." Corinna paused. "I heard that a doctor has been taken for the murder," she said, adding hastily, "But it might not be him."

"Of course it is him! That is why he sent no message!" Tilla sprang to her feet, grabbing the bench before it toppled behind her. "I must go to the fort!"

"Not yet." A figure was climbing down from the loft. To his wife Victor said, "How do we know she won't talk?"

"She is a friend, husband!"

It was hard to recognize this ginger-bearded man as the creature who had begged her for food and then fled across the river. The swelling had gone down and the bruises were yellow stains.

"Her man's accused of murder," he said, placing himself between Tilla and the door to the street. "She knows I'm here, and everyone knows I had no love for Geminus. How do we know she won't betray us to save him?"

Tilla drew herself up to her full height, which was not much less than his own. "Because I give you my word," she said.

"She brought her husband to help Lucios," urged Corinna.

"And if it were not for us," said Tilla, "what would have happened to you when they caught you at the river?"

Victor continued to glare at her as if he were waiting for submission, then closed his eyes. "Forgive me," he said quietly. "It is hard to know who to trust."

"Indeed," agreed Tilla. "Now, may I leave my bags here while I try to help the man who saved you and tended your son?"

"You may," he said, stepping aside. "Holy Bregans go with you."

51

No admission without a gate pass."

Tilla made another show of hunting through Corinna's basket as she stood in front of the archway of the east gate. "I am sorry," she said, scrabbling around under the onions and the wedge of cheese. "It was in here when I went out. I must have dropped it somewhere. What a nuisance."

"No admission without a gate pass," repeated the man. He was wearing the blue tunic of the Sixth Legion, so he had arrived only yesterday.

"No, of course," she agreed. "If you do not know who I am, I will wait while you send a message to the tribune."

The guard glanced across at his comrades, but they were busy arguing with an old man whose donkey had shed a load of firewood and blocked most of the entrance. He said, "Tribune?"

"Tribune Accius of the Twentieth Legion," she explained. "Tell him his house keeper Minna is at the gate and he will have a pass sent down straightaway. If you do not, his dinner will be late."

The guard's eyes narrowed. "You look like a native."

"I am the tribune's personal choice," she assured him, leaving him to decide what that might mean if he annoyed her. The other guards were still busy insulting the old man, whose only hope of clearing up his scattered load any faster was for them to stop complaining and start helping. "You could ask at the Mansio," she suggested. "Or at Headquarters. Everybody knows Minna."

The guard pursed his lips, then stepped aside. "Next time, make sure you've got your pass."

She flashed him a smile of thanks that was much more friendly than anything the real Minna would have given him, and strode into the fort past rows of loaded and abandoned vehicles as if she knew where she was going. Nobody challenged her. With all the recent comings and goings, everyone would assume that somebody else knew who she was. It crossed her mind that a Brigante woman intent on mischief might see her chance to set fire to those vehicles. Today she had more important things to think about.

A slave carrying a basket of loaves on his head gave her directions to the hospital. A heavily built clerk told her that Medical Officer Ruso was not available but he would see if the deputy was free. While she waited outside the office, wondering what she was doing in the fort and how she was going to get back out again, an orderly arrived to deliver linen to the room opposite. She caught a glimpse of a pale figure propped up on pillows. She hoped it was Austalis, because as far as she could see, the figure still had both arms. When she found her husband, she must remember to tell him that. It would be a small piece of good news.

A couple of men dragged a creaking basket of soiled linen all the way along the tiled corridor and disappeared around the corner at the far end. A group of Praetorian guards strolled past. They had the loud voices and confident laughter of men who thought they were more important than anyone they might be disturbing. Tilla kept her head down, and if anyone paid her any attention, she was not aware of it.

The clerk had been gone a worryingly long time when a short young man with dark curls appeared and said, "I'm Pera. Were you looking for me?"

There were times when it was necessary for a woman to shut herself in a room with a man who was not her husband, no matter how alarmed that man might look, and this was one of them. When she told him who she was, he looked even more alarmed. She said, "I need to know what has happened to him."

Pera reached up and rubbed the back of his neck as if it were aching. When he spoke, it was only to confirm her fears.

She said, "Have they hurt him?"

"I don't know. They wouldn't let me visit. I heard the Praetorian prefect's taken charge of the investigation."

"Perhaps he will be fairer than Accius."

"They're talking about a trial before the legate in Deva."

"But he did not do it!"

Before he could reply, the door crashed open. Four legionaries appeared. The one in front demanded, "Name?"

Tilla had been expecting this. She told them who she was, and they marched her away down the corridor. Out in the street, she turned. Pera was standing in the doorway, still watching her.

Accius was looking just as fierce as before, but this time there was no Minna pretending to darn socks in the corner: just the guard at the door, and some sort of secretary with a stylus at the ready.

The tribune's gaze wandered over her as if he were assessing an animal for breeding or slaughter.

It was no good hoping he would be merciful. She had met ambitious men like Accius before. They were so busy watching every move of the people they were trying to impress that they did not notice who they were trampling on.

Finally he spoke. "Were you both born fools, or has he become one because of you?"

"Sir, I am sorry you have lost a relative. But my husband did not kill him."

The scowl deepened, as if he was not used to being spoken to frankly by women. "The Medicus has chosen his own fate," he said. "You need not share it."

She was careful to keep her voice steady. "What do you advise, sir?"

Accius rose from his chair and advanced toward her. "I advise you to obey me in future."

The secretary was so still against the wall that he might have been painted on it. Accius was only a pace away now. He reached out one hand and lifted a curl from her ear. His breath smelled of wine. "I have been watching you," he said. "I am told that you native women will bed any man who takes your fancy, and have no shame."

Holy mothers, he must have spoken to Sabina! She must stay calm. She must *think*. He was trying to frighten her. If she gave way, what would it gain her? He was not the one in charge of the investigation, but he could still make trouble for them both. "Sir," she said, "you were advise—" No, that was wrong. She tried again. "You advised me well before. My duty is to my husband."

"A man of his rank does not have a wife."

Before she could stop herself, she said, "And a woman of my rank does not let the army decide who she is married to!"

She waited for the blow to land. You did not challenge a man like this. You appealed to his vanity. "Sir," she said quickly, "you are an honorable man. I know you will want justice for the death of the centurion."

He gripped her by the shoulders. "Your husband tried to step over me to get to the emperor."

She swallowed. "He did not kill Geminus, sir."

Forcing her back against the wall, he said, "Nobody insults me like that."

"Sir, he was with the doctors last night, and then he was with me."

One hand was groping her breast. "We both know that's a lie."

"Sir, I beg you—"

But it was not her who made him pause. It was the secretary, tapping on his shoulder. "Sir! Please, sir!"

"What?" snapped Accius.

For a moment Tilla thought the secretary might be a decent man who had chosen to rescue her. But what had saved her was an urgent summons from the emperor. The secretary even asked Accius if they should keep the woman here until he returned.

"Don't bother. I don't have time to waste on native whores."

She took a deep breath. "Sir, I will try to find out who really killed the centurion."

"What?"

"The local people will not talk to your soldiers, but they talk to me."

The fierce gaze was leveled straight at her. "Stay out of army business," he said. "If I catch you near any of my men, you'll be executed. Guards!" The door opened. "Take her away."

52

It was not until the soldiers pushed her out of the east gate that Tilla noticed the state of the streets she had hurried through earlier. Parts of Eboracum's civilian quarter stank of urine and looked as though they had been battered by a terrible storm. Flowers and weeds alike were trodden flat. A couple of people were wandering about with buckets, picking up broken glass for remolding. A slave was washing vomit from a wall and two men were removing a shutter that looked as though someone had punched a hole in it. Opposite the temple of Mithras, a thin trail of smoke still rose from a mess of stark black timbers. A man and a barefoot woman stood in front of the wreckage. The woman was crying. Tilla moved on.

As ordered, she would not talk to soldiers. But as for keeping out of army business . . . well, the murder of Geminus was her business too now.

She soon found there was no shortage of people eager to tell her what had happened last night. Many had damage to property or to themselves to show her. For a lucky few, the outrage was soothed by a good evening's takings, but for most, it had been a costly night. For some, the worry was not over yet. They were now waiting for news of relatives who had been hauled in this morning for questioning.

The trouble was, nobody could tell her anything useful about Geminus. Most people assumed he had been killed by another soldier. Few seemed surprised. And as several people pointed out, all soldiers looked alike in the dark.

According to the sleepy girls behind the bruised but defiant doormen at the bar, soldiers didn't all feel alike, but none had seen or felt Geminus last night. None seemed at all sorry about it, nor about what had happened to him. Tilla was fairly certain they were telling the truth.

While she was there, the small boy appeared with a stack of kitchen pans and seemed pleased that the lady whose bags he had carried had come back to visit his mother. Tilla promised two sestertii to be shared between him and any of his friends who could give new information about Geminus's death. With luck, all the children in the town would now be hot on the trail, and a message would arrive at Corinna's house if there was any news. Tilla was slightly uneasy about this part of the arrangement with Victor hiding there, but she could not think of anyone else to trust.

Slipping into the mansio by the side door, she managed to snatch a brief word with the slave of one of the visiting eastern ambassadors. The man spoke just enough Latin to swear that the visiting slaves had huddled indoors, protecting their masters. Nobody had seen any centurions or men with knives, thank the gods.

The gardener looked up from weeding the rose bed, hoped she had found no more pigs' heads, and asked if there might be any more mandrake. Tilla would have fetched the whole bottle if it would have released more information, but the gardener knew nothing about the murder. He had enough troubles of his own with that lot (here he glared at the eastern slave) pinching herbs and pissing in the flower beds.

Before she could escape, the manager appeared, asked after her health, and ordered her to leave in a manner so polite that it almost sounded as though he were sorry. He had not seen Geminus, and his guests and staff had already been questioned by the authorities. He was not able to allow her in at the moment. The guests' privacy had to be respected and the staff were very busy.

"When will they not be busy?"

The manager took a firm grip of her arm and steered her toward the street door. "My staff are always busy."

Tilla moved on down the street. Nobody had anything useful to offer until a sallow-faced woman filling a water jar at the fountain told her that a man had been seen skulking around the ditch in a suspicious manner. He was wearing a red cloak "to hide the blood." This became less credible when she added, "He had a bloodstained surgeon's knife in his hand."

"You saw all this in the dark?"

"Not me. A friend of someone I know."

"Is the friend here now?"

"No."

"Perhaps the person who told you?"

"Why do you want to know?"

"Because my own man will be executed if I do not find out who did this."

"You're the wife!" The woman snatched up her jar and backed away. "I can't help you. Nobody knows anything."

"If nobody knows anything," Tilla called after her, "then stop spreading rumors!"

The shopkeeper's small daughter was helping by passing him the nails one by one while he hammered a diagonal strut across a broken door shutter. He recognized Tilla and offered his sympathies on the Medicus's arrest.

"He did not do it. Does anyone know who did?"

The man assured her that they knew nothing at all.

"No," added the small daughter. "We're not going tell anybody. My da says so."

Tilla laid a hand on the arm clutching the hammer. "Shall we talk in private?"

The truth, once she had managed to extract it from him, was nothing to do with Geminus. Last night drunken looters had smashed their way into his shop, seized anything that took their fancy, and flung at him anything that didn't. While he was begging them to stop, one of them began to climb the ladder to where his wife, his children, and his day's takings were hidden in the loft. The shopkeeper tried to drag him away. Meanwhile, the wife leaned down and cracked the looter over the head with a chamber pot. The man fell senseless to the floor. The others ran off, leaving the shopkeeper and his wife to decide that the safest thing was to haul the dazed man away and dump him outside the temple of Mithras. "I went to look for him this morning," said the man, "but he'd gone."

Tilla surveyed the chaos of broken furniture and cabbage leaves. "I am sorry for your troubles."

The heroine of the chamber pot appeared from somewhere at the back of the shop. "It could be worse." She retrieved an onion and a shoe from under the counter. "Anything worth having was already sold, and they didn't stay long enough to find the money."

"We didn't mean to hurt him," the man said.

The woman said, "*I* did."

The man ignored her. "We don't want to lead off on the wrong foot with the new legion."

"I think," said Tilla, "that he and his friends will say nothing. They know they should not have been here."

"That's what I told him," the woman agreed. "But he likes to worry."

"But they will ask you about the dead centurion," Tilla warned them. "You need to have the girl better trained. Never mind what she is not to say. Think what they might ask, and get her to practice what she will answer."

As she was leaving she heard the woman's voice rise from the back of the shop, "What do you mean, 'much too hard'? Next time, *you* do it!"

53

Ruso shifted in the chains, wincing as the stiff muscles in his neck and shoulders were forced into movement. He wriggled his fingers to bring the blood back, then wriggled them again to disperse the stabs of pain as the feeling returned. What if the injury was permanent? What use was a surgeon with damaged fingers? What use were any sort of fingers if they cut his head off? He shifted his elbows, shrugged his shoulders up toward his ears, clenched and unclenched his fists, and wondered what time it was.

Daylight still bloomed around what passed for a window, but from where he sat with his back against the cold wall, it was as distant as the stars. He closed his eyes. There was nothing to do in here but worry and drift into a fitful sleep, and he knew which he preferred.

Sometime later, as he was floating back to reality, it dawned on him that there were two sandaled feet on the floor in front of him. The pain in his neck and shoulders as he looked up should have jerked him awake, but when he saw who the feet appeared to belong to, he realized this was one of those deceitful, half-coherent dreams that seemed like waking: the sort that the mind sometimes recalled as real even when reason proved they could not be. He blinked. The figure was still there.

"Valens?" The sound of his own voice startled him. Could a man hear his own voice in his dreams?

His old friend and colleague looked down at him with an expression of pity. "Gaius."

This was definitely wrong: Valens was up on the border with the procurator, and nobody outside the family ever called him Gaius.

He tried closing his eyes and opening them again. Above him, the light from the window caught lines on the handsome face that Ruso had never noticed before. Valens looked tired and anxious. That was all wrong too.

Ruso squirmed against the wall and felt the ridges of the stones. If this was not a dream, what was it? A vision? Why a vision of Valens, of all people? Why not a god, or someone useful? Struck by a sudden fear, he said, "Are you dead?"

"No."

This was not entirely reassuring. Valens was alive, and he himself was seeing things.

The vision spoke again. "I've come to try and help you."

"Can you take these chains off?"

It shook its head. "Sorry, old chap. I did ask, but they said no."

Ruso supposed that an apparition's claim to have had a chat with his guards was no more surprising than its initial appearance.

It crouched in front of him. A pair of bleary dark eyes looked deep into his own as if they were searching for his soul. "Gaius, do you realize—"

"Why are you calling me Gaius?"

"Sorry. Ruso. I just thought, since you were a little confused, the family name might—"

Ruso said, "I know what my name is!" before it struck him that if he was rude to the vision, it might disappear. "Sorry."

It brushed away the musty straw with a remarkably realistic swish of a hand and sat on the floor beside him. "You do realize, don't you, that the way you've been behaving lately is rather ... odd?"

"It seemed like the right thing at the time."

"Of course. Look, old chap, you probably don't know this, but your mind has gone."

"Has it?"

"Yes. You're quite crazy. But don't worry. These things often pass with the seasons. In the meantime I'll tell them that you're not quite yourself at the moment."

Ruso closed his eyes and recalled several patients who had seemed to be living in a different reality from everyone else—a reality that, to them, had been utterly reasonable.

How would you know?

The vision got to its feet. "I'll get them to bring you some decent food. How about some fresh air? Shall I recommend to Clarus that they let you out for a walk?"

Ruso scratched one ear and wondered whether a vision that believed it could hold conversations with the Praetorian prefect was therefore as deluded as he was. "Yes," he said. It could do no harm.

"Excellent!" said the vision, with more of Valens's characteristic cheeriness. "And don't worry, old chap. We'll get you sorted out."

Instead of vanishing, the vision banged on the door and called, "I'm done!"

Ruso scrambled to his feet. "It *is* you! You're real! What the—Bugger these things!" The chains had jerked him to a halt.

Valens paused in the doorway. The anxious expression had returned. "Ruso, old chap . . . who or what did you think you were talking to just now?"

"I didn't murder Geminus. And I'm as sane as you are!"

Valens's very best reassuring smile would have been more reassuring if Ruso had not seen the circumstances in which he usually used it. "Of course you are, old chap. Or at least, you soon will be."

"I'm sane now! I was just half-asleep and I thought—Don't leave me here! Valens! Come back!"

But he had gone. Ruso was a lone prisoner in chains shouting at an empty space.

54

The hammering on the door was louder the second time, which was just as well, because it covered the sound of Lucios shouting, "Dada! Dada gone!" as Victor vanished into the loft. Tilla grabbed the child and swept him up into the air, whispering, "Time to play bears sleeping in the trees!" while Corinna tried to peer through a crack between the planks.

"Some Roman," announced Corinna, stepping back. "It's all right, he's gone."

Tilla wanted to say, *What if it is a message for me?* but when she opened the door, there was no one there.

They were about to sit down when someone rattled the back gate and a voice shouted in Latin, "Hello! Anyone in?"

The sleeping bear came down from the trees faster than he expected. Tilla paused to kiss him on the forehead, then rushed out of the back door, leaned across the gate, and flung her arms around the visitor. "Valens! Oh, Valens, it is good to see a friend!"

He stepped back, holding her by the shoulders and looking at her. "Tilla, dear girl, you look exhausted."

"It is not me who is in trouble, it is—"

"I know, I know. I've just seen him."

Tilla turned to introduce him, but Corinna had slipped back into the house.

Valens said, "They don't seem awfully welcoming around here. I just went to ask for you at the mansio and the chap couldn't get rid of me fast enough. Where can we talk?"

The owner of the bar brought them very watered wine with a drop of honey and some sort of hard, flat cake. He apologized for the lack of choice, but his man had gone out of town in search of supplies: The locusts had stripped everything else last night. When he had gone, Tilla leaned across the table. "You have seen him. How is he?"

Valens shook his head sadly. "It was a shock to see him in that state, I have to admit. I've recommended they improve his diet and let him out for exercise. How long has he been like this?"

"They locked him up this morning. They won't let me see him. What will happen?"

"You mustn't despair. I'm going to try and talk to some people before I leave, see if we can get him a medical discharge."

"You think they will let him out?"

"They might allow you to take him back to Gaul. He may well improve, you know. These things often burn themselves out."

She shook her head. "I know you are trying to offer comfort, and I thank you. But you have been out of the Legion for a long time. The army will not forgive something like this."

There was an awkward silence. Both picked up the unappetizing cake. Valens ventured a bite. Tilla noticed the scalded-like-a-pig woman and a friend staring at them from across the street. She waved and forced a smile, and they moved on.

Valens carried on chewing for a while, then pushed the remains of the cake away. "A whole one of those could be fatal."

Tilla remembered to ask, "What are you doing here?"

"The emperor is here, the procurator is the emperor's man, and I'm the emperor's man's doctor. We arrived this morning after a rather hasty journey. The wife would say hello if she knew I was seeing you."

So he was still calling her "the wife." It was as if he might change her at any moment and did not want the bother of remembering a new name. She said, "Please take my greetings to her and the boys."

"I have to say," said Valens, "that finding you here is one bright moment in rather a gruesome few days. I tried to persuade the procurator not to rush down here, but he insisted, even though he's not well. Politics and friendship, you know. An irresistible force. Now it looks as though we're going to be going straight back to the border again in the morning."

Tilla said, "It is a comfort to see you."

Valens nodded. "I was sorry to see poor old Ruso like that. He got quite agitated when I left."

"I think perhaps it is my fault," Tilla confessed.

"Oh, no! Never. Every marriage has its troubles, you know. If you could blame this sort of thing on the wife, I'd have been driven over the edge years ago. No, it would have happened anyway. He's lucky he has you to look out for him. But in time, with the right care, I see no reason why he shouldn't make a complete recovery."

Tilla frowned. "He is ill?"

"Dear girl, hasn't anyone told you?"

"No."

"I happened to spot him by the gates as we arrived this morning. To be frank, he wasn't looking good. So I asked around. It seems he started to think he'd been sent to inspect the entire fort. He's been breaking into buildings and spying on the maintenance crews. Countermanding other men's orders, making accusations, and... well, they should have kept a closer eye on him last night. But you don't think he would have spoken to Hadrian like that if he were in his right mind, do you?"

She wrapped her hands around the cup to stop them trembling. "There was no problem with his mind last time I saw him."

Valens gave her the look he would have given a patient who had disagreed with his diagnosis. "He looked me in the eye and asked if I was dead, Tilla."

"Oh." Gripped by a sudden worry she said, "Is he thirsty? He was bitten by a dog."

"It didn't look like hydrophobia, no."

She said, "I was the one who wanted him to appeal to the emperor. I thought it would help."

Valens looked blank. "Help what?"

It occurred to Tilla later that if the local gossips had enjoyed seeing the wife of the murderous doctor breaking bread with a handsome stranger, they must be even more excited now that stranger and doctor's wife had taken a long and unchaperoned walk together beside the river. The fact that stranger and wife kept a respectable distance would not, of course, be reported. Nor—and this was why they had gone there—would anything that they said to each other on that walk.

"So," said Valens as they passed beneath the trailing willow on their return, "if it wasn't Ruso who cut this chap's throat—which I must say I found very hard to believe when they told me—who was it?"

"Plenty of people had a reason. But it was dark, and there was a lot of fighting going on. How can anyone know which of them did it?"

Valens sighed. "He really should have left all this alone until you got back to Deva. The recruits would have backed him up once the centurion wasn't in a position to frighten them anymore."

"He saw the boy jump from the roof," she said. "And he was angry about the boy who might lose his arm. He could not stand by and watch a patient being treated that way. His student had the courage to write a report, and he did not want to let him down."

Valens's smile was brief but as handsome as ever. "He just can't resist taking on other people's problems, can he?"

"No," said Tilla. "That is why I like him."

55

He had tried shouting for Valens, but nobody took any notice apart from the guard, who yelled back that if he didn't shut his face, they would come and do it for him. So he sat listening to the distant bellow of orders, the scrape of boots on stone, low voices outside, and the occasional sneeze. They should have sounded the change of watch by now. Perhaps he had missed it while he was asleep. Perhaps he had been too busy shouting.

He tried not to think about Tilla, waiting for a message that would never come. There was nothing he could do for her except try to keep her out of this. He should have stayed out of it himself.

Valens was going to tell everyone he was out of his mind.

Perhaps he was.

He squinted up at the window. Was the light fading, or was he imagining it? He squirmed, careful not to knock over the bucket as he tried to arrange the blanket around his shoulders. He supposed he could lie down if he slid the chain through the ring so one hand was in the air. Maybe they would take the cuffs off at night.

Maybe they wouldn't.

Maybe they would feed him.

Maybe the water was all he would get. He should have saved some.

He tried the diversion of reciting all the bones in the body, working down the left side to the toes and then back up. Each toe and finger separately, just to waste time. He lost his place somewhere in the right hand.

Footsteps outside. Someone sneezed as the lock scraped open.

Ruso's hopes of explaining everything to Valens were dashed by the sight of a nondescript figure in a plain tunic who could have passed almost anywhere unnoticed. Unfortunately there was no avoiding him here, and he was the only person Ruso could think of at the moment whom he did not want to see.

Metellus waited until he heard the lock fall into place. "Ruso."

This did not seem to require an answer.

"Your friend is doing his best to convince them you're insane."

"No doubt hampered by my history of violence to fellow officers."

Metellus was either smiling or baring his teeth: It was hard to tell in the gloom. "I felt the events of our last meeting were relevant to the case."

"I'd do it again."

"You aren't helping yourself, Ruso."

"Get me out of here. You know I didn't do it."

Metellus shook his head. "Sadly, I know nothing at all. I wasn't there. And as I'm sure I must have explained to you in the past, it doesn't matter what really happens. What matters is what people believe. Can you imagine what it would do for discipline if the common soldiers believe a man can murder a centurion under the nose of his emperor and escape punishment by pretending to be mad?"

"If they find out that a man who's trying to help them is punished for a murder he didn't commit, that won't do much for discipline, either."

"Oh, Ruso." Metellus sighed. "Sometimes you don't seem to grasp how the world works. Those men out there won't care who gets the blame, as long as it isn't them. Believe me, if I thought it would do any good, I would vouch for you. But the Praetorian prefect needs someone to punish. And you've made yourself very unpopular here. I imagine he's keeping you stored away in case he can't find a better candidate."

"You imagine?" said Ruso. "Have you spoken to him?"

"If he wants you to know his plans, no doubt he'll tell you."

"Answer the question, you slippery bastard."

"There's no need to resort to insults. The question you should be asking is about the welfare of the lovely Tilla."

"Keep away from her."

Metellus opened both hands as if to demonstrate that he bore neither malice nor weaponry. "She has no need of my help. She has the handsome tribune to protect her now."

"Out!" The chains pulled him up short. "Get out!"

The guard must have been listening outside the door. Metellus's teeth appeared for a moment, then he was gone. He had, Ruso knew, achieved exactly what he wanted. And knowing that was even more infuriating.

The substance in the bowl (he would have to slurp it or dig it out with his fingers, since he had no spoon) reminded him of the slop they had been feeding to Austalis. The surface had the texture of goatskin with wet cowpat underneath.

He put it to one side. Stretched out and with his pelvis twisted to one side, he managed to kick the door. "Hey! You with the sneeze?"

No reply, but was that the scrape of a footstep outside the door?

"When you get off duty, go over to the hospital and ask them to give you some bay leaves to sniff. Keep your eyes shut when you do it."

No reply.

"And while you're over there, tell them to get the procurator's doctor to look at Austalis."

Still no reply.

He had done his best. He sat back and contemplated the contents of the bowl, wondering how long it would be before he was hungry enough to eat it.

56

The cell was dark and the slop still untouched when a more welcome visitor than Metellus arrived. Blinking in the lamplight, Ruso said, "I'm quite sane, you know."

"I know," said Valens, lowering the lamp to inspect the floor before committing himself. "Tilla explained. But I'm sticking to the diagnosis. It's your best chance."

"How is she?"

"Worried about you." Valens tugged across enough of the rough gray blanket to sit on.

Ruso felt the warmth of his friend's shoulder as they both leaned back against the wall in the cramped space. "I want you to take her with you when you go."

"It won't come to that."

"Just in case."

Valens said, "She won't want to come."

"Use your charm on her. It works on every other bloody woman."

Valens delved into the folds of his tunic and pulled out something wrapped in cloth. "I brought you this."

While Ruso gnawed the meat from a chicken leg and wished it had belonged to something bigger—a turkey, a swan, an ostrich, a horse—Valens explained the plans that he was no longer important enough to be told.

"Practically everyone's clearing out in the morning. Hadrian's taking his own people and every spare man he can find up to the wall site, but the empress says she's had enough, so she's going across to Deva to visit a friend and wait for him there."

Ruso tried to muster an interest in the imperial travel plans, and failed. "What about me?"

"I'm coming to that. Clarus will have to send half his Praetorians off with Hadrian, so they want what's left of the Twentieth to bolster the escort for Sabina. They've put some chap called Dexter in charge of the recruits. I'd imagine you'll be going with them."

At least he would be traveling with his own unit. Valens would be traveling north with the emperor's party, taking Tilla toward her own people and safely out of Accius's way. It was not good, but it was the best he could hope for. He said, "Geminus had it coming, you know. He and his pals were putting the recruits into danger and betting on the outcomes. Then they tried to silence the complainers."

"I know."

"Did Tilla say if she'd found out anything useful?"

"Not yet. Clarus's men are pressing on with the questioning tonight, but they don't seem to be getting anything sensible out of anyone, either. It was dark, and there was a riot."

Ruso supposed he ought to be grateful that Clarus was bothering to investigate at all, although his witnesses would not be. People who knew nothing did not suddenly discover the truth just because they were frightened of pain. They became people who made things up, and the more desperate the witnesses, the more false signposts began to clutter the road to understanding.

"I'd imagine they all want it to be me," Ruso observed. "None of the commanders will want his own men blamed, and the Sixth won't want to start here by executing any of the locals." He frowned. "In fact, if I weren't myself, I'd be hoping it were me too."

Valens did not contradict him.

"Thanks for coming back, anyway."

"When you get out, you owe me four denarii. I had to give the guards one each."

"You were robbed."

"I know. And I can't stay long. The procurator has a bad attack of gout and he's exhausted after rushing down here. I need to be around if he calls me."

Ruso swallowed. Valens had his own duties. It would be neither appropriate nor dignified to grab him and beg him not to leave. Instead he said, "So you won't be a provincial much longer?"

Valens gave a modest shrug. "The wife didn't want to bring the boys up in Britannia."

"Understandable."

"If Fortune's kind to us, we'll be in Rome by autumn."

"Well done."

Valens retrieved the chicken bones and the cloth. "You're not a bad surgeon, you know. If things had gone differently…"

"I'm a better surgeon than you are," Ruso pointed out, alarmed by his friend's sudden generosity. "I always was."

"Bollocks."

Ruso smiled.

"I wish I could travel with you, old chap, really I do. I'm not happy leaving you like this. If there were something else I could do…"

You could shout louder. Tell the truth to everyone you meet. Scrawl all over the walls of Headquarters, RUSO IS INNOCENT. Harass people until they listen. Tell everyone what an evil bastard Metellus is. And tell Accius if he goes near my wife, I'll kill him. "No," Ruso said. "You've done all you can."

"You know what it's like. Always people waiting to push you aside. If I don't go with the Procurator—"

"No, absolutely. You must go. It's a good opportunity for you."

"If it wasn't for the family…"

"Of course."

They had run out of words. Perhaps Valens too blamed the awkwardness of their parting embrace on the restriction of the chains.

Ruso remembered something. “I don’t think Metellus will bother Tilla now that he’s got me locked up, but watch out for him.”

“I promise.”

Valens was on his feet, and then he and the lamp were gone.

Ruso swallowed hard and began to count bones again in the dark. Then when he reached the right elbow he stopped counting bones and began to count the number of suspects in the murder of Centurion Geminus. Out of the two thousand or so soldiers and the untold number of civilians who had been in Eboracum last night, the only ones he could definitely eliminate were the recruits, Hadrian, Tilla, and himself.

And now that he thought about it, for most of the evening he had no idea where Tilla had been.

57

Lucios saw no reason to linger in bed once he was awake, and it was barely dawn when his father carried him down the ladder and wandered about, bleary-eyed, in search of breakfast. Corinna was still asleep. Tilla, her own blanket already rolled and crammed into one of the bags, found them bread and honey. She wanted none herself. After a sleepless night her stomach felt as though someone had tied a string around it and hauled it up between her lungs. She forced herself to drink a cup of water. She was washing her face when she heard the rap at the door.

Victor leapt up, handed the entire honey jar to a surprised Lucios, and vanished into the loft. Tilla managed to trade the jar for the honey spoon before there was a sticky and costly mess, and waited. The knocking came again, followed by a child's voice calling in Latin, "Message for the doctor's woman!"

When she opened the door, the boy from the brothel held out a grubby hand.

Tilla reached for her purse. "Come in! What have you found?"

"The man says you got to come with me, quick."

"Which man?"

"I got to help carry your things."

"What has this to do with the centurion?"

The boy shrugged.

"Where did you get this message?"

"At the north gate."

"Did the man give you his name?"

The boy closed his eyes. His lips moved as he recited the message, trying to remember. The eyes opened. The words "Doctor Val—" ended in a squeak as a rough forearm clamped around his throat.

They threw Tilla against the door frame. They pushed past her in a confusion of helmets and armor, yelling, "Out! Everybody out!"

Corinna was shouting for Lucios above the crash of furniture being overturned.

"Stop!" Tilla grabbed the nearest arm. "Stop it!"

He did not even turn. The arm shook free, swung back, and hit her on the nose. She staggered sideways, gasping with the pain, her eyes filling with tears. "Stop, please!" she cried again, groping blindly with one hand and shielding her face with the other. She could hear the child howling with fright. "Lucios, where are you?"

Footsteps above her. Corinna screaming. A confusion of angry voices. Thuds, cries of pain—Victor with "Don't touch my family!" and Corinna with "Let him go!"—and then they were gone, leaving Corinna shouting into the street, "Be brave, husband!" and then "Rot and die in pain, you filthy cowards!"

She gave a squeal of terror as the footsteps came back. There was a dreadful moment with a soldier standing in the doorway and no sound but Lucios whimpering and the slow drip of liquid from a broken container. At last Corinna said, "What ever you want. Don't hurt the boy," but Tilla could see well enough now to know that it was not Corinna the man wanted: It was herself.

She straightened up. He was wearing the tunic of the Twentieth Legion, but he was not someone she recognized.

"Are you the doctor's woman?"

A few days ago she might have expected her husband's unit to protect her. Now she was just another native. She should have said something brave like *Where have you taken that man?* but all that came out was a little squeak of "Yes."

He nodded. "Sorry about that, miss, but the tribune thought if we warned you, the prisoner might run off. He said to thank you for your help."

Tilla stared after him, still stunned by the blow in the face, unable to understand what he meant.

"It was you?" cried Corinna.

Tilla turned just in time. The slap only half caught her. Corinna made another lunge and missed. Tilla was out of the door before she could try again. Moments later, one of her bags flew out into the street, accompanied by "Get out and stay out, treacherous bitch!"

Tilla stepped backward, dazed. Even at this hour there were more than a dozen people in the street, staring at her. "It wasn't me!" she said, looking around at them. "I didn't betray him!"

The second bag landed at her feet. Corinna shrieked, "Get away from my son!" and kicked the medicine box, which was too heavy to throw.

One of the onlookers took a step forward. Tilla recognized the scalded-like-a-pig woman, who said, "It was all right here till you and your man started interfering."

"That's right," agreed another voice. "Clear off."

The others were advancing toward her now.

Sensing a movement, she spun round, grabbing for her knife.

It was the boy. He heaved up one of the bags and balanced it across his thin shoulders. "Shall we go now, miss?"

58

The sun was up by the time they reached the north gate. The bags seemed much heavier than when they had set out. Tilla and the boy struggled through the chaos of vehicles and pack animals. Everyone from armorers and ambassadors to jugglers and souvenir sellers seemed to be planning to set off for the border in the wake of the great man. She recognized the two junior officers who had been Geminus's shadows. They looked somehow less frightening now that Geminus was not there to give them orders. She guessed they were heading north, safely away from the recruits who might want revenge.

There was no sign of Valens. A Praetorian who had clambered up onto a cart waved them away. He was busy trying to organize drivers whose vehicles were crammed too close to move no matter how much they were yelled at. Someone told them that the procurator's carriage was still inside the fort. The informant had no idea where—or who—the procurator's doctor was.

Eventually she heard someone calling her name. Before she could respond, several bored travelers took up the cry. There was a mocking chorus of "Tilla! Hey, Tilla! Come on Tilla, you're late!" and a round of applause when she appeared.

Valens too looked as if he had been awake all night. He paid off the boy and seized her bags.

She said, "Is there any news?"

"Not yet." He lifted the bags into the air, maneuvering past a stall where a couple of foreign-looking slaves were haggling over the price of coats with hoods to keep the rain off. Finally he deposited them in the back of a worm-eaten two-wheeler that smelled of sheep. Its lone mule was being held by a boy not much older than the one who had just brought Tilla here. "This is Celer," announced Valens. "He's promised me he's a safe driver. I'll pop back and see you whenever I can."

"But where—"

"Ruso's fine," said Valens. "I saw him last night. He sends his good wishes." Drawing back from the cart, he murmured, "Sorry about this, but it's all I could find. You should be all right: The mule doesn't look capable of running off."

"But where is it going?"

"We're traveling with the emperor," he said, as if he had just told her something good. "Well, a little behind him, actually."

"But where is—"

"I promised Ruso I'd look after you."

"But—"

He seized her by the elbow. "Jump in," he urged. "Get yourself comfortable. The emperor should appear at any moment and then we'll be off."

She stood her ground. "What about—"

"He's with the Twentieth. Give me your arm—"

"We are following the emperor while my husband is going west to Deva?"

"Please get in the cart, Tilla."

"The emperor is going north, to where his wall cuts my people's land in two."

"You'll be able to see your family. How long has it been?"

"But I have to go where my husband goes."

"Dear girl, you don't understand. He doesn't want you there. He made me promise to take you with me." Valens flashed her one of his charming smiles. "You don't think I'd dare to argue with you otherwise, do you?"

She almost smiled back. "You are very kind, but—"

"Tilla, if you don't get in this cart, what are you going to do?" His voice hardened. "They won't let you near him. You'll be alone with several hundred men. He's got no authority anymore and you haven't even got a maid to protect you. This isn't the time to be stupidly brave. This is the time to think, *Poor old Ruso has enough things to worry about, so I won't give him another one.*"

Tilla leaned back against the worm-holed boarding. "There is just me in this cart?"

"There wasn't time to find a chaperone." He gestured toward the melee of vehicles. "But as soon as that lot get moving, I'm sure you can find some local woman who needs a lift."

And you will come back and see me when you can?"

"I promised I would look after you. I intend to take my duties very seriously."

"Then I thank you for keeping your promise." She gathered up her skirts in one hand, seized the side of the cart, placed a foot on the wheel hub, and swung up without his help.

When she was in, she crouched and looked over the side at him. "Valens, did you tell the tribune anything about the people in the house where I was staying?"

He frowned. "Should I have?"

"No," she said. "But somebody did."

59

The hound guardian of the Underworld barked "Breakfast!" and the gates of Hades crashed shut.

Ruso opened his eyes, squinted at the new bowl of slop that had been placed inside the cell door, and realized with relief that he was not being crucified after all. He winced as he eased his stiff body into a new position, trying to angle his raised arms so that the cuffs bit into a different area of flesh. It provided some temporary relief.

There are eight bones in the human wrist. And not enough padding around them.

Very soon the skin would break down. There would be sores. He had tried lining the cuffs with corners of the blanket during the night, and woken up shivering.

Since the only window faced north, he had no idea what the time was, and no way of finding out.

The slop was paler than last night's offering but smelled no better, although it was hard to tell over the stench of the bucket in the corner. He hoped he would be out of here before he was starved enough to eat it.

He had tried asking the guards last night, but if they knew any more than Valens about the travel plans, they were not telling. He realized now what a privileged position he had held as an officer. Of course, he had never known the secrets that were whispered in the legate's private rooms—unless a patient happened to let something slip—but at least he had been entitled to know the official version given out at morning briefings. Now he had no information, no responsibilities, and no right to decide anything. Not even what he would eat for breakfast. From now on, unless he could find a way out of these chains, his every action would be decided by other people.

Tilla was safe: He had seen to that. He was almost certain that Valens would take his responsibility seriously, because he was a friend, and because Tilla was an attractive young woman, and because it would make Valens look like a hero, and that would please him enormously.

There were people outside his window. He caught a snatch of a discussion about the state of the roads. And then a blast from a trumpet, and a voice that said, "See you later," and he supposed Hadrian was about to set off for the border, and Tilla would be going too, and he was reminding himself to be glad about that when the guards opened up his cell and threw in a new prisoner.

⚜ ⚜ ⚜

Ruso waited until they had gone before saying, "You're Victor." It sounded better than *You're the deserter* or *I see they've caught you at last, then.*

The young man shifted until he could reach up a fist to wipe the blood trickling from his left nostril. Then he looked down at the fist, spat on it, and tried wiping again. The streak across his upper lip became a messy smear in the ginger stubble.

Ruso said, "We've met."

Victor slumped against the wall and glared at the army boots that had betrayed him at their last meeting.

"By the river at Calcaria," Ruso prompted. He was not sure why he felt responsible for lifting the youth's low spirits. He was not an officer anymore. Still, a gloomy companion could lower a man's own morale. "Have you any idea what they're doing with us?"

Victor glanced up from his feet. "Leave me alone."

Ruso closed his eyes and leaned back. If the youth wanted to sulk, he was not going to argue. Some people did not want to be cheerful. At the moment he was one of them himself.

An hour passed, or half an hour, or two hours: It was hard to mark the space between the watches when they were punctuated only by the use of the bucket and the frequent need to change the position of his arms. With every passing moment, the absence of a parting message from Tilla became more apparent.

So did his disappointment. It seemed Valens's charm had been so persuasive that she had forgotten about him entirely.

"It was your woman, wasn't it?"

Victor's words startled him out of his thoughts. "What?"

"I knew we were fools to trust her."

"What was my woman?"

"Sneaky little cow. Sits by our hearth, eats our food, and this is the thanks we get."

"You think Tilla betrayed you?"

"Who else?"

"Almost anyone else," said Ruso.

"Well, it didn't work. They haven't let you out."

"Not Tilla," insisted Ruso, but in the silence that followed he began to wonder if he was wrong. Perhaps there was hope. Tilla would never have betrayed the husband of a friend for desertion—but for murder? It was possible. If Victor had been hiding in Eboracum with his family, he could have seized the chance to take revenge on Geminus under the cover of darkness. Perhaps her message was already here, sitting in front of him, while she was negotiating his freedom.

He felt the muscles in his shoulders relax until a stab of pain from his right wrist reminded him of where he was, and that there was still the business of the insubordination. He could, in theory, be executed for that as well. Perhaps that was why they were keeping him here even though Victor had been caught.

"Up!" roared a voice outside the cell door. The lock rattled. The door burst open. Had they come to release him?

"Shift your arses, the pair of you. We don't want the bother of burning your stinking carcasses here. They can do it on the road."

60

There were cheers—perhaps of relief—from the waiting travelers when the soldiers finally cleared the road and the emperor rode out of the north gate of Eboracum. Valens, mounted on a gray horse behind a gleaming carriage, drew admiring glances from some of the local women as he passed through the crowd who had come back to take a second look at the emperor. He caught sight of Tilla seated in the cart and gave a nod of approval. She smiled, knowing the women were looking at her with envy. A woman from these islands who had a man in the imperial party!

If only they knew.

Once the official travelers had set off, the soldiers who were not escorting them marched back inside the fort. The locals scattered. The civilian vehicles made a brief surge forward... and stopped. Nobody seemed to know what was causing the holdup.

Celer tied the reins, jumped down, and ran ahead. Moments later he returned with the news that two wagons had gone for the same gap and were now blocking the road with their wheels locked together. Tilla yawned and rolled up her blanket to make a pillow. This was going to be a long wait. She had grown used to the sheep smell, and there was nothing to do now but sleep.

It seemed only moments later that she was jolted awake. Pulling herself up, she peered over the side. The walls of Eboracum were growing smaller behind them, and her husband was farther away with every bump in the road.

He doesn't want you there. He made me promise to take you with me.

Was this how it ended? With him sending her away?

She curled up again. The sun would bring out the freckles on her nose. It was hard to care. It was hard to sleep too. Finally she gave up and opened her eyes. A figure was sitting beside her in the cart. She blinked. The figure was still there. "Virana?"

"You were asleep," said Virana, as if that excused her inviting herself into someone else's vehicle.

"But what are you doing here?" The pink dress was looking cleaner than before, and as the cart lurched and Virana grabbed the side to steady herself, Tilla could see that the hole was bigger. "Does your mother know where you are?"

Virana wrinkled her nose. "She told me to go away."

Tilla sat up straight. "She didn't mean this far. Get down and go straight home."

"Is it true they've arrested the doctor and Victor and they might cut their heads off?"

"Go home!"

"Corinna wouldn't talk to me. She's upset about Victor."

"Yes."

"She said you were a treacherous bitch. I told her you weren't."

"You are right and she is wrong. Now, go home."

Virana pouted. "I've got money. I can buy my own food."

"Get down!" This was worse than talking to a dog.

Tilla was too busy arguing to notice the roan mare that had drawn up alongside them, and was startled when its rider wished her a good journey. It was another traveler she did not wish to see.

Metellus indicated the road ahead. "North. I think you've made a very wise choice."

Tilla lifted her chin and tried to ignore Virana staring at Metellus with her mouth open. "Was it you who betrayed Victor?"

"Was that his name?"

"Have you been watching me?"

Metellus shook his head sadly. "If only I had the time. I confess I had quite lost interest in you until I heard someone was claiming to have had secret meetings with the empress."

"The empress and I talked about nothing!"

Metellus nodded. "So I hear. But occasionally a surveillance of one person happens to turn up someone else of interest. The informant who was keeping an eye on you started to wonder why the deserter's wife was buying so much food if she was only feeding two women and a toddler."

So that was how it had been done. Corinna would be mortified. She said, "The men who took him came back specially to thank me for betraying him."

"Yes." If a snake could smile, that was what it would look like. "That was a nice touch, I thought." He dug his spurs into the roan's flanks and it sprang forward, taking him away before she could think of a curse foul enough.

"He is not a nice man," observed Virana. She watched the roan ease through a gap. "He is quite good-looking, though."

"Get down, before you have a long walk back."

"You can't throw me out on the road. I'm your patient: You have to look after me."

"We are barely out of Eboracum. And we aren't going to Deva."

"I don't mind."

Tilla half rose, stabbing a forefinger at the ground. "Down! Right this moment, or I will throw you out."

Virana slumped into a corner and folded her arms. "I don't mind not going to Deva. There will be plenty of soldiers at the border."

Tilla leaned forward. "Celer, pull off the road!"

The lad turned. "Here, miss?"

"Anywhere we won't get stuck."

⚜ ⚜ ⚜

Stopping was no problem, but Celer had been hired to follow the emperor and needed to be offered several half-truths and more money before he agreed to turn the cart around. Finally the road cleared of riders and baggage wagons and the number of pedestrians thinned out. Celer was able to swing the mules out onto the hard surface and bring the cart around. Meanwhile Tilla had made two skinny little girls repeat her message in their mother's hearing before handing them a small coin each and promising there would be more when the job was done. "We give him the scroll," they chanted, "and we say, 'Tilla thanks you, Doctor Valens. She says she is not traveling alone and may the gods give you good health and a safe journey,' and we do not tell him until everyone stops for a rest at midday."

Talking was so much quicker than writing. The mother, who was carrying a toddler on her shoulders and now a scroll of Catullus's poems in one hand, seemed grateful for the cash. She hurried the family away to catch up with their luggage.

"You have a choice now," Tilla hissed to Virana as Celer urged the mule back the way they had just come. "You learn to keep quiet and do as you are told, or I take you home again."

"I can keep quiet."

"And leave me alone when I tell you to. I will have things to do that are private, and I cannot always have you trailing around with me like a strand of goose grass."

"What things will you have to do?"

Tilla rummaged in her bag for a spare tunic. "First, I will hold the blanket around you while you put something sensible on."

"Where are we going?"

"Wherever my husband goes," said Tilla.

"Oh, yes!" agreed Virana as she disappeared inside the blanket. "That is exactly what I would do. And I can help you with all the private things!"

61

The Praetorians were streaming out of the fortress in the sunlight like one huge shining creature with many legs. The barbs of spears rose above their glittering helmets like bristles.

"So fierce!" gasped Virana, as if it were a good thing. "What do we do now?"

"More waiting."

"Then what?"

"I don't know yet." Leaving her husband to face trouble alone would be very wrong. Knowing what was right was more difficult.

The carriage that must hold the empress was enormous, pulled by six black horses whose coats gleamed almost as brightly as the freshly washed paintwork. No doubt there would be soft beds inside so the wealthy passengers could rest while everyone else was out in all weathers, escorting them safely across lands where they had no business to be.

"Here they come!" cried Virana. The sound of jingling and clanking pots and pans accompanied the march of the men from the Twentieth: The

Praetorians must have commandeered the baggage wagons, while the Twentieth had all their personal kit slung on their backs or loaded onto mules. Tilla recognized Accius on a leggy bay stallion. The squat centurion riding alongside him was Dexter, friend of the murdered Geminus.

Virana was enjoying herself. "There's Marcus, and... Victor! Victor, it's me! Cheer up!" She turned to Tilla. "They've chained him up like a slave! Do they think he'll run away again?" Before Tilla could answer, she said, "I can't see the Medicus, can you?"

Tilla raised one hand and pointed to a covered wagon that had just emerged from the gates. Behind it was a figure whose bearing and boots said he was a soldier. The loop of chain between the back of the wagon and his wrists told another story. Tilla leapt down from the cart, waited until Dexter was shouting at a man who had dropped something, and then ran across the rough grass toward the wagon.

"Husband!"

He seemed to be concentrating on the uneven stones beneath his feet.

She fell into step with him. "It is me!"

He looked startled, as if he had just woken. "What are you—"

"I am not leaving you."

He glanced around. "Careful. They'll be watching."

"Are you all right? Your hands—"

"Valens was supposed to look after you."

"He did. He does not know yet." Pale faces were peering out at her from the gloom of the covered wagon, where a skeletal young man was lying under a white blanket. "Those are the people who should be in the grand carriage."

He said, "I'll ask the empress to swap."

She lowered her voice so that the patients could not hear. "Victor has been arrested and they say he is accused of the murder."

"I know. He says he didn't do it."

"He is telling the truth. He was hiding in the loft at Corinna's house and I was downstairs. I was awake, listening for rats: I would have heard if he had crept out. They said I betrayed him, but it was Metellus."

"Metellus?"

"He is a slimy liar. If Victor is accused, why have they not released you?"

"I don't know. Probably because Accius—"

"Get away from the prisoner!"

Something hard smacked into Tilla's upper arm. She ducked and ran, leaping across the ditch beside the road. When she turned, a centurion was striding away from her husband, who seemed a little less steady on his feet.

"Do not despair!" she called to him, half running to keep parallel with him, and stumbling in the long grass. "I will do something!"

The wagon moved on, taking him away with it.

I will do something.

What?

What could one woman do to change the mind of the army? Their only friend here—unless you counted Virana—was going north with Hadrian. Meanwhile, now that the Legion no longer recognized her marriage, she would be lucky if she was allowed to speak to anyone with influence. Even if she could, they would all support each other. Look how they had all refused to believe their own medical officer when he spoke ill of Geminus. How could a British woman get a soldier released when he was chained up not for a crime but for speaking the truth about the mistreatment of Britons?

She stood alone by the side of the road, rubbing her bruised arm and watching the lines of mules and pack ponies plodding past. She supposed they would make him walk all the way back to Deva. A hard week on the road, and then someone—Accius, she supposed—would accuse him of murder and the legate of the Twentieth Legion would decide his fate.

While the rest of the baggage train rumbled and squeaked past, she whispered a quiet prayer to Christos. The *Amen* was still on her lips when it struck her that Christos was not known for saving innocent men from suffering at the hands of the Roman Army. Perhaps she should look elsewhere.

She would find a place this evening to make an offering to the Goddess, but it had to be said that the Goddess had not done much to save her people from the Romans, either. Perhaps, if they stopped at

Calcaria, she could make a promise at a shrine to one of the army's gods.

By the time she had decided this, the orderly baggage train had given way to a straggle of hired vehicles and farm carts: slaves following their masters, and families eager not to be left behind. She stepped forward so that Celer could see her in good time to pull in. No sooner had she done so than a familiar voice cried, "That's her!"

It was the scalded-like-a-pig woman.

"Traitor!" cried a voice from another cart.

Someone spat.

"Whore!" yelled somebody else.

Tilla flinched as something more solid than spittle flew past her ear.

"Go back to your fancy man!"

Tilla felt her pulse rise. There was no sign of Corinna. The scalded-like-a-pig woman was seated on the back of a cart, legs dangling. At least, she was until Tilla grabbed both feet and pulled and the woman landed on the gravel, screaming that she was being attacked, and all her friends rushed in to defend her.

In the end, nobody was badly hurt, although clothes were ripped and dirtied and hair was torn out and somebody complained afterward that That Girl had stamped on her toe and ruined her shoe and was Tilla going to pay for it?

No, said Tilla, trying not to sound out of breath: She was not going to pay, because That Girl had only come to defend her when she had been called bad names by women who should have known better. Had she herself not helped when Corinna's son was scalded? Had she not helped Victor to escape when he was caught the first time? They did not know about that, did they? Well, perhaps they should stop name-calling until they knew what they were talking about. Perhaps, if they wanted to know who had betrayed Victor, they should start by asking the shopkeepers.

"Did you hear that, Corinna?" cried the scalded-like-a-pig woman, bold now that she was back in the safety of her own vehicle. "She's blaming the neighbors now!"

"Leave her!" Corinna, with Lucios on one hip, stepped forward from the crowd of spectators. "I will talk to the doctor's woman myself. And if anybody calls her names, it will be me."

"I was not the one who betrayed you," Tilla insisted, pulling her skirts straight and checking that her purse was still tied to her belt. "We are caught in the same storm, you and I. We should not be fighting."

"I wasn't," said Corinna. She turned to the scalded-like-a-pig woman and the others who had come to her defense.

They did not deserve to be thanked, but at least it made them go away—which was a good thing, because if they decided to have another try, Tilla was not sure how long she could hold them off. Not even with Virana's help.

With the excitement over, the crowd melted away. The vehicles set off again. The chatter and the cries of children mingled with the sound of wheels on the road and the calls of drivers urging their animals forward to catch up with the baggage train.

In the safety of their hired cart, Tilla cleaned the gravel out of a graze on Virana's elbow and put some salve on it from the medicine box. "I was glad you were there, sister," she said. "Thank you."

The girl's features were transformed. It was the smile of a child who had just been given an unexpected present. Tilla wondered if anyone had ever thanked her before. "You are a good fighter."

"I have brothers."

"I can tell," said Tilla, replacing the lid on the ointment pot. "And we must let them know where you are."

Virana's face darkened. "Must we?"

"Yes. It is not far to the turn, and we can catch up afterward." Tilla paused. "Or have you lied to me again about them sending you away?"

62

Flat-nose moved toward the gate with a limp he did not have before and glanced across to where Virana was waiting in the cart. "You're wasting your time with that one, miss."

The rude one said, "We've had enough of Romans, all right?"

"It's not her fault!" Flat-nose turned to Tilla. "We told them everything we could, miss."

"That didn't stop 'em," put in the rude one. "Sick bastards."

Tilla said, "You were questioned about the murder?"

"We saw him come out the gate," said Flat-nose, "but we never saw no doctor. Not that I know of. Unless he were one of them fellers with the scorpions."

"A Praetorian?"

"That's them."

"You saw some Praetorian Guards that night?"

He snorted. "Couldn't miss 'em. All over the place like a plague of rats. Them and the new lot with the funny-speaking women."

He must mean the Sixth, some of whose families had followed them from their last posting in Germania.

"Where were you when you saw Geminus?"

The brothers glanced at each other, evidently embarrassed. Finally Flat-nose said, "In the ditch."

"Where Geminus was found?"

"No," said the rude one, "the other side of the gates. It was getting a bit lively out there. We didn't want to get stabbed, so we hid. Me and him and our mate. He's the blacksmith."

"Why did you not tell the questioners this?"

He frowned. "I did."

Flat-nose said, "So did I."

Tilla spoke slowly, just to make sure her meaning was precise. "Did you see anyone near Geminus?"

"I just told you!" The rude one was getting impatient now. "Like I told old Skinny-legs with the fancy sword. I saw the centurions come out the gate banging on their shields. I thought, *Somebody's in trouble now.* Then Geminus come out with some of them Praetorians. I don't know why that's so hard to understand."

"How many?"

"I don't know. Three or four."

"You're sure they were Praetorians? It was dark."

"They had torches."

"And that's how you recognized Geminus?"

"Nah. They all look alike with them helmets on. I heard his voice."

Tilla looked at Flat-nose for confirmation. He nodded. "It was him all right."

"What was he saying?"

"It was in Latin. Something about going into action together again."

"And then what happened?"

"We hid."

"So you didn't see what happened next?"

"No."

"What did you hear after that?"

"*Hear*?" said the rude one. This was clearly something they had not been asked before.

"You knew Geminus from his voice. You must have good hearing."

The brother sighed. "Are you going to call in a man with a whip too?"

"Shouting," suggested Flat-nose. "Grunting. Like a fight."

The rude one said, "Did you hear someone breathing funny?" They looked at each other for confirmation.

"We had a good laugh after," said Flat-nose. "Somebody had the same idea as us, see. We heard him go into the ditch the other side, only that side's all nettles."

"Did you hear him complaining?"

They looked at each other, but neither could remember any complaints. "Well, he wouldn't shout about it if he was hiding, would he?"

Or if he was dead. "And then?"

"We followed the ditch away from the gates, got out where nobody could see, and went back to our mate's workshop to sleep it off." Flatnose rubbed his leg and winced. "Then next day we all got woke up and marched in to the fort to see a man who didn't believe a word we told him."

"Romans do not believe that ordinary people will tell the truth unless they are in pain," explained Tilla. "Did you see Geminus again after that?"

"No. Well, he were dead, weren't he? Lucky they didn't throw him in our side."

"From what I hear," said the rude one. "Good riddance."

Tilla allowed herself a smile. "Yes," she said, "I think we are all better without him. Now, about your sister …"

"How much are you offering?"

"I am not offering to buy your sister!" Tilla was shocked. "I am come to ask your mother's blessing for her to travel with me to Deva. Then I will see to it that she gets safely home again."

Back at the cart, Tilla merely told Virana that she had the family's permission to go to Deva. She left out the brother's demand for money, and the fact that the mother had said she need not bother coming back.

63

One of the chief—one of the few—pleasures of long-distance marching was that it left a man alone with his thoughts. Today, however, Ruso's thoughts were not good company. It was difficult to ignore the fact that every step was taking him nearer to…He was not sure what, but it would not be good. Once they got to Deva, Clarus and Accius would report on events at Eboracum to the legate. Ruso had not had the heart, or indeed the time, to explain to Tilla that it barely mattered whether or not he was accused of murdering Geminus. Insubordination was a capital offense in itself, and there was no shortage of witnesses.

There were also mitigating circumstances, but who would listen? Accius would undermine anything he might say by forewarning the legate that the accused was a known complainer with a history of violence against fellow officers. The legate, with whom Ruso was no better acquainted than he was with the moon, would support his tribune, because that was what officers did. It was called loyalty. Ruso could think of better words.

A painful tug on his wrists brought him stumbling back to the present. He quickened his pace to keep up with the wagon and felt something shift around his left ankle. Trying to adjust his pace to get a better view, he prayed that the knot in the leather thong was just slipping and not working itself undone. If the ends came apart, the lacing would gradually loosen all the way along the boot. He would be left shuffling and hopping and trying not to leave it behind until the order came to halt for water.

He must think about something else.

At least it wasn't raining.

Inside the wagon, Austalis had his eyes closed. The patients seated along the bench had all adopted different poses, trying to brace themselves against the wheels jolting over the uneven road. Their faces spoke of boredom, although there was at least one man up there who should have been looking pleased with himself: If Ruso had been in charge instead of Pera, the slackers would have been walking. The patient at the back, a man with a torn knee cartilage, was gazing out blankly as if he had not noticed there was a doctor attached to the back of the hospital wagon.

Could a soldier appeal to the emperor? And if he could, would the emperor listen—especially when listening would be an admission that he had been wrong not to believe the soldier in the first place? Come to that, how exactly would the soldier go about getting any appeal past his commanding officers?

The boot felt no looser than before. He glanced back over his shoulder. The driver of the hospital supply wagon was keeping his mules at a safe distance, which Ruso supposed was the only kindness he could offer. Tilla would be farther back with the camp followers. He hoped she was not alone. He was in no position to protect her. He had managed to exchange a few surreptitious words with Pera, who had promised to look out for her, but Pera had other duties.

Do not despair. I will do something. The gods alone knew what bizarre plan Tilla had in mind, but what ever it was, he was glad of it. Even if it did not work—and he could not see how it could—at least she was here with him. She had been given the chance to go with Valens, and she had done what he had not dared to ask of her: She had chosen him instead.

He was still warming himself beside this small glow of comfort when the trumpet sounded the order to halt. Somewhere ahead of him, the empress would be treated to the sight of a couple of hundred men guzzling from their waterskins and lining up to pee in the ditch. Here, the not-quite-walking wounded rose stiffly to their feet and were helped out of the wagon by a couple of orderlies. One or two of them murmured, "Thank you, sir," perhaps because he had had the sense to step out of their way. Or perhaps because they could not think of anything else to say to him. What ever the reason, it was good to have his existence acknowledged.

Since nobody else seemed to be paying him any attention, he clambered awkwardly into the vehicle and shook the grit out of his boots before turning to find his former patient reaching a hand toward him.

"Sir..."

"Austalis. How are you?"

"Not too bad, sir," said Austalis, which probably said more about his mental resolve than his state of health. He should have been left in the care of the Sixth until he was stronger.

"I expect Pera will be along in a minute." Ruso was surprised he was not there now. He stretched out one manacled hand and just managed to reach the man's pulse. As he was counting, he heard the scrape of hobnails on wood behind him.

"Can I enter, sir?" Marcus, the recruit whose split lip and splendid tattoos Ruso was ashamed to realize he had forgotten, was already looming over the bed anyway.

"I'll get out," offered Ruso. "You probably shouldn't be seen talking to me. Give him some water if he wants it; there's a skin in the corner."

"Sit down, sir. We respect what you did." He turned to his friend and murmured in British, "I'd have brought you a beer, but there was nowhere to hide it."

Ruso, still in Latin, said, "You shouldn't be calling me 'sir,' either."

Reverting to Latin, the recruit said, "He deserved it, sir."

"I didn't kill anyone, Marcus. I just spoke to people."

Marcus untied the stopper and held the waterskin steady as Austalis tried to tip it with one thin hand. "Did you hear the doctor went to the emperor about Geminus?"

"It didn't turn out too well," said Ruso.

"This is what they did to him," Marcus continued to Austalis, grasping one of Ruso's arms to show the manacle.

Austalis pushed the water away. "Bastards," he said.

"They've put Dexter in charge now."

Austalis's lips moved in response. It was a moment before Ruso realized it was a mime of spitting.

Marcus said, "Sir, the men are asking what will happen to us at Deva."

Ruso hesitated. The Roman officers would find it only too easy to believe the tale that Tadius had been murdered in some wild barbarian ritual and Sulio had killed himself out of guilt. For a moment he considered warning them. But Geminus had been right about one thing: Telling the recruits they were marching into trouble would only make things worse for everyone. Instead he said, "They don't invite me to briefings these days."

"We think they will tell a story about what happened to Tadius," said Marcus, who was evidently not as naïve as he looked. "And we think they will say Victor killed Geminus."

"They may well accuse me."

"We are only recruits, sir. You are useful to them." He nodded toward Austalis, who seemed to have drifted off to sleep. "You are a good doctor."

"On reflection," said Ruso, "I think you were wise to keep those tattoos."

Marcus nodded and got to his feet. "A good choice for a bad reason, sir. We all wish you well."

"That's very good of you."

Stepping over the length of chain that stretched between Ruso and the back of the wagon, Marcus jumped down. On the ground, he turned and put both hands on the wagon floor, leaned in, and said quietly in British, "You speak our tongue, sir?"

"A little."

"I could keep you informed, if you like. We know we can trust you."

"Yes," said Ruso. "Yes, please do." He might no longer be an officer, but it seemed he had become an honorary Briton.

There was still no sign of Pera come to check on his patient. In fact, there was no sign of anyone, since the driver of the second wagon had tied the reins of his mules and left them with hay nets while he went to tend to his own needs. Ruso shuffled as far back as the chain would allow, leaned against Austalis's makeshift bed, and stretched his legs out across the rough wooden floor, listening for the plodding of a horse that might mark the arrival of someone who would punish him for resting.

He gave a guilty start when a shadow fell across the back of the wagon, but it was only Pera arriving at last. He climbed in and glanced at Austalis.

"He's had some water," said Ruso. "Fast pulse but no fever, and he's talking sense."

"Thank you, sir." Pera was evidently satisfied that he did not need to be woken. "Sir, there's a message from your wife."

Ruso sat up straight. "Is she all right?"

"She's fine, sir. She's traveling at the back with a…" Pera seemed to be considering his choice of words. "…another woman." He lowered his voice. "She said to tell you that Geminus was seen with some Praetorians just before he was murdered."

"What? Does Clarus know?"

"She said to tell you Prefect Clarus questioned the witnesses himself not long after the body was found, sir."

Ruso stared at him. "He knows? What did he do about it?"

Pera looked nonplussed.

"Sorry, that's an unfair question. I need to make sure Accius knows what you've just told me."

"She's going to try and talk to him herself."

"Right," said Ruso, pushing aside his unease about the tribune's interest in his wife.

"It might help both you and Victor, sir."

"Yes. Don't say anything to anyone else, will you?"

"Are you sure, sir? I was thinking it might raise the morale of the recruits."

"Exactly. Then the gods alone know what they would get up to."

64

Not like that!" Tilla snatched at the comb in Virana's hand. "Start at the bottom, where the tangles are smaller, or you will pull the teeth out." Virana looked surprised, as if nobody had ever suggested this before.

Tilla was surprised too. She would have expected such ignorance of an empress who only had to call a slave to have her hair attended to, but how could an ordinary girl not know this? Had Virana's mother bothered to teach her anything at all, or just shouted complaints from a distance while her children fought and argued amongst themselves like wolf cubs?

When the hair was combed, Tilla shifted back awkwardly on the seat and styled it herself, winding in a cream braid with blue edging. She pulled the knot tight so the hair was plaited for a handspan, and then hung in a neat tail down Virana's back. "That's better."

Virana pulled one end of the braid round to examine it, then fingered the beads that were hidden inside the plain brown tunic and pouted.

"What is the matter?"

"I look dowdy."

"No, you look how a Roman officer thinks a modest woman should look."

"I don't want people seeing me like this."

People, Tilla supposed, meant the recruits of the Twentieth Legion. "Do you want to meet the tribune or not?"

"Can't I just put the necklace out?"

"No. You are supposed to be my slave: You can't wear more jewelry than I do. And remember, you must stay silent about anything you hear."

"I know."

"If you whisper a single word, the gods will make sure the tribune finds out. Then he will have you tracked down by his torturers before they send you to the slave market."

"I know!"

But knowing was not doing. Of all the women Tilla had ever met, Virana was the last she would have chosen for an escort. Still, it was take Virana or approach the tribune alone, which would give him completely the wrong idea. Virana was worth the risk.

She reached into the food bag and was about to break a piece off one of the pastries she had bought from a roadside stall when a distant trumpet sounded the signal for the second halt of the day. It must be well past noon.

"That's it!" she exclaimed, pushing the pastry down into the bag. "Celer, stop a moment so we can get down. Then stay with the others and we'll come and find you later."

They hurried forward along the verge, passing the baggage wagons now strung out along the road and still moving, the drivers seizing their chance to close up the gaps and rejoin the marching troops.

She felt a surge of pride as she saw him: still striding rather than shambling like Victor, gaze fixed on the uneven road, mind probably somewhere else. She dared not call out in case it brought him more trouble. She hoped Pera had given him the message. It would give him hope.

Virana was more interested in the recruits. "There they are!" she exclaimed, pointing ahead beyond the lines of pack animals munching on their hay nets.

"Don't draw attention," warned Tilla.

"I am not!" insisted Virana. "I am only a slave. Why have they got those guards?"

Tilla was wondering the same thing herself. The recruits were sitting in formation on the ground, munching food from their packs and swigging what she supposed was watered vinegar, and which they probably wished was beer. They were surrounded by the upright figures of officers, with Dexter on horseback. When several men returned from standing by the ditch, Dexter shouted, "Right, next lot!" and another squad rose to relieve themselves. Tilla, who had trailed behind many a military unit on the move, had seen plenty of guards posted during meal breaks, but they had always been looking outward for possible enemies. They had never been turned in to watch the men who were supposed to be their comrades.

Both the Praetorian Guards and the small group of older soldiers of the Twentieth who were returning to Deva were more relaxed. Some were asleep. A few were clustered around some sort of game with counters. Another was whittling a stick. All were evidently enjoying their few minutes of rest in the sunshine.

Sabina's carriage, meanwhile, was surrounded on one side by folding screens. Slaves were trotting back and forth between the screened-off area and the supply carriage behind, carrying trays with cloths over them. "She has proper tables!" hissed Virana as the straight-backed Praetorians on guard glared at them from under their helmets. "You can see through the gaps. Did you see the silver wine flagon? If this is how she eats on a journey, what will dinner be like?"

Tilla could not imagine. It seemed the empress did not share her husband's taste for eating simple fare with his soldiers. She hoped Accius was not behind those screens, helping to empty the wine flagon. He would not want to be called away to be told something that was only going to cause him more trouble. The problem was she could not see him anywhere else.

He had definitely dismounted: The bay stallion was in the line of horses under a stand of trees. She and Virana hurried along the verge, trying to search the crowds of men without appearing interested.

Still, they attracted remarks that she pretended not to hear. Eventually they had to turn and retrace their steps, silently grateful to an officer who barked at his men to shut up and show some manners: Did they want the empress thinking she was guarded by a herd of animals?

The speech about manners might have usefully been given to Minna too. She was bustling toward the screens with a jug of something when she stopped and announced loudly enough for the whole lunch party to hear, "There's the prostitute from the mansio!"

Tilla heard Virana draw breath to reply and jabbed her with one elbow. "You are mistaken," she said, approaching and deliberately speaking a little more quietly than Minna, because with luck around them everyone was listening now. "This young woman you have insulted is my assistant. I am the wife of the Medicus, as you well know, and we are bringing the medicine requested by the tribune." She held out the bottle, chosen not because it was anything he might need but because it had been the nearest to being empty before she topped it up with water.

Minna frowned at it. "What is that?"

"It is a private matter for the tribune only," said Tilla, adding, "We will accept your apology after we have seen him."

"Ha! You think the tribune will fall for that? I know nothing about any medicine."

"It is a private matter," insisted Tilla, hoping he was listening from behind the screen, because she could not draw out this conversation much longer. If a body slave—or indeed anyone more sensible and less nosy than Minna—arrived, she would be expected to hand the bottle over and leave, and there was no knowing whether he would take the hint and come and find her.

"Really, Tribune!" exclaimed a voice Tilla had not expected to hear. "So you too have been having secret meetings with the Medicus's wife!"

What ever the tribune said in reply to the empress was lost beneath a ripple of laughter from the lunch guests. Male hands appeared, grasping one of the screens. Minna gave a squeak of terror and fled. The screen moved to reveal Accius, looking even fiercer than usual. He stepped out. The screen was replaced.

Tilla gulped. Accius was standing over her like an eagle deciding which part of its prey to tear at first. "What?"

"Sir," she murmured, "I have information."

"Not now!"

"Then when?"

He glanced round. "Gods, woman! Do you have no idea how this looks?"

"That is why my assistant is here," Tilla assured him. "Perhaps, sir, you would like to discuss the use of the medicine away from the ears of the guards?"

65

They paused to stand halfway between the road and the line of horses flicking their tails against the midday flies. Anyone watching—and there were plenty of men with nothing much else to look at—would have seen Tilla hand over a small bottle to the tribune and give a small bow of respect. They might, if they thought about it, have seen several other things. They might have seen that neither man nor woman wanted to be thought of as holding a secret meeting with the other. They might also have seen that neither trusted the other—the woman had a companion and the tribune had three guards—and yet that they did not quite trust their own people, either, since the companion and the guards had been made to stand out of earshot.

They could not have heard Accius say, "Another anonymous informer?" and Tilla reply, "They are the best sort. These men have no reason to lie: They would rather not have seen or heard anything at all."

"You expect me to believe that you can get information from these people when our questioners can't?"

"They told what they knew. Your torturers needed to ask better questions. Nobody asked what they heard, and they were frightened of getting involved."

"They're involved now. They're spreading dangerous rumors, and yet again only you know their names. The only evidence that our recruit was at home in bed comes from a wife who is bound to say that—and from you. I have been patient with you. The Praetorians won't be."

Tilla had not thought of that. It was not good. Why did this man always look at things backward? "Sir," she said, squaring her shoulders, "you have a choice. You can hand me over to the Praetorians for questioning and I will give up the names before long, because I am not brave, and they can catch the witnesses and silence them. Or you can bring justice for your lost relative and defend your own men against false charges of murder."

"Don't presume to tell me what my choices are!"

"No, sir. I am sure you can see them for yourself."

Was that a smile? It was gone before she could be sure.

"It's very convenient," he said, "that you should find anonymous informers who point away from your husband."

"Any true witness would point away from my husband, sir."

"It won't free him, you know."

"No, sir."

"Who else knows about this?"

This was it: the tricky moment that she had known would come. Naming Pera might put him in danger. On the other hand, if she said nobody else knew, Accius could find a way to silence her and carry on as if nothing had changed.

"I have sent a sealed letter ahead to Deva with a merchant, sir. It is addressed to the legate."

She might as well have punched him in the stomach. "You've done what?"

"Saying that if anything happens to you, he should know that you were investigating the murder of a centurion by the Praetorians."

"You're lying."

"No, sir. I knew you would not want anyone here to be told, but this knowledge may put you in danger, and you know how easily a bad thing can happen to someone, and then it can be covered up."

The smile was definitely gone now. "So some common scribe knows as well?"

"No, sir. I wrote it myself. My writing is not good but I think he will be able to read it."

He stared at her for a moment, trying to decide whether this ridiculous invention was true, or perhaps whether a native woman really could write. She did not blink.

Finally he muttered, "You stupid, interfering ... A letter like that should be in code!"

Yes! He believed it. Or at least he was not sure it was a lie. She lowered her gaze. "I do not know the codes, sir. I have only just learned to write, and I did not think. I am sorry."

He gave a sigh of exasperation. "This trip has been nothing but trouble."

There was no need to reply to that.

He peered through the glass of the bottle. "What is this muck?"

"A mixture to ease coughs, sir."

He put a thumb over the stopper and shook it in a way that suggested he would rather be shaking her. Then he handed it back.

"Drink it," he ordered.

"But it was only—"

"All of it."

Conscious of everyone watching her, she twisted out the stopper. Then she raised the bottle to her lips, wondering what an overdose of cough mixture might do. It tasted disgusting. She was glad she had not brought the mandrake. That would definitely have killed her.

"If you're still alive later this evening," he said, "report to me. Alone. Then I'll consider what you've said."

66

The gods, Ruso decided, could never be accused of lacking a sense of humor. A few days ago he and Tilla had saved Victor from being locked up inside the fort at Calcaria. Now not only was Victor locked up in a damp and stinking cell at Calcaria, but Ruso was in there with him.

He examined the crust on the chunk of barley bread that had been issued with his cup of water, and which seemed to have been left to mature for several weeks before serving. That mark was probably just a scrape, although it could equally have been the tooth marks of a rat that had made a failed attempt to break into it. It felt hollow as he tapped it on his knee. He wondered how well Victor's jaw had healed and whether the recruit would have to smash off chunks of bread against the wall and then suck them.

At the moment Victor was ignoring the food altogether and sitting with his elbows propped on his knees and his head in his hands. This was not good. He had walked ten miles: He needed to eat.

"You could build houses with this stuff," Ruso observed.

No response.

"I found out who betrayed you," he said.

Victor gave a vague shrug as if he did not care.

"Tilla's doing her best to get us both out of here."

If he was pleased to hear this, it did not show.

"If you want to survive this, you need to eat."

Another shrug signaled that at least the man had heard what he said.

"I believe this is food," remarked Ruso, eyeing the tooth marks again, "although it's rather hard to tell."

He was trying to think what else he could contribute to this one-sided conversation when Victor's head jerked up. "What does it matter? I am cursed anyway!"

Gods above, was he back to that? "If there's a curse, Victor, it's not on you."

"No?" demanded Victor. "Then you know nothing!"

Ruso's reply was formed in British. "So my wife often tells me," he said. "But I am willing to learn."

Victor buried his face again. Ruso had run out of things to say. Perhaps that was why Victor started to talk.

At times his voice dropped to a whisper and it was hard to follow what he was saying, but the outline of the story was plain enough.

It was a sorry tale. Geminus had devised a ruthlessly efficient system of punishment for offenders, of whom there would doubtless be many amongst a bunch of raw recruits. Instead of going to the bother of flogging them, he would gather all the other recruits together and have the miscreant of his choice chained to a block like a baited beast in the amphitheater. The other wrongdoers were lined up to attack him one by one. "He made us roar," mumbled Victor. "Like animals. And if you didn't hit hard enough or roar loud enough, you were the next one chained up."

That was not the worst of it. According to Victor, while Geminus's desperate victims fought like wounded beasts, their comrades were expected not only to cheer them on but to place bets on the outcome. "It could go on for hours." said Victor bitterly. "They called it Sports Night."

Ruso let out a long breath. There were many questions he wanted to ask, but he dared not interrupt.

"Then they let Dannicus drown. Sulio heard the ferryman yelling at Geminus, asking permission to go and get them. Geminus made him stay back, saying it was too dangerous." Victor snorted. "Too dangerous for the ferry, but he still made them swim."

"Why would he do that?"

"Because him and Dexter had money on Dann not making it," said Victor without hesitation. "That was when me and Tad stopped trying to pretend it would be all right in the end. We wrote a letter to the legate."

With each day that passed, their hopes rose that the message had got through. Almost a week had gone by when Geminus announced the latest Sports Night. As they stumbled down the dark streets to the warehouse, they tried To assure each other that tonight would be no worse than usual. It was too soon for a reply, and too long since the letter had left. If it had been intercepted, Geminus would have acted before. But Geminus was a man who enjoyed a slow revenge. When all the recruits were assembled, he called Victor and Tadius out into the center, held their letter up, and made them read it aloud.

"And they kept us there, and Tad was chained, and they… they…" Victor hid his face in his hands. "He was my best friend," he whispered. "But I was too frightened to stop."

Ruso let out a long, slow breath.

"I just wanted it to be over."

"You should never have been put in that position."

Victor shook his head. "Marcus bribed the gate guards to get me out. He said all the lads chipped in. I think he lied." He shifted his position on the damp mud floor. "I wouldn't have bothered saving someone who did what I did."

Ruso said, "It had to be one of you."

But Victor was beyond comfort. "Every morning," he said, "I wake up to another day Tad will never see. And he'll never see it because I was a coward." He looked up. "We were all cowards, sir. One way or another. That's the curse."

Ruso closed his eyes, imagining the shame of men forced to make the choice Geminus had given them. Men made complicit in the deaths of their comrades. How would he feel if he had been compelled to fight for his life against a friend? It was unimaginable. Valens, he supposed, would have fought back. Albanus would probably have apologized for his blood making a mess on Ruso's fists.

Victor was still talking. "I went to see his girl. I told her the truth. I thought perhaps if she forgave me ..."

Ruso already knew that forgiveness had not been granted.

Victor said, "He said it would turn us into men."

It had turned them into beasts. Ruso felt almost a physical ache in his chest at the cruel waste of young men who had joined the Legion eager to better themselves in the service of an emperor who had never heard of them. He asked gently, "Did you kill Geminus?"

"I wish I had."

"Do you know who did?"

"No. And if I knew, I would never tell you."

"Next time they ask, don't say that. Just say what you know. Don't antagonize them."

"Thanks."

"Be a friend to yourself, Victor. If not for your own sake, then for your family."

Victor gave a snort of derision. "Like I was a friend to Tadius?"

Heavy footsteps were approaching. A key scraped in the lock, and within seconds Ruso was being unchained and ordered to his feet.

"Where are you taking me?"

"Tribune wants to see you."

"Hah!" he heard Victor shout after him, his voice suddenly hard. "Tell the tribune his little trick failed. The native didn't confess!"

67

The tribune was a guest in the commanding officer's house at Calcaria, as presumably was the empress. Ruso, whose request to wash had been refused, was led into a dining room whose décor made him think of the insides of a raw chicken: yellow fat, cream skin, pink flesh, red blood. In the midst of this lay Accius, propped on one elbow on a yellow couch. He was surrounded by the debris of a formal dinner. Standing in front of one of the tables was Tilla, looking alarmingly pale. He glanced from her to Accius, slightly reassured by the fact that she was fully clothed and her hair was no more ruffled than usual.

Her eyes widened when she saw him. The quick pout and lift of the eyebrows told him only that he should have learned to interpret her facial expressions by now.

"Ah," said Accius with the languor of a man who had eaten too much and did not want to shake it up with an animated conversation. "Ruso."

"Sir."

"I have decided," declared Accius, "that it is a waste of skill to have a doctor marching in chains."

Ruso let out a secret sigh of relief and offered the obligatory "Thank you, sir" as if it were not Accius's fault he had been chained in the first place. This was probably the nearest he would get to an apology.

"I find myself," said Accius, "in something of a quandary."

Ruso glanced at the scattered remains of the meal. He could smell wine and fish and spice and lavender. He looked at Accius's soft leather house shoes dangling from the end of the couch, and thought of Victor crouched in a malodorous cell not two hundred paces away. It was hard to sympathize with the tribune's quandary.

"I have been informed by this annoyingly persistent young woman"—here Ruso exchanged another uncommunicative glance with his wife—"that there may be further information about the murder of Centurion Geminus. If I tell you that none of this information is to leave this room, do I have the faintest chance of you obeying me this time?"

"Absolutely, sir. What ever it is, it's confidential." Since Ruso already knew what it was likely to be, this was not a difficult promise to make.

Accius turned to Tilla. "Tell him what you told me."

Tilla looked at them both, opened her mouth, swayed, and grabbed at a table for support. Ruso seized her and lowered her onto one of the couches.

"Head between your knees," he ordered, feeling her forehead for fever and scanning the tables for a water jug.

"It is nothing," Tilla insisted in a muffled voice.

"Of course it's something!" Ruso glared at Accius. "What did you do to her?"

"I haven't touched her."

From between her knees Tilla said, "I drank too much cough medicine."

Ruso decided he must have misheard. "You drank too much? Has he been giving you wine?"

"Cough medicine," she repeated, making no more sense than before. "It made me vomit. Can I come up now?"

When she did, he gave her a look that was intended to mean he wanted to continue this conversation later and that they would be discussing more than medicine, but it was too complicated a message for a simple look to convey.

Restored, Tilla perched on the edge of the dining couch and relayed the account of her anonymous witnesses from Eboracum. Three or four Praetorians, recognizable by the scorpions on their shields, and Geminus talking to them about going into action together again. Then the sound of a struggle and someone landing in the ditch.

When she had finished, Accius said, "Some of us believe in knowing all the facts before we draw our final conclusions."

Ruso bit back *Then why did you send me down the sewers?* and said, "I thought the Praetorian prefect was in charge?"

"Prefect Clarus is in overall charge, yes."

A misdemeanor in the Legion would normally be dealt with by a tribune. Possibly Accius had not taken kindly to having the investigation snatched away from him.

"It has come to my notice, Ruso, that you seem to have the knack of persuading men to confide in you."

"It's my job, sir."

"Yes. It has also occurred to me that a doctor can move about freely amongst all classes of men. And since you are the senior medical officer on this march, you need not confine your attentions to your own unit."

"Yes, sir." Or should that be *No, sir*? Was he being released? What the hell was Accius playing at?

"Do you think you could perhaps attempt the art of being discreet?"

"I'll do my best, sir."

"Good. I shall deal with your insubordination when we get to Deva. Meanwhile, just carry out your medical duties as usual."

Tilla's face brightened. Ruso looked from one to the other of them. "Thank you, sir."

"I don't want our men—or any of the men—more agitated than they already are. Do you understand?"

"Yes, sir."

"Good. Should you happen to discover anything interesting in the course of your duties, I expect you to report it to me—and only me—immediately."

So that was it. Accius didn't trust Clarus, and Ruso the Insubordinate had become Ruso the Useful.

"If you get into trouble, you will deal with it yourself."

And also Ruso the Expendable. He stifled *What do you actually want, sir?* There was no point: Accius would not—could not—tell him to make inquiries about the unknown Praetorians. If indeed that *was* what Accius wanted. It was certainly what Ruso wanted, so the vagueness of the instructions suited him nicely.

"Is that clear?"

No. You're being deliberately evasive, you pompous, self-serving... "Absolutely, sir."

"Good."

"Just one thing, sir?"

Accius waited.

Ruso gestured toward a dish still half full of small cakes. "If you aren't going to eat all of those, can I have them?"

"Haven't they fed you?"

"They're not for me, sir."

Accius sighed. "Very well."

As Ruso lifted the dish, something else occurred to him. "Sir, one more thing."

"You're not having the wine."

"Am I right in thinking Centurion Geminus joined the Praetorian Guard straight after the return from Dacia, sir?"

"Yes."

"So that would be ... how long ago?"

"I was eight," said Accius. "Sixteen years ago."

"Thank you, sir. And when did he leave them?"

Accius frowned. "I can't remember. He served in Judaea and then transferred to the Twentieth. Does it matter?"

"Probably not, sir."

"Good. You can go."

Ruso glanced at his wife.

"Not her," said Accius. "She will be traveling with my household."

Ruso tensed. "Sir—"

"You can't expect me to release a prisoner and not retain a sign of good faith." Accius turned to Tilla. "My guards will arrange for your vehicle to travel with mine. You will lodge with my housekeeper, and you will be treated with respect unless you make trouble, in which case my guards will restrain you."

"Yes, sir."

"You are not to speak to me again, do you understand? You have embarrassed me enough. Now, get out, both of you." Accius reached back to slide his shoes on. "The staff need to clear up."

In the lamplit corridor outside, at last able to rub his sore wrists, Ruso whispered, "Are you all right?"

She nodded.

"You were right about the betting. Geminus got what he deserved." Before she could reply, a gang of slaves who had been waiting somewhere discreet bore down upon them carrying trays and cleaning cloths. He said, "Cough medicine?"

"A mistake."

"What if it had been the mandrake?" he demanded. "You must read the labels, Tilla!"

68

Ruso rolled onto his back, realized where he was, and smiled to himself. He spread his fingers wide and stretched up into the cool morning air. His fingertips brushed the cover of the wagon. He moved them about, pushing against the rough underside of the leather. He had never before thought to celebrate such a simple freedom. It did not matter that he had spent the night adjusting his sleeping position around the hard corners of boxes of hospital supplies. Briefly, nothing else mattered except the fact that his hands were under his own control once more, and seemingly undamaged.

Several things would matter in a moment, not least the question of how he was going to worm information out of the Praetorians—if indeed the soldiers he wanted were here, and not marching north with the emperor and Valens. But first, he must make himself look like a man who was supposed to be carrying a medical case, rather than a man who had just stolen one.

He dealt with his hair by running both hands through it and with the stubble by ignoring it, a habit that had helpfully come into fashion with a bearded emperor. Most of his kit could stay with Tilla and the girl that he was sure he recognized from somewhere, but he needed his belt. He had not seen it since they took it from him at the guard house in Eboracum.

It took half an hour of negotiation and the last three slightly stale cakes from the empress's dining table (Victor had eaten the rest) to get it back. As the march set off once more, he slipped the leather tongue through the heavy silvered buckle with a sigh of relief. Without it, he had felt half-dressed. And without it, nobody would take him seriously as a soldier. Now he could face the Praetorians and…

And what? He had dismissed this question several times, telling himself that when the moment came, so would the inspiration. With luck, one of them would report sick. But the moment was here, the inspiration wasn't, and the guards that had streamed out of Calcaria's west gate ahead of the Twentieth all looked disappointingly healthy.

Still, he was not going to find anything out by spending the morning hanging around the hospital wagons of his own legion. "If anyone wants me," he murmured to Pera, "I'll be with the Praetorians."

Pera grasped the significance of this immediately. "Do you need any help, sir?"

"Probably," Ruso admitted. "But I think it's best if one of us stays with the patients, don't you?"

✤ ✤ ✤

"A memorial to whom?" demanded the Praetorian officer, looking down on Ruso from the height of his horse, the gleam of his armor and the superiority of his education.

"Centurion Geminus," repeated Ruso. The man could hardly have failed to hear about Geminus: He was just being deliberately awkward. "He used to be with the Guard in Rome. The tribune wants me to check the details with men who served with him. Probably just after the end of the fighting in Dacia."

"Hm." The officer eyed the case in Ruso's hand. "And you say you're a medical officer."

Ruso saw himself as he must appear: a man with no armor whose wrists betrayed the fact that he had recently been chained up, and who had now appeared clutching a nonregulation case and asking to be allowed to move freely amongst the empress's guards.

"You're the one they locked up for murdering him," observed the officer. "I heard you were insane."

Ruso was very much wishing he had not started this. "I'm innocent," he insisted, "and I'm as sane as you are. They've arrested one of his own men instead."

"What's in the case?"

Ruso unfastened it one-handed and held it up. The small probe slipped out of its clip as usual, and he noticed one of the scalpels was missing. How had that happened? He propped the lid awkwardly with his elbow and put the probe back. There was the empty bottle of cough medicine, clearly labeled. What had Tilla been thinking of? Come to that, what was he thinking of himself, bringing a case full of blades?

"Knives for cutting flesh," observed the officer, who had obviously had the same thought. "Keep them sharp, do you?"

If he said no, he was a bad surgeon. If he said yes, he looked like an armed lunatic trying to get near to the empress.

"Very," he said. "And they cost a small fortune, so I keep them where I can see them."

The officer said, "Hm."

Ruso closed the case. The horse plodded on.

"I heard you had a grudge. Why are you doing his memorial?"

"Because our tribune has a sense of humor," said Ruso.

The man glanced over his shoulder at a subordinate. "Go and get Fabius," he said. "We'll see if he wants to talk about the old days." He turned back to Ruso. "Fabius might remember more than I do," he said. "All I can recall is that Geminus didn't make very many friends. The tribune may not want that inscribed on his memorial."

69

The empress's carriage had been parked on the verge at the crossroads and again screened so the sight of her protectors did not put the great lady off her lunch.

Ruso found Accius deep in conversation with Dexter. They were casting occasional glances at the recruits, seated just out of earshot. In return, several of the recruits were staring at their officers with expressions of glum resentment. Marcus was watching them intently over his waterskin as if he was trying to work out what they were saying.

Accius waved Ruso away with an impatient flick of the hand. Ruso was not sorry to make his way back to the hospital wagons. He was not sure how to tell Accius what he had found out.

The tribune appeared at the wagons a few minutes later. He paused to speak to the patients and had the sense to move well away from Austalis before remarking to Pera that the lad was looking very ill. To this Pera replied that had it not been for Doctor Ruso, he would be dead. Thus Pera unwittingly provided the cue for Accius to move on and engage Ruso in a conversation during which they strolled away from the others.

"So?" demanded Accius.

"Sir, could you just describe for me—without looking—the doctor and patient on the wagon?"

Accius's scowl deepened. "What?"

"It's important, sir."

"Have you found out anything or not?"

"Yes, sir. If you could just describe for me—"

"The doctor had curly hair. The patient was all skin and bone, with bandages on his arm. Get to the point."

"Hair color? Eye color? What were they wearing? What color was the blanket?"

"The mens' blankets are gray. Get on with it."

"Thank you, sir." Without explaining, Ruso began with the easy part. There had been four Praetorians with Geminus as they marched out of the east gates. Two had been old comrades of his and one of those was currently traveling north with Hadrian, but he had spoken to the other one, a man called Fabius. Fabius said he had lost sight of Geminus just after they began to advance down the street. He had thought it would be wiser to stick together, but he assumed Geminus had gone to find the men from the Twentieth, and he was not concerned when he did not see him again.

Ruso could see that Accius was impatient for him to finish. The moment he stopped speaking, Accius demanded, "How exactly did you go about this conversation?"

"I told them I was researching Geminus's life for a memorial, sir."

"And they believed you?"

"No. They thought I was there trying to clear my name."

"As long as you didn't involve me."

"No, sir. What was really interesting was what Fabius said next." Ruso paused, hoping Accius was going to listen to all of it and not just what he wanted to hear. "He said he's thought more about that evening and now he remembers seeing a native hanging about by the ditch, off to their left. He didn't seem to be causing trouble so they left him alone. When I asked for a description, he explained that it was dark, but they were carrying torches and he thought the native had pale coloring and his hair was unusually short for a Briton."

"Victor!" exclaimed Accius, as Ruso had known he would. "Excellent!"

It was not excellent for Victor, but Accius was not the sort of man to worry about that. "Then he referred me to the other two men who were there as well, sir. And this is where I think it all gets rather strange."

"Never mind what you think. Tell me what they said."

"The two men I spoke to gave exactly the same description as Fabius."

"Good! A description of the murderer, and three witnesses. You're a lucky man, Ruso."

"It's too good, sir."

"How can it be too good?"

"Sir, Pera has dark hair and eyes and he's wearing chain mail. Austalis is blond and blue-eyed and he's got a green tunic over his good shoulder. The blanket isn't gray, it's white."

"Get on with it!"

"People don't remember things accurately. Were you present when Clarus interviewed his own men, sir?"

"Of course not! Otherwise I wouldn't be—" Accius stopped. "There was no need for me to be there."

So Accius's interest in this was definitely unofficial. "Did he say anything about his men seeing a native?"

"His men must have seen dozens of people. He would hardly tell me about all of them."

"Yes, sir. Yet these three all said exactly the same thing in the same order. It was as if they'd rehearsed it." He paused to let that sink in. "I'm willing to bet that none of them remembered the native before Victor was arrested."

Accius sighed. "I should know better than to listen to a doctor. You people see a pimple, call it a deadly disease, and prescribe six weeks in bed with daily visits."

"They're hiding something, sir."

"They're describing the same man! Besides, they couldn't have known you were going to come asking. Why would they all get together and make something up?"

It was a fair point, and one Ruso had already considered. "Sir, think back to your childhood. When my brother and I did something we weren't supposed to, we agreed what we'd say in case we got caught."

"I wouldn't know," said Accius. "I don't have any brothers."

Ruso was struck by a picture of the lonely young Accius wandering through a large house, wishing he had somebody to play with, and suddenly thrilled by the attentions of a storybook war hero. No wonder he had been determined to defend him. "The point is, sir," he said, "we only ever did it when we knew there was something to cover up. And the more clever we tried to be, the more likely we were to trip up. If they said they hadn't seen anyone—which I imagine they told Clarus—they'd have been fine. But they decided to embellish their cover story when Victor was arrested."

"Or they could have discussed their memories around the campfire one night."

"Then they would have gone to Clarus, sir. And Clarus would surely have told you that he had evidence against one of your men."

"Hm."

"One of the other veterans told me that Geminus wasn't popular when they served together. I think this may go a lot further back than we realize."

The silence that followed was interrupted by the trumpet signaling time to move on.

"Well," said Accius, "that's something to think about." He took a step back toward the road. "Thank you, Ruso. You will now forget everything you have just told me."

"Yes, sir. Sir, the recruit under arrest is—"

"He's none of your concern. If you want to do something useful, help us get the rest of them to Deva."

"What about my wife, sir?"

"Just stop her from making any more trouble." Accius strode away to deal with more important matters, leaving Ruso wondering how to carry out that most challenging order of all.

70

Ruso was trying to find out who he should ask about borrowing a horse when he found Dexter riding alongside him. The man had never been friendly, so he was surprised to hear a greeting. He was even more surprised when Dexter said, "You did a good thing, Doctor."

"I did?"

"Somebody should have done it way back."

"Geminus?"

"Me, I was never happy about him. You just turned up and dealt with it. Like that." He snapped his fingers. The horse tossed its head.

"I didn't do it."

"Shame about young Victor, but he's not the sharpest tool in the box, is he?"

"He didn't do it, either."

"I bet you're thinking, *How did the old man get away with it for so long?*"

"*Sports Night*?" said Ruso, unable to keep the disgust out of his voice.

"You know, then?"

"Where did you think you were, the amphitheater?"

"It was just a bit of harmless fun to start with. But the old man didn't know when to stop. And I didn't have the authority to stop him."

"Men were being injured!"

"They weren't my men."

Perhaps not, but Dexter must have been betting on them.

"Then he went and lost that lad in the river. Even Geminus could see he'd gone too far there."

"But by then he'd implicated everyone else," Ruso surmised.

"He was a clever bastard."

"Was it you who told the maintenance crews to follow me?"

"We had to know what you were up to. They were keen enough to help. Nobody likes an inspector."

"You could have backed me up!"

Dexter shrugged. "What's done was done. The old man said if we talked, we'd all be thrown out with no payoff. Or worse. So we decided to keep the lid on it."

And they said centurions were the bravest men in the army.

"You don't how it was," continued Dexter, as if he had guessed what was in Ruso's mind. "You weren't there.

"I got the general idea from his dog. Where is it, by the way?"

"Still with him," said Dexter unexpectedly. "We couldn't have a dangerous dog on the march, so it went on the pyre."

Ruso pictured the wolf dog standing calmly alongside its master and felt more kindly disposed to it in death than he had in life. "Bella," he said, as if he felt he should mark its passing by naming it, and then tightening the muscles in his leg so that the stitches pulled. "How much does the tribune know?"

Dexter shrugged. "That's what he'll be trying to decide, ready for telling his story at Deva." He paused. "Nobody meant it to end like it did, you know. It was just a bit of fun."

"I didn't kill Geminus," Ruso repeated. "Neither did Victor. So where were you that night?"

Dexter was staring ahead to where the recruits were marching in ragged lines four abreast. "Busy knocking heads together," he said. "But if that's the way the wind's blowing, maybe I'll take the credit." Urging his horse into a trot, he moved forward to ride alongside his men.

Ruso watched him trim the lines and fall in beside some of the junior officers. According to Pera, Geminus's shadows had managed to get themselves sent north with Hadrian, but he supposed most of the officers had been tainted by Sports Night in one way or another. No wonder they were keeping a close eye on the recruits. They were terrified of them.

71

The tribune's guards had shown little interest in Tilla, but Minna seemed to be taking the duty very seriously. Her approach to guarding a hostage who might yet turn out to be an officer's wife was to travel behind, watching her every move, ask from time to time if she was quite comfortable, and then do very little about it if she wasn't.

Tilla was bored, frustrated, and still feeling faintly queasy from the cough medicine. Only the fear of causing more trouble for her husband had kept her in her seat all day, watching the land gradually begin to rise and fall as the convoy trudged toward the hills at the speed of the slowest ox in front.

From time to time she had sent Virana to find out what was going on. There was no good news. The Medicus was busy. Victor was spending another day limping along behind a supply wagon. He must be in agony: Already his wrists were rubbed raw and his feet would be blistered where he had been unable to shake the grit out of his boots yesterday. The medics had bound them up, but another day of marching must have made them much worse. There were at least eighty thousand paces between here and Deva, and Victor would feel every one of them.

The sun was well past its midday height when the convoy ground to a halt yet again for no apparent reason. Tilla had had enough. Without glancing back at Minna, she and Virana jumped down and went forward to see if there was anything interesting happening.

By the time they got there, the empress's painted carriage had been unhitched and was propped on stacks of wood by the side of the road. The front wheels lay in the grass. As was the way with breakdowns, there were a lot of men standing around pointing at various parts of the carriage and telling each other what had gone wrong and how to fix it. Several more were crouching by the props to hold them steady, and offering advice to the one man underneath who was actually trying to do something. As Tilla approached, a loud and very rude word suggested things were not going well down there.

"Really!" Minna, of course, had not been able to resist following them. "Fancy speaking like that in front of the empress!"

The empress, seated on a folding stool under a parasol held by one of her slaves, looked weary rather than shocked. Minna managed to corner another of her slaves and ask if there was anything the tribune's household could do to help, and that was how, somehow, the empress, the parasol, and the first slave ended up in Celer's smelly cart while Tilla and Virana walked behind them the mile to the Falcon's Rest.

Tilla remembered the Falcon's Rest from their journey to Eboracum. It was the sort of inn that was only there because it was on the way to somewhere else. It squatted on a minor crossroads and scowled down from its high barred windows at any travelers who might be approaching in search of a meal and fresh horses. Its defensive stance had made her feel oddly cheerful. It was a reminder that, without soldiers to hide behind, the Romans were frightened people.

There was no fort here, and the air was already filled with the clatter of mallets on tent pegs by the time Celer delivered his important passenger to the front door of the Falcon's Rest and Tilla and Virana scrambled back in for the short drive past a straggle of smaller eating houses to the stable yard at the back. Tilla had already worked out that there would be a shortage of beds, and she was not going to risk being turned away.

As soon as they were in, she sent Virana off to buy something to eat and looked around for somewhere better than the cart to spend the night. The main mansio building formed one side of the stable yard: two stories pierced with more mean little windows, those of the better rooms glassed to protect the guests from smells and flies and drafts. By the time the empress and her hangers-on were installed, there would not be much room in there. The rest of the yard was surrounded by stables with what must be stores above.

She thought about mice and rats. Then she thought about sharing a room with Minna.

She climbed down so Celer could unhitch the mule, and slipped a couple of coins to a stable hand. He directed her to the corner of a hayloft and then went back to dealing with more horses than they probably saw in a month.

Tilla was unloading their luggage and wondering whether it had been wise to send Virana out on her own with money when Minna arrived to ask if she had found a comfortable place to spend the night. Finding that Tilla would be out of her sight, she promised to come and visit her again very soon. Meanwhile she would "ask the stable hands to keep an eye on you," as if it were a kindness.

By the time all the luggage was hidden in the hay, Tilla was beginning to wonder whether Virana was coming back at all. So it was a relief when the girl finally reappeared with a triumphant smile, four sausages, two apples, and a jug of beer. "The Medicus says," said Virana, lifting one hand out of habit to push away hair that was no longer in her eyes, "he will talk to the tribune as soon as he can."

"You have seen him?" asked Tilla, wriggling to get comfortable on the hay and reaching for the beer. "How is he?"

"He is still walking around free. And he made me swear to tell him truthfully whether the tribune is trying to bed you. I said he was not, and he said he was glad you are safe."

"What use is being safe? I have wasted a whole day with that woman watching me!"

"He says he knows it is very annoying for you."

Then why, Tilla wondered, did he not speak to the tribune straightaway and demand her release? Corinna must be frantic with worry about Victor. She could be doing something to help. Instead, here she was, sitting in the cozy gloom of the hayloft drinking beer, because the master of that stupid Minna had the power to have her husband locked up again. Maybe she could sneak out after dark.

"But the Medicus is doing things!" said Virana brightly. "He has been talking to the Praetorians and trying to find out what they know about the murder."

Tilla frowned. "Who told you that?"

Virana took a bite of apple and paused to chew it before saying, "Everybody knows."

" 'Everybody?' "

There followed a list of names, some of which Tilla vaguely recognized as the putative fathers of Virana's baby.

"They're very cross. They don't want to go to Deva. They think something horrible is going to happen."

It was doubly annoying to be stuck here when Virana was able to wander about, spreading gossip. "What makes them think that?"

"Marcus complained to the centurion about being watched by guards, and the centurion said, 'This is nothing. You wait till you get to Deva.' "

"Perhaps he meant things would be better at Deva."

Virana shook her head. "That is not the way Marcus heard it. It was 'You wait till you get to Deva and then it will be much worse.' So Marcus asked him what was going to happen at Deva and he didn't answer."

It might be something; it might be nothing. Tilla said, "If the recruits are under guard, how were you talking to them?"

Virana grinned. "The guards are very nice if you're friendly. They let me talk to Marcus. He's the one I like best. And he still talks to me, so when we get to Deva—"

Tilla put her head in her hands.

Virana paused. "Are you all right? Is it the cough medicine again?"

"No."

"Are you sad about Victor? Corinna says he can hardly walk and please, please, can you tell the tribune again that he really didn't kill Geminus?"

"Virana, I am supposed to be looking after you for your family."

"I thought I was here to help you."

"Yes, but... I am older! I am responsible! You must stop going round the camp, being friendly with the soldiers! What will—" Tilla stopped. Virana would not care what her mother thought. "Marcus won't want to marry you if he sees you with other men."

Virana's mouth rearranged into a pout. "You think I am stupid."

"Yes."

"Well, I am not. I made sure Marcus didn't see us."

Tilla fought back a wish to fling herself backward into the hay and scream. As calmly as she could manage, she went back to her first question. "Who made the recruits think that the Medicus has been talking to the Praetorians, Virana? Was it you?"

Virana squared her shoulders and gave a little wriggle like a hen settling down over her eggs. "I shan't tell you things if you get cross with me."

"If you don't tell me anything useful," said Tilla, "I shall have you dumped at the side of the road and you can walk home."

"It is not my fault you are stuck here with that woman! Why is everyone horrible to me?"

"Because you are very annoying. Do you know who told the recruits, or not?"

"Yes."

"And?"

"One of them heard some of the Praetorians talking at the latrines. They said the Medicus was snooping around, asking questions, but it was all right: The native would get the blame. Now Marcus and the others are all arguing about what to do." She glanced up. "They told me to go away. But I'll go back if you like. If you give me my dress—"

"No," said Tilla. "It's bad enough that you go wandering alone amongst the soldiers, without wearing that." Seeing Virana's face fall, she added, "But you have done well, and I thank you."

Again Virana's expression changed to one of plea sure and surprise. It was as if nobody else had ever taken the trouble to encourage her.

Tilla pushed aside a faint sense of foreboding. Virana had been told she would be sent home after this. That was what was going to happen. She would worry about how to do it later on.

72

The owner of the sheep had been warned in advance. Ewes and lambs had been driven into another field beyond the immediate reach of hungry soldiers, leaving a fine swath of cropped grass for the rows of goatskin tents and a fine scattering of droppings to be kicked aside before the occupants of those tents wished to lie down in them. The tents were set out in neat blocks, reproducing the layout of the barracks the men had occupied in Eboracum. The horses and the draft animals were grazing under guard in an adjoining field, and the vehicles had been drawn up on a patch of dry, gravelly ground not far from the gate.

Ruso sat on the back of the hospital wagon, swinging his legs and surveying this scene of impressive organization and calm. Dexter had men patrolling the hedges and ditches of the perimeter, and the smoke from a dozen cooking fires was spiraling into the fading sky. One thing the army knew how to do well was pitch camp. Even the laziest man was spurred into action when his nocturnal comfort depended on his own efforts, and as usual the only complaints came from the squads who found themselves allocated a damp patch. No one would suspect that the men in the tents over by the oak tree had murdered the centurion of the men who were camping by the hawthorn hedge.

With luck, the Praetorians would believe that he had swallowed their implausible account of events on the night that Geminus was killed. If they thought he suspected them, venturing anywhere near their tents after dark would be a very big mistake.

Ruso slid down from the back of the wagon. Austalis was settled. Pera was doing his best to tend to Victor's wrists and swollen feet, and there was nothing more anyone could do to help. He really should go and rescue Tilla from the custody of the tribune's housekeeper and see that she was settled with the other camp followers. He could hardly keep up the pretense that she was still a hostage, even if it was for her own good.

"Food!" The voice of the hospital cook rose from behind the wagon. "Come and get it!"

On the other hand, he was very hungry. Perhaps he would just have a bite to eat first. Then maybe he would stay with her in the civilian camp, leaving Pera in charge here. Otherwise he might find himself compelled to make a lone nighttime visit to the Praetorians. He could hardly refuse to answer a call to a sick man just because the messenger who summoned him might be luring him into a trap.

The beans were hot and filling and surprisingly tasty. By the time he had finished a second helping, the evening star had appeared and the fires were points of glimmering light with shadowy figures moving around them. Ruso collected his case and the few possessions he had on the wagon before telling Pera an edited version of the truth that made it look as though he were abandoning his duties for a night with a beautiful blonde. The instruction not to tell anyone where he had gone only made it worse. "But if there's a problem with Austalis, send someone across. The code word is *snake tattoo.*"

"*Snake tattoo,* sir?" Pera sounded doubtful.

"Yes," said Ruso, hoping he would have the chance to explain. Otherwise he would drift into the future as an anecdote. *Poor old Ruso. Began to think everyone was out to get him. Used to hide behind his wife and make you say the password before you could speak to him.*

He was almost at the entrance to the campground when, instead of the expected challenge from the guard, he felt a hand on his shoulder. He spun round, grabbing at his knife.

"It's Marcus, sir!" hissed a figure whose face was invisible beneath a hood.

"Marcus? What are you doing wandering about?"

"Visiting Austalis, sir."

The coat was hardly necessary on such a fine night, and nor was this circuitous route. Ruso guessed that Marcus was trying to avoid being caught by Dexter.

Still, that was not his problem. He had more important things to do.

"He's still doing well, but don't tire him," he said. "Just a quick visit. And if he's asleep, don't wake him."

Instead of replying in Latin, Marcus spoke in his native tongue. "Don't worry about your wife."

Ruso frowned, thinking he had misunderstood. "Sorry, Marcus. My British is not as good as I thought."

"Your wife. She will not be harmed."

"But—"

"We are not as foolish as they think."

"Marcus?"

But Marcus was gone into the night, and any sound his footsteps might have made in the grass was covered by a shout of laughter from a distant campfire.

Ruso strode out through the entranceway and turned left toward the faint glimmers of light that marked the buildings. As he did so, it occurred to him that not only had he not been challenged on leaving, but there seemed to be no guards covering the gateway at all. Dexter's men were slipping. And the Britons were up to something.

He turned and walked back into the camp, still unchallenged. He would go and find Tilla in a minute, then come straight back. Meanwhile, Dexter needed to be told.

73

Sabina tried a mouthful of the soup, confirmed that it tasted exactly how it looked, and pushed it away. Still, what could you expect from a place that thought it was acceptable for guests to dine upstairs in a room overlooking the stables?

If only she had insisted on keeping the head cook.

If only she had been traveling in a roadworthy carriage.

If only Julia had not been so inconsiderate as to fall pregnant. At least they could have assured each other that one day they would look back on this and laugh.

Separating from the emperor's party had been a mistake. This was only their second night on the road and, breakdowns aside, it was already clear that her companions had more important things on their minds than entertaining a lone empress. There was plenty of wine, and the innkeeper had found a couple of moderately attractive girls to tootle on flutes, but the scowlingly handsome young tribune of the Twentieth Legion still reclined so stiffly on his faded couch that he might have been lowered in through the ceiling. Meanwhile, Clarus glanced up every time someone entered as if he was hoping to be called away at any moment. Even the wild, murderous doctor (not present, of course) proved to be less wild and murderous than she had hoped: Apparently he had been released and a native arrested in his place.

"So you were both wrong?"

"There will be a trial at Deva, madam," explained the tribune.

"And was he right about the evil-minded centurion?"

The two men exchanged a glance. Clarus said, "We will see at Deva, madam."

Both men returned stoically to the soup and offered no further information. The flutes trilled on in the corner.

The door opened. A slave placed an item of no obvious origin in front of them and proceeded to cut it into slices that steamed gently in the light of the lamps. Having established that it was a pig's stomach, stuffed and roasted in bran, they ate it in silence.

Sabina sighed. The emperor never had this problem at dinner. No one would dare to look tired or distracted in his presence, and besides, since he had an informed opinion upon everything, the room was never short of conversation.

There were two more courses to get through before she could spend the rest of the evening composing another bland letter to Julia (she was sure someone read them before despatch) and beating her staff at board games. She considered pleading a headache, but to leave in the middle of a dinner could look like an insult. Clarus would understand, but it was never a good idea to insult the son of a potentially useful politician... although, since the emperor vastly outranked them, it was possible the other two were equally worried about insulting her. Meanwhile someone had to tell those annoying flute players to stop blowing and go away. And then someone was going to have to make conversation.

"Perhaps," she said to the tribune, aware that she should have asked this before, "you could tell us what we are to expect in Deva. Apart from my cousin Paulina and a murder trial."

At least that got him talking. His tactical briefing on the fortress at Deva lasted through most of the fish course. Had she been planning to lay siege to it, the construction techniques currently being used for the stone curtain wall would have been of enormous interest. Unfortunately she was not, and there was still an egg and milk sponge to get through.

This was desperate. Either she would be forced to plead a headache, or...

"That Briton," she said. "The one who lent us her smelly cart. Married to the wild doctor. She was rather quaint. I think we should invite her in to keep us entertained."

The tribune was too busy wiping the wine he had just spilled down his chin to reply.

Sabina smiled. "Did her medicine work, Accius?"

"I needed no medicine, madam." He snatched a towel from the hand of a hovering slave. "The woman wanted an excuse to appeal for the release of her husband."

Clarus said, "She does not know her place."

"She'll be busy serving her husband's dinner," put in Accius, who evidently thought she did.

One of his staff raised a hand. Accius snapped, "What?"

The woman whispered in his ear. The tribune's scowl deepened to the point where he was no longer handsome. "I told him to take her back hours ago! What's she doing in the stables?"

Sabina smiled. This would serve them both right for being such poor company. "Let's ask her, shall we?"

They were still waiting for the egg and milk sponge when the Briton arrived. If she was pleased to be rescued from a stable yard in the middle of nowhere, she did not show it. She had not even bothered to comb the hay out of her hair, but at least this time she did not stare in that insolent fashion. Sabina said, "I am pleased to hear that your husband's difficulty is resolved."

"I thank you, madam. But the man they now have in chains is not guilty, either."

"I see you are as refreshingly forthright as before."

The young woman looked up. "I said some wrong things before. I did not mean offense."

"Not at all. You were most entertaining. And are you still finding useful things to do?"

Accius burst in: "Madam, this woman should not be in the mansio!"

Sabina said, "The tribune thinks you should be busy serving your husband's dinner."

The Briton looked confused, as if this were some sort of trick.

"But before that, perhaps you could tell us about all the things we have to look forward to in Deva."

"Deva?"

"You have been there?"

"I live there." The woman thought for a moment and then said, "The cheese is salty, but very good."

Sabina nodded to Clarus. "We must try the cheese. Which reminds me..." She beckoned the serving staff with one finger. When nobody approached, she turned to see two of the mansio slaves staring vacantly across the room. She sighed. She should have insisted on bringing more staff too.

"You there. Have they forgotten us down in the kitchens? Go and see where the next course is." To the Briton she said, "Go on."

"The best bakery is the one opposite Merula's bar, and the baths are open to women in the morning." She paused again, then added, "But I think the legate has his own baths."

"I do hope so."

Clarus was poking at an olive with his knife as if he were trying to goad it into life. Accius was having his wine refilled. The woman seemed to have run out of things to say about Deva.

"There must be something else."

The woman met her gaze. "Madam, I go to market and talk to my friends and deliver babies and keep house for my husband and try not to anger the gods. I do not know what would interest a lady like you in Deva. You must ask the legate's wife."

"You were more helpful in answering my questions last time we met."

"You asked better questions."

Sabina chuckled. At last! This was more like it. "So, what else should we travelers know about the Britons? Is it true you that you believe chickens are gods and nobody should eat them?"

"A chicken is a not a god, madam. It is a bird that lays eggs."

"And your warriors—" Sabina stopped. "What is that?"

Everyone looked up as it came again: an irregular cracking and scraping somewhere above them, almost as if someone were walking about on the tiles.

The woman said, "Perhaps there are rats in the loft, madam."

Sabina shuddered, imagining the size of a British rat. She would have to make sure every hole was stuffed with rags to night, and one of the girls would have to lie across the gap under the door. The others could take turns to keep watch. "Is it true," she said, making an effort to regain her composure, "that your warriors fight naked and live in bogs?"

"I cannot speak of warriors, madam. The tribune has ordered me to speak only of matters concerning civilians and women."

Sabina exchanged a glance with Accius. "That is very good advice," she said, wondering exactly what had gone on between them. "I believe I told you something similar."

"But I can tell you about a woman and child from the Dumnonii people who are traveling with your escort, who will soon be left widowed and fatherless because—"

"The empress does not want to hear idle gossip!" Accius interrupted.

"But you are the one who ordered her not to speak of anything else," Sabina pointed out.

Now the scowl was positively sulky.

She turned to the Briton. "Why will this woman be left widowed?"

The Briton lifted her chin. "I cannot tell you, madam." She pointed to the other two dinner guests. "But your friends can."

There was no shortage of conversation now. The awkwardness was forgotten, as were the rats. Clarus and Accius both hastened to explain that the Dumnonii woman's husband was a murderer, that this Briton did not know what she was talking about, that a full investigation had taken place, and that Britons always made trouble. Meanwhile, the source of all the upset was glancing from one to the other of them with a small smile of triumph on her face. Nobody seemed to have noticed the legionary standing in the doorway.

"Stop!" Sabina cried. "Both of you!" She nodded toward the legionary. "Speak."

"Message for the tribune, mistress."

What ever the message was, it sobered Accius immediately. He excused himself and left in the man's company.

Sabina addressed the Briton. "You and your husband seem to enjoy stirring up trouble."

The woman bowed her head. "I am sorry to have disturbed your dinner, madam."

"On the contrary, you have helped to pass the time in a most entertaining manner—which is just as well, since it seems the wretched staff have forgotten us entirely." She frowned at the one remaining inn slave. "Go and fetch your master, girl. This is ridiculous!" To Tilla she said, "Unfortunately, I am not in a position to do anything about your friend from the—who are they?"

"The Dumnonii."

"The Dumnonii. I can do nothing about anything, because I live perpetually surrounded by spies." She gestured toward her own slaves, lined up against the wall. Nobody flinched. They were used to it. "Rest assured that one of them will be reporting this evening's conversation. For all I know, all of them will. So I never interfere in military or political matters. I leave all that to the emperor's men. Clarus, I'm sure you can deal with what ever it is?"

Clarus stood and began to make his way—none too hastily—around the outside of the couches. "With your permission, madam, I will hear what this young woman has to say."

"Please do."

He seized the Briton by the arm and led her out of the dining room.

Sabina, alone with her staff, held out her glass for more respectably watered wine. "The emperor's health," she said wearily, raising her glass. As she did so, she glanced at the badly painted ceiling and wondered if even Julia would have found it possible to laugh about rats.

74

Marcus's words might have been intended to reassure, but they had the opposite effect. As he strode toward the lanterns that marked a feeble welcome to the inn, Ruso asked himself what the recruit might know about Tilla. Why would she not be harmed? Why might any harm have come to her in the first place? Why might harm come to anyone?

He should have stayed in the camp. He had done his duty: Dexter had leapt to his feet and said he would check on the absent guards straightaway, but the more he thought about Marcus's words, the more uneasy he felt. He would just make sure Tilla was safe, then go back to the men.

Finding Tilla was not as easy as he had thought. The innkeeper denied all knowledge of her, and refused to summon the tribune's housekeeper so she could be asked.

"But she must be here. She's traveling with the tribune's party. Blond, in her twenties, probably with a local girl with—" He extended his arms, fingers splayed, in an exaggeration of the girl's assets.

"I'd have noticed, sir."

"Let me in and I'll find them myself."

But the innkeeper was not inclined to let him in, and the doorkeeper was very inclined to throw him out, so he made a tactical retreat with "When you find her, say her husband's looking for her."

With the brisk stride of a man caught between anxiety and irritation, he headed down the road to where the civilians had set up a makeshift campsite. Tilla had gone missing.

Something had happened that might put her in danger. Something that Marcus, up to no good, had tried to warn him about. Where was she? Why had he not had the sense to grab the tattooed Briton by the throat and demand to know what the hell he was talking about?

Tilla was not missing.

Any minute now he would find her amongst the camp followers, curled up beside a fire and wanting to know why he was making such a fuss.

Tilla was missing.

She had found out that she was no longer the tribune's hostage, realized her husband had failed to come for her, and taken herself off somewhere that the Britons knew about and he didn't.

Tilla was missing.

Still clutching his case and the blanket he had brought thinking he was staying the night, he picked his way through the huddled confusion of vehicles and makeshift shelters and guard dogs and murmured conversations and crying babies and cooking smells that made up the civilian camp. None of the voices that responded to him in the darkness would admit to having seen her. The girl Corinna called out from somewhere to ask how her husband was. He reassured her as best he could, wishing he had better news.

Finally he resorted to shouting, "Tilla!" in the hope that she was hiding and might relent. The only reaction was a cacophony of barking and voices telling him to shut up: People were trying to sleep.

He glanced down the road to where the black shapes of roofs were silhouetted against the starlit sky. Had she taken a room somewhere? There was only one way to find out. Slowly, so as not to trip over tent pegs invisible in the dark, he began to make his way toward the buildings. That was when a movement caught his eye. A figure creeping along the grass verge, just this side of the ditch. Then another. And another. He ducked down, ready to raise the alarm. Then he saw the glint of metal from some idiot who thought he could skulk around unseen in shiny parade armor.

Suddenly, the blast of a trumpet set a dozen dogs all barking at once. The soldiers leapt up, looking like monsters in the starlight, and began a rhythmic, relentless crash of sword hilts on shields. Ruso could sense movement all around him as cries of fear and protest rose from the camp.

"This is an inspection!" roared a voice that had been educated in Rome. "Everyone stay where you are!"

It was the Praetorian officer he had met this morning, but... an inspection? Of a civilian camp in the middle of the night? What was the matter with him?

Children cried. Dogs barked. Adults muttered and cursed as they fumbled with covers and tent ties in the dark.

"The camp is surrounded! Nobody is to leave! Stand still outside your own shelter!"

Gods above, was he going to perform a roll call next? And why, having made his point, did he not stop that awful thumping beat?

"Keep those dogs under control!"

Somebody protested, "There are children here!" and several other voices rose in support.

"No one will be hurt!"

The beat was silenced at last. All around Ruso, whisperers were asking each other what was going on. One brave soul shouted, "What have we done, then?" and a bolder voice ventured, "Clear off back to Rome!"

"Silence!" roared the Praetorian. "Everyone onto the road in an orderly manner! My men will be performing a search. As soon as we have finished, you may return to your beds."

Was that supposed to be reassuring?

Eventually everyone seemed to be moving toward the road, although in a manner that was far from orderly. Ruso went with them, hearing the sound of soldiers crashing about behind him. The search did not sound too orderly, either.

He joined the disgruntled and shivering collection of civilian travelers lined up for inspection by the flare of torches, and was taken by surprise when the officer ordered him to step forward. Surely the Praetorians had not arranged this search just for him?

No, they had not. When he responded truthfully to "Name?" the officer peered at him and said, "Ah. You again," and looked down at his medical case. "Another memorial, is it?"

Before Ruso could reply, another voice called out his name.

"Sir?"

The torchlight picked out the gleam of Accius's armor. This was turning into a very strange night.

Leading him away from the melee on the road, Accius said, "What are you doing out here?"

"Looking for my wife, sir. What's going on?"

"Your wife is over in the empress's dining room, upsetting people as usual. Where's your kit?"

"On a wagon, sir."

Accius sighed, as if Ruso were being deliberately unhelpful. "Never mind. Arm yourself with something and get down to the camp. The British recruits have deserted."

"What?"

"Centurion Dexter is also missing. I don't care about the recruits, but if Dexter's not already in a ditch with his throat cut, I intend to get him back."

75

Angry thin men were always more frightening than angry fat ones. This one hauled her out of the dining room with "The empress does not want to hear your nonsense about the Dumnonii woman!" and waited until they were out in the corridor to add, "And neither do I!"

"But Victor—"

"The deserter murdered his centurion, and he'll be made an example of. If his family are foolish enough to follow him, the legate will decide what to do with them."

There were no servants about as Prefect Clarus hustled her toward the stairs. She said, "Sir, I must speak with you!" but he was not listening. "I am on your side, my lord! You cannot trust the tribune!"

That stopped him.

"Sir, the tribune—"

He said, "Nonsense!" but instead of pulling her down the stairs, he seemed to change his mind and bundled her into the next room.

In the gloom she stumbled and fell out of his grasp, colliding with a bed and scrambling to her feet before he could pin her down there.

But he seemed to have no interest in the bed. Instead, he stood between her and the door and said, "If you lie to me, you will be punished."

She moved closer to whisper, "You cannot trust the tribune, sir." He had been to the baths: She could smell the oil. "He is making his own separate inquiries into the murder."

She heard him draw in his breath. "You're lying."

"It is true." She placed a hand on his shoulder and stood on tiptoe to whisper in his ear. "He is trying to prove the deserter did not kill his centurion. He is using my husband." She moved away slightly, leaving one hand at his throat. "And I"—she pressed it against his skin—"am using his scalpel."

She felt the blade rise and fall as Clarus swallowed. He had not seen her slip it out from under her skirts as she pretended to fall.

"You could shout for help," she murmured. "But before anyone hears the words, your windpipe will be sliced in two and your blood will be spraying on the walls. I am the wife of a surgeon, and I know how these things are done."

"You said you were on my side!" His voice was hoarse, and he sounded aggrieved.

"I lied."

"I am a guest here! It is inhospitable to lie to me!"

"I lied about that too." She was not going to waste time arguing. "The men seen with Geminus just before he died were yours," she said. "I know you have been told that, and I know you said nothing about it to the tribune. So what I am asking myself is: *Why is this man saying nothing? Why is he letting an innocent Briton be punished for a murder done by Roman men? Does he have no shame?*"

The blade lifted and sank again, but he said nothing. She pressed it a little harder above where she thought the artery might be, hoping her hand would not slip before he answered her questions.

"Is it no shame for Romans to murder each other?" She could not feel any blood yet. "Answer me!"

"Of course! We are not—" He broke off. Men were shouting in the courtyard. A woman screamed. There was a juddering thud and a cry as if someone had been thrown against the wall. More voices. They sounded like soldiers but they were shouting in British.

"You are not barbarians?" she suggested, keeping his attention on the scalpel. "No. Your guards obey orders. So did you give the order to kill Geminus, or are you protecting the one who did?"

"I cannot say."

The door burst open. "No swords!" she cried in British, hoping she had guessed right. "I am Darlughdacha of the Corionotatae, and this man is my prisoner."

There was a moment's hesitation, then a voice said in the same tongue, "Need any help?"

"He is asking if I need his help," Tilla translated into Latin. "Do I? Or will you speak?"

From outside the room came more cries and the crash of overturned furniture. The air held the sharp stink of something that should not be burning. She could feel Clarus trembling. Not wanting to admit that she had no idea what was happening, she said to the Briton, "How is it out there?"

He laughed. "Easy. They'll be renaming this place the Eagle's Downfall."

"You are taking prisoners?"

"I wouldn't," he said. "But Marcus says we've got to."

So Virana's friend Marcus was giving orders. But why bring the recruits here? Surely they had not come to take the empress and her guards hostage? It was madness. Still, she might be able to use it to her advantage. She reverted to Latin. "My people want justice," she told Clarus. "With every painful step they have seen Victor make, their anger has grown."

"My men—"

"Your men have been dealt with," she said, hoping it was true. "We are not afraid of death as you are. Our men are in charge here now. If I hand you over, my people will sell you to the hill tribes for their sport. Perhaps they will impale you on a tall stake stuck in the ground. Perhaps they will roast you alive." She hoped Christos was too busy tending to some other follower to be listening to this. This was a matter for the old gods. "Even if you live, you will be praying to die." She gave him a moment to frighten himself with any other gruesome tales he might have heard. "Tell the truth, and I will order them to keep you here unharmed."

She could not order the recruits to do anything, but that did not matter. The tales of British warrior queens haunted the nightmares of every visiting Roman.

A terrified shriek rose from the direction of the dining room.

Clarus cried, "The empress!"

The shriek died into a rasping gurgle.

"Oh, Sabina!"

Tilla said, "You can do nothing for her now."

Slowly, he let out his breath. "I will speak."

The recruit backed out and closed the door.

"Well?" she asked.

"I passed on the order."

"Who gave you this order?"

He did not reply.

"Tell me, or I will hand you over to my men."

It was barely more than a whisper. "It was Tranquillus."

"Tranquillus?"

"The emperor's correspondence secretary. But it could not have been his idea."

"Whose idea was it?"

"I don't know. He said it was a secret."

"Do not lie to me!"

"I am not lying. I was told to get rid of Centurion Geminus in a way that would not be traced back."

"And who wanted him dead?" If the murder had been ordered by the emperor's trusted secretary, it could have nothing to do with the recruits. Nor with an old grudge amongst the Praetorians.

" I—I think my poor empress ..."

He must have felt the startled shift of the blade. "The empress?"

"I may be wrong! Tranquillus is the only one who knows."

"Tranquillus is not here. You are." Was it possible that Sabina interfered in her husband's business after all?

"Oh, my poor lady! To end in a place like this!"

"Tell me about the empress."

"You will all die for this!" said Clarus, recalling his dignity. "The emperor will take such a revenge on your tribes that—"

"If he does, you will not live to see it." She had to get rid of this man and pass on the news. She hoped the recruits had listened to Marcus and taken prisoners. She could leave this one with the rest. "Move slowly and do as I say. If you do anything that makes me think you are trying to escape or call for help, I shall kill you. Do you understand that?"

"Yes."

The men guarding the entrance to the dining room stepped aside to let them pass. At the sight of Clarus, four men lined up across the far corner snapped to attention: Praetorians, looking half-dressed without their armor and their weapons.

Beyond them, a couch had been tipped over and pushed into the corner. Several heads popped up from behind it. A voice cried, "Clarus!"

Clarus stopped dead. Tilla almost stabbed him in the back of the neck by accident.

"Clarus," cried the voice again. "Thank the gods! Where are the rest of my guards?"

"Madam! Oh, my lady, I thought—"

He did not say what he thought, perhaps because he now realized Tilla had never exactly told him the empress was dead.

"Clarus, what ever is happening? These ghastly natives are all over the place!"

As Tilla pushed him forward, she heard Minna cry out, "Do not trust that woman, sir! She is one of them!"

The Praetorians took a pace toward her. A couple had armed themselves with chair legs.

"Tell them to stand back," Tilla said. "They should guard the empress, not waste their lives trying to defend you."

Clarus did not sound pleased to be reminded of his duty, but he gave the order.

Tilla stepped away from him. "Now go and join the others."

She retreated to talk to the nearest man on the door. To her surprise, he raised his sword. She whispered in British, "I am with you. I am a friend of Corinna and Victor. What is happening?"

"Buggered if I know," he said. "I just got told 'Don't kill nobody and don't let nobody out.' "

"That doesn't mean me, you fool!"

"Nobody," he repeated.

Perhaps it was safest to wait here for a moment. There were, or there should be, armed men all over the building. In the dark, it would be easy for one of them to make a mistake. Tilla nodded for the benefit of the watching Romans, as if she and this idiot had just been having a discussion rather than an argument. "If they come near me," she murmured, "it will be your job to defend me, since you made me stay here." She left him to think about that. Still clutching the scalpel, she walked across to peer through a crack in the window down to the courtyard below. She was almost as much of a prisoner as the Romans now, but she was not going to let the Romans know it.

76

A couple of fast-moving flares in the distance traced the progress of the search along tracks that the Britons might have taken. Meanwhile, the peace of the camp was a distant memory. A volley of shouts was followed by silence: Someone sensible had decreed that the searchers should allow themselves time to hear any replies to the cry of *"Dex-ter!"*

As they approached he saw lights bobbing about above the ditch, picking out the shapes of soldiers hunting for a man who, not half an hour ago, had been sitting by a campfire, eating bacon.

Ruso felt sick.

He should have told Dexter that Marcus was wandering around where he shouldn't be. Instead he had pointed out that the captain of the watch was slacking, mentioned vaguely that the recruits seemed restless, and then left the centurion to deal with forty-six armed and resentful men while he wandered off to look for his wife.

Someone arrived to tell Accius that several guards had been found dumped under a hedge.

Ruso felt his stomach shrivel.

"Dead?" demanded Accius, voicing his own fear.

"Just knocked about a bit, sir."

Clinging to this small shred of comfort, Ruso followed the tribune to the hospital wagons and joined Pera and the orderlies in checking the injured men as best they could by the light of the one remaining lantern. To Ruso's relief, none of the victims was seriously hurt, although there was an impressive amount of blood and all had nasty rope burns around their necks. It struck Ruso that their accounts of the attack were as graphic as any man might offer if he were trying to avoid being flogged for not paying proper attention on guard duty. They must have been negligent. How else could the deserters have managed to overpower, tie up, and gag all half a dozen of them without anyone noticing?

Accius's eager questioning revealed nothing new. None of the guards knew anything about Dexter. He told them they would be dealt with in the morning, and left them to worry.

Ruso got up to leave with him. None of this was helping to find either Dexter or Tilla, and now he was afraid for both of them. What the hell had Marcus meant when he said she would come to no harm?

"Sir?" Ruso hurried to catch up with the tribune, who was doing a good job of striding purposefully about and looking as though he knew what to do next. Ruso felt almost sorry for him. "Sir, has anyone checked the inn?"

"They haven't popped out to dinner, Ruso. Just thank the gods the empress is well away from all this."

"Just a thought, sir." He was going to have to explain. But not truthfully. Not now. Besides, he might be wrong. Marcus's promise might not mean they were planning to enter the building Tilla was in. But if it didn't mean that, what did it mean? Had they disappeared into the night and taken her with them?

Accius was still pointing out the stupidity of his first idea. "The empress has a guard, and I was there myself just a few minutes ago."

"Sir, they could have taken Dexter as a hostage in the hope of doing a deal. And that's where they think the officers are."

"The place is packed with staff, man!"

Ruso did not want to have to say it, but it was true. "Most of the staff will be natives, sir."

77

It was scant satisfaction to be proved right. The native recruits were not only in the inn: They had taken control of it. Outside, at a safe distance from anything that might be thrown from the roof, the centurion of the Praetorians was briefing his junior officers. In the absence of his commander he seemed to have taken it upon himself to do what ever was necessary. What he deemed necessary was a diversion, so that a small party of his best men could climb over the stable walls and open up from the inside. Accius's few remaining men from the Twentieth could provide one of the diversions by storming the front steps. Clearly the Praetorians were excited at the prospect of some real action.

In response to Accius's question he retorted that, yes, he had tried negotiation already. The only response had been a hail of insults and roof tiles. "How many of your barbarians are in there?"

"I'll talk to them. They're my men."

"They've got my prefect. And the empress. It's too late for talking."

Nobody seemed to notice when Ruso faded back into the darkness, leaving his tribune to a dispute that might be about saving lives, or about not being told what to do by a mere centurion, or about the Twentieth drawing all the fire so the Praetorians could perform the rescue. Whoever won the argument, it would do no good. He was not sure the recruits would believe anything Accius told them.

They might not believe anything he said himself, but it was worth a try.

The feeble lamps still burned on either side of the front doors, an odd reminder of normal business. As he approached he could hear some sort of native chanting going on inside. The sound brought back memories he would rather not think about.

There was movement up on the roof, a hollow scraping sound, and then a crack, as if someone was shifting and then breaking up a heavy clay tile. He stopped and called out in British, "This is Ruso, the healer. Let me talk to Marcus."

Behind him he could hear the Praetorian centurion demanding to know who that idiot was, and Accius ordering him to come back as if he were a disobedient dog. With luck, the men on the roof would hear them too.

"I'm coming forward!" he called, then ducked and made a quick sidestep.

In answer, something flew over his head and thudded into the gravel. Broken roof tile was not the easiest of missiles to aim, and they would be throwing toward the sound of his voice in the dark, but Geminus had trained his men well. With no armor or helmet, he was a soft target for anything with sharp edges.

"Marcus will talk to me!" he shouted, dodging again and wishing he had had the sense to borrow a shield. "Go and ask him!"

There seemed to be more movement up there, but no reply came. Perhaps Marcus was not in charge after all. Perhaps he was dead. Perhaps Tilla...

He could not think about Tilla. He needed to concentrate.

More movement, and a voice shouting in Latin this time. "Bring the tribune. Just you two and nobody else. No weapons. We are watching."

To Accius's credit, his footsteps were crunching forward over the gravel even before Ruso could turn and ask him. They walked forward slowly, far enough apart to make two small targets instead of one large one. The chanting grew louder. Ruso was conscious of being watched from behind and from above. This was very different from the last time he had seen a recruit up on a roof.

He murmured, "The Praetorians aren't going to try storming the place as we go in, are they, sir?"

"Not unless they want to kill us," observed Accius.

They passed between the lamps. Ahead of them, one of the double doors swung back. Ruso led the way forward. The chant was pulsating through the darkness. It was like walking under an amphitheater with the crowd above roaring for blood. The heavy door slammed shut behind them. He heard the bar scrape across into the socket. Someone called, "Put down your weapons."

Ruso lowered his knife to the floor. He was aware of Accius bending down beside him. Hands moved over his body, checking for concealed blades. Then the voice that had spoken before said, "Welcome to Sports Night."

78

If she closed one eye, Tilla could see down into the stable yard through the gap in the glass. The chant was coming from the men crowded around the outside. One man knelt in the middle, head bowed. He wore only a plain tunic and boots. His hands were tied in front of him and there was rope around his chest. Above him stood Marcus, the tattoo twisting up his arm like a live snake in the flickering torchlight.

"Silence!" Marcus bellowed in Latin to the crowd. Then when this had little effect, he added in British, "Shut up! We haven't got long!"

Finally the chanting died down. Turning to look round at his audience, he shouted, "Men, we are honoured by the presence of Tribune Accius and Medicus Gaius Petreius Ruso!"

Tilla stared in horror as Marcus saluted two of the figures standing in the shadows. The rest of the men followed suit. "For your entertainment this evening, sirs, we present... Centurion Dexter!"

What ever the guests of honor might be saying was lost beneath the roars of approval. Marcus stepped back, raising his right arm. He held a spear. The point hovered just above his victim's head. The audience cheered. Ignoring shouts of "Spike him!" Marcus eased the spear down behind Dexter's back. Dexter glanced round in alarm and Tilla saw the fear on his face. For a moment she was puzzled. Then she realized.

"Stand up for the tribune, Centurion!"

Encouraged by a kick, he staggered to his feet.

"How many turns before he tells the truth about Sports Night?" yelled Marcus. "Place your bets!"

Men were shouting out numbers. One roared, "Kill the bugger!"

"Are you ready?"

"Yes!"

"Are you ready?"

"Yes! Yes! Yes!"

Tilla realized the empress was calling to her from the corner of the room, asking what was happening. Without taking her eyes off the figures in the courtyard she said, "They are trying to get justice."

She wished they were not so very obviously enjoying it.

Marcus bent sideways. He seized the spear by both ends and turned it upside down as if he were winding up a crank. Dexter jolted. The rope around his chest tightened. "One!" roared the audience, with several immediately adding, "Two!" and "Get on with it!"

Marcus bent down to his victim. "Anything to say?" From the way he jerked his head away, Tilla guessed Dexter had spat in his face.

"You must stop this!" cried a voice from the shadows.

Accius was no coward. Even outnumbered by wild barbarians, he was doing his best to defend his man. "This is mutiny! Stop now, before—"

"Before what, sir?" demanded Marcus, one hand on the spear and the other wiping his cheek. "Before he tells the truth?"

"Men, this is Tribune Accius!" As if they would not recognize the cultured tones of his Roman education. "Listen to me. I order you to release that centurion and disband immediately!"

"We would, sir," Marcus told him calmly, "but this is Sports Night. Normal rules don't apply. Do they, Dexter?"

He upended the spear again.

"Two!" roared the crowd.

"This is outrageous!" cried Clarus from the safety of the corner in the upstairs room. "The empress can't be expected to listen to this! Tell your men to stop immediately!"

Tilla glanced back into the room. "They will stop when he confesses," she said, wondering if they would.

"I confess there was gambling, sir." Dexter's voice was clear, if not as strong as before. "Betting on fights. Harmless fun."

Several cries of "Ha!" and "Liar!" from the crowd almost drowned out Dexter's next words: "Geminus took it too far."

"Only two turns!" Marcus called out. "Pathetic." He looked around at his jeering comrades, though Tilla supposed he could barely see them in the darkness around the pools of torchlight. "I'm betting one more and he'll tell the tribune all about Dannicus. What do you think?"

79

The spear had turned five times now. Dexter could hardly stand. He had confessed about the betting on Dannicus and Sulio crossing the river. He had admitted that Geminus had forced Tadius and Victor to fight to the death and that he had done nothing to stop it. The crowd seemed to be growing restless.

The men who had been holding Ruso back against the wall next to Accius ("for your own safety, sirs") had slackened their grip and were looking round as if they were not sure what to do next. Accius had fallen silent as he listened to Dexter's confession. For once he seemed to have nothing to say.

Ruso elbowed his way out of the men's grasp and stepped forward into the torchlight. "Let him go, Marcus. He's told you everything he knows. He had nothing to do with Geminus's death."

"We know that, sir. He is a coward who left the killing to the Praetorians." Marcus turned to address the tribune. "Sir, even now this man has not told the whole truth. Ask him about tonight."

Ruso lowered his voice. "Marcus, have some sense! This is suicide. You can't get away from here, and the Praetorians are waiting outside. Do what the tribune tells you: Stop now and some of you might live."

"It is suicide to stop now," Marcus retorted.

"Let me pass!" Accius's voice cut through the rising discontent of men whose entertainment had been interrupted. He appeared at Ruso's side. "Centurion Dexter, I order you to tell me about tonight."

Dexter mumbled something.

"What? The watch captain let you down?" Marcus shouted in his ear. "I don't think so! Speak up so the tribune can hear!"

The crowd hushed to listen. But all anyone could hear was the centurion gasping to Marcus, "Should have—run when—you had the chance. You're a—dead man."

Marcus leaned down and hissed to the sagging head, "And so are you!" He looked up at Accius. "We are not as stupid as he thinks, sir. He is afraid of what we will say about him to the officers at Deva. He tried to frighten us about what will happen if we go there and then arranged to have the gates unguarded so we could desert."

It sounded ridiculous, but suddenly several things made sense. The sight of Dexter sitting calmly by the fire, eating bacon, while the watch was nowhere to be seen. The amazing ability of the Britons to overpower half a dozen guards in complete silence. The curious lack of any serious injuries amongst the guards, none of whom had managed to wriggle out from under the hedge until they were found.

Ruso took hold of the spear and prised Marcus's fingers away from it. Dexter, wheezing, slumped sideways as the rope slackened around him. Several hands caught him and lowered him to the ground.

"We are tired of being afraid, sir," Marcus was saying above him. "We will go to the next world as men rather than live in this one as cowards."

Crouched beside Dexter, concerned about broken ribs and internal injury, Ruso heard the centurion mutter a feeble, "Fools."

"Does it hurt when you breathe?"

"They'll be sorry—they were born."

"They had reasons. What happens when you cough?"

"Half-wits!" Dexter gave an experimental cough, took another gulp of breath, and carried on talking. "They'll be—nailed up. Threatening—the empress." He rolled over and swore. "Hercules's balls, that hurts."

But clearly it didn't hurt as much as broken ribs would. Ruso left him to recover. The recruits were milling about in the faltering torchlight, not sure what to do now that their complaints had been heard. The smell of beer wafted across the courtyard and a scuffle broke out in a dark corner. There were a few halfhearted cries of protest, but nobody seemed interested in imposing order. There was a crash and cheering as something was knocked over and shattered. Somewhere deep in the stables, a girl screamed. Accius, busy listening to some earnest discourse from Marcus, paid no attention.

Having realized he was not about to be butchered, the tribune had evidently decided the safest course was to concede what ever the men wanted. And Marcus, who seemed to have forgotten that the Praetorians must have the place surrounded, was falling for it. Ruso glanced around, wondering what to do. When the Britons realized they were trapped, this shambles was going to turn very nasty indeed, and the place was packed with civilians who would make ideal hostages for men with nothing to lose.

Dexter was back on his feet now. "Did you let these men out?" Ruso demanded.

"Me?"

"Stay out of sight or they'll kill you."

"I'm not afraid of—"

"Or I will." Ruso pushed his way forward. "Marcus! Get these men under control. Quickly."

Marcus ignored him and carried on berating Accius. Ruso gripped his earlobe and twisted, digging in his thumbnail. Marcus let out a yell of pain.

"You started this!" Ruso shouted. "Get them under control or we'll have a bloodbath!"

For a man who was ready to face the next world, Marcus suddenly looked very frightened. He turned to Accius. "Sir?"

Accius raised both hands in surrender. "They won't listen to me!"

To their left, a couple of drunken recruits had clambered onto the mounting block and were attempting a dance. Somewhere in the darkness, the girl screamed again.

"One of us," said Ruso grimly, "had better think of something."

Marcus stood on tiptoe and shouted in the direction of the stable, "Lads! Oi! Leave the girl alone, lads!"

Someone shouted, "Wait your turn, mate!"

The dancers stumbled off the edge of the mounting block and crashed into the crowd.

Ruso shouted in Marcus's ear, "Is the empress safe? And my wife?"

Marcus yelled back, "Upstairs. The lads were told not to touch them."

Ruso glanced at the row of upstairs windows. Was that a blond head behind one of them? He could not tell. He reached out and seized Marcus with one hand and Accius with the other, dragging them round the fallen dancers toward the vacant mounting block.

"Tell them they must listen to the tribune," he urged, pushing Marcus up the narrow steps.

"But, sir—"

"Do it!"

He did it. Either the men were eager for leadership or a powerful god was with him. Ruso neither knew nor cared which. The confusion died down for a moment while the crowd waited for the next part of the show. Pushing Marcus toward the stables with "Go and help that girl," Ruso urged a reluctant Accius up the steps of the mounting block. "You're good at making speeches. Tell them you understand why they're angry. Tell them you respect their loyalty in not deserting. Tell them—oh, tell them any old bollocks. Then tell them you're supporting their appeal to the empress."

"But the emp—"

"Now, Accius! This is what all that training was for!"

80

"Sa-bi-na!" roared the men down in the courtyard, stamping and banging anything within reach in time with the rhythm of the name. *"Sa-bi-na! Sa-bi-na!"*

In the upstairs room, a grim-faced Clarus had joined the line of men guarding the corner. He was clutching a metal jug in one hand and what looked like a woman's hairpin in the other. If it had not been so desperate, it would have been funny.

Behind them, some of the huddled women were weeping. Then Sabina cried, "Do not let them take me, Clarus! Kill me now, I beg you! I know what they did to those poor women in Londinium!"

"Madam, I cannot—"

"Then somebody give me a knife!"

"Madam!" Tilla abandoned the window. "They do not want to hurt you. The tribune has made his speech, and the men have listened. Now they want to present a delegation."

Sabina's squeak of "A delegation?" left Tilla wondering if she had chosen the wrong word.

"They want to ask for justice."

"But the emperor is not here!"

Clarus said, "The empress cannot grant petitions."

"Madam," said Tilla, ignoring him, "these men are Britons. They do not know who can grant what." In truth they probably did, but Sabina did not need to know that. "What they know is that you are the wife of a great leader. You have traveled all over the world with him, and between you, you have won many victories. They believe you are a noble warrior-queen like the ones they honor amongst their own people."

There was a pause while Sabina and Clarus thought about that. The chant of *"Sa-bi-na!"* still rose in the yard, embellished with whoops and whistles.

The empress said, "Can their officers not get them under control?"

"They are loyal to the emperor, madam," Tilla reminded her. "But they have been badly mistreated."

"That has already been dealt with! What is the matter with these people? The man is dead: What more do they want? I shall tell Paulina about this when we get to Deva and her husband will have them all flogged."

"Sa-bi-na!"

"We are not in Deva to night. You do not need anyone's husband. Not even your own. Tonight everyone here is depending on you."

"Stay here, madam!" urged Clarus, glancing over his shoulder. "My men cannot defend you out there. Stay here and wait for rescue."

"Sa-bi-na!" The chant was beginning to sound ragged. The men would not wait much longer. Some of them would be drunk, and Clarus was right: Any minute now, the troops outside would find a way into the building and there would be an end to this, but neither a quick nor a happy one.

Tilla said, "Madam, they are calling for you. If you listen to them you can save us."

"Do not believe her, Madam!" It was Minna's voice. "She's one of them: You can't trust her!"

"Very well." A figure rose from the corner. "I will do it."

Several voices began to object.

"Thank you, but I have made my decision."

Clarus said, "Then I shall come with you, madam."

A voice from the door said in British, "We was told not to let nobody—"

"Have some sense!" Tilla snapped. "How can Marcus present anything to her if you do not let her out?"

"Just you and her, then."

None of the Romans liked that very much, but the Britons were the ones with the swords. Sabina's hand was trembling as Tilla led her along the dark corridor and down the stairs toward the barbarians.

Down in the courtyard, the chant of *"Sa-bi-na!"* gave way to cheering and shouts of "Make way!" as the two women appeared and were hustled across to the mounting block. Tilla felt a hand on her arm and turned to see her husband mouthing something she could not catch. Marcus was standing next to him with the snake arm around—was that Virana?

Accius was helping the empress up the steps of the mounting block. There was a confusion of shouting and shushing as everyone told everyone else to shut up and listen. Finally a hush spread across the courtyard.

Sabina's earrings glittered as she looked over the heads of the crowd and waited for someone to address her. "Well?" she asked. "You had plenty to say just now. I am listening."

There was nervous laughter. Tilla felt her arm released as some sort of whispered argument erupted between her husband and Marcus. Then Marcus stepped forward. "Empress," he said, and bowed to the figure above him.

Someone shouted, "Good start, mate!"

Marcus hesitated, clearly unnerved. "Madam Empress, three months ago there were fifty of us, recruits to the Twentieth Legion. Now three are dead, one is sick, and one is in chains."

Sabina said, "Who are you?"

"Oh. Yes." Marcus cleared his throat. "Marcus of the Regni. Tonight Centurion Dexter tried to get rid of the rest of us, but we came to report to Tribune Accius instead, because we want to serve the emperor."

Sabina inclined her head.

"And you," he added quickly.

She inclined her head once more.

Marcus said, "We wanted the tribune to know what really happened to the men who died. Dannicus and Tadius and Sulio. And now he does. And ... ah ... we're sorry about spoiling your dinner."

A cry of "No we're not!" was followed by a scuffle somewhere in the darkness and hissings of "Shut up!"

"I see," said Sabina. "And what is your petition?"

There was another pause. Tilla could hear whispers of "What's he saying?" but Marcus seemed not to know how to explain what his men wanted.

Suddenly Accius stepped forward. "Madam, if I may..."

"Please do, Tribune."

"Madam, these men are proud to be citizens of Rome, but they are also natives, and they are overwhelmed by the honor of speaking with the greatest lady in the known world. Even here in the wilds, everyone has heard of your great virtue and beauty and your many achievements..."

So that was how you were supposed to talk to an empress. No wonder she always looked bored. Finally he seemed to be getting to the point. "They ask your full and absolute pardon for their behavior this evening, for safe conduct to Deva where they can present their case to the legate and receive justice—"

"Proper justice!" shouted someone. There was a chorus of support. A small chant of "No more lies!" broke out and died away again as Sabina raised one hand for silence.

"—and for the immediate release of their comrade Victor, whom they believe is innocent of the murder of Centurion Geminus."

Tilla noticed that he did not say what he thought of Victor himself.

Sabina said, "That is it?"

"Yes, madam."

She held out one hand. "I will receive their petition."

Accius looked around wildly. "Madam, my men have not yet—"

"Here you are, Empress!" Virana stepped forward, tugging a little scrap of rolled-up parchment out of her cleavage. Sabina took it between finger and thumb as if she were holding a dead rat by the tail. She teased it partly open with one fingertip and frowned. Then she lifted her head and said in a voice that was clear, but without the strength of one used to making speeches, "Men of the Twentieth Legion, on condition that you leave immediately and peacefully and return to your camp, I, Vibia Sabina Augusta, am pleased to grant a full and absolute pardon for your conduct this evening and to grant your petition."

As the cheers gathered into a fresh chant of "*Sa-bi-na!*" she handed the parchment to Tilla. "Look after it. I can't read a word of it in this light. I shall have to sign it in the morning."

81

Ruso watched the recruits march out of the stable entrance behind Accius, the odd drunken stumble the only hint of the chaos they had caused just now. They appeared to have taken to heart the tribune's warning that the first man to step out of line again would be crucified, and so would his comrades on either side of him.

Just before they formed up he had murmured to Marcus, "You're a different man from the one I met at Eboracum."

"It was you who gave me the courage, sir." Then he grinned as if Ruso would be pleased with the compliment, and as if everything would be all right from now on, and wisely pulled the shoulders of his tunic down over his tattoos before merging in amongst the other recruits.

Meanwhile, Clarus had rushed outside to ensure that the Praetorians who had been spoiling for a fight didn't pick one, and then returned to resume his anxious guard over the empress.

A couple of slaves crept out from wherever they were hiding, barred the gates, and disappeared again. The clearing up would have to wait for daylight.

Ruso sat on the mounting block, folded his arms, and gazed up at the stars. A horse stamped over in the stables, no doubt relieved that the terrifying humans had all gone away. Tilla had whispered a hasty "Wait for me!" but she had gone inside with Sabina and was probably still trying to smooth ruffled feathers. He should probably go straight to the camp, but he doubted the men would dare cause any more trouble now. He would just enjoy a few more moments of peace, then get out before everyone here locked up and went to bed.

There above him was the Great Bear, and above it the North Star and the Little Bear, and around them all the constellations he should remember the names of but never could. Through all the madness of this evening they had been shining there, constant, hidden only by the confusion of light and smoke made by humankind. No doubt there was a lesson there that he ought to ponder on the road tomorrow. To night, he was merely relieved that the crisis was over.

Between them, Accius and Sabina had managed to convince the recruits that they should proceed peacefully to Deva. If they were lucky, the legate would uphold Sabina's unauthorized pardon—it might be politically awkward not to—and withhold the charge of mutiny. Victor, now amply punished for his desertion, would be free from the unjust accusation of murder. And if Clarus chose not to prosecute the Praetorians who had apparently settled an old grudge by murdering their former comrade, that was his business. Even Accius would have to admit that it was a kind of justice.

A distant owl hooted. Something changed in his peripheral vision, and he realized the light in one of the windows above him had gone out. As he watched, another light died. He got to his feet, noticing for the first time that he was cold, and made his way across the yard to where the lamps were still glowing in the main entrance hall.

He was almost there when a figure stepped out of the shadows. He had sprung back and grabbed his knife before reason pointed out to instinct that the blond hair belonged to his wife.

"Husband!" she hissed, raising both hands. "It is me!"

It occurred to him that "It is me!" was unnecessary, since no one but Tilla was likely to call him "husband." Next it occurred to him that only a very tired mind would notice that sort of thing when there were far more pressing matters to attend to. Like Tilla assuring him that nobody was dead.

He was pleased she was safe, and that no one had been killed, and he thanked her for the good news.

"It was Marcus."

"What was?"

"The horrible screaming and the—" She broke off to give a muted demonstration of a ghastly choking gurgle.

"I see." He had no idea what she was talking about, but Marcus had looked perfectly healthy just now and no doubt the explanation would be more complicated than it was worth.

"One of his friends told me. He learned it from a charcoal burner who used it to frighten off the soldiers when they came sneaking through the woods to steal his fuel."

"Ah."

"And I can tell you something else: The scorpions from Rome had orders from the emperor's secretary to kill Geminus."

"I see."

"How can you see? I have not told you yet. You are just saying "I see' without listening."

"Yes."

Then she told him. And then he did see, and he wished he did not, because what she was so proud of having found out was something that would be much, much better left hidden. And the way she had gone about finding it meant that she now had an enemy far worse than Metellus.

"But I did it to help!"

"I didn't ask for your help, Tilla."

"You wanted to know who it was. I have found out for you. It was not some old grudge after all.

Someone gave the order through Tranquillus. I think the empress was trying to help us."

He doubted that, but what Tilla thought did not matter much as long as she kept it to herself. "Who else knows that you know?"

Tilla gave a huff of exasperation. "You think I am fool enough to go around telling everybody?"

"If it's just Clarus, we might be safe. He won't go round saying he was overpowered by a girl. If you just stay out of his way..." He stopped. How likely was it that Clarus would believe his secret was safe with someone like Tilla?

Not very. And now Tilla was saying "There is just one other person..." in a tone that suggested he was not going to like this very much.

"I did not mean to say anything," she said. "It just came out."

"What did?"

"It was just me and her, alone on the stairs, and she was frightened, and I tried to cheer her, and I think I said... oh, dear."

"What?" he demanded.

"I made sure to whisper. Nobody else heard."

"Just tell me what it was!"

She sniffed. "I said something to the empress about knowing she was on our side. And if the men knew what she had done, they would be grateful."

"Oh, gods above!" Ruso ran one hand through his hair. "What ever possessed you to say that?"

"I am sorry! I thought..." She shook her head. "I felt sorry for her. She is never allowed to do anything and when she is brave enough to try, nobody knows, so nobody can thank her." She looked up. "Anyway, I did not say what I was talking about."

"You really imagine she didn't guess?"

She lowered her head. "She did not question it. I think she knew."

While part of Ruso's mind was praying, *Holy Jupiter, let this not be true,* the other part was reasoning that it made far more sense than some ancient Praetorian grudge that could surely have been resolved years ago.

"This is very bad, Tilla."

"I will stay out of sight."

He sighed. "The damage is done now. Clarus will assume you were acting for me."

"I am sorry, husband!" He could tell from her voice that she was close to crying. "I was trying to help. I am so tired, and so very... oh, why does nothing go right?"

He put his arms around her, because that was the only answer he had. The hot tears soaked though the shoulder of his tunic. He thought of other times when he had told Tilla to stay out of something, only to find that he was glad of her help. This time it had gone wrong, and it was his own fault as much as hers, because instead of being grateful to her in the past, he should have insisted that she learn the first duty of a wife: obedience.

When she lifted her head and sniffed he murmured, "We both need to be careful now. We know too much, and we're more expendable than Geminus. Don't imagine that because you've helped the empress, she will help you."

"But…what are we going to do?"

He stroked her hair. "You're right," he said, not because she was but because he could think of nothing better. "We'll both keep out of the way, and we'll keep quiet. The empress will leave and life will go back to normal. All this will all blow over."

She wiped her eyes on a fistful of his tunic. "That is what you said before." She released him and reached down to pull something out of her boot. "I have this."

He caught a glint of light on the bronze handle of his missing scalpel. "Careful with that!" He tried to take it from her, but she bent to slide it back into its hiding place. She was lucky she had not sliced herself open.

This was ridiculous. Mixing up medicines, stealing dangerous equipment, assaulting a close friend of the emperor…Why had he not had the sense to do what other men did: to buy a slave and leave his wife at home?

Somewhere across the yard, a door scraped open. A voice said, "There you are!"

"Virana," Tilla sighed as the girl approached. "Are you all right?"

"Marcus came to save me! Did you see? And the empress will sign my petition in the morning!"

"I think," said Tilla acidly, "it is time for bed."

"Yes, that is the other good news! Celer is guarding our space in the hayloft." She looked at Ruso. "There is room for another one, sir."

Ruso shook his head. "I'm going back to the camp," he said. Before he left he squeezed Tilla's hand, glad that the girl could not see she had been crying. "Be careful."

"Don't worry, sir," put in Virana. "I will look after her for you."

As he made his way back toward the entrance hall, he heard a loud whisper of "Oh, isn't he kind! You are so lucky!"

No, he thought. *She is not. She is cursed with knowing too much. And so am I.*

82

Alone as usual, Sabina lay in the comfort of her own fragranced sheets and savored the silence. The women bedded down on the floor around her would not dare to speak into the darkness unless she gave the order, and of course there were no rats. It had been the sound of mutinous Britons creeping across the roof.

The tremulous staff from the inn were long gone, as was the dreadful woman from the tribune's household who had the nerve to ask the slaves—in her hearing!—if the empress was really as all right as she claimed to be.

Clarus had been harder to get rid of, but he had finally stopped making a fuss when she compromised: no Praetorians standing guard in the bedroom, but however many he wanted outside the door. She heard a floorboard creak as one of them shifted his footing. It would not surprise her if Clarus, ever loyal and now unusually flustered and apologetic as well, was lined up out there with them.

Safely returned into the care of her staff, she was finding it hard to believe what had happened this evening. All those men chanting her name! She could not restrain a smile. *Her* name. Not that of the emperor. *Sa-bi-na!* Raw and raucous and potent.

For a few brief minutes, she had been more than an unloved wife trailed in the wake of the most powerful man in the world. More than a woman with thinning hair and a tooth held in by gold wire whose slaves tactfully buried her deeper each year in layers of jewelry and makeup and hairpieces.

They had called for her. They had cheered her. They had listened to her. They had even laughed at her joke. She had felt a thrill run all the way through her as she knew for the first time what real power was like.

If the men knew what you had done, the Briton had said, *they would be grateful to you.* What did the Briton know about the murder of the centurion? What exactly had Clarus told her when they were alone together, and how much had she passed on?

It was a problem she would consider tomorrow.

To night she would enjoy being Sa-bi-na, Warrior-Queen of the Britons.

83

Morning came, and with it the sound of birds singing and broken things being swept up. The Warrior-Queen of the Britons pulled the sheet up over her face, wishing away the knocking on the door and the urgent whisper of "Madam!"

The wishing did not work. Sabina, empress of Rome, flapped the sheet back down and said, "What?"

"Madam, Prefect Clarus is here to speak with you."

"Tell him to come back at a sensible hour."

"We tried, Madam. He won't go."

She ran her fingers through her thin hair. He could not be allowed to see her like this. Gesticulating to the other slaves to fetch her clothes, she said, "Ask him if the carriage is mended, and whether—" She stopped herself just in time from calling them *my men.* "—and whether the soldiers are behaving themselves, and how long it will be before we can get out of this dreadful place."

The questions were conveyed, but instead of answering them Clarus called through the door, "Madam, the emperor is in the camp. He will be here at any moment."

"Here?" She sat bolt upright. "Why did nobody— What is he doing here?"

"I sent a message last night, madam."

What would people tell him about yesterday? Would anyone tell him how much she had enjoyed it? She turned to her slaves. "Clothes, quickly! Fetch my hair!"

"Madam, if I could speak with you a little more privately…"

"In a moment!"

When she was sufficiently clothed and coiffed to be decent—although the perfect lead-pale skin was still in its pot and the curling tongs were heating in the brazier—she finally allowed him to enter.

Clarus looked even more cadaverous than usual. "Madam. I am glad to see you looking refreshed and well this morning."

"I wish I could say the same of you."

"It has been a long night," he conceded. "But now that the emperor is here, I'm sure all will be well."

"No doubt he will enjoy setting us all straight. What do you want?"

"I thought you would like to know that the officers were very grateful for your help last night, madam. The camp has been peaceful all night."

"Good."

He lowered his voice. "Although some of the Twentieth seem to think that my men murdered their centurion."

So the woman had talked. Already rumors were spreading among the soldiers. "Well, you're in charge of the investigation," she told him, settling herself on the stool as the slave approached with the first pot of skin cream. "It's nothing to do with me. I thought you had some suspects under arrest."

"The Briton's husband and the recruit. Both have been released. You agreed to the release of the recruit last night."

"Ah, yes. So I did." She sighed. As usual, plea sure was followed by regret. "I still haven't signed anything."

"I think it would be unwise to retract now, madam."

"Well, what can I do?" She pushed the slave's hand aside. There was no sense in letting her get cream all over the hairpiece.

In front of her, Clarus was looking genuinely worried. She said, "I never interfere, as you know, but if I were you, I would consider rearresting the other one."

"Yes, madam. That was what I was thinking also. I shall see to it."

"Now, go away. I have to get ready to receive the emperor."

Clarus did not seem in the least offended at being sent away. He seemed to have grown in her presence. He had to duck to get out of the doorway.

84

Valens? "

"You're not going to ask if I'm dead again, are you?"

"No, but what are you doing here?"

Valens yawned and let the tent flap fall closed behind him, cutting out most of the light. "That was quite a ride. I don't know how Hadrian does it at his age. I thought that little secretary chap was going to expire before we got here. Have you got something to sit on down there? I don't want a damp backside."

"On my left." The chains rattled as Ruso patted the torn goatskin.

Valens settled beside him with the weary grunt of a tired man whose muscles had begun to tighten up. "I'm sorry to see you still in this state. I was hoping they'd have sorted it out by now."

Ruso said, "So was I."

"I did my best with Tilla, you know."

"That's all any of us can do with Tilla. Have you seen her?"

"They said she's over at the inn. I'll go and find her in a minute."

Something else occurred to Ruso. "Aren't you supposed to be with the procurator? Or is he here too?"

Valens yawned again. "The gout's settled down. I've left him in good hands."

"But aren't you—"

"The truth is I'm not sure I really want to go to Rome."

"What about the family?"

"The wife won't like it," Valens conceded. "But she's marginally less frightening than a couple of people I might run into back there."

"What sort of people?"

"You'd think they'd have more important things to worry about, wouldn't you? I mean, look at you. Still stuck here in chains on some ridiculous murder charge. You've got a real problem."

"Thank you."

"Oh by the way, the tribune says he'll do his best for you. I don't know why he's changed his mind, but he seems to be a sensible sort of chap after all."

"Good."

"Anyway, Rome: You know how you get chatting to people on a journey? It turns out one of Hadrian's grooms has a cousin in the household of someone I used to know years back, and apparently I'm still mentioned."

"Ah."

"It's hardly fair. Her father told me to clear off, and I did. It's not my fault she's gone and divorced some stuffy old politician because she's still in love with me, is it?"

Ruso shifted to ease the stiffness in his back. The chains tumbled into a new position.

"Look, is there anything I can get you? Are they feeding you properly?"

Ruso, who had only been rearrested half an hour ago, had not had time to find out. "Go and find Tilla," he said, "and tell her that I've got a plan. Tell her it depends on her staying out of it, whatever happens. Tie her up and gag her if you have to."

"She won't like that very much."

Ruso managed a smile. "Get the scalpel out of her left boot first."

"So what's the plan?"

"I'm appealing to Hadrian."

"Can you do that? You're supposed to go before the legate."

"Hadrian knows me. We were stationed together in Antioch. We worked together on the earthquake rescue."

"Really? You never said."

"My stepmother says I only have to ask him for a favor and he'll grant it."

Valens said, "Your stepmother? Does she know him too?"

"Mm," said Ruso. "Apparently."

85

A traveler approaching a small staging post on the Eboracum Road at about the sixth hour that day might have noticed two soldiers strolling westward along the road toward him. As they grew closer, he might have been mildly surprised to see that while one was a well-built bearded officer whose outfit was respectable if rather dusty, his companion was chiefly notable for the heavy chains linking both wrists to his left ankle. Should he have happened to overhear any of the conversation between this odd couple as they passed by—which was unlikely, since their voices were low—he might have been further surprised to note that in this westernmost province of the empire, they were speaking Greek.

He might or might not have associated the dusty officer with the four cavalrymen riding slowly along a hundred paces behind, but by then his attention would have been diverted by the unusual spectacle of soldiers still striking camp at such a late hour. Whereupon all other thoughts would have been pushed aside by the pressing question of whether the Falcon's Rest would still have anything decent left for lunch, or whether the soldiers had scoffed the lot.

"Your tribune tells me," said Hadrian, "that he refuses to accuse you of murdering his relative because you didn't do it. Meanwhile, my prefect seems to think he has plenty of grounds for an accusation, and you tell me you're willing to confess."

"Yes, sir."

"Explain."

"I'll confess if it keeps the peace, sir. But I didn't do it."

"Do you know who did?"

"Yes, sir."

"Well?"

"I can't say, sir."

"I've ridden most of the night to get here, Ruso. I've got gritty eyes, stiff shoulders, and a bruised arse. Don't annoy me."

"Sorry, sir."

"Who did it?"

"I'm sorry, sir. I can't tell you."

"You'll tell me soon enough if I hand you over to the questioners."

"Probably, sir. But I don't think it would do either of us much good."

Hadrian sighed. "And you imagine I won't accept your confession?"

Ruso swallowed. "I'd very much rather you didn't, sir."

"But it would be very convenient, wouldn't it? The native suspect will remain free, his mutinous comrades—whom your tribune tactfully describes as "boisterous," by the way—will stop getting themselves into more trouble by accusing my Praetorians of murder; and it will be clear to everyone that the Twentieth Legion answers to its officers, not to some uppity medic and his native girlfriend."

"On the other hand, sir, you know you would be punishing an innocent man for somebody else's crime."

"Given the scale of the convenience, and your apparent willingness to be an unsung hero, that may be a price worth paying."

"Perhaps, sir." Ruso swallowed. This was not the way he had imagined the conversation going. Maybe he really had been influenced by his stepmother's ludicrous presumption of—well, not of friendship, of course; perhaps *comradeship* would be the word. But back in Antioch, he and Senator Publius Aelius Hadrianus had both been on the same side. Now one of them was the most powerful man in the world, while the other was a nuisance.

Hadrian untied the stopper of his water bottle and took a swig like any common soldier. "I should have Clarus arrest that woman of yours. I hear she's behind all this."

"Absolutely not, sir!"

They stepped aside as a rumble of wheels announced the approach of a post carriage. Ruso hopped awkwardly over the ditch and Hadrian busied himself tying the thong back around the stopper. The carriage thundered past, driver and courier oblivious to the fact that they could have halted and delivered many of their messages in person.

"Sir," put in Ruso as soon as he could be heard, "my wife has nothing to do with it. Nothing at all. I won't confess anything if you arrest her." Not willingly, anyway. The gods alone knew what he would say once the questioners got to work.

"Hm." Hadrian stepped back across the ditch. "Let me propose a hypothetical situation. Let us suppose that there are two wives. Neither wife trusts her husband to get on with his own business without her help. I take it you can imagine this situation?"

"Yes, sir."

"The first man's wife goes bleating to the second man's wife about some difficulty her husband is having. The second man's wife, who has a tendency to exaggerate her husband's shortcomings, expresses some surprise that he has done nothing to help the first man in this situation—a situation about which, of course, both of the wives have only the barest understanding. Are you with me so far?"

"I think so, sir."

"This is, of course, purely hypothetical."

"Yes, sir." If only this whole mess were hypothetical. If only Tilla had held a hypothetical meeting with the empress. If only she had threatened the prefect of the Praetorians with a hypothetical scalpel.

"Now let us say that the friends of the second man's wife, some of whom are rather more eager to impress her than they should be, listen to this complaint and take it to be an expression of her wishes. So, in a misguided act of loyal service, they arrange for the problem to be dealt with."

Gods above, the emperor knew the whole story! Everything he and Tilla had risked their necks to find out. Was there anything this man's spies did not tell him? "If that were to happen, sir, it would be very unfortunate."

"Especially since, if this came to light, people might mistakenly assume that the wishes were not only those of the wife but of her husband."

Of course. That was what interested Hadrian. If word got out, people would assume that the murderer of inconvenient senators had now become the murderer of inconvenient centurions. The emperor, whose power traditionally rested on the tripod of the Senate, the army, and the people, would appear to have kicked away a second prop. If his enemies managed to exploit this apparent weakness, he could be in real trouble.

Unfortunately, it was hard to imagine Hadrian confiding any of this to a man he didn't intend to have safely executed by lunchtime.

Ruso took a deep breath. "Personally, sir, I think if the second husband were going to deal with the problem himself, he would have found a better way."

Hadrian grunted. "I suppose that's a compliment."

"To the hypothetical husband, sir."

"Yes. Anyway, were someone to come along who was willing to assume the blame for the whole fiasco, I'd imagine that—for the sake of peace and quiet—any sensible man would let him get on with it."

Put like that, his impulsive offer to confess—which had started out as a way of silencing a few recruits and getting Tilla out of trouble—sounded less like a fatal mistake than a heroic act of self-sacrifice to save the stability of the empire. He said, "Probably, sir, yes."

"We've gone far enough. Turn around."

Ruso pivoted round his chained ankle and faced back the way they had just come. The cavalry escort now facing them urged their mounts across onto the opposite verge and waited at a respectful distance for the emperor to pass. Ruso eyed the road ahead, unable to repress a hope that Tilla might have defied his wishes and Done Something. She could be galloping toward him right now on a stolen horse, ready to drag him up behind her in some miraculous feat of weightlifting, and...

"I have given this matter considerable thought," Hadrian announced.

He had said he wanted no help from her. He had told Valens to tie her up if necessary. It was not the sort of request Valens would be likely to ignore.

"As you are no doubt aware," Hadrian was saying, "I have never sanctioned the killing of innocent men."

"Yes, sir." Or should that be *No, sir*?

"Contrary to what I've been told, you seem to be a man who knows when to speak up and when to shut up."

Was that an acknowledgment that he had done the right thing at Eboracum? "I try, sir."

"Good. Because if you speak of this conversation to anyone, I shall find out, and neither you nor that woman will live long enough to regret it. Is that understood?"

What Ruso understood was that the great man was speaking as if he had a future. "Absolutely, sir."

"I am therefore pleased to tell you what my prefect has discovered." Hadrian paused, as if he was enjoying the moment. "You were all mistaken. There was no murder."

Ruso swallowed. "No, sir?"

"No. Centurion Geminus diligently carried out his duty at Eboracum despite knowing that he was incurably sick—a fact that he hid even from the medical service. Satisfied that his recruits had passed their final tests, and not wanting to burden his comrades with a long and debilitating illness, he bravely committed suicide. With his own knife, as I'm told you can confirm."

"Ah—yes, sir."

"Which only leaves us, Ruso, with the question of where you wish to be posted next."

Ruso gulped. He was still taking in the barefaced lie that would save his life, and wondering what other fantasies this man had foisted onto the citizens of Rome in the name of decency and stability.

"Pay attention, Ruso. I'm offering you a favor."

"Yes, sir. Sorry, sir. I didn't expect it." Although if he had listened to his stepmother, he should have.

"Where shall I send you?"

Where did he want to go? Somewhere warm and dry and civilized. He could go home to the family in Gaul—or, then again, not. He could go to Rome and look after—no, not rich people. But maybe glamorous ones. Gladiators. Charioteers. Healthy young men who suffered from nothing tediously chronic and incurable but had plenty of interesting accidents. He could try new surgical techniques. Make advances. Pay someone—his old clerk Albanus, perhaps—to write down his every thought and publish it. He could become the World-Famous Doctor Ruso. He could finally clear off the family debts. He could buy so many slaves that Tilla would never have to polish his armor or light a fire or interfere with his medical case again. Or cook. Now, there was a thought. He was definitely going to buy a cook.

"I hear my outgoing procurator is looking for a new doctor."

The words interrupted his reverie.

"I believe he is a generous patron."

Had Valens really abandoned the procurator's service because of some old quarrel in Rome? Or had he sacrificed his position out of friendship? What ever the reason, it would not be fair to take advantage of it.

And then there was Tilla. Tilla, who had been homesick in Gaul. Tilla would be miserable in Rome. And when Tilla was miserable, nothing else was a pleasure, either.

Britannia did not have enough gladiators and charioteers on which to build a career. But it did have plenty of healthy men who had interesting injuries. Soldiers were frequently unlovely, uncouth, and ungrateful. On the other hand, they were mostly young and lively and entertaining, and somebody had to be there to protect them from their own stupidity and that of their officers.

"Well?"

"Sir, I think..." He stopped. "I'd like to keep my current posting with the Twentieth, sir. But can I ask something for my wife?"

Hadrian's silence was not encouraging.

"She's somehow ended up on a list of doubtful persons, sir. It was all dealt with years ago, but we can't seem to get her name off the list."

"Ah, the wretched lists. A necessary evil. Hard to believe, but there really are people who don't appreciate the benefits of our rule."

"Tilla's very appreciative, sir." If emperors could lie in a good cause, so could their subjects.

"In that case, I see no difficulty. A native woman married to one of my officers. A fine example to the Britons. Yes. I'll have the document drawn up straightaway."

"Document?"

"Citizenship, man!" Hadrian's heavy features broke into a smile. "Personally granted by the emperor. That should deal with it."

Ruso blinked. Citizenship of Rome. The privileged status that outsiders could only earn after decades in the army, or keeping order and collecting taxes on behalf of the treasury, or a life of slavery, or performing some outstanding act of service to the emperor or his cronies. It was the one freedom Tilla would not have wanted, and he had just arranged to have it foisted upon her. "Thank you, sir."

Hadrian turned to beckon his cavalrymen forward. "Have this doctor taken back to his unit," he said. "And tell them to take those ridiculous chains off. I want him busy looking after my men."

86

Ruso stood waiting to be assigned a horse from the lines, and running over his conversation with Hadrian with increasing unease. He had been offered the chance to heave himself out of the muddy rut that was Britannia, and he had turned it down. He had just demonstrated the depths of cowardice to which his family and his first wife had always known he could sink. *You're hopeless at putting yourself forward, Gaius.*

Think of other people and make an effort.

"Ruso! A word!"

Accius was striding toward him across the grass. "I got you released. Have the decency to tell me what's going on."

"I think there'll be an announcement, sir."

"There's already been one. Geminus killed himself, the empress is going north with Hadrian, and Clarus and Tranquillus are being sent back to Rome in disgrace."

Ruso stared at him. "Why?"

"For being overfamiliar with the empress, whatever that means. Anyway, it's none of our business. What did the emperor say about me?"

"He said you'd told him I was innocent, sir. I'm grateful."

"So you bloody should be. What else?"

"Nothing else, sir."

"So what did he talk about?"

"I can't tell you, sir."

"Did he mention my family?"

"No, sir."

"What did he say about the Twentieth?"

"Sir, I'm really sorry, but I can't tell you what he said."

"I see." The tribune lowered his voice. "So, it seems the Praetorian Guard get away with murdering another of my relatives."

Across the field, the mules had been hitched to the hospital wagons. Ruso could see Pera helping Victor up to keep Austalis company. Dexter, relieved of duties pending trial, was just visible behind one of the supply vehicles. The remaining junior officers were yelling at the recruits to get a bloody move on. Apparently they had never seen such a bunch of ham-fisted layabouts. Ruso said, "In Geminus's position, sir, I believe taking his own life was the most honorable thing he could do."

"But you and I both know ..." Accius paused. "Yes. Yes, I suppose you're right."

A groom was approaching with two horses. "Someone also just passed on a curious rumor about your wife," murmured Accius.

When Ruso did not respond he said, "You need to get that woman under control, man. She's a menace."

"I'll see she keeps out of your way in future, sir."

"The last thing she needs is to be honored with citizenship. I take it that's one of your rewards for silence?"

"Silence, sir?"

"Oh, I give up!" Accius seized the reins, spurned the assistance of the groom, and vaulted into the saddle unaided. "I suppose you're just glad to be alive."

"Always, sir," said Ruso, who wasn't, but who was beginning to think he really should be, when he noticed another man approaching across the grass. He tried to hide his surprise.

Metellus waited until Accius had gone. He did not bother with a greeting. "It wasn't my idea to have you arrested the second time."

Ruso took the proffered reins of a bay mare from its groom. "Well, you can't have all the good ideas."

"I suppose you think you've won."

Ruso teased the mare's forelock out from beneath the brow band. "Frankly, I'm happier when I don't think about you at all."

"Then you'll share my pleasure in the news that a promotion will be sending me to Rome in the next few days."

Ruso paused with one hand on the girth. "You're going a long way away? Very good."

Metellus said, "I only did what I did out of duty, you know. It was never personal."

"Wasn't it?"

"You know damn well your wife was withholding information."

"My wife has just been made a citizen of Rome by the emperor himself." Ruso pulled the girth tighter. "What we know or don't know doesn't matter anymore."

"Exactly." Metellus gave one of his rare and unnerving smiles. He said, "I would offer to shake hands, Doctor, but that would give you the pleasure of refusing."

Then he turned on his heel and strode away, leaving Ruso to wonder whether Rome was really a promotion, and glad he wasn't going there too.

87

It was a subdued pair of passengers who sat in Celer's cart, waiting for it to set off behind the official transport of the Twentieth Legion. Tilla had heard nothing from her husband since his release. Before that, the only message had been an order to stay away from him. Valens, who knew nothing of the trouble she had caused by trying to help before, had seemed surprised and relieved when she promised to obey.

The news about Sabina had dampened her spirits further. She could not say good-bye, of course, but Tilla had gone to watch her carriage pulling away. The empress had enjoyed one brief moment of glory. Then her man had arrived out of nowhere, banished the people who seemed to be her only friends, and ordered her to accompany him. Tilla could not help thinking that if Hadrian had married a woman of the Corionotatae, she would have put him in his place many years ago, and they would both have been much happier for it.

Or perhaps not. She should have rejoiced when Valens came back with the good news that her husband had been set free, but still there was no message, and the silence grew louder with every moment that passed.

Virana had troubles of her own. She had scrambled down from the cart when Marcus and the other men emerged from the camp, only to return with the news that he was being horrible to her. "He told me to go away."

"He cannot speak with you when he is on duty."

"He says he won't marry me and he only saved me because the Medicus told him to."

"Oh."

"Why can't the Medicus tell him to marry me?"

"Because he can't! Think of something else to talk about!" As soon as the words were out, Tilla wished she had not spoken them. "I am sorry. But wishing for something will not make it so, and besides, being married to a soldier is not the wonderful life you imagine."

Virana was still thinking about that when Corinna arrived to say how pleased she and Victor were that the Medicus had been released and everything had worked out so well. "I am sorry for the harsh words I spoke back in Eboracum."

"They are forgotten," Tilla assured her.

"And I shall forget that you were cross with me," put in Virana, pushing herself up to peer ahead. "Is that the nice doctor? Is he coming with us to Deva?"

Tilla said, " 'The nice doctor'?"

"The good-looking one. The one who is getting divorced."

"Valens? Divorced? Never."

"He says his wife is always cross with him."

"His wife is also very rich."

Virana slumped back into her seat. "So what am I going to do? I was only going to Deva to help you, and now I shall be stuck there and nobody will want me!"

"But you were the one—"

"And my baby will starve and I shall end up being a slave in a whorehouse!"

"Don't be ridiculous!" snapped Tilla, remembering too late that that was exactly where she had thought Virana would end up.

"Of course you will not!" Corinna assured her. "The Medicus and his wife would never let that happen. They are good people." She turned to Tilla. "You will look after Virana, won't you?"

Tilla sighed. "Virana, I do not know what is waiting for us in Deva. But you can help me until your baby is born. Then you must either go home or find respectable work."

"Oh, thank you, thank you!" Virana's troubles were forgotten. "I know how to work hard. I will fetch the wood and the water and light the fires and cook and clean the house and milk the goats, and I promise I will behave myself, and—"

Tilla stopped listening to the promises the girl would probably break within a week, because she had seen who was riding back along the verge toward them.

She gathered up fistfuls of skirt, leapt down from the cart, and ran toward him. "Husband!"

He leaned down from the horse and held out one hand to seize her own.

"Are you really safe this time?"

"I am," he assured her, bending to kiss the top of her head.

"What did the emperor say to you?"

He swung down from the horse and they fell respectably into step, a glance the only further sign of affection between officer and wife: nothing to entertain the drivers of the baggage train.

"You've heard about Geminus's suicide?"

She said, "I do not care about him. The important people to remember are the three boys who died."

He nodded. They walked together in silence. Then he cleared his throat. "There's something I need to talk to you about. We can stop worrying about Metellus's wretched list from now on."

"This is good news, husband!"

"Yes. I was hoping you would see it that way."

"Why would I not?"

He seemed to be having some trouble with his throat. "The emperor didn't arrange it in quite the way I was expecting."

"Do we have to go to Rome?"

"No. Metellus does, but I expect his lists will continue to circulate after he's gone."

"Like the lady with the sparrow."

He said, "You don't have to learn to read if you don't want to."

"I want to. So I will know what it says on the all the labels and you can teach me how to be a medicus."

"How to be a—"

"And when you go away, I can write and nag you, like Marcia does."

His eyes widened. "Gods above. I saw him twice and completely forgot. She wanted me to ask Hadrian for a job for her husband."

"She does not need to know that you met him."

"But how else do I explain why you're a..." He paused, looking round. "Who *is* that girl that keeps hanging around? She reminds me of somebody."

Tilla turned. "Do you not remember Virana?"

"The pregnant tart from Eboracum? But she's—"

"Wearing something respectable."

"What's she doing here?"

Tilla took a deep breath. "There is something I need to explain to you."

"Yes. There's something I need to explain to you too."

Their eyes met. "You first," she said.

Author's Note

This is a story about filling in gaps.

Eboracum (York) is known as the home of the Ninth and Sixth Legions, but the last record of the Ninth there is in the year 108. Where it went after that is a question for other storytellers, but we know the Sixth Legion did not arrive until 122. Somebody must have garrisoned York through the lean years in between, when a British rebellion early in Hadrian's reign reduced the Roman numbers so far that reinforcements had to be brought in from elsewhere.

Hadrian made a tour of Britannia in the summer of 122, but the details are tantalizingly sketchy. We know he made "improvements" but have no record of where he went, although he must surely have visited the troops who were building the Great Wall to mark the edge of the empire.

The unhappiness of the emperor's relationship with his wife, Sabina, is a matter of record, but they remained married until her death—although there was a suggestion that he had her poisoned. Meanwhile, the outcome of the trip for imperial biographer Suetonius Tranquillus and his friend and patron Septicius Clarus was exactly as it is described in the story, although much else about them here is fiction.

Readers in search of more facts and less embroidery will find them in:

Hadrian: The Restless Emperor by Anthony R. Birley
Hadrian: Empire and Conflict by Thorsten Opper
Roman York by Patrick Ottaway
The Ordnance Survey Map of Roman and Anglian York

The Yorkshire Museum does a fine job of commemorating some of the real inhabitants of Eboracum, a fortress whose Roman walls still dictate the layout of the city that grew up around them. The Roman Headquarters Hall (Basilica) mentioned in the story is long gone, but a lone column still stands, and visitors to the York Minster undercroft will find the stone foundations of the original building upon whose roof Sulio sat.

ACKNOWLEDGMENTS

A novel is never a solo effort. At least, mine aren't. I'm grateful to Benjamin Adams, Peta Nightingale, Araminta Whitley, George Lucas, and David Chesanow for encouragement and for helping to beat the manuscript into shape. Guy Russell, Kathy Barbour, Carol Barac, Caroline Davies, and Andy Downie bravely read and commented on the first draft.

Sandra Garside-Neville kindly recommended source material on Eboracum; the organizers of This Is Deva provided the inspiring sight of a "real" century on parade; and Lindsay Powell reassured me that, despite much research and experiment, nobody really knows how the Romans cleaned their armor. All the surrounding speculation and invention is my own, and so are the errors.

A Note on the Author

Ruth Downie is the author of the *New York Times* bestselling *Medicus, Terra Incognita, Persona Non Grata,* and *Caveat Emptor.* She is married with two sons and lives in Devon, England.

Printed in Great Britain
by Amazon

44176857R00290